CeeCee
Shades of Black

By

ELLEN M. FOSS

CeeCee Shades of Black is a work of fiction. Names, characters, places and incidents are products of the author's imagination or are used fictitiously. Any resemblance to actual events, locales or persons, living or dead, is entirely coincidental.

Library of Congress cataloging – in – publishing – data
Foss, Ellen M., 2020 – CeeCee Shades of Black
2020910313

ISBN
978 – 1 – 7348904 – 1 – 9
First published in 2020 in the United States

ACKNOWLEDGEMENTS

I want to thank my husband for his years of patience, as he listened to me developing my Characters, Plots and Story Lines.

Thank you, Barbara McGarvey,
for all your input and editing support.

Thanks to all my family and friends
for your continued support and encouragement.

CHAPTER ONE

Sometimes life's choices are not ours alone. Then..., sometimes they are, and we have no one to blame but ourselves.

Juliet maneuvered the fiery red Saab into the empty parking space and grinned with satisfaction as she murmured a gleeful, "Wonderful! Life is so good, no traffic and a good parking space, along with the best story of a lifetime. All I can say is my career angel must be smiling upon me."

Yes, today Juliet was in a jubilant mood and her excitement was evident as it burned brightly across her face. She hesitated only a moment to compose herself before she grabbed her purse from the passenger's side of her car, then immediately reached down for the briefcase that laid on the floor below. This large attaché' was her office; it carried all her notes, questions, plus all the recording apparatus she thought she would need for her assigned interview. Once again, a shiver tickled her spine. The anticipation was exhilarating, and she gained energy from it.

Juliet inhaled a deep breath and whispered, "Here you go girl; now go get that Pulitzer." She dramatically swung the car door wide open and started to exit. Before she stepped out of the vehicle, she checked the contents of the case to make sure everything was there. It was, just as she knew it would be. Since she had already checked it four times that morning and umpteenth times yesterday and the day before. Again, her skin prickled with expectation and silently she said a prayer of thanks for her good fortune as she questioned outwardly, "Why would Cecilia Kempe choose me? Me, why?" This, she had no answer for. Especially since her Editor had told her that Mrs. Kempe had specifically asked for her. And at that time, she asked him the same, "But, why me? I mean I'm a novice; I barely have my feet wet." Once again, she pictured her Editor's Gus Hampton expression when she said those very words. He immediately replied, "I agree and I said the same thing at the time the request was made, but I was duly informed by Miss Darnell Weaver, *'Sir, Juliet's inexperience doesn't make a damn bit of difference; she is who Cecilia Kempe wants.'*

Even if none of that mattered to Mrs. Kempe. This fact still puzzled Juliet, particularly since any journalist worth their weight was after the Kempe story. Especially all the top reporters..., she mumbled to herself "But, I guess that is neither here nor there, for once all is said and done, I'm the only one standing, the chosen one, the one and only reporter granted an interview..., me..., future powerhouse journalist, Juliet Powers."

After today she will no longer be the rookie, the unknown, inexperienced dilettante, *a greenhorn;* that's what all her cohorts loved to tease about. Most just in fun, some because she is black and they decided that she had been hired entirely because of her color, or, and gender. As one unkind soul put it, 'why not kill two birds with one equal-opportunity-stone when you can.'

But today none of that mattered, since Cecilia Kempe decided she would speak with only one reporter on her one-hundredth birthday and she was the lucky one, inexperience and all. "Wow! What a break," she sang.

Again, she moved to scoot herself out of the car, then stopped and jerked the makeup mirror down to take one quick peek at her appearance. She grinned back at her beauty and noted that her light tawny skin was rosy pink with excitement. She stifled a giggle and winked at her own reflection before she slammed the mirror shut. Finally, she bolted from the car and headed in the direction of the affluent Georgian retirement home. She knew she was a bit early but what the heck, she told herself. *I'm too damn anxious to just sit in the car and twiddle my thumbs while I wait for the minutes to tick away. When I can just as well wait in the lobby and watch their clock tick instead. Besides on the flip side, if my luck holds out, maybe I can see the illustrious CeeCee Kempe earlier than scheduled. Either way I much rather sit in an air-conditioned lobby than an overly heated car.*

Juliet informed the attendant who was perched bird-like on a stool behind the front desk that she was here to tape an interview with Mrs. Cecilia Kempe. The young lady smiled as she coolly requested in an unimpressed voice, "Yes, I see, can you please take a seat in the visitors' lounge."

Juliet slightly deflated settled herself in a courtly, though cheery overstuff armchair, and unloaded her camera. At which time, she heard a loud bang and glanced up to see two men hammering a nail into a banner across the way. It was being hung on the wall inside a large open space. The room itself was filled with all the ceremonious paraphernalia which indicated a promise of a festive celebration. When the men backed away to admire their work, Juliet saw the banner was chocked full of squiggle marks that represented ribbons and confetti. Attached to each end were several colorful balloons with streamers surrounding the words, ***HAPPY 100TH BIRTHDAY CEECEE KEMPE.***

Juliet twisted, then stretched her neck to see inside the room. There were more banners inside, some with reminders of the many achievements CeeCee had accomplished throughout her years, including a picture of her when she joined the march on Washington for equal rights. *Yes,* Juliet thought, *if it wasn't for women like you, I probably wouldn't be here today.*

Juliet stood to move closer, the large red print beneath CeeCee's name read, **August 23, 1886-1986=100 years of outstanding achievements, CeeCee Kempe.** From what she could see, it looked like Cecilia Kempe was well liked by the other residents.

As she started to turn and go back to her seat, she noticed a woman in a tailored black suit that was full of oddly sized purple shapes. It was her animated jesters that caught Juliet's interest, and she watched her as she hurriedly approached where she stood. The woman who she estimated was near forty and from what Juliet could tell, she seemed to be in a weary state. Despite the woman's apparent distressed her face still beamed happily as she greeted several guests that she passed along the way. As soon as she stopped in front of Juliet her smile softened, and her voice held a warm charm as she introduced herself. "Hello, I'm Mary Lou Appel, Director of Pleasant Haven Manor."

While the efficient, though extremely attractive brunette spoke, she nervously patted Juliet's hand as she briskly pumped it up and down. At this same time she sweetly added, "I'm so sorry for your wait, but it looks like you are going to have to wait a little longer, Miss Powers. From what I understand CeeCee is having a bad hair day." Laughing as she continued, "I can tell you from experience, she is not about to come out of her room until she is perfect in every way." Juliet noted that when Mary Lou Appel laughed, she appeared much younger than she first had.

Mary Lou shook her head and again laughed at CeeCee's rascality, as she put in, "CeeCee said to let you know that she will meet you in the garden on the swing in about fifteen minutes. In the meantime, why don't I entertain you by showing you around the Manor?"

"That would be nice," answered Juliet.

Mary Lou wrapped her arm though Juliet's and led her down the hall. "We are very proud of our facility; it is by far one of the most luxurious guest homes in the nation. Why don't we start in the Solarium?" She stopped and stepped aside for Juliet to move in the direction her hand indicated and offered, "We have around the clock medical assistance, but not all of our residents require this, and many have their own live-ins, such as CeeCee does. Her personal secretary, Darnell Weaver also helps with her minor nursing needs. She's a woman of many vocations and aids CeeCee in all her affairs. Before we start, can I get you something? Coffee, water, or maybe a soda? This heat has just been atrocious this year."

"Thank you, but I'm fine."

Mary Lou's prior offer of information gave Juliet the opening she was looking for. It seemed Mary Lou Appel knew Cecilia Kempe, aka, CeeCee well enough to answer a few simple, but none the less; essential questions that she needed for her piece.

"Miss Appel, how long has Mrs. Kempe been a guest at the manor?"

"Oh, please, I rather you call me Mary Lou. And if you don't mind, I'd like to call you Juliet?"

Juliet smiled, her manner was relaxed and full of confidence even if her insides were a bundle of nerves. She hoped her smile would help hide this fact. "Yes of course, Mary Lou. That would please me very much."

"Wonderful and as for your question, Juliet, I believe CeeCee has been with us just shy of ten years. She is one of our most honored guests. And as you can imagine, here at Pleasant Haven, we have had our fair share of prestigious clientele over the years."

Mary Lou's eyes twinkled with pride as she continued to boast proudly, "Yes, we have a waiting list that measures several years. And we're quite picky as to who we choose from the applicants." She stopped and offered, "Here we are," and Juliet followed her into the room.

The Solarium was beautiful. Its garden-like appearance glowed with sunlight which burst brightly through the ample windows that shone crystal clear. In spite of the pristine glass most of the broad windows stood wide open so the soft summer breeze could flow unimpeded throughout the room. The soft fragrance that wafted throughout the room was wonderful, and the open windows made it easy to hear the musical chirps from outside in the garden. Juliet laughed out loud as she watched several birds flutter about happily amongst the flowery bushes.

Mary Lou urged, "If we stand in one place for several seconds, before you know it the birds will grow brave and enter through the windows."

Juliet burst into a pleasure filled giggle when a small brown bird flew pass her, soon followed by a larger more colorful breed. Her laughter disturbed both birds and they immediately exited a window across the room.

"We try not to discourage their soaring flights since they bring us so much enjoyment. This, Juliet, I can see you will agree with."

"It's wonderful. It makes you feel...well cheery and contented at the same time."

"I agree," smiled Mary Lou.

Again, Juliet caught a scent of sweetness and took several deep breaths of the fragrance that blew softly into the lustrous room. Her eyes moved around the large area; it was lovely and reeked of an extravagance she would never afford.

"Come along," said Mary Lou, "I'll show you more." As she led her into an open suite across the hall. "This chamber doubles as my office and a model for potential residents. As you can see its setup for both functions though no one lives here."

Juliet caught her breath. The lavish beauty of the room was majestic, and the suite's vastness was even more impressive. The ceiling seemed to be endless and midway, there was a floral trim that overhung almost to the point of being obnoxious, yet it was perfect for its setting.

Mary Lou smiled with self-satisfaction, "It is exquisite, isn't it? This suite is very much like the one CeeCee lives in, of course, excluding her personal touch and belongings. Our tenants usually prefer to have their own furnishings, so all the suites show quite differently, including CeeCee's which essentially has a strong English flare. It's full of wonderful old English art as well as antiques from all around the world. Yet it is still surprisingly spacious and open; not at all like you'd expect a two-bedroom suite full of heirlooms to look like." Glancing at her watch Mary Lou finished, "Well, it looks like I better get you to the garden. We certainly wouldn't want to start your interview off on the wrong foot. CeeCee doesn't mind being late but rarely tolerates others who do the same. She says, it's something I will learn to understand when I am older." Laughing at her own surmise, Mary Lou briskly moved forward to lead Juliet through the elegantly spacious mezzanine. Then she headed in the direction of the porch and to an extremely sociable looking swing. The huge porch was perched in the middle of a beautiful side garden that was filled with sprouting summer blooms.

Again, Mary Lou glanced at her watch then apologized, "Juliet, I hope you will not mind waiting alone for a few minutes. I have a meeting that will be starting with or without me in about three minutes. And since I am the Director of this facility, it would be wise for me to be on time. It sets a good example," she whispered. Quickly she shook Juliet's hand and without another word rushed off in the direction of the main lobby.

Juliet watched Mary Lou until she was out of sight, then turned her attention back to the humongous swing that took up a good portion of the porch. After a quick inspection, she decided it was too big for the area. It could easily seat four or maybe even five skinny people. Any which way, she decided not to sit in it for fear of being swallowed whole. Instead she took in the view that encompassed the area, while she jotted several notes to her pad, then quickly shot a couple of pictures. At this time, she noticed the heat had lessened somewhat; this she realized, was due to the garden's full lush greenery. It gave the area a dampness which in turn, gave the area a much-welcomed coolness. A gazebo that stood boldly centered within all the lushness made the area even more amiable.

"Well," she uttered as she twirled around full circle. "This certainly is a welcome change in climate; if not to mention environment."

Last night, in her hotel room, the Georgia heat was insufferable. "I guess I forgot how humid it feels in Georgia's stifling heat."

She hadn't been home since her parents were killed in an auto accident fifteen years prior. Their faces flashed across her mind, and she sighed mournfully since she still missed them terribly. Though instead of feeling sorry for herself she threw the strap of her camera over her shoulder and sat her briefcase on the table in front of the swing. She had been raised by her grandparents after the accident, and for this she was thankful, and as she grew up, she recognized she had had the best of both worlds.

Juliet closed her eyes as she inhaled a large draught of the garden's bouquet. A sweet smile covered her lips while she listened to the musical tunes of the varied chirps and immediately, she felt refreshed.

"Tis lovely isn't it?"

Juliet jumped, not from fear, but from sheer unforeseen surprise.

"Oh..., my, I am so sorry child, I did not mean to startle you." Putting her hand outward she hurriedly introduced herself, "Hello, I am Cecilia Kempe; please call me CeeCee. Most all do."

By now Juliet realized she was standing there gaping at the old woman, and at once she attempted to pull herself together in hopes of behaving like the professional, she was supposed to be. "It..., it is genuinely nice to meet you Mrs....I mean, CeeCee. I'm Juliet Powers. And I'm sorry, but the beauty of the garden and its sounds are so harmonious..., I guess I sort of got engrossed and didn't hear your approach."

Waving her hand in the air CeeCee replied, "Nonsense. No reason to apologize child; it's quite understandable. That is one of the reasons I chose to be interviewed out here. I love all the sounds and life's movements. The beauty here is even more enchanting in the evening."

She grinned slightly and arched a brow before she went on, "I believe it's because you can hear the crickets at night fall." Dreamily she added, "I just love the sound of crickets, though it does seem to give me a terrible yearning inside."

CeeCee hesitated then suddenly declared, "I believe we are going to have another scorcher of a day." Her face lit up and she asked, "Can I get you something to drink before we start? I think I am going to get me some lemonade; how about you my dear? Doesn't that sound good?"

CeeCee's voice almost carried a childlike tone and her accent was a cross between English and a Southern drawl. Which sounded strange to Juliet's acoustic organ.

"Yes," piped Juliet, "lemonade does sound good. Yes, that would be perfect, but I can go get it."

"Nonsense, child. I might be an old lady, but I can still carry a pitcher of lemonade. You just set yourself up, and I'll be back in a jiffy."

Juliet smiled as she pulled the equipment out of her bag. CeeCee was everything she thought she would be. Spunky and alert, just as she heard she had been her entire life. But her soul magnificence was even more beautiful in person than in any of the pictures she had ever seen of her. Even though she is a hundred years old today and her dark chestnut hair had turned a solid white, her face and stature still held a youthful appearance. It was plain to see she also possessed a significant amount of elegance and grace. Clearly a sign of good breeding, decided Juliet.

As far as Juliet could see there was no doubt about CeeCee's intelligence or wit being as sharp as ever. Yes indeed. She was very pleased that she was not disappointed as some suggested she might be.

When she returned, a servant followed CeeCee with the tray of lemonade and glasses. Juliet could tell that the girl had to quicken her stride to keep up with the old woman, and she wanted to laugh at the pleasurable sight. At that instant Juliet decided, *I think I'm really gonna like this lady, the woman the world addresses as CeeCee Kempe, Crusader for Minorities.*

While the lemonade was being poured, Juliet snapped several shots of CeeCee, and the area that surrounded them. "Perfect," said Juliet as she set the camera aside and readied the switch on the recorder. She sat, then sipped at her lemonade and pondered a question before she asked, "CeeCee, before we get started, can I ask one personal question?"

"Why of course you may, sweet child."

"Why did you decide on me for this interview? I mean, there are so many more experienced writers out there to choose from. All have done this sort of interview before, and I know you know, I haven't. So why me?"

CeeCee's answer surprised Juliet. "Child, please, don't ever underestimate your abilities. You are a gifted journalist. Yes..., and it is true that any number of writers could tell my story, but none as good as you will, my dear." CeeCee tilted her head slightly then smiling she added, "You are in so many ways like me. As a matter of fact, I would say so much so, that you could pass for my great-great grandchild."

"Hardly," spouted Juliet. "I don't know if you noticed CeeCee, but even though I'm terribly light skinned, I am definitely an Afro American."

CeeCee noted the pride in Juliet's voice and smiled. "I have indeed noticed, and that was the first thing that drew me to you."

She wavered briefly, then added, "Juliet, it would be wise for you to understand..., and always try to keep in mind what some might label as a couple of old nugatory quotes. You cannot judge a book by its cover, and you cannot always believe what you see. I imagine those quotes are much more valuable than many people may realize. You see, one cannot always be sure of what they believe they see is truth."

Juliet nodded in agreement but added nothing, since she didn't really get where CeeCee was going with these excerpts and she didn't want to distract her from her thoughts.

Earlier that day Juliet decided she wanted the story to be from the old woman, in her own words as well and at her own pace so she would listen and record in silence.

CeeCee sat quietly for some time before reaching out and patting Juliet's hand while asking softly, "Juliet, I hope you will be open- hearted...and please, after you hear my story try not to judge me too harshly. Things were different back then... when I was a young woman. Blacks, especially black woman, were not free to be much more than the slaves they were brought here to be. And please... do not misunderstand me, I realize that that was slightly different depending on which part of the country you were from. But still in all...education was nearly out of the question for most and position was even more unattainable."

Juliet looked at CeeCee... questions were shooting through her mind. She wasn't quite sure where the elderly lady was going with this, and she wondered if maybe she had been wrong and CeeCee didn't have all her wits about her after all.

The old woman recognized the look of incertitude and laughed lightly then smiling tenderly said, "Honey child, why don't I just start from the beginning. Then you will understand what this old woman's jabbering about."

Immediately she saw the relief cross over Juliet's lovely, but slightly distraught face, and she smiled again at Juliet's innocence. It was refreshing to see such purity of heart and trust in a black child, not all have achieved this equanimity yet.

Once again CeeCee reached out to pat the girl's hand as she called to mind, "Let's see, in all honesty; I guess I would have to say it started way before the day I was born." Juliet watched CeeCee as quietly, but prudently as possible. She did not want to miss a word, an expression or any crucial significance, and she had no intention of distracting her or leading her away from her thoughts and memories. This was CeeCee's story and she would tell it in CeeCee's words.

Juliet could see the instant the mist touched CeeCee's dark yellowish-brown eyes as they moved to a memory long, long ago. Juliet thought, *I can almost see her mind moving back in time. She is extraordinary.* At this same time, she also recognized that some of what she was witnessing was sorrow and realized this glance into the past brought about a feeling of sadness for the old woman. But soon Juliet became intrigued when a sudden change crept in CeeCee's well educated enunciations. Her accent in some ways sounded different. However, Juliet held back any comment and recorded CeeCee's every word.

"Yes, I guess that's when it started; way, way, back then, all those years before I was even born. When my Grandma Letia was just a young girl, not more than twelve or thirteen, if I recollect right. My mamma's Uncle William used to say, *'Yes, Letia was such a pretty lil thing. She loved to sing and dance around, ever since she was a knee high to a grasshopper.'* I just loved that tale. I could almost picture her singing and whirling around as she danced about for her mamma and her brothers.

There was six of them, and Letia was the only girl my great grandma had. Anyhow from what I was told, eventually her beauty and all this high spiritedness brought about some unwanted attention from their master's young son. At the time, he was just coming into his manhood and was looking for somewhere to experience his fruition.

And since my grandma was almost thirteen years old and was sprouting her womanhood, she became the prime choice for this young man. She had barely finished her thirteenth year and she was full of child.

The story passed on, told that she was deathly ill most the time she carried the child. I guess being not much more than a babe herself, it was just too much for her small body to handle. And by the time the baby was coming she was near death's door. Uncle William said she fought like the dickens to stay alive and deliver that child, and sure enough, that's when my mamma came into this world, Spring 1865.

Only she didn't look much like anybody but my grandma. It wouldn't have made a bit a difference if she had looked like the master's son, because he wasn't interested in no baby and especially a Negra baby from some slave girl. Neither were his folks. But be as it was, Mamma said Grandma never fully recovered and died several years' pass.

Letia named my mamma, Flower, and she was raised by my,

Great-grandma until she married or was promised to my Papa, Ely Brown. Papa was about the age of sixteen, in 1881 or 82. And after the loss of two girl babies and my brother that died soon after birth, she had me. Then not long after; come my sister. As you can see, I come out looking more like the young man that was supposed to be my Granddaddy, than most of his owned kin. But no matter, my mamma and papa loved me. Though most colored folk did shy away from me. I guess they thought it was catching or something like." CeeCee laughed as she shook her head at such a notion.

In the beginning when Juliet noted that CeeCee's enunciation had changed, she found her manner soon followed. Now, both had become more prevalent and she seemed to have forgotten she was being interviewed, or that Juliet was even there. Yet, none of this mattered, for now Juliet was sure the old woman had lost her mind, since she was saying she was a child of a Negro family. Juliet had done her homework, which included a background check, and she knew CeeCee Kempe was a distant cousin of the Roberts Family of Virginia....or ...

Suddenly CeeCee refocused on Juliet's face, though after only a brief hesitation she continued, and Juliet noted that CeeCee's phrases at time were broken, but she continued to record.

"Of course, by this time slavery was a thing of the past, but a lot of people were still bond-servants. Some was given a piece a property from their owners and was working for nothing to pay for it, which I guess was slavery in its own right. Needless to say, many others didn't know what or how to do anything else, so they choose to stay with the families they'd grown up with. Though even if they did choose to try and make it on their own, they were often held back by the very people they trusted.

I recall being told from the older folk, that was there at the time, that more times than not, white folk told them to keep in mind their standing and no Nigger was to own much of nothing."

She took a deep breath before continuing, "We, on the other hand, was luckier than most, since my papa's family worked for an upright family that took good care of their slaves. And when free-

dom was announced, they offered them slaves pay for their services, and just as soon as Papa married Mamma, in ritual only, the
Roberts offered her a position in the kitchen. We lived right there
behind the big house, next to the carriage house, where Papa
worked. We had plenty of food, plus a good place to stay warm
from the cold Virginia winters. Though some others weren't as fortunate. I still recall, not far down the road, where the Hopkins
workers lived. It was disgraceful, barely shacks, with nothing more
than four walls and a roof. Although, the Bradford workers had it
much worse. I mean, they had no more than a lean-to and them
youngsters didn't have a hoot to eat. I remember the oldest girl,
Myrtle and her younger brother, Tomboy, working in the fields till
their hands bled, and them not more than seven and eight at the
time. But most awful, there was times when those kids didn't get
anything more to eat than left over pork fat; and they lapped that
up on a dried-out biscuit.

So, you can see why we felt the Lord was taking good care of us
by letting us live behind that grand old house. Course, Mamma reminded us often to count our blessings which we did. Mamma was
always a staunch supporter of the Lord.

Yes, that grand old house was splendid. The land had been in the
Roberts' family for generations. Years before, it was one of Richmond's largest working tobacco plantations. However, by the time I
was old enough to start to remember, it had slowed down to barely
anything more than just a beautiful mansion sitting in the middle of
a lavish patch of green pastures. My first memories were of those
pastures..., and of course, the lady of the house, Mrs. Ollifrey
Roberts. She sure was a pretty woman, and my, oh my, she was
such a dainty thing."

Again, CeeCee's diction changed and once again Juliet heard the
woman she recognized and had listened to so many times in the
past. CeeCee Kemp had spoken out on behalf of the migrant workers across the nation. And attended rallies that supported women's
rights and the Black women's deliverance. She, repeatedly, over the
years heard her speak on television in support of women's right to

choose. CeeCee had always been her role model, and now here she was trying to say it was all a lie. That this white lady from England was, in fact, an Afro American woman, hidden behind an easier color. Juliet struggled with disappointment, then anger. Yet she still was not believing what she was hearing. As a Result she, at last, decided to concentrate on CeeCee and her words and not to evaluate the message. *Maybe this is CeeCee's misguided attempt at humor*, thought Juliet. *Maybe I misunderstood.*

CeeCee's face brightened as she went on, "My Lord, Mrs. Ollifrey Roberts loved to picnic and often did so. Many of the local ladies who lived nearby joined her regularly, and many more that lived miles away or in town, looked forward to receiving an invitation. Her favorite place was by the creek; it ran right through the middle of the property. She also enjoyed fancy tea parties under the large maple tree out back of the house. My Mamma would have my Papa, who was the carriage and stable hand, but also helped mamma in the kitchen when needed, set up large tables for Mrs. Ollifreys' guests. Then Mamma would arrange white lacey tablecloths with fancy dishes on top. Just before the ladies arrived, Mamma would place a large urn filled with water and flowers in the center of each table. Yes, it was always so lovely to see. The ladies were served tiny cucumber sandwiches with tea and decorative cut cookies all fancy and pretty for dessert.

My job, as far back as I can remember, was to stand quietly off to the side of where the ladies sat under the maple tree and cool them. I used this huge fan that Mamma made up of branches and such. She would braid the twigs together and sweeten them with berry and flower juices. Then just before the ladies arrived, she would dampen the fans, so the air was sweetened with their scents as we waved them up and down. The ladies simply loved the fresh sweet fragrance that cooled them."

CeeCee laughed as she pictured two scrawny looking colored kids, but when she spoke her tone was filled with emotion as well as indignation. "We must have looked silly to those cultivated ladies, of well-to-do genteel families. The fan was almost bigger than me, but surely bigger than my little sister Viola, who was almost two years younger than me. She helped hold it while we fan the ladies, sometimes for hours at a time. Why, it was often that I felt my arms ache with fatigue, and more than once I was sure they were going to fall right off. But that made no matter, we weren't allowed to stop till the last lady left the field.

Those hours in the sun beating on Viola, whose skin was darker, more like Mammas' and Papas', turned her even darker. But not mine all it did to me was turn my skin a pitch more golden.

She hesitated as she pondered the vision briefly before moving on, "Sometimes the ladies' voices would carry, and I could hear their words. I always wished I was a lady too and could speak just like them."

CeeCee laughed out loud and added, "My how them ladies loved to talk, and they would carry on as if they didn't even know we was standing there. Why they paid more attention to the flies than they did to us kids. Although I guess we was used to that, because me and Viola paid no attention to it anyhow. Especially Viola, she never listened to their conversations, she had no interest. But me on the other hand was bright as all get out and too smart for my own britches. And it didn't take long for me to figure out that I could mimic these ladies' voices and gestures with just a little effort. From then on I spent a good portion of my days practicing being just like Mrs. Ollifrey."

She chuckled when she added, "I tell you; it was as if I was born to it. It came so easy and since I dreamed of being a lady, I pretended to be one every chance I got." 'Viola, please pass the sugar, my it is a sweltering day, much warmer than usual, would you not agree, Miss Tanderman? Why, where in the blazes is that colored girl with my glass of lemonade, mine as you can clearly see is nearly empty?'

"I could always hear the pleasure it bought these women when they called us colored instead of Negra, so when I parroted them, I too held that same tone of satisfaction in my voice. I was really good at it, but without fail Viola would whine, 'CeeCee, you stop tat now.'

Viola at a younger age could never pronounce Cecilia so that's how everyone started calling me, CeeCee. Yes, each and every time, she would angrily wail, 'I'm tellin mamma, yous gonna git a wipin for talkin like a white lady. Just cause ya look white, ya cain't talk white. White folks ain't gonna put up with it, CeeCee. Ya hear me, I is tellin mamma?'

"Viola, I is just playin so don't ya go off in a teether and ya better not tell mamma." Then I'd go right back to practicing my walk and talk so when I grew up, I could be a lady just like Mrs. Ollifrey.

In my opinion Mrs. Ollifrey looked and was, at all times everything a lady should be, and of course her husband, Hershal Roberts, was always the perfect Virginian gentleman. Kinder than most though."

CeeCee sighed and fell silent for a moment, then quickly added a memory as though she had just recalled it and it needed it to be voiced right away. "He..., Mr. Hershal Roberts worked in town where he owned his own bank and several properties. And since he was very wealthy, he gave his children most everything they wanted..., especially Winnifrey. Winnifrey Roberts," she shook her head, "now there was a handful....

Anyhow they had two children, Abigail who was six at the time, two years older than Viola and same as me. She was very close to being a lady just like her mother even at six, and that fascinated me..., yet I dare say I was a bit envious, too. Occasionally I played with Winnie, that's what we called her back then, but we didn't play very often."

CeeCee groaned, "It was only permissible if the white child asked you to play with them and with Winnie that didn't happen often. Yes, indeed, from what I remember she was a handful even way back then. So, I didn't mind if she ignored me, since I did my best to avoid her anyway.... when possible.

Now Abigail was a different story, though at times she was a little crybaby, still in all she was much more preferred than Winnie who was always thinking of something to get us into trouble. She was what my mamma called a '*fistful of woe.*' I didn't know it back then, but Winnifrey was the one who was going to point my life in the direction it eventually went. Yes undeniably, Winnifrey Roberts herself...."

Suddenly there was silence. Juliet waited... she still felt disturbed, although, even more, she was extremely filled with doubt that CeeCee was lucid....

CHAPTER TWO

"Ely, ya needs to get down to the cold cellar and brings me a ham, so I's can cut the meat for the lil sandweches the Mrs. wants. This is gonna be a big ta do, so we is gonna need some sausages and somewheres near fitteen chickens. So best git them picked and feathered fore mid-day, ya hears me, Ely? And Ely; I see ya eyein them pies, don't ya go gettin no ideas about touchin none of them pies coolin.

Mrs. Ollifrey, she wants this sociel-git-tagather, ta be the best this town ever seen. 'She says, Flower, I don't want no missaps, does ya hear me, Flower?' So, I is tellin ya the same, Ely, no missaps. We is gonna make Mrs. Ollifrey proud, ya hear me, Ely, proud?"

Laughing and scratching his head as he answers, "Yes em, I hears ya, Flower."

"Mamma cain't we's go ta da sociel too?" whinned CeeCee.

"Child what ya thinkin? We cain't go ta no sociel. That's for gentlemans and ladies. No Negras cain't go, sept for servin."

Flower shook her head back and forth and headed for the wood burning stove that stood in the corner of the hot kitchen. The fire had been going inside it before daybreak and the pies aromas were wafting throughout the house since long before breakfast. Flower mumbled under her breath while she moved across the kitchen, "Wha a scrambled brain child I has gone and borned. This child Lord, what ya think she be thinkin? We is Negra folk. Negra folk cain't go ta no white folk sociel. With this young'un Lord, I fears I is failing ya."

Flower glanced over and noticed Ely was still standing in the corner of the room and she immediately ordered, "Ely gets movin, I needs them meats now."

Flower was a stern woman who took great pride in her position and counted on the respect she earned to keep her in good standing with the Roberts. Her husband, Ely, was full of pride for his wife. She was not only in charge of the kitchen with a girl helper; she was also in charge of the two girls who cleaned the house, and tonight, she had two more helpers for serving. Moreover, Mrs. Ollifrey had given Flower a free hand to run the house anyway she saw fit. In the Roberts' house, Flower Brown's word was law. She took special care in her work and preached that the workers below her do the same. Her aim was to run a gracious house, and she expected everyone, including her young'uns to help in any way they could. Everyone was called upon to make life easier for Mrs. Ollifrey and her family. And on a day like today, Flower did not take to young'uns under foot.

"CeeCee, take ya sister out backs ta play, I don't need ya under foot, now scoot, gowan, git out a my kitchen. And ya don't go gettin in no troubles either, ya hears me, and keeps ya sister close, I don't want her go wanderin off someswheres when I's got no time ta be lookin fer her."

CeeCee's face registered disappointment, yet she knew her Mamma was in no mood to argue with so she only answer, "Yesum," and quickly moved towards the door. As always once the door slammed behind the two girls, they stepped up their pace and snuck around to peek in the side window of the big house to see if anything was going on.

All this ado was something that only happen two times a year, once at Christmas and on the Fourth of July, which was the big cook-out Flower was preparing for right now. This affair was the one that CeeCee always dreamed of attending. There was plenty of music and dancing, too. Plus, from what she had witnessed from under the large Lilac bush last year, most folks not only joined the dancing, but sang their hearts out as well.

Her and Viola never was allowed to join in the actual fun when the Roberts threw a party, but still in all, they did feel the joy and excitement from afar.

"Wellll, at leeast we gits ta help wit some of the readiness," mumbled CeeCee. "Come on Viola, we can peek in the windo, that's one way ta sees whats goin on. I'is already feelin som of the xcitment ain't you, Viola? I is sure Mrs. Ollifrey and the girls is feelin it, too. Comon Viola, you can help me up. Ya knows Viola, its a big ta-do to choose a dress and all and I wanst ta see Winnies. Yes ser, a lady's gots ta look her best, I hear-say. Viola come on hold the box."

CeeCee pulled her scrawny body up to stand on the old weather worn crate that she kept hidden in the bushes on the side of the big house. Viola shoved at her sister and attempted to climb on top as well, and when she couldn't see, she started to whine. This caused CeeCee to teeter. Quickly she caught herself, then shushed her sister with one finger to her lips while mumbling harshly under her breath, "Viola you is gonna git us caught, naw hush up, girl."

"I wanna sees toooo, CeeCee."

"Shish...an stop ya whining, I'll let ya sees in a minute. Shish... I wanta hear what Winnie is sayin." As she moved her ear real close to the window and whispered, "Somptens reeal bad happenin Viola, cause Ole Winnie sure is doin som sulkin an cryin."

CeeCee could see that Winnie had her lips pursed way out like when she didn't get her way, and her arms were wrapped angrily across her chest. From CeeCee's experience with Winnie this meant she was put-off and one thing Winnie did not stand for, was not getting her way. CeeCee pushed her ear harder against the glass so she could hear what was being said.

"Mother has one, so whyyy caiiiin't I.....," whimpered Winnie's little southern voice. "I am a lady, and all ladies have personal maids, so why Father, why cain't I."

"Again, you are much too young for such a maidservant. You are barely out of a nanny, what are you nine, ten? Anyhow I do not want to hear another word of argument from you, young lady. This whole thing is nothing more than plum nonsense child."

Scarcely letting her father finish his exasperated declaration Winnifrey jumped in, "Father, you know very well that I am soon to be eleven and that is my very point. I am approaching womanhood and I do not have anyone to take care of my needs. And, as you were so kind to point out, *Father.* I no longer have the aid of a nanny. So, I am forced to dress and take care of my own self," answered Winnie in her most indignant grownup tone. "Why, I think it is utterly disgraceful that I have to pick up after myself."

"Winnifrey, you have the house girls to help you dress if it is needed. And as for your other needs, such as picking up after you or your bath water being heated and poured, those are also taken care of by the house staff. So my dear daughter, lets' not hear anymore conversation on the subject."

CeeCee could see Abigail and her mother standing to the far side of the room as they watched the commotion. Mrs. Ollifrey fought her smile, yet it was quite evident that with all the effort she imposed, she was not successful. CeeCee could see the composed smile from clear across the room and outside the window.

"Faaather...."

"Winnifrey, I do not have time to deal with this absurd notion, I have an appointment to get to."

"Father... pleaseee hear me out. If I cain't have a woman, how about a child to pick up after me, you know someone like CeeCee."

Her father stood firm, "No, Winnifrey, No."

Though this did not falter Winnifrey or her pleas. "Maybe for my birthday gift, oh please Father, please do not say no, please. This means everything to me."

Hershal Roberts said nothing but stood there staring at his daughter Winnifrey, the apple of his eye. Finally, he concluded that it was senseless to argue with the child, since he knew very well that she would eventually get what she wanted, as she usually did. Suddenly his heart wrenched as he watched his eldest daughter give him her biggest smile, and she clasped her fingers tightly together and pleaded once more, "Ooh... pleaseee... Father, pleaseee..."

He pretended to be aloof as he picked up his papers that were strewn across his desk and headed for the door. When he opened it, he turned and replied, "Have Cecilia in my office tonight at six o'clock sharp."

CeeCee gulped, as she watched Winnie jump up and down and squeal like a pig. Quickly she hopped off the crate and choked the words, "Ohhh dear me, Viola..., I thinks I is in real big troubles, a whole lots a troubles, if I knows Miss Winnie. Ooohh my, Viola, Viola."

CeeCee tried to go about her business that day and pretend that she had not heard what she heard. But despite her attempts to avoid thinking about it, her mind kept wandering right back to the very thing she hoped to avoid. At last, out of desperation she cried out for help, "I cain't say notin to Winnie, since I ain't spose ta be lisining at da windo, so tells me, Viola, what's I gonna do?"

Viola stood there staring wide eyed at her moaning sister. She had no idea on how she could help her with her plight. But since she didn't get to see inside the big house and CeeCee did, she decided her sister deserved to get whatever befell her.

"Oh Viola, Miss Winnie's she such a demandin child, and if I is ordered ta pick up aftar her, she could work da skin right offs of my very bones."

CeeCee didn't know what a personal maid did, but she knew Mrs. Ollifrey had Mab to take care of her. *But the Mrs. is a lady,* she thought, *and ladys needs things.* "What is Miss Winnie gonna need, sept ta boss me round?" She wailed at the disinterested Viola.

Before the sun was pass mid-day, Winnie came to CeeCee and ordered, "CeeCee I want you to go and clean yourself up, *real good*. And put a comb through that hair of yours." She studied her up and down then handed her something and said, "And put this on, we cannot have you looking like some rag a muffin. And when you are all finished, I want you to come up to the house at six sharp. Father wants to talk with you. And CeeCee try to stand straight, and I ex‑ pect you will not be ill mannered."

Sadly, CeeCee nodded her head as she unfolded the garment that Winnie had handed her. Suddenly she gasped, "Oh my..., Miss Win‑ nie, you's lettin me wear ya blue dress. It sure is pretty. I always liked it best?"

"It's old, and I of course, would not want it back after you have worn it. Besides, I do not wear it any longer, so you can keep it. I certainly can't have my personal servant looking like some poor beggar now can... well, never mind. I shall bring you some shoes and more dresses tomorrow." She considered the gawking girl for a few seconds, then before she turned to march back to the main house, she asked, "Do you know how to tell time? I mean should I send someone to fetch you at six?"

CeeCee felt embarrassed. She didn't know if Winnie was belit‑ tling her or not, but she answered her question truthfully, "No, Miss Winnie, and I gots no time piece, Mam."

CeeCee stood there for some time after Winnie walked away. She was in complete awe of her new predicament and after spend‑ ing some time thinking she began to realize, "Tis ain't gonna be bad. Tis is the prettiest frock I's ever got."

Suddenly she turned and ran towards home as she giggled with pleasure, "I better hurry yup, cause it sure ain't proper ta be late. Then one more thought shot through her mind, *what if Mr. Roberts thinks on it and changes his mind? Oh, I sure hopes Miss Winnie wont's forgit ta bring me them shoes tomarro.*

C eeCee stood as straight as she could in front of Hershal Roberts and his large desk, while he evaluated her new polished gleam. She was as self-satisfied and as nervous as he had ever seen any one person. She looked as stiff as a board standing there before him. Her wide eyes never left his face as she rigidly waited for his decision. Her lips grinned wide and her eyes beamed jubilantly at him, as she held solidly for him to inspect her new look. The blue dress she wore he noted was one of Winnifrey's old dresses. Suddenly he had a sense that some of her profuse excitement was for this very fact, and for an instant he felt sad that a discarded dress could bring the girl so much pleasure.

Hershal considered the face that looked more white than colored. Then after a minute or so, he concluded that CeeCee was high spirited enough to handle the abuse he was sure his daughter would bestow. At this time, he smiled and said, "Cecilia, I have asked you here because my daughter Winnifrey's birthday is in two weeks, and she has asked to acquire a personal maid for her gift. Do you know what that is? A personal maid I mean."

"No Ser," she insecurely answered.

"Well, to put it simply, it would mean that you do anything the child request you to do. Do you understand?"

"Yas Ser."

"Do you think you could handle that job, Cecilia?"

"Yas Ser."

"Well, I know Winnifrey is quite indomitable at times, so I imagine she may be a handful and quite demanding."

"Yas Ser."

"It was for this reason that I was not inclined to agree with her or grant her request. I have since reevaluated the situation and decided that she may very well be correct. She may indeed need someone to take care of her and her daily needs. So, I am inclined to take the gamble and give you a chance for two weeks. After such a time, if I decide that you have done well enough, I will begin to pay you for your services. Does that sound agreeable to you, Cecilia?"

Her eyes suddenly grew even larger, once she heard the word pay and it registered. And her grin grew wider as she stuttered her answer, "Ya...yas Ser, I...I's sures do understand and yas Sers, I's sur do agrees."

Holding back a smile Hershal added, "Well, since you are here and already all dressed up, I guess there's no time like the present to get started."

"Yas Ser."

"Follow me, Cecilia."

"Yas Ser."

CeeCee was so excited by the time their meeting was finished she was afraid she would pee in her britches. And when Mr. Roberts said to follow him, all she wanted to do was run past him and out the door to share her good fortune with her Mamma. But she didn't, instead she followed his footsteps out the door into the parlor, where the rest of the family sat while they waited for his decision. It was this very night that Cecilia Brown began the journey that changed her life forever. ******

Immediately after Mr. and Mrs. Roberts excused themselves, Miss Winnie's ordered, "CeeCee fetch my nightclothes and after I am readied for bed, I want my hair brushed one-hundred times."

Yas Miss Winnie," answered CeeCee, but she thought to herself, *'I gots no idea what a hundred is and I sure hopes Miss Winnie don't eithar.*

It didn't take long to find out that Mr. Roberts was right about Miss Winnie, she was one demanding girl.

"But tat's all right," she told Viola, "cause I gots me this dress. And shoes, Miss Winnie promised me shoes, and soon I's gonna get a pay. And as far as I can tell Viola, more clothes is sure to come my way. Cause Miss Winnie gots a whole bunch a dresses. Yes ser, and she told Mrs. Ollifrey tat she aint got nothin to wear but ole rags, and she needs new dresses." CeeCee's eyes shone bright when she added, "I sures hopes Miss Winnie gits what she wants."

It was a few weeks after she began to get her wage that CeeCee confessed. "The days is long, Viola, but I pay no never mind, since I is learnin things. I learned how ta be a lady, Viola, like white folks. I can even hold a teacup, jus like one a them ladies. I could shows ya how, but I's don't got me a teacup."

"CeeCee wat good is known tat?" spouted Viola?

"Never mind, Viola."

"CeeCee."

"Just listen, Viola. Miss Pediwhopper; ya know the teachar that comes ta da house, she teachs Miss Winnie and Miss Abigail. Well, she's a mite puff out, Viola. Miss Winnie bringed me ta class and Miss Pediwhopper, she turned red in da face and puffed out too. Right off she ordered me out of da room. She sure was mad and yelled, 'No colored girl is sittin in ma classroom.' And Miss Winnie, oh my, Viola she was even madder en Miss Pediwhopper. And she runned from that room cryin, 'Fatha, Fatha.' And not mor en a breath latar here come Mr. Roberts. I tells ya,Viola, he was stumpin his feet ta da floor as he moved ta stand face ta face with Miss Pedi-whopper. And Miss Winnie was grinin like a fool standin at his side, and when Mr. Roberts, hollered, "*Miss Pediwhopper, what is the meaning of this? I's sees no harm in lettin a child sit quietly ins a cor-ner if it pleases ma daughter*'. I tells ya, Viola, that Miss Pediwhop-per's face almost turned white as da chalk she writ on da board wit. And after that no more was said bout me leavin, so's I stayed." From that day forward CeeCee was allowed to sit way back in the corner of the room, in case Miss Winnie needed her for anything.

"The whole matter should never have been mentioned in the first place," said Miss Ollifrey to Miss Manny, a friend of hers from Town.

"After all it is not like the child's going to learn anything. Every-one knows a colored child cannot learn much more than the sim-plest things. Why it is hard enough for them to understand the concept of taking care of themselves, let alone education."

These words where overheard by CeeCee who fanned the ladies while they sipped their minted tea on the veranda one afternoon.

She pretended she was not listening, but she heard their words. And after they left, she wondered if this were true. She knew no one who had an education, nor anyone who could read or write. Yet she knew what they said had to be wrong because she was already learning from what Miss Pediwhopper taught. *Am I brighter than most?* She thought to herself. But this she doubted even more. Though in truth CeeCee was far brighter than she realized. She had a gift for recall. And as soon as this fact became clear to her, she reported that to her only ally, "I's learns real easy, Viola. And I's learnin all about the world. White folks travel across the seas ya know, and tat's amazin, tat's what I's heared Miss Pediwhopper say. I's also learnin how to spell words, like my name..., and potatoes. Viola, I always thought it was tatoes, but it ain't, Viola." CeeCee shook her head in wonder, then a new excitement took over and she hurriedly went on, "Oh and I's learnin how to count numbers and add. Best though, I's learned to read som words." She looked dismal when she added, "I gots me no paper or pen, so I's practice on da dirt." Suddenly her face brightened, and she said, "Even so, it comes out real good if ya press hard."

CeeCee thrust her hand outward, "See Viola, I's borrowed one a Abigail's books. I don't gots me a book either, so I just listen real good to what Miss Pediwhopper is tellin the girls. That's how I's learnin all bout places. Oh Viola, I nevar would a guessed of such travlins, would you Viola?"

CeeCee waited but she could see Viola didn't care about learnin or travelin, so she moved on. "But I guess its common amongst the white folk. Some of the places are so far away, ya has ta take a ship ta. Viola..., I surely would like ta go."

Viola's face wrinkled with disproval, "Not me, I don't wanna leave Mamma."

"Viola, ya can't stay a baby fer-ever," shouted CeeCee.

Anger fired up in Viola' and she growled, "CeeCee, yous is gonna git in trouble. You is colored, and colored folks aint pose ta learn things. An ya betta face it, cause you aint goin no wheres. You a colored girl CeeCee Brown, an when Mr. Roberts hears yous' learnin, you is gonna be throwed out of his house."

"No, I's ain't Viola; cause I's hidin all my learnins. Viola, I don't want Miss Pediwhopper to send me out of da room, or Mr. Roberts ta throw me out." CeeCee shook her head and a strong emphasis filled her next statement, "Cause if that evar happens, Viola, I's nevar gonna gits ta come back, nevar." Her face relaxed and she searched for the right words that could explain her feeling to her sister, "Viola, I likes learnin, is real impotant to me. Please don't be mad at me cause I wanna learn."

It was almost a year before anyone found out that CeeCee had benefited from her hours in the classroom, and as she put it. "It was only cause of my own pridefulness."

The discovery took place upstairs in Winnie's room. At the time CeeCee was brushing Winnie's hair while she studied her geography lesson. Both girls had to learn every State in the Nation, and for the life of her Winnie could not remember the full list. She continued to mis-spell or misplace the same state over and over and over again.

CeeCee listened to her stumble over the lesson for more than an hour before Winnie began to whine. For CeeCee this was the last straw; she had had enough. Her temperament was usually tolerant, but after all the whining Winnie was doing her nerves had worn thin, and before she could stop herself, she burst out angrily. "Miss Winnie, ya knows very well that Georgia was the last of the thirteen colonies, and it was the fourth to become a state, now what is so hard about remembering that, huh?"

Winnie and Abigail both sat there with their mouth hanging open wider than a rain barrel. Their eyes darted back and forth in confusion, as they searched CeeCee's face. CeeCee wanted to laugh since they both looked as if they just witness her eat a June bug on purpose, but she was too scared. However instead of getting in trouble as CeeCee had feared, the girls jumped up and down, giggling. Then stopping abruptly, they immediately began to ask all kinds of questions. "CeeCee, how do you know this, you are a colored girl? Do you know how to spell Georgia?"

Cautiously she answered, "Yes...G E O R G I A."

Both girls clapped as they squealed with pleasure.

"Can you write, can you repeat the poem we need to write?"

CeeCee nodded that she could, and Winnie hurried on, "What about our arithmetic problems, can you do those?

"Yes, them is easy," spouted CeeCee proudly.

With this announcement, Winnie handed CeeCee her books and ordered, "Good, then you can start with mine."

Of course, she also ordered, "CeeCee Brown, you are to tell no one about this, it is our little secret. And if Father finds out he will send you away. No one wants a colored girl that knows how to read because they cannot be trusted. Besides no one will believe you anyway," threatened Winnie.

Since CeeCee believed everything Winnie told her, she told no one her secret, except Viola. "Cause, I always tells you evarthing Viola, evarthing. And you better nevar say a word to nobody cause I's will surely be sent away."

Keeping the secret never bothered CeeCee, especially since her life was better than it had ever been before. And with all the lessons she was doing she was getting smarter and smarter day by day. "My favorite thing," she whispered to Viola while lying in the darkness of their tiny room, "is the readin...and I's like poetry, too. I tell you Viola; that poetry sure hurts a mind, but I's tryin to do my best to learns it well. I likes to hear Miss Pediwhopper read it to us. Still readin to maself is the best, my favorite book, Viola, is called, *Little Women*. It was wrote by a woman, her name is Louisa May Alcott. Viola, ain't that a prutty name? Yes ser, that book is my favorite readin. I can't even guess how many times I's read Miss Winnie's copy. She borrowed it ta me. Viola, Miss Winnie is becoming more like a friend ta me than the bossy girl she started out to be. We do just about everthing together. I guess she's just thankful fer all my help."

Once CeeCee started doing most of the studying she rapidly grew far smarter than either girl. She was very proud of this fact, yet it also bought new fears. She worried about what might happen to her if anyone ever found out, particularly Winnie. She did not take kindly to being less than anyone, especially a colored girl. CeeCee was certain that if it was ever learned that she was growing smarter than Winnie, the girl's anger would be more than she could handle, and no telling what she would do. So, she avoided the rivalry by pretending to be less than she was.

Only to her sister did she guiltily confess, "With all the studying I's doing, I is learning more than Winnie or Abigail. Viola, they don't do squat; they gives it all to me. But this time I is keeping my mouth shut; I aint tellin them, cause I is scared. I am fretful of what Mr. Roberts might do, if he finds out his color girl is smarter than his Winnie."

Sadly, all CeeCee's new knowledge was upsetting Viola. She never had a mind for learning and the thought of it frightened her. *'She was a Negra girl and learnin ain't right.'* She said these very words to her sister over and over, but nothing slowed CeeCee's hunger for education.

Finally, one night out of frustrated fear Viola cried, "CeeCee, jist white folks should be readin an writton. An if yas don't stop, I's gonna tell Mamma." As the years past CeeCee heard this threat more times than she could remember, but Viola never told and CeeCee had always known she wouldn't.

'I *guess everthing changes,'* thought CeeCee, '*and time does move on.'*

As the girls grew older things began to change, and as they entered their womanhood there was a definite difference between the three.

Eventually Winnie began to except visitors and have her own tea parties with white female friends from town. Soon she spent more time with them, than she did at home with CeeCee. It was not long after this inception that Winnie ordered, "CeeCee, you are not to address me as Winnie any longer. I want to be called Miss Winnifrey. Do you understand me, Miss Winnifrey?"

Sadly, she acknowledged, "Yes...Miss Winni...frey, yes I do's understand."

Later that evening she grumbled her despair to her sister as she worked the polish wax into Winnifrey's shoes. "She's just puttin on airs to impress her new friends. All this goin to music recitals and church socials, and leavin me home alone with idle time. It is all just her way to show her friends she's uppity. That's what I understand," she mumbled to herself.

Though ultimately after so much time spent alone CeeCee faced the fact, Winnifrey was no longer her friend, she had turned into a lady. And no matter how much she learned she was never going be a lady or get invited to a white girls party.

It was Viola who finally put it into the hurtful words that she herself, had tried to avoid thinking. "CeeCee, yas learned to read and acts likes a lady, but yas still just a colored servant girl. And thats alls ya ever gonna be, so ya better gits use to it. Yous is just a colored girl and ya ain't goin or doin anythin more than what color folks do."

The next day Viola's enlightenment was still heavy on CeeCee's mind and she felt gloomy most the morning. Though her day grew worse when Winnifrey informed her that she was going away. She was nearing her sixteenth birthday and her mother and father decided it take her to England to visit a distant relative for her gift. CeeCee wanted to be happy for Winnifrey, but she was too full of envy. Together with a new worry that lingered in the back of her mind. *Maybe Winnifrey was growing to the point that she would not need the aid of a simple colored girl. Maybe she is gonna need a lady's keeper, and she herself would be sent a packin.*

The two months Winnifrey was away, CeeCee did little else but read and dream of the pleasures she herself would never enjoy. And as she feared with Winnifrey's return everything changed, only not in the way she had imagined. Winnifrey herself had changed; she had grown and filled out enough to be called a full fledge woman.

Furthermore, CeeCee noticed there was a new aura about the girl. She could not easily put the new look into words, but she did try to explain it to Viola while they sat under the persimmon tree that evening. Though after some time was spent searching for the right description she finally gave up and blurted, "It's only that she's different. She aint the same girl that left here two months ago, thats all."

Winnifrey was bursting to tell someone about her trip. And after several days of keeping it in she finally chose to entrust CeeCee with every little detail.

"Since," she said, "there is no one else I can confide in... well, not without them spreading derogatory gossip about me and my actions," she giggled then blushed slightly. "You see CeeCee, most of my friends are a bit jealous of me, as I am sure you can understand why. So, I usually try not to add to their discomfort by flaunting my personal accounts."

CeeCee had no idea what Winnifrey was talking about, but she nodded none the less.

"I simply had a wonderful time in England, CeeCee. And while I was in London, I went to my first opera and I also saw a wonderful play." She giggled again then continued. "I even sat next to a young man. He is three years older than I. And when he said good night, he touched my hand ever so lightly with his lips. Oh, CeeCee, it brought such feelings...feelings I never experienced before. It was wonderful, the whole evening was wonderful."

Winnifrey spoke the boy's name, "Mr. Henry Dauber," and her eyes twinkled and began to take on a dreamy faraway look as she whispered to herself, "He was completely infatuated with my beauty."

Then to CeeCee she gushed, "Why I say, he could barely restrain himself. It was quite exhilarating and a feeling I long to experience again."

The look on Winnifrey face almost scared the dickens out of CeeCee. She never saw anything like it. Concerned, she asked, "Winnifrey..., you sure look sick, maybe you shoultn't be sittin next ta no boys, I heared you can catch things. Do you think you caught somptan?"

Later CeeCee grumbled as she told Viola, "Winnifrey just giggled like an ole fool and pretended to be all grown up when she said, "Why..., why how simple of you, CeeCee, you silly little colored girl. You cannot catch anything from a gentleman."

As soon as Winnifrey had finished her tale about her excursion, CeeCee had once again faced that Winnifrey's trip was far more than she herself would ever see. Not in her world..., no matter what she told herself, there was no way she was ever going to be a lady like she always hoped. She was a color girl, just like Viola and Winnifrey said, and color folks do not travel the world.

She tried hard not to feel sorrowful for herself and she put forth an effort to be happy for Winnifrey's new life. But this was harder than she thought it would be. Her mind kept bringing the same words to light,

'I ain't nothing but a Negra girl and that will never change. I is gonna end up just like Mamma and work my fingers ta the bone for Winnifrey while she's out havin fun.'

"Well, no, never mind," she told herself, "I still have my books Abigail gave me, and even if I can't travel across the seas, I can still see the world in my mind. I can go to parties too, jes like the ones Winnifrey talks about. Alls I has to do is read about them and pretend, and if I listen to Winnifrey's stories, it'll be just like I was there."

And this was something CeeCee did every night. As soon as her head touched her wooden bed, she began to dream of a life she would never exist in. She told herself, *I may never be invited to a real party. Or sit in the front row to watch a play, but I can surely live these affairs through Winnifrey's eyes.* And in fact, she did this so often that sometimes she forgot it was Winnifrey who lived them and not her.

CHAPTER THREE

During the next few weeks following Winnifrey's trip to England, CeeCee noticed several more changes in the girl. Some were so small they did not bear mentioning, but the biggest and the most obvious, was that she had become just plain boy crazy. There was not a place she came away from that she did not bring back a tall tale of some boy thinking she was the prettiest girl in the room. And before long, she was expressing a lot of interest in the boy down the road. His name was Christen Hopkins. CeeCee had seen him around, though him being a white boy she had never spoken to him. But now with Winnifrey talking of nothing else except Christen this, and Christen that, she soon started to think she knew him long before she ever made his actual acquaintance.

The thing is, considered CeeCee, Mr. Roberts and Mr. Hopkins, Christen's papa, were the closest thing there is to an enemy. Their feud started way back when both of their papas came near to blows over some tabbaca crop. Since then there never was any kind a friendship between the two men. Then of course years later there was that colt thing, which didn't help none....

From the beginning by way of stories, CeeCee was put right in the middle of Winnifrey's flirtations. Yet as time moved on it grew worse. It all began when Winnifrey arranged to meet a boy unaccompanied by a chaperone. She ordered CeeCee to accompany her and to be the lookout for her. CeeCee was against her sneaking off to see a boy, but Winnifrey threaten to fire her if she did not promise her allegiance. The liaison continued for weeks. Though, things got even worse when one morning CeeCee was folding the girl's undergarments in the clothes room, and Winnifrey came running into the room. It was easy to see the girl was frazzled and immediately she screeched, "CeeCee! CeeCee, you have got to help me. There is no one else I can turn to."

"Yas, Miss Winnifrey," was all CeeCee got out before Winnifrey grabbed her by the hand, then jerked her all the way up the stairs into the bedroom. When the door was shut tight, Winnifrey twirled around and started to speak rapidly. Then, instantly, she halted all speech and started to pace the floor. Back and forth she went from one side of the room to the other, as she wrung her hand nervously and fretted to herself, "Oh, oh, oh."

Finally, she faced CeeCee and cried out, "Oh my, oh my, CeeCee, How, just how can something like this happen to me? I never meant it to go this far. What am I going do? Surely Mother would understand, if she were here. Why did Father insist Mother accompany him on this business trip? How selfish of him, doesn't he know a young lady needs her mother around to care for her, not out gallivanting around the world? Oh, CeeCee, what am I to do?"

CeeCee said nothing for several minutes, as she strove to stifle her fears. She was scared witless, for anyone she growed up with there was only one fear that was this dreadful. At last she put into words her suspicion, "Winnie, Miss Winnifrey you's not with child, are's ya?"

Staggered by CeeCee's question, Winnie who by then was pacing once again, stopped in her tracks. And for an instant she looked as if CeeCee had slapped her. Suddenly she burst into laughter, as she choked to get the words out, "Of, of course I...I am not with child. Whatever would make you think such a thing? CeeCee, you are one foolish colored girl. A lady does not get herself in such a predicament, though I doubt you would know that."

This hurt CeeCee's feelings, but she only bowed her head and said, "Yas Mam," and nothing more.

Suddenly Winnifrey asked in a voice laden with anger, "CeeCee, I want to know why you ask such a hideous question? Certainly, you realize I am a lady, and I would never do anything so awful." She waited for an answer and when nothing came forth, she snapped sharply, "Speak up, you foolish Niggar girl."

Winnifrey had not made her feel this bad in years, and she almost choked on the tears she was holding back, but she stood tall and faced her straight on as she confessed, "It was just the way yous been behaven, as if you was scared beyond anythin I ever witnessed. I knows you is a lady, Miss Winnifrey, I guess I jes wadn't thinking."

"I certainly would say not," burst Winnifrey in a passionate snit. "Afterall, it is not like I am some back road colored girl, lifting her skirt for every boy who walks her way."

Again, CeeCee bit her cheek, so not to feel the pain that Winnifrey's words brought forth.

The two girls stood facing one another without either uttering a sound for what seem to be forever. Finally, CeeCee said, "Miss, you said yous needed me ta help ya."

Winnifrey tossed her hair back and answered, "Yes. Yes, I do. Truly I do. You see, CeeCee I have been writing this gentleman I met in England last March, Mr. Dauber..., Henry Dauber. And now he is here in Richmond and has written me a note, asking to see me at two o'clock today. This has bought about a predicament for me. Though I have come up with a brilliant plan and I need your help to carry it out."

Winnifrey's voice lowered as though she was speaking more to herself than to CeeCee who still stood disarmed and confused. "Luckily Mother and Father are out of the country, and we only

have my feeble minded Aunt Isabel here to contend with. Yes...,
with your help I am sure this can work."

Still very hurt from Winnifrey's earlier outburst CeeCee did not
feel obliged to help unless it was an order, so she asked hesitantly,
"I don't understand..., Miss Winnifrey. What can I do? I don't know
nothin about mens."

Winnifrey stared at CeeCee as if she could see through her, then
babbled hastily, "Well you know that Christen and I have been
spending some time together. Yet, entertaining Henry today is very
important to me..., though you see I am to meet Christen by the
creek around the same time Henry is to arrive. There is absolutely
no way I can tell Christen I can not meet him because of another
gentlemen caller. He just would not understand, and of course I certainly do not want to discourage Mr. Dauber. I fear if I do not receive him, he will lose interest and began to pursue other young
ladies...."

"Miss Winnifrey, if you aint interested in 'em, why do it matter
if he wants ta see other ladies?"

"Oh, CeeCee you are so simple, of course I care. You see Mr.
Dauber is quite the catch. He is definitely marrying material, and I
do want to keep him chasing me until I am ready for him to catch
me. But right now; I am enjoying the company of Mr. Hopkins."

"Hows you gonna be in two places if ya don't want to disap-
point either gentlemens, Miss Winnifrey?"

She looked CeeCee up and down before she responded, "Well, I
think I can fix a situation where Mr. Dauber will be distracted,
while I am out seeking the attentions of Mr. Hopkins."

CeeCee was still standing in the middle of the room gawking at
her bewildering charge who in turn, was looking at her strangely.
This only added to CeeCee's confusion as she started to feel awkward under the harsh gaze of Winnifrey. All at once the door
swung open and in entered a flustered Abigail who immediately
yelped, "Well, Winnifrey, I did my part, did you tell her? Did you
tell her what we are going to do?"

Without waiting for Winnifrey's answer she spun around to face CeeCee and continued, "CeeCee, ooh CeeCee, I truly do not feel good about this, but Winnifrey says this is the only way." She twirled back around to face her sister and beseeched, "Do we have to do this Winnifrey? Please say, no. Winnifrey she is a colored girl, surely anyone can see that."

"Abigail hush now, I was just about to tell CeeCee when you interrupted us, so go sit down and let me finish." Once more Winnifrey turned her focus back to CeeCee and quickly added, "You see, CeeCee, I figured I could fix you up in one of my finer dresses and do your hair up in a fashion that would make you appear a little more sophisticated and hopefully attractive." She frowned slightly at CeeCee and her all around appearance before she quickly babbled, "Then of course when Mr. Dauber gets here, I will introduce you as my cousin from out of town. That way when I excuse myself with a vile headache, he can sit with you while I go meet Mr. Hopkins. I shall not be longer than thirty minutes or so. Surely you can sit and keep your mouth shut that long."

CeeCee's mind was not working, all thought ceased, and not a word Winnifrey uttered was processed into its gist. She could not comprehend what the girl was inferring, or what her intentions were. Winnifrey without further consideration accepted CeeCee silence as agreement. Though in truth it did not matter if she agreed or not, Winnifrey had already made up her mind and intended to carry out her contrivance either way.

"See, my plan is very simple, CeeCee, and you should have no problem carrying it out at all. All you have to do is sit there and listen. And pleaseee...try not to speak, because that colored accent of yours will surely come through."

CeeCee's eyes bulged wide and she gaped like a fool at both girls. She was sure that this time Winnifrey had lost her mind, cause there was no way that this colored girl was gonna pass as her white cousin. Finally, her mouth dry as a withered corn husk, she gulped a mouth full of air and choked, "Wh... why can't Abigail entertain Mr. Dauber?"

"Do not be silly," replied Winnifrey, "Abigail is much too young and inexperienced to be left alone with a man."

Without waiting for any further discussion both girls turned and headed out the door for the stairs, as Winnifrey snapped back at CeeCee, "So come on girl, we have no time for dallying. We must begin at once if we are to get you cleaned up in time. Come along, CeeCee, I do say you are slower than molasses on a cold day."

CeeCee forced her body to move forward as Winnifrey continued. "I am afraid we will need all the time we have before Mr. Dauber gets here to fix you to some kind of acceptable appearance, and of course, you will need to practice your lines. We certainly can not have you stammering about like some ninny, now can we?"

CeeCee started her protest once again, "But Miss Winnifrey, I is the same age as Abigail, and I ain't got no experience either, you cain't put me wit a man." CeeCee could see her pleas were falling on deaf ears, yet she continued. "Winnifrey please, I cain't pretend to be yous cousin, he'll know. And your Aunt Isabel..., she is here and she's gonna know that I's aint yous cousin. What kind of fool plan has you cooked up Winnifrey...?"

"CeeCee listen to what you are saying. Have you forgotten everything you have learned these past years? Why I say, you are sounding no better than some ordinary niggar worker. Now I know as well as you, that when you put a mind to it, slow down and pick your words, you can sound as well-bred and white as Abigail or me. Now stop and think before you open your mouth. CeeCee, think before you speak."

"But Miss Winnifrey I is scared, and I don't wants ta do this."

"Hush now, Cecilia. Cecilia, that is what I will call you, cousin Cecilia, and do not call me Winnie, or Missy or Miss Winnifrey. Remember to call me Winnifrey, do not forget..., W-i-n-n-i-f-r-e-y."

CeeCee wanted to cry, but she followed the determined girls up the flight of stairs to the girls' mother's room. There they picked a simple brooch and a hair-bobbin. Afterward back in Winnifrey's room CeeCee stood in silence, as she nervously moved from one foot to the other while Winnifrey went through her closet. It was full of dresses and it took the determined Winnifrey several minutes before she decided on a lovely brown taffeta frock. It was trimmed with a light creamy lace and cinched tightly at the waist. She held it up and studied it. Then to get the full effect she held it against CeeCee as she smiled and whispered to herself, "Perfect, absolutely perfect. The lace brings the gold out in your eyes. You know Cecilia, I never noticed, but I do believe your eyes have several different colors in them. That is quite peculiar, do you not agree, Abigail?"

Disinterested in the conversation Abigail nodded her head. She was more interested in how to fix Cecilia's thick mass of shiny chestnut hair. Which once released from the tight sash she wore to hold her braids, fell softly into loose curls. Abigail mumbled to no one in particular, "CeeCee, your hair is not at all like a colored girl's should be."

Holding the dress out and against CeeCcc's again; Winnifrey nodded, "Yes, yes, this will do fine. Try to remember Cecilia that a lady does not babble. If you remember this, you should do fine. So, keep your mouth sealed and speak only when it is necessary, simply try and play demure. Oh, and smile a lot while you shyly nod your head every so often. That always works. Are you listening to me? Do you understand, Cecilia?"

CeeCee spoke slowly and listened to what she was sayin, "Yes, Miss Winnifrey, I believe I do."

"Cecilia! I told you to address me as, Winnifrey, simply Winnifrey. Can you remember that?

"Yes..., Wi-Winnifrey." Without warning CeeCee's eyes filled with tears and once again she wailed, "But whats about Miss Isabel, she's gonna know? I's really gonna git in trouble, Miss Winnifrey. Your Mamma and Papa is gonna send me away for sure. No color girl can git away wit passin white, and I's could git in real trouble. I's don't wanta do this."

"Ohhh, hush your whining, and stop those tears Cecilia before your eyes puff. Abigail pass me the wash basin." Winnifrey scolded as she grabbed a brush and started to clean CeeCee's nails. "I have a plan for that too. Aunt Isabel will be no trouble at all. As a matter of fact, it is already in place as we speak."

Abigail giggled, and soon Winnifrey joined in. Poor Aunt Isabel. She has such an incapability for spring flowers and their fragrant bouquet. It seems that they make her sneeze just awfully, and quite often it is so extreme that she ends up in her bed for hours. It is pitiful, but at times her eyes nearly swell shut and the light is extremely painful. I believe that is where we shall find her if there is a need. It is truly an embarrassment that our poor little Abigail had forgotten Auntie's aversion to the lovely posies, and without thinking she ordered flowers to fill every vase in our dear Auntie's outer-rooms as she lay asleep last night." Again, both girls burst into a mischievous laughter.

This further distressed CeeCee, although her dread was mostly for herself, and not their dear sweet Aunt Isabel. Yet still and all, for one fleeting instant she did feel grim for the poor elderly Auntie Isabel.

While at the same time both girls worked away on their separate task, CeeCee sat quietly and continued to fret. This was all too frightening for her. *I is a simple hired girl*, she groaned to herself. *Ever-body's gonna find out, and I is the one that gits in trouble, not Winnie or Abigail... just me."*

But there was not a single thing she could do about it, because Mr. Roberts himself said: it was her job to do whatever Miss Winnifrey said, and that is exactly what she was doing.

Once CeeCee was bathed and dressed, she could not believe the reflection in the mirror. She had a desire to look longer, but she felt discomfit with the image she was confronted with.

Even Winnifrey who rarely saw anyone's beauty but her own, whispered before she caught herself, "Ooh...ooh my lord...CeeCee, if I did not know you were a colored girl, I would never be able to tell, and I most certainly would not let you near any beau of mine."

Abigail echoed her sister's retort, "Oh CeeCee, you are as exquisite as anyone I have ever seen. You surely resemble no colored girl I have ever seen." Her sister's declaration did not please Winnifrey at all.

CeeCee practiced her walk until her feet ached in the fancy shoes Winnifrey gave her to wear. She also worked on what Winnifrey said was looking demure, which was not as hard as she thought it would be, since she felt awkwardly shy and unseasoned with her new look.

At last Winnifrey announced, "Mr. Dauber should be here any minute. We better hurry and get downstairs. Abigail, I want to seat CeeCee outside in the garden before anyone can see her, so you go get the lemonade and cookies for our guest.

Now remember Cecilia, Mr. Dauber is very wealthy, and a highly educated world traveler. So, I am quite sure he will discuss his many adventures. So, if I were you; I would simply sit as quiet as a church woman and let him reminisce about his travels. If you do this, you should not have any problem. Just remember, all you need to do is every so often nod your head and pretend interest. If you must speak, please ask a clear question and talk softly. And pleaseeee... ask it as casually and with as few words as possible. Just do not go into any lengthy discussions. Do you hear me, do you completely understand what I'm telling you, Cecilia?"

Winnifrey did not let CeeCee answer, but continued, "Not that I would expect that you could possibly add anything to Mr. Dauber 's reflections, but just do not get all immersed in his conversation and forget yourself. I know that imagination of yours, and I can only guess what you believe you have done or what stories you may come up with along the way....but...well never mind, come along."

Minutes later when CeeCee was seated alone on a bench that was situated among the lush greenery and out of view of anyone in the house, she reflected on the day's events thus far. She was still hurt by the cruel things Winnifrey had said. She had inferred several times that she was stupid or less than she was. CeeCee understood her place with most white folks, but when it came to Winnifrey she always felt close to being equal. Now she feared that that feeling was gone forever. She now realized that in Winnifrey's eyes, she was nothing more than just some ignorant colored servant and nothing more. She scooted closer to the edge of the seat and then looked around the garden. She was wholly familiar with it, yet this was the first time she had ever sat on a bench to observe the scenery. It was lovely and very different when you sit and look around without being disturbed. She closed her eyes and inhaled the sweet blossoms that surrounded the bench. At the same time, she continued to practice her pattern of speech in her head. She wanted to do her best, even if she was still angry with Winnifrey for forcing her to do this absurd thing. CeeCee pushed her lips forward to mimic Winnifrey's pout. Then once again she practiced her proper speech in silence as she reflected on Winnifrey and her crazy antics. After she had considered her plight, she quickly moved back to the situation at hand and muttered, "Sometimes that girl comes up with the wildest notions. I am not at all sure why she can not be just a little more customary like her sister, Abigail. Why one of these days, one of her plans *is gonna*, oops, is going to plain blow up in her face."

Yet what CeeCee feared most is *if* this ever happened, she would be the one to suffer. She opened her eyes and peeked to see if anyone was nearby and heard her words, and then closed them again. With her eyes shut tight she crossed her fingers and whispered a little prayer, "Please lord, not today. Please let today be as wonderful as it can be. I want this one chance to feel like the lady I look and smell like." She inhaled a deep breath then whispered one more, "Please Lord, let today be as lovely as the stories I read."

"Or as least as lovely as the creature who is whispering the prayer."

CeeCee almost jumped out of her skin she was so startled. Immediately her face turned a bright pink, and she wanted to run and hide. But instead she stood and covered her faced with a nervous smile. Speechlessly she waited for Winnifrey's introduction. Though not too surprisingly, once Winnifrey opened her lovely little mouth, her plan quickly began embellishing. And once more

CeeCee felt the weight of imaginary sandbags pulling her deeper and deeper down into a swamp filled with Winnifrey's lies.

"Mr. Dauber, I would like you to meet my dear cousin, CeeCee... cilia....," she stuttered for a second then continued, "Cecilia Roberts." She is visiting while her parents are abroad. I believe they are traveling through Africa on some outrageous safari. Can you imagine?"

Mr. Dauber's interest was plain to see. His eyes lit up and he asked, "Really? Where abouts in Africa? I hope not South Africa, I hear there has been an uprising there abouts."

Mr. Dauber's speech held a strange accent which wholly surprised CeeCee and she held her tongue while she pondered its pertinence. After a short delay she started to speak. But Winnifrey cut in with a flirtatious laugh and asked, "Why Mr. Dauber wherever are your manners?"

Catching himself he also laughed at his impropriety. Immediately he reached out and politely took Cecilia's hand in his, he bowed slightly and asked, "Please do forgive my rudeness, I assure you my parents did teach me better. I believe my lapse in deportment is due to the fact, that these past months have been primarily spent amongst the male species at Oxford. Miss Cecilia Roberts, it is extremely nice to make your acquaintance. Again, I do hope you will forgive my harshness. I am extremely interested in travels, that at times I get carried away and forget all aside from that fact."

Cecilia instantly became breathless when his lips touched her hand. She had never been this close to a man and certainly not a white man. She was so nervous her mind ceased to work, and her voice was lost completely. With her mind so benumbed, she, for an instant, almost forgot herself and started to curtsy. Yet, before she did so she caught herself with a nervous cough, and hurriedly gathered her thoughts before she could embarrass herself or anger Winnifrey.

At that moment and without conscious thought she became one of the ladies she always dreamed of being. "Why thank you, Mr. Dauber it is indeed a pleasure to meet you. I have heard so very much about you from my dear cousin Winnifrey, that at times I feel I have already been acquainted with you. Oxford, you say?"

Winnifrey's eyes widen with surprise as they sent a swift warning to CeeCee.

"Yes," answered Mr. Dauber, "and prior to that; I spent two years at Harvard University..., before I was escorted back to England. My dear parents had doubts that any school in the States could do justice for their sons' education. I am studying law."

When CeeCee sneaked a quick look at poor Winnifrey, her face still held a blend of a smile and disbelief as she stared at CeeCee.

Whom, Winnifrey noted, had already distracted Henry's attention. *This, she thought, is going to be much easier than I had anticipated.*

Though as soon as she recognized the look of interest in Henry's eyes; she began to wither as she stuttered, "I... I... I shall...", but instead of saying anything distinguishable she simply seated herself on the bench.

Mr. Dauber concerned asked, "Winnifrey, are you all right? Can I get you some water or something? My dear, you look ever so pale." This did little to relieve Winnifrey's stress. Since she never wanted to look less than perfect, especially in the light of another beauty, and she immediately began to moan as she fanned herself with her hand.

With Henry's show of concern Winnifrey promptly heeded to herself; *I must have misread Henry's interest in CeeCee,* and instantly she felt better, although she noted, *his obvious concern certainly will help make my exit effortless.* "I am so sorry, Henry; I do not know what has come over me. I feel slightly dreadful and lightheaded. Maybe I better lie down for a minute or two."

"My word, perhaps I better leave and we can do this another day."

By now Winnifrey was fully in control of her wits, and immediately sat her back straight and answered, "No. No please, I have truly looked forward to your visit, Mr. Dauber. I shall be so distressed if you do not stay. I am sure I will be fine in a matter of minutes. Cecilia, if you will not mind awfully, I would appreciate if you could sit with Mr. Dauber for a spell while I rest for a time. Then as soon as I feel better, Mr. Dauber we can continue with our little visit. Do you mind, Cecilia?"

Cecilia took her cue and happily bubbled like so many of the ladies with class seem to do, "Well, I would be extremely delighted to do so, that is, of course, if you do not mind, Mr. Dauber?"

"I would also be delighted, and if I may be so forward, I would like it very much if you could call me, Henry."

"Henry, you will also honor me greatly if you will merely call me Cecilia."

"Cecilia," he whispered her name, then decided, "it fits, for it is as lovely as you."

CeeCee smiled but said nothing.

Winnifrey stood to leave then hesitated momentarily. She was not at all comfortable with how well CeeCee was handling the situation; she was much more convincing than she ever expected her to be. Yet, before she could remind herself that she had not a thing to worry about, her vying nature reared its ugly head and she wondered if she should stay. But no, CeeCee was no competition at all. She was nothing more than a colored servant girl, play acting. Tomorrow she will go back to doing exactly what she does every day, taking care of her charges' needs, and nothing more.

With this thought in mind Winnifrey smiled meekly, then apologized again before she made her hasty exit. As soon as she was out of sight of Henry and CeeCee, she headed straight for the front door and her rendezvous with Christen Hopkins.

Winnifrey loved the feelings that Christen brought to light within her. Her entire body tingled at his every touch. She realized it was wrong to be sneaking off to meet him, but when it came to being with him, all common sense just flew out the window. For an instant she felt a tiny bit shameful for poor Henry sitting there alone with CeeCee. Poor man, how unfair of me to put him in such a distasteful position. One day after we are married, I will have to make it up to him.'

Indeed, he, as of yet has not revealed his full intentions, or asked for her hand in marriage, however she had no doubt he would one day.

CHAPTER FOUR

C eeCee looked in the other direction away from where Henry
sat. She could not think of a single thing to say, so she did as
Winnifrey had advised, and kept her eyes diverted and her mouth
shut tight. After a long awkward silence, Henry asked, "So
Cecilia..., have you been to Africa?"

Flabbergasted by the question she blurted without any
forethought, "Ooh my..., heaven's no, I never even been out...." Then
conscious of her dull-witted response, she instantly fell back into
silence.

Henry fought to hide his smile, though his eyes revealed the
pure pleasure of her. He liked her shyness; it was puzzling as well
as pleasing. He started to ask another question and then promptly
decided, if he talked of idle things for while it might help ease her
discomfort.

"You know my homeland is England and I have been to the
States many times. As well as France, Italy, and even the Alps, along
with a couple of the Middle Eastern countries, but never have I ever
thought of going to Africa. Not that I am opposed to it, mind you. It

simply never occurred to me. Yet now I believe it might be worth considering..., the trip I mean."

At once CeeCee's curious nature was awakened. She quickly turned to face him and asked eagerly in a strained voice, "Ca... can you please tell me about your travels..., Mr. Dauber...Henry. I would love to hear about them?"

Again, he grinned at her guilelessness and noted how refreshing it was. Then without further ado he set off into his many adventurous journeys.

While CeeCee listened attentively, she discreetly watched his jaw muscles move up and down as he spoke. His facial expressions filled with passion and excitement with each absorbing tale. For some reason this bought a feeling of yearning in her. At one point she realized she was closely evaluating his handsome looks, along with his mannerisms and a feeling of warmth spread throughout her body. This was something she never experienced before and she wondered if her face was flush, because she felt a tinge heated. At which time she admitted to herself, *he sure is truly pleasin lookin.*

Uncomfortably she shifted. He was white and this she was quite aware of, but in spite of that, he was still wonderful to look at. His hair was dark and wavy, but just slightly, not tightly like a colored man's. His cheeks and forehead were broad, and this created a look of virility. Suddenly she felt her heart give a flutter and she diverted her eyes. They immediately rested on his hands which were also large. Yet she noticed their largeness did not impede their gracefulness, and when he moved them around in the air as he spoke of places she only read or dreamed about, he did so with a courtly flare.

At one-point Henry stood and walked around the area in front of her as he talked and she noted that his shoulders were broad, almost surprisingly so. But since he was so tall, they did not seem to make him look clumsy like her Papa's did, maybe because Papa's was hunched, and Henry's was erect and strong looking.

She watched his mouth move and she faintly colored when she wondered if his lips had ever kissed Winnifrey's. She had never been kissed and chances are she never would be. Many colored boys wanted a lighter skin Negra girl, but not someone who looked more white than Negra, like herself. Nearly all the boys she knew seemed afraid of her, and that was not likely to ever change, so being kissed was not....

Henry sat down on the bench and this drew her attention back to him. She could see his stories were drawing to an end and Winnifrey was still not back. She wished she would hurry because she did not know what she could say to him.

At the conclusion of his tale he sat back against the bench and silently smiled at her. She smiled back in her inexperienced way and in turn she stood up and walked over to the flowers that seemed to be in full bloom. She smelled one, then turned and said, "Henry, thank you, that was a splendid adventure. I feel as if I have just returned from a voyage around the world and yet I never left my garden."

For CeeCee this was true, but not unusual. This is how she lived her life, through dreams of other peoples' experiences. That, no doubt would never change.

"Have you traveled much, Cecilia?"

"My family travels often, but no, they never take me along. They feel that my schooling is all too important to be wandering the lands with them. Although I do agree with them to some point, I also believe that one should never underestimate the value of travel." She read that very commentary in a book that belonged to Winnifrey's Aunt Isabel, and she hoped it sounded right vocalized.

She needed not to worry, for as far as Henry was concerned, she could have spoken in gibberish and he would not have care. In his mind she was the most bewitching perfection he had ever laid eyes on.

Her beauty was magnificent, although it seemed not to faze her in the least, and he found this more seductive then if she flaunted it. *Though,* he reasoned, *could she simply be unaware of her beauty, this was surely how it appeared to be.*

He was unaccustomed to this kind of behavior. In his world, most of the young women Cecilia's age, were, more often than not, in search of a husband, and they were very well aware of their physical assets and displayed them most freely. Though from what he could tell of Cecilia, she was very close to uncomfortable with her splendor. He had noticed when he flattered her; she immediately withdrew within herself, and she certainly did not exhibit or openly display any pageantry. At this point he decided more women should follow her lead, since her comportment was most enticing.

Henry Dauber, as all young men of his station, was quite confident of the catch he would be for almost any of the young women he met. His family's name along with their assets were vast and far outweighed nearly all, not excluding Winnifrey's family. In any case, thus far, he had not run across one that has made his heart skip a beat like Cecilia did. And when she turned and fixed her dazzling gaze upon him, he wanted to fall to his very knees, and kiss the lovely long fingers she so nervously wrung, until they relaxed their stressful grip. He wished he could think of something to say that would help ease some of the strain she so unequivocally, yet unconsciously felt. Nevertheless, he stood in silence and simply appreciated her extraordinary sweet beauty.

After another awkward moment he gave a light, laughed, then started to speak. At that very same moment Winnifrey rushed out of the side door of the drawing room into the garden. Briskly she headed straight in their direction while criticizing herself all the way, "Oh my, how deplorable. I am so sorry, Henry, you must think me awfully rude. Wretchedly I must have fallen to sleep the second my head hit the pillow. I can not think whatever came over me. I am sure you are as bored as a turnip Henry. Cecilia knows so little about entertaining a gentleman."

"No...no, my dear Winnifrey, I would say to the contrary. Cecilia and I have had a wonderful visit. Though I regret to say it must come to an end, and a truly sorrowful reality from my standpoint. Though nonetheless as disheartening as it may be, I am afraid the time has gotten away from me and I must leave at once, or I will be late for another appointment."

Winnifrey's expression instantly became dread filled; she could not believe her ears. Immediately she jerked her head in the direction to where CeeCee stood amongst the flowers. Her biggest fear was that the cat was out of the bag and that Henry was angry with her. If CeeCee spoiled her plan and failed to give an effective performance as her cousin, she, Winnifrey Roberts, will be ruined forever, the laughingstock of society. But no, CeeCee looked fine, though her face did hold a stupid dreamy eyed expression.

Quickly she glanced back to where Henry stood gawking at her colored servant and her heart fell to the ground. *He is smitten with her, a simple little nigger girl. Well I never,* she grumbled silently to herself. However, I must bear in mind, he has no idea of this fact and that is something I best not alter. I will certainly fix this silly predicament later, surely in some other way, beside the truth.

Abruptly Winnifrey changed her expression to a flirtatious smile. Suggestively she moved a few steps closer in his direction and when she was closed enough, she clasped his hands in hers. After she locked her gaze on his, she tipped her head slightly and giggled, then scooted an inch closer. This, she told herself, is as close as I can get and still remain respectable. She pushed her lips into what she always thought was an attractive pout and said, "Mercy no, dear Henry, you must not leave? I have yearned for this visit." Suddenly her eyes lit up, and she added in pretended annoyance, "As a matter of fact, I have thought of little else since this morning. Why that alone may be the very reason I felt ill." Again, her lips fell into the pout, as she waited for him to apologize. When no apology came, she pushed on with a whine, "Henry, if you leave so soon it will simply break my little heart in two." At this time, she confidently gave him her biggest smile, while she waited for him to concede.

Henry's green eyes twinkled with enjoyment at Winnifrey's obvious plight, and he weighed whether he should give in to her or not. Yet he disliked her prior remarks about Cecilia. He thought them rude so he decided against staying. However, he did decide to play along with her silly flirtation. *Yes*, he thought, *this might prove to be a pleasurable game.*

"That my visit made you ill, Winnifrey, I am truly remorseful. For my intentions were never to cause you unfavorable wellbeing. Though, I do fear far worse may befall you, since I have heard one can easily perish from a broken heart."

Henry wanted to laugh at Winnifrey's dumbfounded expression, though he did not and he continued his remarks, "I hope you realize Winnifrey, that I would not wish to cause discomfort..., for you *or* that little heart of yours. Still before it gets any later, I do have to leave."

"Henry, I must insist...."

"Winnifrey," explained Henry as he cut her plea short, "I am afraid I will be forced to bring you even greater sorrow, for tomorrow I shall be leaving the States and returning to England."

"Henry Dauber, how could you? Why we have not even begun our visit."

"Yes true, that is true, and that is one reason why I left my morning hours free."

Winnifrey's eyes suddenly lit up, though her triumph was purely delusion because Henry immediately turned to face Cecilia and asked, "Cecilia, I would be honored if you would permit me a visit, before I leave."

Henry saw the instant look of discomfort that crossed CeeCee's face and he added, "Even if it can only be for a brief period, it will still be greatly appreciated."

Winnifrey pushed herself between the blushing CeeCee and Henry and forced her tone to be cheery considering the situation, "I will be pleased to spend some time with you Henry. Moreover, first thing in the morning I will have a couple of steeds saddled and ready for a leisurely ride. Why, I will even have a bountiful picnic basket packed for our pleasure. However, unhappily Cecilia will not be accompanying us, she will have to ready herself for her trip back to school. I fear she will have little time for anything else."

"Oh," moaned Henry, "I am terribly sorry to hear that, Cecilia. Maybe next time I visit friends in the States, we can continue with our adventurous journey."

Fearfully CeeCee nodded and glanced demurely down at her feet. His obvious look of interest made her feel happy yet afraid at the same time, since Winnifrey's angry glare was scaring her silly.

Winnifrey knew Henry was delighted with the girl he thought CeeCee to be, and deplorably it was quite clear CeeCee wished in her heart that she could be this girl, the white girl she appeared to be in all aspects, except reality.

Suddenly Winnifrey had enough of the two ogling each other, and she grabbed Henry by the arm and led him towards the door. She gushed with pretended excitement as she chattered all the way to the foyer.

CeeCee hesitated near the gardenia bush. Taut and short of breath she silently prayed before she moved forward, *Lord, please do not let him ever find out that I am no more than a colored servant...please Lord, please?*

Once the door closed behind Henry, Winnifrey angrily turned and faced the distraught CeeCee. *Her look,* CeeCee thought, *resembles a male cat who's about to fight over a female cat in heat.* With this thought her fear grew greater. But no past assault prepared her for Winnifrey's wrath. Her voice was shrill, and it echoed throughout the room when she screeched, "What have you done, CeeCee Brown? Did you forget yourself and not behave like a lady?"

CeeCee stepped back in fear, then shakily she answered the accusation, "Na...na Ma..mam," she stuttered, I, I bahaved."

"Then why was Henry looking at you like that? Tell me girl, what did you do? Did you go lifting your skirt? You niggars are obscene."

With her last statement Winnifrey's face scrunched up, and her eyes expressed the same disgust as her voice. CeeCee at once became even more frightened then she was, and she stumbled and emitted a low cry as she searched for the right words to answer the allegation. She was not quite sure exactly what Winnifrey was asking her, but she knew whatever it was, it was not good, and when she fully comprehended the implication; she turned a bright red. Her embarrassment was soon replaced by anger, and she expressed it with an indignant wail. "Miss Winnifrey Roberts, I ain't did nothin wrong, I is just as much a lady as you is."

This time it was Winnifrey who turned a bright crimson, since the one thing she was not today, was a lady and even if CeeCee did not know this, she herself did, and this enraged her even more. With an offended snort, she gave CeeCee a hard slap across the face. CeeCee held back the cry of pain as Winnifrey gave her one more disgusted look. Then she threw her head back, and in a huff stamped, across the room and all the way up the staircase. She was livid and she wanted this colored girl to know that she was never again to forget her place, and she certainly best not ever compare herself with the likes of her again.

That night when CeeCee lay her head back against the thin frayed excuse of a mattress, the first thing that came to mind was Henry and how special he had treated her. *Just like a real lady,* she thought, *my, that sure is a good feelin.* Very soon her mood changed when her mind settled on Winnifrey and her slap. This was the first time Winnifrey had ever hit her, yet her revile hurt as much as the blow itself did. She reached up and felt the welt on her cheek and thought of Henry. He was going to spend the morning in the company of Winnifrey. Herself, she was ordered to stay out of sight. Winnifrey said, *I want you completely out of my, or Henry's sight.* Even so, she had no wish to see Henry, especially with the large welt Winnifrey's slap left across her cheek.

A cry almost escaped her lips, and her chest felt full of shame as she remembered Winnifrey's accusations. Suddenly CeeCee's anger for Winnifrey swelled, and in her mind, she mocked the girl's indignant attitude while she mimicked her ill behavior. *CeeCee Brown, did you forget yourself and not behave like a lady? Did you go lifting your skirt? You niggars are obscene. How can she accuse me of that behavior...the... the very thought of it is..., well she should know me better,* CeeCee silently cried?

CeeCee felt Viola stir as an elbow jabbed her side and she moved so her sister could turn over. There was little room in the small makeshift bed and CeeCee did not wish to wake her, she wanted her solitude so she could think further on the days' events.

The brightness from the full moon outside filtered through a crack in the ceiling that her papa hadn't had time to fix, she hoped he would before the rains. She wrenched her head to see if Viola was still asleep. After she heard several even snores, she knew it was safe to go back to her earlier reflections. *Winnifrey is the one whose behavior should be questioned, not mine,* she mumbled. *Though it's ain't no mystery why Winnifrey's conduct has become so appalling. Since she spends so much time with Mary Lavine Johnson. That girl is a dreadful person. To most it was no secret that Mary Lavine is and always has been plain spoiled. She certainly doesn't take kindly to not gettin her own way.*

CeeCee knew better then to blame Mary Lavine for *everything,* since Winnifrey herself had always been as least as selfish and difficult, as the pretty Miss Mary Lavine. But lately she did seem to be out of control, and she treats everyone, *especially me,* with no concern. "I think Winnifrey has begun to act more like Mary Lavine, than Mary Lavine herself. Except Mary Lavine ain't so boy crazy like Winnifrey," grumbled CeeCee louder then she intended. Quickly she looked over to check to see if she woke her sleeping sister. Viola was still resting peacefully, so CeeCee added. "And if she don't stop chasin that Hopkins boy like she's been doin, she is gonna be in some big trouble. No, lady I ever sees acts like she been doin."

As soon as her conjecture was aired, her anger dissipated and she moved to scold herself instead, "CeeCee listen to your words, speak proper. How you ever gonna be a lady if you can't speak well." However, she knew speaking properly took a concentrated effort, and right now she was just too tired to think that hard. Half asleep her mind drifted towards Christen Hopkins and she shuddered. Winnifrey was messin where she should'nt be and this worried her. If her Papa ever finds out, she is gonna be in more trouble than a fat goose at Christmas time. *Yes ser, Mr. Roberts hates Mr. Hopkins as much as the other way around. All cause of that blamed colt that wandered off and mixed with the Hopkins' herd. Yes, I guess that's when things got worse than it was*, settled CeeCee. She never heard the whole story only bits and pieces over the years, so she didn't know for sure what was fact or fib. Some say Mr. Roberts confronted Mr. Hopkins to ask for the pony's return and his request was met with a hostile refusal. Of course, this angered Mr. Roberts who immediately accused Mr. Hopkins of pilfering. In return and in a fit of anger he bellowed, "Roberts, I am not in any way a thief? You, like your father before you, are no gentlemen. And you proved that the very day you deliberately sat out to steal my beloved fiancée,' Miss Ollifrey...." About that time, he came to realize that Mrs. Hopkins was standing in the doorway. Her look of disdain was said to show all that needed to be said, and at that time both men dropped the discussion. No more words were ever spoken, and to this day the breach continues.

"So," CeeCee advised the flickering light that still shone in her room, "if Winnifrey has a lick of good sense, she'll stop actin so vulgar and stir clear of that Hopkins boy before her Papa finds out."

CeeCee's eyes felt heavy and she began to doze yet one thought came to mind as her proper words began to fade. *On the other hand, it should all be over soon enough. Winnifrey don't know, but the boys she heard talkin behind the carriage house, said that Christen had a yearnin for the lovely Mary Lavine, and she for him. Their very words was, 'we expect one day Christen is gonna ask Mary Lavine to wed him.'*

Sleepily she thought, *that, possibility alone should be enough to keep Winnifrey away from Christen Hopkins.* "Yes, when it comes to gettin what Mary Lavine wants, she is a fierce girl to contend with. I doubt Winnifrey is gonna have a blaze of a chance against her. But I guess that don't matter none, cause Winnifrey is gonna do just as she pleases, anyhow."

CeeCee rolled over and closed her weary eyes as she sighed, "as for her being uppity like she been, that most likely aint gonna change either, so I best get used to it if I wants to keep my job. Yes, I best not go forgettin my place no more..., though it sure was nice bein like a lady today....

It was about a week or so after Henry left to go back to England that things started to get back to normal. Winnifrey pretended that everything was the way it used to be before Henry ever came for his visit. She never once brought up the fact that she had slapped CeeCee, or that she believed the girl had misbehaved. She simply dropped all mention of the situation. Yet for CeeCee, the fact that Winnifrey and Abigail had deceived Henry Dauber by passing her off as their white cousin laid heavy on her mind. She was full of fear that someone would find out and blame her for the deception. Nonetheless, with Winnifrey acting as if nothing ever happened CeeCee soon began to relax her guard and think of other matters, which mainly turned out to be Winnifrey and her wild behavior.

Once Mrs. Ollifrey returned home from her travels abroad, the jaunts Winnifrey made to the lake became naught since it was more difficult to carry them out. In CeeCee's mind this was a good thing since she felt so uncomfortable with all the fibs, she had been forced to tell Aunt Isabel and now Winnifrey's mother to cover for her charge. Yet soon after Mrs. Ollifrey returned Winnifrey's lies and the jaunts returned. CeeCee herself stood witness to her false-hoods more times than she could recall and each time she witnessed the lies she was amazed by Winnifrey's ability to embellish her falsehoods. She never even winced when she told her Mamma a bold-faced lie. CeeCee wanted no part of the lies, but she had no choice and became an accessory to them when Winnifrey ordered her to. As hard as she tried, there was nothing she could say to sway the girl's bad behavior. Particularly now that Winnifrey knew what CeeCee was capable of, she used this knowledge to get what-ever help she needed to achieve her frolics. She threatened to di-vulge her secret so often that CeeCee lived in constant fear of being exposed. She did not want to be sent away, and this is what Winnifrey said would happen if anyone guessed that she was so clever or that she had passed for white.

To justify the support Winnifrey reminded CeeCee that she was there to do her bidding. No matter what the request she was to do as she asked, as per her Father's orders from the very beginning of her employ. So, CeeCee was forced to give credence to Winnifrey's lies and antics.

CeeCee reminded herself day after day; like it or not without question; her job was to do whatever Winnifrey demanded. Of course, almost daily Winnifrey repeated, "CeeCee, you should be utterly indebted to me, for it is I, who gave you all that you have, and undoubtedly it is I, who can take it away."

It was only a month later that Winnifrey received a letter from Henry. After the normal salutations he requested CeeCee's address at school. After reading that in her letter, Winnifrey was fit to be tied. She was even madder than the first time when she thought CeeCee had raised her skirt for Henry. She screeched CeeCee's name so loud it could be heard in the yard out by the stables.

When CeeCee heard the scream; she thought something awful had happened and she took off in a dead run towards the wail and the main house. She was met by Winnifrey at the front door as she swung it open with a bang and screeched her name one last time. After that Winnifrey stared wide eyed, her face quivering with anger. CeeCee was terrified; she had no idea of what she might have done to have induced such anger.

Winnifrey said nothing for what seem like an eternity, then she started to stutter, while her head bobbed up and down. "Up...up...Up upstairs," as she pointed and jerked her arm angrily towards the stairwell. The look on her face sent shivers up CeeCee's spine, and she stood frozen on the outside step. Again, in a huff Winnifrey pointed violently towards the stairs to indicate that she wanted CeeCee to move immediately. Cautiously CeeCee moved inward, then followed the stumping girl up the stairs to her room. As soon as they entered Winnifrey slammed the door and turned to tear into CeeCee. She yelled, "You little Jezebel, you...you.... you... What did you do to my Henry? What...CeeCee? You tell me. You had to have done something disgusting. That is the only reason he would be interested in someone like you."

CeeCee was scared. She did not know about the letter and her mind did not know where to go with Winnifrey's question. Her mouth opened and moved up and down, but no sound came out. Her first instinct was to cry, then she wanted to run, but her legs wouldn't move.

Finally, full of fiery anger Winnifrey ordered, "You..., you little tramp, sit down." She pointed to the other side of the room and continued, "I do not need to hear your excuse. I... I just want...."

Suddenly she stopped and inhaled a deep breath, then in a controlled, yet wrath filled voice she explained. "I received a letter from my dearest Henry today, and....and a request," she screeched. She stopped long enough to take another breath then ordered, "CeeCee, I want you to sit down and you will write everything I say, do you hear me?"

CeeCee still stood stiff by the closed door. She saw that Winnifrey was pointing towards the chair by her desk, but she was too scared to move. Winnifrey hollered, "CeeCee move and sit down, and I want you to write what I tell you."

Slowly CeeCee moved to the chair and picked up the pen and paper that sat on the desk. The incensed Winnifrey stood right behind the chair that sat in front of the fancy writing desk. CeeCee kept her head downward as her eyes peeked upward and waited for Winnifrey's words. Winnifrey thought for a minute, then began to dictate the words she wanted CeeCee to write to Henry. CeeCee wavered then slowly she began to fill the paper with more of Winnifrey's lies.

"Dear Henry.... Stop," said Winnifrey, "First I want you to listen to every word I tell you, CeeCee Brown. Then I want you to write it exactly like I say. Do you understand me?"

"Yas, Miss Winnifrey, I do."

'Dear Henry,

I truly enjoyed your social call, though I feel it would be best if we do not enter into any kind of an attachment; by letter-writing. This, I fear could be insinuated as a relationship, and I have already been promised in marriage to a gentleman from Carolina, who I fret may consider our friendship to be an act of betrayal. I wish you well, and hope you continue to derive joy from your travels.'

"Now," continued Winnifrey, "I want you to mention how much I, Winnifrey, enjoyed his company and how I am looking forward to his next visit, and end it with, Regards, Cecilia Roberts."

Winnifrey was delighted with the letter though CeeCee never felt worse for lying in her life. She wanted to weep when Winnifrey grabbed it from the desk and shoved into an envelope to mail off that very day.

That night CeeCee said a prayer and begged for forgiveness. She also prayed that Henry would never find out the truth then she cried herself to sleep.

CHAPTER FIVE

The summer was hot and just about everyone around had a short temperament. The intense winds whipped through Virginia with a vengeance and by the time the weather showed a lick of change, there had already been more than a few fist fights amongst the Negro workers.

Even if the summer was blusterier and hotter than normal, they were ultimately blessed with a shorter duration than normal and with this change in the weather brought the much-needed change in dispositions.

Soon things began to get back to normal and everyone welcomed this openly. They thanked the Lord for his kind favor and cool air, as well as praising him for giving it mercifully before anyone got killed.

CeeCee sighed and rubbed the dampness from her brow as she laid back and rested against the large tree trunk. She took a bite of the pie her Mamma had cut for her and Viola then said, "This sure is a hot summer, Viola, but I has to say the wind that's been tearin through Virginia is nothin like the fury Miss Winnifrey's been throwin out. I would say she's been madder than a Mamma bear lookin for her missin cub. She is downright basides herself. She just cain't believe her Papa and her Mamma is sendin her off to finishin school. I sure would like to go to finishin school, but only white folks, git to go."

She pondered the possibility as she watched Mr. Roberts get out of his carriage and head for the front door before she moved on, "Well anyhow, her arguments ain't done her a bit of good, but she's still fightin like a chicken abouts to git its head chopped off. I tell you Viola, the look on her face when Mr. Roberts said, 'that is my final decision...Winnifrey.' Well... there is no words to describe it, Viola, none at all." She shoved the last bite of her pie into her mouth and sat the tin aside as she grabbed Viola's hand and said, "Come on Viola, let's go hear whats goin on."

CeeCee pushed the box closer to the structure of the house then climbed up, as she mumbled, "It don't look like Winnifrey's gonna git her way this time, Viola. All the same she is still gonna fight, and I am guessin she will till the end." Thereupon she laid her ear against the window and shushed her sister to silence as she listened to the arguments inside.

"Winnifrey, do we have to go over this, again? You are going to Georgia and finish your education at Brenau Women's College. That is final, young lady. I do not wish to hear any more of your arguments."

Winnifrey turned on her heels and faced the only person she felt would support her pleas. "Mother..., pleaseee, you tell him he can not do this. You can not let Father send me away, Mother. Why I will die from severe loneliness! Can you explain this to him?"

Ollifrey smiled her understanding; nonetheless she agreed with her husband. "Winnifrey, you will like the young ladies that attend Brenau. The school is one of the most prestigious southern schools in the States. These girls have come from the same social background as you my dear, and from each, you will learn as they will from you."

Winnifrey was disappointed by her mother's words of betrayal. She had hoped she would support her and not her father's ridiculous plan. Finally accepting her impending defeat, she twirled around and faced her father who was busy readying himself to leave for another appointment.

"Father, please, you have to understand. I am much too young to be away from my family. And...and Abigail...she is just starting into womanhood and she is going to need her older sister close by. You must see this, Father. This is so wrongful, and Father I shall miss all that is dear to me. Father, can you please understand this? Pleaseee, let me stay home. I truly cannot bear the thought of leaving."

Without a pinch of concern her father stood firm and answered, "You, my dear will be going away to Brenau. And you will take part in the sort of life that any young lady of your social position should. You will meet and become friends with the most exceptional young ladies of today, and I dare say, I suspect they will remain important to you throughout your life. And Winnifrey, I expect I will hear no more of this discussion... do you hear me, not another word." Winnifrey's mouth flew open to speak and Hershal ordered, "Winnifrey, not a word." He hesitated while he evaluated her tears along with her supposed sisterly concern, then continued once again. "Moreover, as for Abigail, I assure you she will do fine without your sisterly guidance. That my dear is exactly why she has a mother."

He had arched a brow as he was slightly ruffled by his daughter's pretend concern and asked, "I trust you do believe your mother is capable of taking charge of Abigail's individual requirements.... without your assistance?"

Hershal Roberts waited for his daughter's validation, but none came. Only tears drifted down her lovely face and she bowed her head in disappointment. At this point her father added. "And if concern for your sister truly distresses you, the fact that Abigail will also have CeeCee at her disposal should help ease your mind greatly." Hershal was miffed at his daughter's feeble attempt to use her sister's requisiteness to sway him. "However," he laughed lightly as he finished his remarks. "You see, Winnifrey my dear, you can leave for school with freedom of mind and light heart. There is no reason for you to worry while you are away, because Abigail will be just fine without her big sister's tutelage."

Once his words had sunk in Winnifrey's face turned a bright red and she burst, "What! Father no..., no Father you can not as well take CeeCee, how will I manage without a girl to look after me? Oh Father...think. Me... me away from my family and no one to care for my essential needs. What Father, what shall I do? I can not take care of myself."

Hershal sighed; he was near the end of his patience with Winnifrey and her arguments. The rumors he had heard lately already sealed her fate and no number of quarrels will change his mind. Nevertheless Winnifrey did not know of the rumors, or her father's resolution, yet she could hear the finality of his decision in the tone of his voice. Especially when he bellowed, "Winnifrey, mercy sakes alive, we are not sending you out into the wilderness to fiend for yourself. You will be attending one of the South's finest finishing schools. Which I might remind you, only takes girls from the best families, and I am sure these girls know as little about taking care of themselves as you do. So, I imagine the staff is fully adequate."

Unaccustomed to, yet not overwhelmed by her father's anger, Winnifrey made one last attempted. "But...Father, I will have to leave all my friends. Mary Lavine's not going and neither is Ola Florence, I will be the only one."

"Which is my point exactly child. You will be among young ladies of the best lineage instead of socializing with those of *questionable* standings. And as for your daily needs, that will be properly taken care of by the staff at the school. Now if you do not mind, I have more demanding business to attend to? Ollifrey my dear, where is that contract? I left it on the breakfast table this morning."

"On your desk, Dear."

Winnifrey started to protest once again and her father immediately cut her off with, "I refuse to hear another objection Winnifrey. This is not open to further discussion, and you, young lady, will began to prepare for your departure in two weeks' time."

CeeCee felt bad for Winnifrey, though she was extremely relieved to hear that she was not going to be accompanying her. For she knew as well as she knew anything, that the girl would surely get her into more lies along the way. She was also aware, even if the Roberts were not, that all the wailing and whining Winnifrey was doing; was mostly because she was leaving Christen Hopkins behind. Of course, the prospect of leaving him to the beguiling charms of Mary Lavine added greatly to her distress.

CeeCee made a silent wager, *Why I would put a penny down, that the very idea of leaving Christen Hopkins alone, is what is frightening Winnifrey so. Far, far more than the thought of her leaving her family behind.'*

For the next two weeks Winnifrey went about the business of laying things out for CeeCee to pack. She had three large chests and a smaller one for her personal items. Throughout this duration she never once replaced her fretful look with a smile. Even when Mary Lavine visited, and brought her a lovely going away gift of lace handkerchiefs!

She told CeeCee after Mary Lavine left, "I am doomed... I am to be an old maid and live my life in loneliness because all the young men I know will be gone by the time I get back from school. Everyone will be happily married."

Ollifrey tried to console her daughter and reassured her, "Your beauty, my dear, will last at least until you find the man of your choice. So please do not fret, your life is far from being over. One day you will see that this was for the best." She patted her daughter's hand, and soothed, "Sweetheart, most gentlemen of any kind of status want to marry a well-bred, educated woman. The Georgia's school for young women is just the kind of school to produce such a desirable wife. This, I assure you, you will one day be thankful for."

But these sentiments fell on closed ears. There were no words to console Winnifrey. She knew her life was over, and she had barely begun her seventeenth year.

Abigail was much easier to take care of than Winnifrey. She had a sweet disposition and was not at all demanding. At times she even attempted to help CeeCee when she was folding her personal articles and several times, she assisted in putting them away. CeeCee could not help but become flustered when she was treated in such a manner. She knew her place and she feared if anyone saw Abigail caring for herself, she would surely lose her job. After all, it was her duty to tend to Miss Abigail's needs, not the other way around.

Mostly what CeeCee liked about Abigail was her even temper, and that she never once asked her to lie or do anything that she did not feel was right. All the years she had known both girls, she never before realized how different they were. While Winnifrey was full of herself and boy crazed, Abigail was exactly what CeeCee thought a lady's nature should be. Slightly shy, with a softness about her, that made you like her even if you did not want to. Which is what CeeCee suspected was the case with Abigail's new-found friend, Ola Florence, who up to this point, had always been more Winnifrey's friend and companion.

Still and all the improved situation did not last long since Winnifrey cried so much in her weekly letters, that Mr. Roberts decided that maybe his daughter was right. She did need a few comforts from home, and by two months' time he told Mrs. Ollifrey, "Get CeeCee ready to send down to Georgia. Meanwhile, I will deal with the Headmistress and all her objections. See that she is ready to leave by next Tuesday morning."

CeeCee stayed in a little room behind Winnifrey's. She ate and stayed pretty much alone, since only one other girl had brought a servant with her. She was French and didn't speak very much English.

The first two weeks away from home CeeCee spent day after day yearning for Viola and her company. Everything seemed so strange. Nothing was like the plantation in Richmond, and since this was the first time she had ever been away from her family, she was frightened and homesick.

As for Winnifrey, nothing changed. She was still up to her old habits which meant CeeCee did most of her studying, and all her written works, plus handling the chores. The studying part, CeeCee never minded and as time went on, she missed her family less and less as she learned more and more about the world.

She also started to enjoy the other girls, especially when Winnifrey invited them to her room to practice their etiquette together. CeeCee loved to watch as they all sat tall in their chair with their backs straight as an arrow. They sipped their minted teas and took tiny little nibbles from the small cookies that lay on the fine China plates. The room would ring with laughter as they chitchatted gayly about their past and daily events.

She loved to hear all the wonderful tales the girls talked about while they practiced being a lady. Her favorite stories where the accounts of their lives back home. Their portrayals were full of abounding wealth and sophistication. Far more elegance than CeeCee ever knew existed, and certainly more than Winnifrey and her family enjoyed.

She would listen quietly from across the room while she pretended to be busy with some other chore for Winnifrey. At times, she would have to strain to hear every word, especially when Miss Elizabeth Bartlett was speaking. She was such an elegant young lady and always spoke softly. Her stories were never lusty like some of the other girls; instead, they were full of courtly activities, and fun filled affairs.

Every time Miss Bartlett reminisced about her life in New York it was so vivid that CeeCee would close her eyes to listen. And as she cordially expressed the events, the pictures in CeeCee's mind became so real it was as if she was truly there. Miss Bartlett would recount every detail, no matter how trivial, yet her stories were never tiresome. And through her minds-eye, CeeCee enjoyed strolls in Gramercy Park in the early morning mist and took horseback rides through Central Park in mid-afternoon. The trips to the Art Museums were so detailed they included the description of the artist's personal signatures and CeeCee was sure she could see their very inscription. The operas and plays on opening night, were so astonishing they were illuminating. Moreover, at times, her stories took CeeCee's breath away as she pictured the actors when they bowed to the audience's applause.

Every one of Miss Bartlett's depictions produced the most magnificent pictures in CeeCee's mind, and in the accounts, she delightedly immersed herself wholeheartedly. In fact, for CeeCee, even the simple luncheons she described at the Grand Hotel were far more intriguing than the more flamboyant stories depicted by the other girls. Even Ida Folk, whose life came very near to the same extravagance, couldn't compare to Miss Bartlett's tales.

Her trips to Europe and cities like Paris and London, where the ones CeeCee looked forward to hearing the most. And at night when all had gone, she would lay in bed and pretend it was she who had lived this refined life with all its extravagances. It was she who had experienced all the wonderful treasured memories that Miss Bartlett expounded on, as she became the young lady in the stories.

With the scope of these tales, for the first time CeeCee realized, that all life was not lived as it was in Virginia. As grand as the Roberts lived, it was far less than most of the others did. *No wonder Mr. Roberts wanted Winnifrey to experience their lineage,* she thought, *for this can only benefit Winnifrey and her privilege.*

The eighteen months CeeCee spent with Winnifrey were the most enlightening she ever experienced in her sixteen and a half years. She not only learned about the finest china, silver and best crystal; she learned the difference between tasteful art and what some called crude art. She also found that there was a great difference between old things and antiques. As well as the different furnishings a proper household should possess, and what the lady of the house should strive to provide. She discovered there was a world of fine music and dance, and what women of good breeding should know of them. And eventually she even learned how to speak French, although she was not very good at it because as hard as she tried, she could not get the accent down. Nevertheless, whenever she was alone, she practiced the tongue. She also rehearsed her walk and how to seat herself like a lady. There were times when she snuck into Winnifrey's room and fixed her hair like Elizabeth Bartlett's.

For hours at a time she worked on her diction along with her French. And day after day she looked in the mirror that hung before Winnifrey's vanity and weighed whether her smile was too forward or not friendly enough. At times, she evaluated the stance of the head: did she carry it well like a lady of well breeding would, or did she hang it downward as most of the colored people she knew did?

As time went on CeeCee became aware of her face and she focused on its peculiar shape. It was longer than her sister's or Mamma's. She studied her high aristocratic cheekbones which she was told she had inherited from her white Grandpapa. The bones created a facial structure that appeared refined and delicate. Her skin was clear and soft and a pinkish glow colored her cheeks. She smiled and rubbed the tips of her fingers over the smoothness of her cherry red lips and recalled she had overheard Winnifrey say that colorful lips were the envy of any lady.

Yes... if she looked hard into the mirror, she could see all the semblance of a well-bred lady. Though, after a time she came to realize that the image that stared back at her was nothing more than an imposter, a beautiful stranger with dark chestnut hair that surrounded a deceptive facade.

Several times she tried desperately to detect herself in that face, but in the end when she looked deep into those yellowish-brown eyes, all she could see was a colored girl staring back. "A Negro girl," she muttered sadly, "with all this splendor and knowledge and no place to go."

CeeCee loved her parents and sister, but for her she felt between two worlds. She was a Negro, but she looked more like a white child, "So I don't fit nowhere," she grumbled to the image in the mirror.

As much as CeeCee missed home she loved her newfound culture more, but Winnifrey hated Georgia. She whined constantly about the moistness, the insects and being locked away. She said she was missing all the fun a girl her age should be having. She said she longed for her family and wanted to go home. But CeeCee knew it was the boys she missed most, since the only male person she got to see was the colored grounds keeper, and that did not make Winnifrey happy at all.

Winnifrey's disposition changed and was cheerful when she received her weekly letters from her mother, father and Abigail. She never shared the letters with CeeCee. And since she herself never heard from her mamma and papa or Viola, Winnifrey's letters bought her a feeling of lonesomeness. Even if she never expected a letter, since not a one knew how to read or write. Besides, as far as anyone back home knew neither did, she. In fact, the entire eighteen months she was away, the only people she saw from home were the Roberts. Even if they did not spend any time with her, it was still nice to see a familiar face.

Surprisingly time passed fairly fast, and with all the studying and work taking care of Winnifrey, before CeeCee knew it, it was time to pack their belongings and head back home. Winnifrey was so excited those last few weeks before departure, she could scarcely stifle her nervous giggles. And for days all she talked about was seeing Christen Roberts again, and not a mention of her family passed her lips.

CeeCee was also excited. The thought of seeing Papa and Mamma again was filling her heart with happiness, but mostly her mind was set on Viola, she had missed her sister greatly. Nonetheless she came to realize that she would miss Brenau along with the hours of study she had become accustomed to, and of course the ladies and their stories. Especially Miss Elizabeth Bartlett's stories, which by now CeeCee had adopted to identify as her own tales, but only in her mind and to herself.

Winnifrey and CeeCee were escorted back to Virginia by Miss Virginia Waters. She was one of the mistresses from the finishing school. She said she had always wanted to see the state that was her namesake. And since Mr. Roberts asked if someone was available to see the girls safely home, she thought this was an occasion heaven sent.

The girls were excited and chatted and laughed all the way home. CeeCee thought, *"This is the way it used to be. I enjoy Winnifrey being her old self again."* The entire train trip was a pleasure and when CeeCee saw her Mamma at the train station, it was more satisfying than she thought possible. However, her biggest surprise was seeing how much

Viola had grown up.

"Why Viola, you is a eyeful to behold. You is almost a woman." For a second, CeeCee was startled by the words that rolled off her tongue. Then she realized she spoke them from habit, because her Mamma would not understand or like that, she had become educated. She herself had changed greatly, but nothing at home had changed; so no one was to know about her knowledge. She realized this will take even more watchfulness than before, because her secret must never be discovered.

Mamma hugged her though she was not a cuddlesome person, so it was short, nonetheless sweet. When she awkwardly pulled away, she immediately explained, "Papa wanit ta come. All ta same he coundn't makit, cause hes ben feelin pruudy poorly as a late. The mans been ailin an we caint guess why."

CeeCee could see her Mamma was worried. But regardless she was bent on making this CeeCee's day, and after the warm welcome home there was no more mention of worrisome details. Everything was as Viola promised, "Gossipin, eeatin, sangin and dancein, with a whole lota smuuchin and a huggin."

All the workers joined together that day to welcome Flower's eldest daughter back into the lot. CeeCee never felt so much love in her entire life and she told Viola that very thing that night as they laid in bed, "I ain't ever gonna leave this place again."

Soon as the welcome home was over and she and Winnifrey were settled in, Winnifrey had the shock of her life. It was Abigail who brought the news, and at first Winnifrey refused to believe it. She even called her sister a liar.

Abigail looked at Winnifrey as if she had slapped her hard across the face. It was plain to see she was confused, yet dreadfully hurt. And after a minute or so, she innocently asked, "Why, why would I lie to you, Winnifrey? I do not see where it has anything to do with me, that it would benefit me to lie to you. I just thought you would want to know that Christen and Mary Lavine married three weeks back. I would have written you of their engagement, but it frightened me to do so. I knew it would hurt you terribly, especially knowing that there was not a single thing you could do about it..., since you were in Georgia and all."

Abigail puckered her face for an instant. She was fretful and fear-filled as she cautiously continued her explanation, "Winnifrey they had a very short engagement. There was not all that much time between the announcement and vows. Ola says she thinks it was because Mary Lavine wanted to marry Christen before you got back. Sadly, I am inclined to agree with her. Winnifrey, I hope you will not do anything harsh, because Mary Lavine can be frightfully mean if you cross her, and I fear your supposed friendship would make no difference."

After Abigail's announcement, the joyous homecoming was tainted, and resembled a wake far more than any happy occasion, and for the next week and a half Winnifrey went about weeping like an ole fool. Her Papa and Mamma had no notion of what was going on, so eventually they came to the conclusion; she must be sadden because she missed school and all her new acquaintances. Only CeeCee and Abigail knew the truth, and they kept their mouths shut as Winnifrey so irately ordered.

A short time after Winnifrey's homecoming, Mr. and Mrs. Roberts were again in the process of leaving for England. He on business, and she for pleasure. Though Ollifrey Roberts worried whether it was a wise time to leave their poor Winnifrey alone, and after much consideration, she asked Hershal, "Dear, do you think without her mother here to comfort her, our dear little Winnifrey will make herself ill? Maybe I should stay home to tend to her."

Hershal was not as sympathetic as his wife and declared, "Winnifrey is no longer a child, Ollifrey, and she must learn to take life as it comes."

"Yes, I suppose you are right Hershal, though I do hope she does not make herself ill from her constant misery."

"Ollifrey, if you feel you must stay home to tend to our daughter's needs, then I shall understand, even if I do not agree with the action."

Except after hearing Winnifrey's wailing for a month, Ollifrey Roberts decided that she too would go to England, and she asked Aunt Isabel to come and stay with the girls while she and Hershal were away.

Aunt Isabel had always been available when needed in the past. Unfortunately, this was not one of those times. She said she would be pleased to stay with the girls for the first two weeks, but after that she too would be leaving on her own three-month excursion abroad. This was a problem since Ollifrey and Hershal had not planned to be back for at least two months. For days, they considered all their options, before they came up with a final decision. It was an unexpected surprise that Hershal and Ollifrey truly hoped would pull their daughter Winnifrey out of her downhearted state.

That very evening after dinner Ollifrey called the girls together, including CeeCee. The gathering was held in Mr. Roberts sitting room off the office, and after everyone was comfortably perched upon their chosen seats while CeeCee stood in the corner, Mr. Roberts said, "We have an announcement," then ordered, "Ollifrey my dear, make your announcement."

Ollifrey stood and smoothed her skirt. She was unaccustomed to the roll of a speaker, especially when her husband was in the room. He was most always her voice as well as his own. But she did as he requested, "Girls, I have some wonderful news..., Well, I hope you will think it is good news..."

Hershal coughed and Ollifrey glanced over then hurried along, "You will be joining us in England. You will accompany Aunt Isabel on her voyage since we have been unable to procure you a suitable compartment on our ship."

Hershal Roberts moved to his wife's side and continued, "Yes, when the ship lifts its anchor from New York harbor, the three of you will be on board." Facing Winnifrey he laughed and teased lightheartedly, "Winnifrey, I say the three of you, because we know how dependent you have become on CeeCee. Mother and I want to assure you, you will have continued comfort while in England."

Winnifrey gave a gleeful yelp, and her father added, "Of course, on the ship she will not be on the same deck. She will be placed with all the other colored folk. Still in all, when the ship pulls into port in Liverpool, England, you will all be on board. Mother and I will meet you, unless business will not permit. If this happens, we will make appropriate arrangements. Your Mother and I will be at the Dauber Estate until you arrive; after that we will all stay at an Inn.

Winnifrey again gave a shriek, and it was plain to see the news of her impending departure had once again put her in an elated state. Her dreadful mood had instantly been replaced by a new enthusiasm for life, and this cheered and relieved Mrs. Robert's earlier concern.

Later that night Winnifrey confided in CeeCee, "If I can not have Christen at least I can have Henry. Maybe I will even decide to let him marry me now. After all, why should I foolishly wait for a later date? Especially since I do not have any other prospects to dally with. Why, CeeCee I may not even need to return to Virginia."

Winnifrey might have been delighted with the prospect of their forthcoming adventure, but on the other hand CeeCee and Abigail were dreading it. The emanate threat of boarding a ship and heading out to sea chilled them to their very bones. And once CeeCee had taken into account that she would not be allowed on the top levels where Abigail and Winnifrey would be; her fear deepened. More than the apprehension of her voyage, she was tormented by the fact that she was about to come face to face with Henry Dauber, as a Negro servant; this realization terrified and troubled her fiercely.

Though Winnifrey immediately attempted to put her fears to rest. "Do not be foolish you silly colored girl, you are not going to be anywhere near Henry, and besides, I am sure he has long forgotten all about you. As a matter of fact, even if he so happens to run across you, I am sure he would not so much as give you a second glance. This you can be sure of."

CHAPTER SIX

C eeCee hoped Winnifrey was right, and Henry would not remember her, because if he did, she would surely die of embarrassment. She said those very words to Winnifrey. Who, in return
immediately laughed at such a ridicules idea, and declared in a
righteous tone, "Why you little Negra girl, you cannot possibly
know embarrassment? Winnifrey giggled, then added, "Why I have
never heard of a colored being embarrassed. CeeCee Brown, you do
come up with the silliest notions! Colored people simply do not
have such feelings."

Winnifrey's hurtful words stayed with CeeCee throughout her
packing. At times, she recalled the train ride home from Georgia
and how she thought Winnifrey was her friend. Sadly, she had
made that mistake before. "When am I ever going to learn? Winnifrey is never going to be my friend." She had asked herself this
question many times in the past and the answer was still the same,
Winnifrey will never be her friend. "She does not think of me as
anything other than her servant."

Still she yearned for the impossible, unexpectedly her eyes filled
with tears, and she felt the urge to weep. For this was the first time

it registered that all she had worked so hard for, all that learning was for naught. All would be wasted and one day forgotten, she was no lady and never would be.

Viola saw this years ago. She tried to make CeeCee see the truth when she advised, 'CeeCee all yaur learnins is gonna gets you in ta trouble. Yous is nothing buts a colored girl and ya's better gits use tas it.' Yet at the time she stubbornly refused to believe it.

"Viola's words were right then and she is right now, I am a colored girl and I am not even allowed to get embarrassed," CeeCee grumbled as she shoved the last garment into the carpetbag that Miss Ollifrey had given her when she went to Georgia. "Winnifrey is a mean, hateful girl, not at all like her sister Abigail. Abigail is kind and never says mean things like Winnifrey, so why do I care if she's my friend or not?"

CeeCee studied the contents of her bag. She had three dresses, plus the lavender one she was wearing and one pair of shoes and a shawl. She rambled over to the table and picked up the hairbrush Abigail had given her, then hesitated. Viola used the brush as much as she did; maybe she should leave it for her. Though she should look her best even if, "I ain't nothing but a Negra servant," she mouthed a dejected, disgruntled retort.

CeeCee glanced at the mirror piece that hung on the wall. She saved the broken fragment after Winnifrey threw the mirror across the floor in a flair of anger. She looked around the room. Everything she owned were remnants from the Roberts girls. Not one item she owned was new or had ever been when she received it. The bed shoved in the corner of the room that she and Viola shared was tattered and broken. It too, at one time, belonged to the main house. She studied her surroundings. There was no window and the walls were all colorless worn wood, not at all like the wallpapered walls of the big house.

Winnifrey's room was bright with sunlight from the large widows. The walls were covered with little yellow flowers against a pail blue background and throughout ruffled curtains to match that blue. Abigail's was all pink with white butterflies that adorned the walls. Spread over the feather bed was a comforter of soft pink ringlets and lace, it was all so lovely and warm.

"Oh, what I would give to sleep in a room like that," she cried. CeeCee laid the hairbrush in her bag and slammed it shut. "Only ladies gets rooms like that CeeCee, so stop your moanin, cause ya ain't gonna change it," she lectured herself purposely in her pidgin tongue. Again, she checked the room, all brown and dreary. The crack in the ceiling was still not fixed or had it simply worn through again? She did not remember and truly did not care.

Mr. and Mrs. Roberts set out with a promise that, if at all possible they would meet the girls' ship in Liverpool, and as their own departure grew nearer, Aunt Isabel's excitement duly increased. She repeatedly told Winnifrey and Abigail, "Girls, this will be an adventure you will never forget." Then once again she would explain how the ship was laid out, and after that she described the array of pleasures they would encounter. Her eyes sparkled with such delight as she spoke and with each narrative the melodrama stimulated the girls into an uncontrolled frenzy, and their titters and laughter filled the parlor with joy.

Although before the departure day Winnifrey came to realize that CeeCee was not going to be at her beck and call. Again, she was beside herself and she screeched, "Aunt Isabel, no, I need CeeCee nearby. I thought that at least I would have her services in the daytime. How will I care for myself? With all the parties I will be attending, I need to have my servant girl to prepare my garments. You certainly can not expect me to do it for myself."

Aunt Isabel tried to explain that a ship's hands would attend to all their needs. But Winnifrey refused to hear this; she wanted CeeCee nearby. Exasperated Aunt Isabel bluntly put into words what she was trying not to voice since CeeCee was within ears range, "Neggars are simply not allowed on the same decks as whites, my dear. It is unheard of; surely you can understand this. So, you will have no choice other than to accept a ship's helper, my dear Winnifrey."

Two nights before their trip was to begin, Aunt Isabel fell ill. Her chronic asthma attack was to the point of deathly. The doctor advised the girls, "No trip, the stress will be too great for the elderly woman."

Abigail was frantic with worry for her aunt; however, Winnifrey was beyond caring for anyone but herself. She wailed, "Auntie Isabel, Henry is expecting me. How can you do this to me? What I am supposed to do?"

This is when Aunt Isabel became even more fretful. "Oh, dear me, your parents will be expecting to pick you up at Port. I have no way of knowing where they are until that time. I received a telegram the day before yesterday that said they would be in route constantly over the next few weeks. They are visiting many sights, and their itinerary indicated no special order. Oh my, what will I ever do?" Aunt Isabel fell asleep with this worry on her lips, and Abigail and Winnifrey tiptoed from the room.

"Poor Auntie Isabel," whispered Abigail, "she looked so forward to this trip."

Winnifrey burst, "Abigail! Aunt Isabel has been on hundreds of these trips. It is not like it is her first, and may I remind you, that we also are stranded. How could this happen? I yearned for this trip. Now I will never get to see Henry. And soon he will find someone else to wed just like Christen did, all because I am not there to claim his heart. Oh Abigail..., I am destined to be an old maid like, Aunt Isabel? How can I face a life like that?"

"Winnifrey, listen to yourself. Auntie is very ill, and here you are wailing about your own woes."

"Abigail, Aunt Isabel is old, and she has had her life. Mine is just starting, and she is ruining everything with her illness."

Abigail released a little moan as she shook her head in disbelief, then stomped off in a huff. Her sister's selfish spirit never fluctuated, and this often shocked her. Yet this time it was even more disheartening to witness, since she herself was so worried about Auntie Isabel.

She breathed a heavy sigh then admitted, although she wished she did not feel this way since she loved her sister, but Winnifrey was frightfully selfish.

Abigail was in her room reading when Winnifrey burst through the door and yelled, "I have it, Abigail. We can still go on our trip as planned."

"Whatever are you talking about Winnifrey? You know very well that Auntie Isabel can not travel?"

We do not need Aunt Isabel to accompany us. We have three boarding passes for first class. We simply assure Auntie that we hired a woman to escort us."

"Winnifrey where are we going to find a woman on such short notice?"

"CeeCee."

"CeeCee is not a woman. She is only out of girlhood. Besides, she is a Negra. She can not escort us anywhere. You know very well what Auntie Isabel said about Negras and Whites not being on the same levels."

"Yes, and that may be normally true, Abigail. Then, if we dress CeeCee up, she can once again pass for white, and we get to go on our trip. Plus, we will have CeeCee to care for us. It is a perfect plan."

"Winnifrey, we cannot do such a thing. Remember all the risk we took last time. Why, it nearly backfired with Henry's infatuation."

"Oh paah, that was merely a young man's need to soar. This time CeeCee will not even be near a man. She can simply stay in the cabin and tend to us."

Appalled by her sister's resolve Abigail stared at her in disbelief, while Winnifrey continued with her contrivance, "So first...we must fill a suitcase with the right items for CeeCee's trip. Then, of course, fix her to look like a lady. I am sure this will take a little more work than it did the last time. I am afraid not everyone is as gullible as Henry."

"Winnifrey!"

"Hush, Abigail, I am thinking. Why don't you go get CeeCee, and we can tell her all about it? Abigail get, we have no time to waste! We have no time whatsoever to spare. Meanwhile I will pre-pare our story for Aunt Isabel. She is so stupefied with those pills the doctor gave her, I am sure she will not be too hard to convince."

"Dear Winnifrey, you are overlooking one *very* important detail."

"And what might that be, Abigail?"

"*Mother* and *Father.* How do we explain no escort to them?"

Winnifrey thought for a second then burst excitedly, "Not a problem, little sister. We will simply tell them that the escort fell deathly ill which I hear some do on an ocean liner, and she was im-mediately rushed off the ship as soon as it docked. See, all will be fine, Abigail. Now let us have no more deliberation, and scat, go, go get CeeCee!"

"Miss Winnifrey, I don't wanna do this." Without even acknowledging CeeCee's pleas Winnifrey continued, "Now, remember to call yourself Cecilia and hold your head up. Why do you coloreds always have to hold your head down? Well never no mind, it certainly does not matter. Open your mouth and let me see your teeth, huhhh."

"Whys do we have to do this again, Miss Winnifrey? We is gonna get caught."

"CeeCee, listen to your diction. With such talk we are surely to get caught. Now get hold of yourself and pay close attention to all your words, and *please* try to carry yourself as an adult would."

When Abigail had informed CeeCee that Winnifrey was up to her old tricks again, she wanted to run and hide. But when CeeCee found out that she was planning to pass her off not only as white, but a white caretaker, she almost dropped right where she stood. She was much too young to be a caretaker, and a white one.... but here she is all over again, doing just what Winnifrey tells her to do.

CHAPTER SEVEN

"Cecilia, listen, hush up and listen to me," Winnifrey grabbed CeeCee by the shoulders and gave her a shake, "listen to what I am saying Cecilia. I do not want you to say a word unless you have been asked. Then merely answer the question. Short and sweet. Always keep your answers short and sweet."

Immediately upon Winnifrey's directions CeeCee's expression turned to stupefaction. The suggestion was unnecessary, and her order would certainly be easy enough to carry out. After all that's what Negra people did. They never spoke to white folk unless they were spoken to first, and most always only answered what was asked.

"Turn around, CeeCee, turn around," spouted, Winnifrey. "Humm, humm," she uttered to herself. "Now walk..., I want to see how you hold yourself. Well, I guess you can continue to practice...walk, CeeCee walk, shoulders back, straighten up."

CeeCee walked from one side of the parlor car to the other, then back again, and continued several more times. She had practiced this walk to the point of exhaustion, but Winnifrey was relentless.

The train ride to New York was long and heated, but CeeCee was in a state of exhilaration and did not mind the activity or the heat. Whereas, Winnifrey and Abigail were noticeably heated and groaned their discomfort with each stop the train made. Though once the train came to a halt in New York, their dispositions changed to a more agreeable one. Winnifrey, at once, pushed ahead of Abigail to take charge of the baggage that was being unloaded and carefully loaded onto a fancy buggy. After watching from the sidelines, it was plain to see that Winnifrey took great pleasure in her new perceived position and disrespectfully, she ordered, "Porter, get a move on... you lazy bag of bones."

The man stopped and studied the woman that he regarded as a child but decided against any deliberation.

"Stop your dawdling and get these aboard the buggy, we must be on our way," shouted Winnifrey. Embarrassed, CeeCee fell back and stood in the shadow of Abigail until all bags were in their place, and the girls were properly seated across from each other. Abagail patted the seat next to her and said, "Come, Cecilia. Sit next to me."

The buggy pulled to a stop in front of a grand and impressive building. CeeCee gawked at its enormity and her eyes bulged as they moved upwards to the top of the structure where a sign announced to the world, Plaza Hotel. "Oohhh... my," she murmured.

Winnifrey mumbled, "Shish," under her breath as she gave CeCee's shoulder a shove. By this time, the doorman had opened the carriage door and bowed. Then he boisterously welcomed them to the most elegant establishment in the city as he immediately offered Winnifrey a hand and assisted her exit. CeeCee awkwardly followed suit after Abagail had done the same.

The uniformed man moved to the front of the line that they stood in and announced, "Ladies, the Bellboy will get your luggage." At this time, a young Negro boy scooted up from behind and grinned wildly. CeeCee smiled back and Winnifrey pinched her arm and gave her a warning glare as she quickly moved forward.

New York was much bigger and busier than she ever imagined. And its streets were filled with an assortment of impoverished nationalities, although the city's wealth was quite evident amongst it all. The enormous difference between the two worlds astounded CeeCee. She glanced back at the young boy once again then forced her feet to follow Winnifrey's lead. Her body felt heavy and she thought, *this feels like a dream. Ooh, please don't ever let me wake up.*

As soon as she entered the hotel lobby all else was forgotten. She was immediately overwhelmed by its beauty, and at first, it took her breath away. For several seconds' she stood fast and could not move. She remained motionless for a complete minute before Winnifrey noticed and gave her ribs a poke. Flustered CeeCee stepped inward when Winnifrey obliquely squinted and sharply nodded for her to move forward. Her movement was slow, and her eyes filled with caution while they darted around the room in insatiable scrutiny.

This she, recognized, was the opulent world that Elizabeth Bartlett had described in her extraordinary stories at Brenau.

It was only minutes later that CeeCee stared down at the streets below from a spacious room on the eleventh floor. She could see the carriages below along with several store fronts. One in particular caught her eye with its grand window display. She had never been to a store in her life, though she had seen catalogs. But a store such as this, well she never would have guessed one even existed.

Sternly Winnifrey's voice interrupted CeeCee's assessment of the street and its many stores below. "Cecilia, I do not want you to leave this room. We will bring you food after we eat dinner. Now hang our clothes before they wrinkle beyond return."

Abigail smiled softly to reassure CeeCee, who was obviously feeling overwhelmed by her new surroundings, not to mention Winnifrey's suggestion that she stays in the room alone.

"CeeCee," encouraged Abigail, "this will give you time to get used to the extravagance you will be encountering. For I am sure the ship is as elegant as your immediate surroundings, so please do not fret. Your confinement will only be for a couple of days. Then we will be on board ship and you can walk as freely about the deck as you please."

"That we will have to see about," imposed Winnifrey, "as for now we will simply have to tell CeeCee about our sightseeing adventures."

Abigail threw an annoyed glance in her sister's direction but opted not to get into any further discussion at this point. Consequently, after the short deliberation CeeCee simply nodded that she would do as she was told. Yet in all honesty she longed to see the city for herself.

The two days locked in her room were long though wisely used for her trial performance. Since her returned from Georgia, CeeCee had not outwardly uttered a word of proper English, nor had she practiced her French. Both she was sure were rusty. Moreover, she had not arranged her hair into one of the many fancy styles most of the ladies wore since before they left Georgia.

'Hair,' Winnifrey always said, 'is truly a way to distinguish a lady's standing.' This CeeCee believed was true, though she decided to start with something simpler such as sitting and walking.

A real lady's life is much more complicated than most colored folks is, thought CeeCee. *We don't have to worry about sitting properly.*

Once she felt comfortable sitting with her back straight and her head held high, she worked on walking tall with her head held upward and shoulders back. *This, she decided, is much more strenuous then one might believe.* "CeeCee," told herself, "hold those shoulders back. Straighten up, back straight, shoulders up, back straight, whew", she breathed.

Afterward she moved to practice her speech in front of the mirror while she arranged and rearranged her hair in different styles. "Good morning. Good evening. How are you this fine day, Miss....? Remember a lady speaks softly and more clearly than most Negros," she chided. "This" she reminded herself, "is going to take some effort and I am sure I will need to remind myself often." Before long she realized that she was still quite good at mimicking the words she so often heard from the likes of Mrs. Ollifrey and her friends. This was a great comfort and the knot in her stomach soon relented.

By the time, the three young ladies followed the shipmate aboard the huge vessel, CeeCee felt quite confident. "Yes," she told herself, "No one is going to guess that I am not what I pretend to be, a lady…, a white lady with good breeding." She immediately stretched her thin frame taller as it filled with pride. Surely, at this very moment, she was all she had ever dreamed she could be, even if it was only pretend, she appeared to be a lady.

Despite this self-satisfaction and her new confidence, it was short lived. For as soon as they boarded the ship CeeCee was immediately shuffled off to the suite. There she was ordered by Winnifrey to stay put. "We will be back, but right now we are going to enjoy the ship's departure from the top deck. You can busy yourself with the arrangement of our fineries and make sure we are ready for tonight's gala; we will want to look our absolute best." Winnifrey's pleasure filled her face and she declared, "Oh, dear Abigail, we are going to have such fun."

Before she began to unpack the trunks, CeeCee peeked out the door, then decided to leave it cracked open slightly. That way, she too could hear the merriment from inside the suite. The laughter and excitement filled the air as well as the music from the orchestra that played across the ship. Suddenly she heard laughter and several people shuffled though the hallways, and a woman's voice gayly sang out loud, 'Bon voyage.' And CeeCee wanted to weep. All of life's pleasures were just beyond her door, "Yet out of my grasp as always. Just the same as it's been my entire life," she moaned.

She pulled the dress from the paper wrapping and started to hang it up. It was one of many beautiful gowns that already hung in the tiny closet of Winnifrey's chamber. At that time, she realized that the girls would probably require the use of her closet too. Dejected and disappointed she threw herself on the bed and wept, "I am no lady. I'm not a part of this world, and never will be. I am CeeCee Brown, a colored girl and no color girl gets ta be a lady.

They only get to be a servant or a mother and most the times both. Their life is spent working, not playing and seeing the world."

She shuddered when she thought of all she had learned over the years. Yes, her type of enlightenment was unheard of amongst her people and now she knew why. "Because once your eyes are open to the other side of life's delights, it truly makes you ache inside knowing its unattainable."

It was after she had washed her face and tidied herself up a bit that Abigail and Winnifrey barged into the room. They were talking rapidly, and their faces shined with gratification and excitement. Their open gaiety intensified CeeCee's pain, though she pasted a smile upon her lips. And even laughed when Abigail giggled and fell back against the well-padded chair and declared, "This is the most pleasure I have ever encountered. Cecilia, everyone is so gracious and at your beckon. Why you simply give your hand a wave and at once champagne comes, and of course, they continue to pour until your head is light and the room is swaying."

"Although," said Winnifrey, "I promise, I only tasted a few sips," she giggled.

Abigail jumped to her feet and continued excitedly, "CeeCee, you too must try a taste..., at supper time we will order you a glass...."

With this suggestion Winnifrey who sat on the settee grinning at her sister, leaped up and declared, "Abigail!"

Still laughing Abagail demanded, "What, Winnifrey?"

"Stop, encouraging Cecilia. You know very well that she can not eat with us. I mean it is bad enough that we must share a suite, I... I have no intention of eating with her. Anyway, I decided it would be safer to keep her in the cabin away from respectable people so she will stay in her room."

"But Winnifrey, I believe they said this is a twenty-eight-day trip. You can not expect Cecilia to stay locked up like a caged animal the entire time."

"Oh, Abigail do not be silly. Of course Cecilia can go out. Though I consent only if it is in the evening time, and she does not speak with anyone."

Abigail screeched, "Winnifrey! What kind of trip is that?"

"My dear untainted sister, are you forgetting what Cecilia is? Why she should be on her hands and knees this very minute to praise the Lord for such an opportunity. Now I refuse to discuss this matter any longer. Cecilia will only go out after dark and that is it, no further discussion do I want to hear. As well, I ask you, Abigail, can you please watch calling her CeeCee?"

"Winnifrey you are not Father and you can not rule us...."

"I must be in charge, Abigail. There is no other way we will get away with this contrivance."

With this declaration, Abigail fell silent. She knew Winnifrey had a point. For there was no way she could ever match her sister's forte in deceit.

That evening Cecilia sat alone while she nibbled at her cold unfamiliar meal. After a bit she pushed the tray aside and grabbed a shawl then hurried out the door. She told herself, "I cannot wait another minute to explore the ship's decks."

With less clutter and no people about, she could see the ship's immensity for the first time. It was endless and she was amazed at its great elegance. After she walked the decks for about thirty minutes, she realized it was far larger than she had first believed. The booklet she read had not done the ship justice; it was more luxurious than it had described. There were long padded chairs everywhere and a few people were seated upon them. She moved to the far corner and sat. Slowly she leaned back against the soft cushions and listened to the ocean sounds, as well as a small groups while they carried on an energetic conversation. Their laughter filtered through the breeze and CeeCee watched with hunger while she envied their freedom.

Eventually she stood and moved to an opening where she felt the damp wind against her face and inhaled deep. The air's freshness was wonderful to breathe. She could hear the splash of water as it hit the sides of the ship and realized she was closer to the railings' edge then she thought. Quickly she stood back from the deck's banisters, though soon she wavered and moved forward again. Her desire was to be brave and venture out to see the water as the boat floated atop. Her heartbeat so loud she swore she could hear its very thump against the hand she held there. Swiftly she decided to move back in the shadow and gaze at the shimmering waves from afar. They were beautiful and time seemed to stand still. She had no idea how long she stood there, but eventually she felt as though someone's eyes were upon her. For an instant she grew frightened, then remembered where and who she was supposed to be. Slowly she turned her head to view the open deck. From where she stood, she could not see anyone. She turned around and faced the now empty lounge chairs that were lined up in a straight row. One by one, row after row she viewed emptiness. Finally, she saw a light from the end of a cigarette. Her first instinct was to move away; then the silhouette of the man caught her interest. He was facing her as he leaned against the banister casually. She was quite sure he was watching her. Nervously she moved a step back then stopped. She wanted to divert her eyes, yet before she did, she caught herself, then shifted her shoulders back as she firmly stood her ground. *After all,* she assured herself, *this is for any guest to enjoy and I am a guest, camouflaged or not.*

Unexpectedly the gentleman straightened his tall frame and moved closer. CeeCee immediately felt her stomach flutter but she refused to show her fear. A second later she heard her name, and this startled her even more than anything prior to its utterance. "Cecilia? Cecilia Roberts?"

When she did not answer, he moved into the light and quickly apologized for the mistaken identity. "Please excuse my forwardness Miss....for an instant I, I thought I recognized an old friend."

CeeCee smiled to herself. Winnifrey was wrong, Henry Dauber did not forget her. She stood silent and evaluated how she could escape without revealing that she was indeed, *as he knew her,* Cecilia Roberts.

Finally, she bravely stepped out of the shadows and announced, "Good evening, Mr. Dauber. I am sorry for not answering right away. I am afraid you frightened me a bit."

"Well, I will be dammed..." He caught himself, the asked, "Please Miss Roberts, you must excuse my harshness, but...but I am truly surprised to see you." He laughed, then said, "It looks like every time I see you, I put you in the position that you are obliged to deal with my bad manners. Though I am afraid this time the only excuse I have is I too am a tad overwhelmed with surprise. I had no idea you were on board. It was only minutes ago that I spoke with Winnifrey, and she did not mention a word about your presence."

CeeCee smiled at the mention of Winnifrey's name, and at the same time remembered what she so often advised, *CeeCee, do not speak unless it is necessary.* And since she had no idea how to answer Henry's remark, she stayed silent.

By then Henry had regained his composer and asked, "Cecilia, please come join me for a glass of champagne. I would love to spend some time and catch up on all that has happened in your life since our last meeting." Unexpectedly he hesitated, then asked, "Or is it, Mrs. now? If I recall, you did announce that you were promised to a young fellow..., from...from Carolina, I believe."

Cecilia almost choked and she gulped a huge swallow of air as she muttered under her breath. *Winnifrey, you and your lies, now you gone and done it. What am I supposed to say,* she asked herself? *How can I get out of this...should I run? No, that will make it worse, and....*

Henry moved to close the space between them, "There I go again, I am sorry for being so forward. It seems I am forever forgetting my manners whenever you are about, Miss..., Roberts?"

CeeCee wanted to melt into the floorboards, but instead she placed a nervous smile on her face and said, "Thank you for your offer, Mr. Dauber, however I must decline. I am merely out for a breath of fresh air and I must get back before I am missed."

"I see. Then is it possible that I may sit with you at dinner tomorrow night?"

"Well...no. I mean I plan to take my meals alone in my cabin, Mr. Dauber."

"Miss Roberts..." again he asked, "it is Miss Roberts, is it not?"

When Cecilia nodded yes, his smile broadened and he continued, "I *advise* you, do not attempt to hide yourself in your cabin for you will surely get cabin fever. And I dare say, I hear that can be fatal. So please say you will join me for dinner tomorrow evening. I promise you, I will be a gentleman at all times, and if that does not ease your fear of spending time alone with me, I will ask my good friend, Ellington Kempe to join us, so to keep me in line of sorts," he teased. When CeeCee still did not laugh at his quip, he quickly added, "And of course you may bring Winnifrey to chaperone."

This concept did bring a giggle to CeeCee's lips, and before she realized what she had said she had answered, "Yes." But then before she could lose her nerve she continued, "We will be delighted to join you, and your friend Mr. Kemp. Although, for now I must be going..., goodnight Mr. Dauber."

CeeCee hurried away and her mind instantly filled with terror. *How am I going to explain this to Winnifrey? She will be beside herself with anger. Dear, dear me, why did I say yes?*

When CeeCee stepped into the room she heard the excited chatter of Winnifrey's voice. She was finishing her tale to Abigail, "Oh, Abigail he is *soooo* handsome and I could see right off he still desires me. Why I would not at all be surprised if Henry asked for my hand in marriage before we even hit port." She stopped speaking when she noticed CeeCee had entered the room and immediately began a reprimand her. "CeeCee, where have you been? Why I have had to ready myself for bed... all by myself...."

Winnifrey paused when she noticed the glow on CeeCee's face, then asked in a sharp voice, "Where have you been girl?" You have not been tramping about the ship, have you?" She turned toward Abigail and threw her arms in the air as she screeched, "My word, the girl cannot be trusted Abigail. I mean I should have remembered that, and my Lord, with all the crew scampering about deck...well she is surely to get herself into trouble, and we certainly don't need a Negra baby to tend to."

CeeCee's anger emerged with a vengeance when she grasped what Winnifrey was insinuating. This was the same accusation she had made years before, when she first forced her to pass for white and entertain Henry Dauber. In Winnifrey's mind Negro's had no decency and would lift their skirt for any man who asked. The thought of her disrespect infuriated CeeCee, and suddenly she decided she was not going to stand for it any longer. She may be Winnifrey's colored maid, but even coloreds deserve to be treated decent.

CeeCee moved to stand face to face with her accuser and said, "Winnifrey, we do not all live by your standards."

Winnifrey reached for her throat and gasped, she could not believe her ears. Miffed she stammered, "Why, why, I... I never. CeeCee, have you been drinking liquor..." and she sniffed the air before her? Then immediately continued, do you realize to whom you are speaking?"

CeeCee wavered but refused to back down completely. She had been belittled by Winnifrey her entire life and now she wanted the respect she thought she had earned. "Winnifrey, I do know who I am speaking too. However, I do feel you have no right to accuse me of such lowly morals. I have done nothing to deserve it. Moreover, I have always done exactly what you have ordered me to do. Which, if I may say, many times have been against my high integrity. Now here I am in a predicament all because of your amoral orders and I am duly upset. For which you immediately misread and began to accuse me of low morals."

CeeCee abruptly stopped and drew in a deep breath, but before she could continue the outburst Winnifrey screeched, "CeeCee! Whatever are you talking about?"

"Winnifrey, when I was out for my walk, I ran into Henry Dauber, and you..., I am afraid were mistaken, he did not forget me. He not only remembered me, but he remembered the imaginary beau you conjured up for me from Carolina."

Winnifrey screamed, "Oh! Oh, my Lord. See I told you Abigail, she should have stayed in the cabin. Now what are we to do? This is awful! Now what? Oh my! CeeCee, once, again, you have ruined everything. Why do you have to be so...so...oh...oh, oh damn you?"

With this remark, Abigail came to CeeCee's defense. "Winnifrey this is not CeeCee's fault. She did not ask for you to dress up like a white lady and she certainly did not ask to be paraded around as your cousin, so stop screaming at her. Besides, all your whining as well as your distasteful language, is not going to help a thing."

Turning, Abigail faced the now completely deflated CeeCee and asked, "So from what I gather, you did speak with Henry Dauber?"

"Yes, Mam," murmured CeeCee.

"So, tell me everything that was said. CeeCee, everything and do not leave a word out"

Once all was revealed Abigail exhaled a sigh of relief. "See Winnifrey, you can stop your pacing; this is not at all as bad as you imagined. We will simply have dinner with the gentlemen and that will be the end of it. From then on CeeCee will plead ailment and have her trays in the cabin."

"Father and Mother will surely find out, Abigail," cried Winnifrey.

"No Winnifrey, do not fret. If Henry does happen to say anything, we will merely brush it aside by explaining that Cecilia Robertson was the name of our chaperon and Henry mistakenly took it as Roberts and her as a relative. Afterwards it will all be forgotten because Mother and Father will not wish to embarrass Mr. Dauber. Now surely you agree, Winnifrey."

"Yes," whimpered Winnifrey, "yes, I guess I do agree, Abigail..., That is up to the point of Cecilia having dinner with us. Why we have no idea how much she has told Henry. Or, how far this little dalliance has gone. As well if I may say, this has put me in a very peculiar situation, Abigail. After all, I do not want my husband to be amorously involved with my colored maid."

This time CeeCee held her tongue and did not let her anger escape. She knew it would be wasted on Winnifrey anyway. *Winnifrey only sees what she wants to see or what she thinks is important to her,* CeeCee thought, *which right this minute is Henry Dauber and his impending marriage proposal.*

Abigail stroked her sister's cheek and whispered, "Now, now Winnifrey, you know better than that, and besides your beauty can put CeeCee's to shame." Abigail winked in CeeCee's direction as she gave her sister a comforting hug.

CHAPTER EIGHT

CeeCee spent most of the next day readying Abigail and Winnifrey for their dinner engagement with Henry Dauber. The final hour was put to use working on her and her de-coloring. She was full of nerves and antsy by the time the last puff of powder stained her face. With this last application, she noticed it made her face look overly white and without forethought she voiced her opinion and was immediately sorry. "Winnifrey please pay attention, I look pallid. This is too much powder... it makes me look ghostly."

Winnifrey put her hands on her hip and countered, "CeeCee Brown, I have come to the conclusion that you are beginning to believe you are white, and this I will advise should stop, along with that disrespectful mouth of yours."

"I mean no disrespect, Miss Winnie."

"Do not call me Winnie, CeeCee, or you will find yourself pulling weeds in the back fields at home. Do you understand CeeCee Brown? I am about to my wit's end when it comes to you and your misbehaving."

Annoyed, Abigail interrupted her sister with a plea, "Please... will you stop, will the two of you just stop? We need to be on our best comportment tonight and your constant bickering is.... Well, we simply do not need discord amongst ourselves. Cecilia, come here so I can fix your face, then I will do your hair." Abigail wiped at CeeCee's face and softly murmured, "Now let me see a smile."

Winnifrey moaned, "Abigail, your overindulging does not help matters one bit."

When CeeCee finally stood in front of the mirror, her pride swelled twofold. This was the first time she had seen herself fully transformed since the first time Winnifrey dressed her up years before. Now things were different; she had grown into a woman and filled the dress out accordingly. The burgundy dress she wore held golden threads throughout its design and was beautiful. Winnifrey had declared that the dress was unbecoming to her own skin tone, and this is why she gave it to CeeCee. Still, now seeing the full effect, Winnifrey had her doubts that this had been a wise decision.

Abigail gasped after she stepped back to get the full view, "Cecilia..., you are simply too beautiful to be a colored."

CeeCee understood that unlike Winnifrey, Abigail meant no insolence by her comment, so she took none and only mumbled, "Thank you, Miss Abigail, though I think it's you who will receive all the attention tonight. You are as lovely as any woman could ever be."

Suddenly Winnifrey froze, then snapped her head around to survey her sister's appearance. She had not noticed her sister before CeeCee had said anything, and now after a full scan she became noticeably unhappy. Her lips at once formed an anxiety ridden pout, and she turned to study her own reflection in the mirror. Her eyes bounced from her face to her sister's entirety. Then she took in CeeCee's superficial exterior and immediately moved her gaze back to Abigail. The question on her face was obvious, when had Abigail become so splendid? She had never noticed this before. As far as she was concerned, Abigail was her little sister and nothing more, and certainly not someone to contend with. Somewhere along the way this had changed for now she was a beautiful young woman.'

Yet again, Winnifrey moved to study her own face and after several minutes she decided she was still more beautiful than either girl. And as for Abigail it was probably the sky-blue gown, she wore that made her appear so attractive and grownup.

Abigail reached over and made one last adjustment to CeeCee's cinch, then stepped back and announced, "There, that should do it. Cecilia Roberts you are now ready for the world."

With this announcement CeeCee felt her stomach wrench. This was everything she dreamed, yet she had to admit it was moving a bit too fast for her to get a steady foot.

C eeCee waited in the doorway as she marveled at the crystal chandeliers that hung from the vast ceiling above. The beauty of the room shimmered beyond description, and its occupants were remarkably close to the same. All the women were dressed in long lavish gowns that accompanied an adornment of jewels of every sort. The men wore tuxedoes, the first CeeCee had ever seen, and they all looked so wonderfully refined. For a moment CeeCee mused then decided, her father, Ely, would never feel comfortable in such an excessive garment. She also guessed he would never want to wear such a thing nor would her mother be inclined to wear an elegant gown. Flower's only aspiration in life was to care for the Roberts every whim. *So why am I so drawn to this life, she asked?*

Abigail moved closer to CeeCee's side and took her arm to lead her in the direction of Henry's table. Winnifrey made no haste and rushed to the forefront to reach the table first. At once she took hold of Henry's hand as well as the chair next to his as she worked desperately to draw his attention to her. She was already in conversation before Abigail and CeeCee drew near though none of that made a bit of difference because a soon as Abigail and Henry's eyes met, he was lost to Winnifrey forever.

Abigail stood silent while she waited for her sister to properly introduce her to Mr. Henry Dauber. But at this time, he was openly gawking awkwardly at Abigail, which made her feel awfully ill at ease.

Once Abigail realized her sister was not paying her any mind and had no intention of introducing her; she quickly glanced over to CeeCee. She hoped she would understand her look was a plea to receive a proper introduction. Her pretty face relaxed at once when she saw that CeeCee understood her message and stepped forward to make the overture.

Abigail recognized that there was a flicker of fear in CeeCee's eyes, but soon she found her voice and began to speak, and it was as if she had been in this situation a hundred times before. "Mr. Dauber, I wish to acquaint you with, Miss Abigail Roberts..., my...my cousin and Winnifrey's sister."

Henry gaped in open appreciation at the beauty that stood before him. At first, he was speechless; nonetheless, he fought to find his voice and he bowed respectfully and declared, "I dare say we have met years ago, Miss Roberts. However, I doubt you would have remembered, since I believe you were only six or seven at the time, and I of course, was at the ripe old age of eleven and a half. I would guess that at that time we had little in common though I certainly doubt that to be true today. Plus, if I may say so Miss Roberts, you have positively grown into an exquisite young woman and I am extremely glad to make your re-acquaintance." At this time, he kissed her hand and Abigail's cheeks turned a charming pink while Winnifrey's turned a scarlet red.

CeeCee smiled with pleasure since she liked Henry and thought Abigail would be a much nicer companion for him than her hard-hearted sister.

For a moment, Henry drew his gaze off Abigail to smile at CeeCee and thanked her for bringing such a lovely being to his table. Thereupon he moved his attention back to his other guests which included several ladies who sat eagerly waiting to meet their competition. At this same time two young gentlemen stood up and smiled their eager anticipation of meeting the new guest. Winnifrey repositioned uncomfortably; this is not at all what she anticipated, and she was at once troubled.

Henry patted CeeCee's hand and at the same time he bowed, then kissed it. After which he announced, "Miss Cecilia Roberts, tonight you are even more stunning than usual, and if I may say my dear friends here, have been keenly awaiting your arrival. By this time, I am sure they are ready to make you and Abigail feel welcome...and of course you as well, Winnifrey. May I present, Miss Mary Pettitree." He extended his hand in preamble and then continued, "Sara Green, in the middle and Doreen Casler is to her left." Turning to face the two gentlemen he added, "And of course let us not forget my brother, Howard Dauber who is betrothed to the lovely Sara. And this is our everlasting friend, Ellington Kempe. This is Cecilia and Abigail Roberts and Winnifrey, who is Abigail's sister."

At once everyone shifted a seat while at the same time, they welcomed the girls. CeeCee moved to sit next to Ellington who stood holding a chair for her. Abigail was offered a seat near Howard since

Winnifrey was not about to move for anyone and the serving cart was on the other side of Henry.

After all were seated, Winnifrey immediately aspired to draw attention to her side of the table. All eyes fell on her as she openly attempted to claim Henry's affections. She giggled and flirted while she leaned forward so Henry could enjoy her well rounded and overly exposed cleavage. Her voice was overly loud when she declared, "I was so thrilled that you invited me to join you tonight, Henry? I assume you have missed me as much as I have missed you these past months." She fluttered her eyelashes and asked, "Whatever have you been up too, Henry?" Clearly, she was attempting to leave all who sat around the table out of the conversation.

Smiling he kidded, "Winnifrey, I am sure you were far too busy at school to think about missing me."

"Oh paah, I will never be that busy, Henry" she grinned and again openly ignored everyone else at the table. Henry smiled back then without further ado moved his attention across the table to CeeCee and Abigail. "Cecilia, I have just recently returned from Africa. The last time we spoke, I believe your parents were on a Safari in that region?"

CeeCee felt an immediate panic and as it emerged it took over all intelligent thought. This was another lie that Winnifrey had told Henry, and now she was caught in the middle and forced to add to its fabrication. *What can I say...?* She watched in silence as Winnifrey touched Henry's hand and whispered something in his ear. Slowly Henry looked up and his face had paled, his eyes held such sadness that it indubitably added to CeeCee's panic. Her mind at once began to dredge up all sorts of fearful thoughts, the worse and most frightful was that, *she told him; he knows I am a Negro.*

Henry coughed lightly into his napkin before he began to speak. CeeCee held her breath until she heard his first words. "Cecilia, I am truly sorry. I had no idea. I heard of many such occurrences and I guess when a country is so uncivilized...one, one can expect that there will be carnage. So..., so maybe one should not be surprised by such incidents, though still.... Well... my condolences on your parent's deaths."

CeeCee almost gagged and her eyes darted from Winnifrey's smirking face to Abigail's aghast look; that was soon followed by a frown. Abigail's eyes then filled with rebuke though she remained silent. Winnifrey was her sister and she had no wish to embarrass her. In Abigail's opinion, Winnifrey was doing a good job of that on her own.

At last Winnifrey broke the silence, "Cecilia, I know this must be very upsetting. Even though Henry did not know about the slaughter of your dear family, his words have brought back a sad time. So, if you have a mind to go back to the cabin, I will have a tray sent posthaste."

CeeCee stared back at Winnifrey's serious face. Her lips held a small understanding smile, but her eyes glared back with intensity as she waited for CeeCee to answer.

Hurriedly CeeCee considered the situation and her alternatives, then returned a smiled and replied, "That is truly kind of you dear cousin, though it is not necessary. You see, I have come to terms with my parents' deaths. I realize that they with all their adventurous spirit, would have wanted to meet their creator in the fashion that they had lived."

She then turned her attention to Henry and continued, "And Henry I accept your condolences..., please do not feel uncomfortable. As Winnifrey so kindly pointed out, you had no idea."

Winnifrey simpered as she glared in CeeCee's direction and Abigail was relieved and smiled slightly. There was a mild discomfort at the table; then Abigail came to everyone's rescue with a change of subject. She smiled demurely as she spoke directly to Henry who still seemed somewhat flustered. "Henry, we had no idea you were going to be on this ship. Our parents are visiting your parents as we speak."

Henry was thankful for the diversion, and this was revealed in his voice when he answered with a released sigh. "Is..., is that so..., Abigail? Howard and I have been in the States these past several months. Sara has been acquainting us with her family, which I might add is very large and widespread. For this reason, we have not kept up with our family's gatherings at home. As for finding us aboard, we six decided at the last minute to take a holiday. My parents have no idea that they are about to be blitzed by such a frolicsome group."

Everyone laughed and CeeCee for the first time since boarding the ship relaxed. Throughout the rest of the dinner CeeCee added nothing to the conversation. She nodded several times in agreement and laughed when it was appropriate, but as for conversation, she had not comfortably achieved the art, so she avoided its engagement.

After dessert Winnifrey suggested, "What do you say we all go to the ballroom? I hear the music is wonderful and the room has a perfect dance floor." The women all enthusiastically agreed while the men grumbled their reluctance and Winnifrey concluded, "Of course we will understand, Cecilia, if you wish not to join us, after all you are barely out of mourning."

CeeCee understood this was Winnifrey's way of excusing her and since she had no idea how to dance with a man, she accepted the out.

"Yes, thank you Winnifrey. I appreciate your concern and if everyone will excuse me, I would very much like to retire."

All nodded their understanding and CeeCee stood and acknowledged, "Henry, thank you for a delightful evening. I will forever hold it dear. It was wonderful to meet all of you, and your company was truly entertaining."

At this time, Ellington Kempe stood and proclaimed, "I will escort you to your cabin, Miss Roberts...that is, if you will permit me?"

CeeCee hesitated then decided it was best not to argue. Beside she knew a lady would not think twice before agreeing. "I would be honored, Mr. Kempe."

Once Ellington placed the wrap across CeeCee's shoulders he whispered, "It is such a beautiful night. It would be a shame to at least not view the moon before retiring, Miss Roberts."

Winnifrey started to speak, but CeeCee hurriedly accepted the considerate offer. She was not in any hurry to end this wonderful evening for she was sure it would be the only one she would ever have.

Abigail stood and said, "That sounds like a wonderful idea. I am sure we all can use a breath of fresh air before we move to the ballroom, so let's all take a stroll around the deck."

With her suggestion Henry eagerly pushed his chair back and rushed to her side and asked, "Abigail, if I may I would like to escort you, and I would be honored if I can have your first dance..., an...and your last," he hesitantly stuttered.

The look, Winnifrey, threw her sister was filled with daggers, yet Abigail smiled sweetly and granted, "I would be delighted, Mr. Dauber." She took Henry's extended arm and move briskly out of Winnifrey's fire site.

Winnifrey, Abigail decided, had been truly annoying the entire evening, and she was not about to encourage her misbehavior by backing down and giving her what she so obviously wanted..., Henry along with all his attention.

Ellington respectfully stood beside CeeCee. However, his desire to reach out and touch the softness of her golden skin was great. This hunger was aroused the moment he laid eye upon her. He thought she was the most glorious woman he had ever met, and his heart pounded with desire.

CeeCee stood tall with her back erect as she had rehearsed time and time again. Her wish to appear a lady had cost her hours and days of rehearsal time, and now here she was in the middle of the ocean, next to the most handsome man she had ever seen. Moreover, she was scared out of her wits.

Ellington broke the tension by pointing up at the stars and remarking, "Years ago when seaman traveled these seas, they depended on these very stars for their bearing. Can you imagine they had nothing as sophisticated as our devices of today? Yet they discovered the lands across the seas."

CeeCee noted the change in his voice, and immediately recognized he had a love for the sea as well as an earnest respect for the stars. This pleased her and she listened intently as Ellington talked about the stars, the sea, and ancient times. In conclusion he asked, "Is this your first trip across the Atlantic, Miss Roberts?"

"Yes, yes' I have never..." CeeCee caught herself, for she was about to say, *I have never been anywhere besides Virginia, except Georgia when Winnifrey went to school.* For an instant her voice teetered, and she felt a pang of indecision. She did not know where to go with the remark and uncomfortably she left it hanging in midair. Finally, she remembered what Winnifrey said, '*do not say anything more than you have to. A lady does not need to be overly spoken.*

Ellington waited and when CeeCee did not continue he assumed her shyness took over, so he added, "Well, I know you were in New York, for that is where you boarded the ship. I hope you took the time to enjoy their great many interests. I, myself," he chuckled, "was fortunate to attend, Harvard University and I spent many a day unearthing the joys of New York. Again, he laughed when he explained, "Sadly much of it was at my parents' dismay. They believe New York, crude."

CeeCee smiled, but since she knew nothing of New York she could not add to his comments. Though she thought of the stories she heard when she was at Brenau with Winnifrey and before she analyzed what she was about to say she began to reveal a tale that Elizabeth Bartlett had lived. However, in her version it was she who enjoyed the ride through Central Park.

Ellington listened to her every word. He enjoyed the sound of her voice, and the way she clearly expressed her seat of passion. It was plain to hear her love for horses and this pleased him as well.

CeeCee described Central Park in a way he had never heard before, and after a while he caught himself watching her lips as they moved. They were full and seductive and promised ecstasy, with this thought he felt embarrassed, and tried to concentrate his efforts on her words instead of her beauty. Soon he came to realize that the words she used to describe the simplest factors showed she had an appetite for adventure, and in her very next statement she proved this conjecture.

"I have a yearning, Mr. Kempe, to experience the world and all its delight"

He smiled at her divulgence but did not comment for he did not want to interrupt her eloquence. Her voice was like a lullaby and her recital was as if she were telling a bedtime story, and he wished she would never reach its ending.

After the portrait she painted of her ride in Central Park and the visit to the Metropolitan Art Museum she fell silent. For a short time neither said a word as they watched the waves and the stars above. Finally, Ellington turned to face her and asked, "Do you ride often, Miss Roberts?"

In truth, she answered, "Not as much as I would like."

"Do you think I might be able to convince you to go riding with me one day?"

When she did not answer, he continued, "I have a mount I am sure would be perfect for you. She is beautiful and as even tempered as you, Miss Roberts."

Smiling CeeCee answered, "Thank you, Mr. Kempe." She did not acknowledge the invitation and instead asked, "Although, I am interested in knowing how you think you know I am of even temper, Mr. Kempe."

"That my fine lady, was easy enough to discern. For your cousin, Winnifrey, as lovely as she may be, was not a very agreeable person towards you this evening. However, you were undeniably pleasant."

"Why thank you, Mr. Kempe."

"Please, will you call me, Ellington?"

With his request CeeCee realized the conversation was getting too amicable and her apprehension returned.

"Mr. Kempe, I fear I am much too exhausted to continue our conversation. So, if you do not mind, I would like to return to my cabin."

Ellington at once felt a tinge of regret. He could hear the change in her voice, and he worried if his assertion had offended her in some way. He hoped not, yet he decided to apologize just in case, but before he could; she had turned to move in the direction of her cabin. So, without further dictum he followed her.

CeeCee lay awake for hours reliving every word spoken that night, and when Winnifrey and Abigail entered the suite she pretended to be asleep. She wanted to stay in her reverie without their infringement, and as soon as the lights went out, she returned to the evening and relived her memories once again.

It was far into the night before she neared sleep, at which time she decided Ellington was the kind of man she had dreamed about her entire life. He was pleasing on the eye, and she knew any lady would love to be acquainted with such a gentleman. It was clear to see he was kindhearted, and at dinner he appeared sophisticated and often charmingly witty. For an instant she wished she could know him better, and then recognized the idea was preposterous. She was a Negro and he was a white gentleman. He was not a person who would ever enter her life and stay, especially if the truths were known.

CHAPTER NINE

Winnifrey was cool towards CeeCee the next morning and barely directed three words her way. She never mentioned the night before until she and Abigail were ready to leave the cabin after breakfast. At that time, she pushed the chair back from the small table where she had been sitting in the corner of their room. CeeCee watched her from where she stood out of Winnifrey's eye view. She had been playing with the leftovers on her plate for some time while she distastefully eyed the half-eaten meal in silence. CeeCee feared she was in trouble but prayed for mercy. Finally, Winnifrey looked her straight in the eye and declared, "Cecilia, I want you to know you were wickedly ungracious last night, and I will not stand for it. Last night we were forced to include you in our invitation, but that will cease as of today. I have given it some consideration and decided, you will stay in the cabin and eat your meals alone..., away from decent white folk. This entire deception was for my..., and Abigail's comfort, not for you to galivant around the ship after the male passengers. Your behavior is becoming more and more unsettling, and I have decided to tell Father to find you a position elsewhere. I no longer need your assistance. I wish to have a personal maid who is more experienced in womanly care and less man crazed."

She stood and move to snatch her parasol that rested against the wall and took one step towards the door before she continued, "Abigail and I are going to watch Henry and Ellington play shuffleboard this morning. While we are out, you will get our dresses ready for this evening. I will wear the green gown and Abigail, the ivory. We will be having dinner with Ellington and Henry and I want us to look our most charming."

When the door closed behind Winnifrey and Abigail, CeeCee burst into tears. She realized at the time she was pushing Winnifrey too far, but she never weighed the possibility that she would be replaced. Viola was right; she had forgotten who she is and her place in life. What will she do now? Where will Mr. Roberts send her?

The next several hours she put an extra effort in making sure every wrinkle was out of Winnifrey's gown. *Maybe she will change her mind if she knows I am sorry. I will promise to work much harder and do a better job at keeping my mouth shut.* "I really did not wish to be so disrespectful," defended CeeCee, while she continued to work.

She tried hard to fight her sorrow, but as soon as she thought the tears were contained, her throat felt full again and a new batch would gush forth; stronger than before. She polished and re-polished both girls' shoes and laid out all the accessories to accompany the garments. At last her work was finished, yet Winnifrey and Abigail had not returned so she decided a walk might do her good. "Surely a walk will not upset Winnifrey," she told herself as she vacillated between desire and doubt. At last desire won out and she grabbed her shawl and headed out the door.

CeeCee moved slowly down the corridors until she reached the open air. There were groups playing shuffleboard and others shooting rifles at plates that the attendant shot into the air. Laughter was everywhere, and she yearned to be a part of it. But she could not guess what would happen if she ran into Winnifrey, so she decided it was best to walk away from the crowded areas.

She walked to the furthest point of the ship where she knew Winnifrey or Abigail would not go. There she leaned against the railing and dreamily admired the thunderous waves. The ship rocked with each wave that hit it. Afterward the crest swirled and formed a white foamed trail behind the steamer. For an instant CeeCee wished they could engulf her and take her away from all the pain of Winnifrey's threats. Her heart felt so heavy and for an instant she was sure it was going to stop beating.

She closed her eyes and said a prayer before she opened them and studied the waves again. After a time, she decided they were somehow comforting her. Yet they also brought a forsaken uneasiness that made her want to shed a tear.

Under her breath, she murmured, "I do not belong in Winnifrey and Abigail's world." This is a possibility she faced for the first time, and it was shattering all her hopes. No matter how hard she tried to be a lady, she was still a Negro girl. They were white and no matter how dressed up and well-mannered she became, she was still just what she was, a colored. *But then, I no longer belonged in the colored world.*

She is educated and knew far more than anyone she knew. Why, no one in her family could even read or write, and here she is as educated as Winnifrey...or Abigail. I can not go back to being ignorant even if I wanted to. "Oh..., where am I to go? I do not belong anywhere; I might as well be dead."

"Cecilia?"

She jumped with a start; she did not hear anyone approaching, and at recalling her last words that she feared she spoke aloud, she felt an instant embarrassment. Slowly she turned to face the voice.

Ellington's concern was all over his face as he took several steps closer. "I am sorry, Cecilia I did not intend to impose, but your words...."

He wavered for a second or two then continued, "Cecilia, it is quite common to feel such dread after a death in the family and with two...well, I imagine it would be far worse. But please believe me when I say the pain does lessen over time."

Cecilia felt foolish. Ellington was talking about her make-believe parents that Winnifrey had killed off last night. She had no idea of how to answer his kind words, so she remained silent.

"Cecilia, you only think you have no place to go. You do have, Mr. and Mrs. Roberts, plus Abigail. And even if Winnifrey is a snot, pardon my language, I am sure she does love you. You are part of her family."

"Mr. Kempe, I assure you, you have no idea of what you speak."

"Oh, but I do. You see, when my mother passed on seven years ago, I was broken hearted. Then when my father remarried six months later, I became quite devastated. I, too, felt lost and had no idea of where I belonged in their life.

Fortunately, the woman my father married is a dear, and she understood my misguided feelings. She explained that life goes on, and my mother would have wanted my father to fill the void in his life. And yes, I must say she was correct when she said my mother would have wanted the same for me. Of course, with all my pain and sorrow still fresh, I fought her kindness. As a matter of fact, at first, I did not believe a single word. Although her sensible compassion eventually won my trust and I opened my heart to her fully. And now I can honestly say, I have never been sorry." He gave her a crooked smile and softly added, "Cecilia, she was right, you know... life does go on and you must do the same..., You need to open your heart to the Roberts. If you let them help you; your grief will lessen and eventually heal."

A tear slowly crawled down CeeCee's cheek and she quickly attempted to wipe it away before he could see it. At this time, he reached forward and held out his hand for her to take. She stood there staring at it as if it were an object she did not recognize. Ellington coughed under his breath but remained standing firm with his hand extended until CeeCee seized it. This was the first time she had ever felt such warmth, and her tears fell suddenly without warning and she collapsed into his arms and cried for several minutes. After she shed her tears of misfortune, not grief; as Ellington still believed, she lifted her head and immediately backed away from his hold. Self-conscious she asked, "What are you doing here? Why are you not where all the activities are?"

"Winnifrey," he replied.

CeeCee arched an eyebrow in confusion and he went on with his explanation. "Well, it seems that since Henry is completely infatuated with Abigail..., Winnifrey has set her sights on me."

CeeCee's eyes still held a question and he added, "So I am hiding..., I thought this was as good a spot as any and a place where someone like Winnifrey would never venture."

CeeCee burst into laughter. She could just imagine ole Winnie chasing poor Ellington around the deck of the ship. When she finally released her last giggle, she admitted, this was the first real laugh she had in a long time. At that moment, she realized that she was still standing too close to Ellington, and quickly backed away. Shyly she begged, "Oh my, Mr. Kempe, please forgive my impudence?"

"Do not be absurd, Cecilia. You were upset, not brazen. And besides, this was an opportune time for me to be chivalrous, so please do not take that away."

CeeCee smiled at his attempt to lighten the tension and her eyes filled with gratitude for his kindness. Suddenly her smile disappeared and without warning she asked, "Mr. Kempe, did I hear you address me as, Cecilia?"

"Well... yes... you did. I hope you do not feel me cheeky. Nonetheless, since I was about to save your life, and you were in my arms; I thought you may at least allow me to call you by your first name."

Again, CeeCee laughed at Ellington's wit. She liked his gentle waggish approach and did not feel at all threatened by his nearness. Suddenly with this thought, her prior self-pity returned. She was not what Ellington believed her to be, and she had no business being here with him. He is a white gentleman and she is only a colored maid. She must remember that even if she is dressed in a lady's fancy apparel, this did not make her a lady. Despite this fact she faced Ellington's handsome face and said what was expected if she truly were what she appeared to be. "Thank you for your concern and thoughtfulness..., Mr. Kempe. But I assure you I had no intention of throwing myself into the sea. Though I do appreciate your intended effort I will take no more of your time. She stood taller and straightened her shoulders, then asked, "If you will excuse me, Mr. Kempe, I have many things that require my attention. Good-day..., Sir." CeeCee's walk was very close to a run when she hurried out of Ellington sight.

He stood there for several minutes staring at the now empty deck. "This woman," he stated, "is the most intriguing I have ever come across. She is utterly disarming." He had schooled several years in the States and so he was aware that the American women were more dimensional. However, Cecilia seem to be a tad more complicated than most and completely genuine. With a fleeting chuckle, he decided, "This, I frankly like."

In fact, most of the ladies he met where sadly more interested in his wealth than in him. Where Cecilia seemed quite unaware of his holdings and in no way was, she attempting to attract him. "Umm," he grumbled, "if anything she is working extremely hard to keep me away. This is pleasantly puzzling..., I must learn more."

Quickly he stepped forward in hopes of catching up with her as he declared earnestly, "I hope I can at least convince her to sit with me at dinner this evening."

Abigail and Henry had eyes for no one other than each other, and this was beginning to upset Winnifrey greatly. After they returned from their days' amusement to rest before supper, she said as much to her sister. "Abigail, you have been repulsively boring all day long."

"Why do you say that, Winnifrey?"

"Why dear sister, because you have not shared Henry's attention with anyone. Not even for a minute. I am sure by now he is extremely weary of your childish vigilance. Though this, you do not seem to notice one bit.

Why Father and Mother would simply die of embarrassment if they saw your behavior, Abigail. Plus I am certain; that they would have you off to boarding school, if not a convent, before you could flash one more of those flirty little smiles you so freely bestow on any gentleman who looks your way."

CeeCee folded the last garment and laid it in the drawer as she peaked sideways to get a gander at Abigail's reaction to her sister's accusations. She was not disappointed, for Abigail's face was white with anger and she turned on her sister and asked, "What do you suppose I do, Winnifrey? Do you think if I hide myself, like you did CeeCee, then Henry will suddenly become infatuated with you? Dear Winnifrey, I am afraid that is a self-deception; if this is what you believe. Henry has no interest in you whatsoever, dear sister. He is much too kind to be involved with someone so self-involved."

"Why Abigail, I never, you...you, young lady better watch that mouth of yours. I am your older sister, and I demand respect, do you hear me, Abigail?"

"I am sure the entire ship has heard you Winnifrey, and respect is earned, not demanded. And as for Mother and Father, if...if they knew half of what you have done these past years, they...they...." Suddenly Abigail broke down in tears, she had never been much of a fighter, and therefore Winnifrey always got the best of her. However, this time something was different, and her tears only shed a minute before she faced her sister once again and warned, "Winnifrey, you will not interfere with my and Henry's relationship..., or I will never forgive you, do you understand? This is not a game of flirtatious rivalry between you and your girlfriends. This is the beginning of a serious coupling between a man and a woman."

Winnifrey laughed loudly and snapped, "Abigail... do not be ridiculous! You are much too young to have a serious relationship. Henry is just tinkering with your childish infatuation. And as for Father, I am sure he will put an end to this as soon as we step foot on England's soil. So, my childish sister, in my opinion all this ado is about nothing, nothing at all."

Abigail's confidence wavered and Winnifrey smiled slightly when she thought she was getting the upper hand, and for an instant she believed she had won the fight with her last declaration.

Still and all Abigail was far from defeated, and she proved this when she announced, "Winnifrey, please do not bother me with no more of your jealous ravings; I need my rest. Henry is picking me up at six, and I do want to look my best. Though I dare say if I did not, he probably would not notice." She grinned at her sister along with a winked in CeeCee's direction before she laid herself on the daybed and her head against the pillow and immediately closed her eyes. CeeCee wanted to yelp with joy, for Abigail had finally succeeded in making Winnifrey speechless.

Winnifrey saw the look on CeeCee's faced and turned her anger on her. "Niggar girl go fetch me a pot a tea and make it snappy. Also, I want you to bring me a cold pack for my head and while you are at it, I suggest you best order your supper. For you will be staying in tonight and every night after until we reach port."

Fighting her smile CeeCee mumbled "Yes, mam." Then hurried out the door to escape Winnifrey and further wrath. If she knew Winnifrey, and she sure she did, she would take her revenge out on her. And the plain truth was, she never knew what form Winnifrey's anger would take, so it was best to avoid her anger when possible.

As she hurried down the corridor, she made a wish that Winnifrey would not learn that Ellington had spoken to her today. *If she finds out*, thought CeeCee, *it will surely provoke her further and with that temper of hers, she might reveal the truth about me without even intending to.*

CeeCee was carrying the tray back to Winnifrey when Ellington and Henry crossed her path. She halted abruptly and spilled a portion of the tea. Without meaning to her eyes registered fear, and Ellington noted this and asked, "Is everything alright, Cecilia?"

She nodded, but said nothing, so he continued, "I see you are taking your tea to your room. Can we persuade you to join us instead?"

"No...no thank you; this is for Winnifrey...." Hurriedly she added, "She has a headache."

"Oh, I see," said Henry. Then perhaps you can join Ellington, Abigail and I for dinner this evening."

Ellington saw her look of refusal register before CeeCee put it into words. "Yes please," he pleaded, "Please, Miss Roberts, I so would like to spend some time and get to know you better."

CeeCee wanted to say yes more than she ever wanted anything before, but her fear of Winnifrey was far greater than any desire she possessed. Therefore, instead of stating what she wanted she rapidly replied, "I must hurry, the tea is getting cold and I am sure Winnifrey would much rather have it hot." She started to step around them, then hesitated and added, "And I do thank you for the invitation though I am afraid it is impossible. See Winnifrey might need my attention. Ah...with her headache, I should be at hand." Without another word; she scurried away.

At six-fifteen when Henry walked into the dining room, he proudly escorted Abigail on one arm and Winnifrey on the other, yet CeeCee was nowhere in sight. Ellington stood and greeted the ladies, before he asked, "Is Cecilia on her way?"

Immediately Winnifrey exaggerated a fret, "Oh no, I am afraid not. Cecilia is..., let me see... how do I put this delicately, she is not of healthy mind and often has days when she prefers to stay alone. So, she is taking a tray in our cabin."

"Really," queried Ellington? "She seemed quite healthy to me this morning."

Winnifrey's cheeks colored and she asked, "This morning?"

When Henry did not answer, she said, "No never mind, tonight she will stay in. Now if you will be so kind, Mr. Kempe, I would like to sit down."

Ellington pulled a chair outward for her to be seated next to Howard and he moved to sit next to Sara. Winnifrey hastily moved toward Howard's side and asked, "Do you mind, Howard?"

Howard sat there for a moment her request did not register. Then suddenly he reacted as he grasped her intention, "Oh, oh by all means, of course."

Winnifrey moved her chair closer to Ellington's and asked. "Mr. Kempe, are you of the Kempe shipping lines?"

Ellington discontentedly answered, "Yes, Miss Roberts, it's been in our family since its' inception; my father is sole owner as was his father before him." His mind was on Cecilia and Winnifrey's obvious disrespect and mistreatment of her irritated him; yet he answered her inquiries politely as he would any other guest.

"Please, Mr. Kempe call me Winnifrey. May I address you by Ellington?" She fluttered her eyelashes while she waited for him to agree, "I would be honored, Winnifrey."

"I hear your father's fleet is quite large. I imagine one day you will take over its operation. That is, when he decides to relinquish his control, after all from what I understand, you are his only son."

"Yes, this is true Miss..., Winnifrey. Indeed, my father does plan to pass along the fleet's supervision to his eldest son, in which case is I, his only son, his child. That is the family tradition, and I too plan to do the very same thing myself one day..., for my son."

Winnifrey scooted her chair even closer towards Ellington, "Oh my, that will be a very large inheritance, Ellington."

Suddenly Ellington stood and said, "If you will excuse me, Winnifrey, I have an errand I must attend to?"

"Right this minute, Ellington? Why, we are in the middle of dinner."

Ellington smiled at Abigail, nodded to his friends, then rapidly moved away from the table. While he did so, he heard the disgruntled Winnifrey mutter, "Why I never."

CeeCee heard the knock and waited to see if whoever it was would go away. When the knock persisted, she finally made herself answer it's call. It was probably her supper tray and hungry or not it looked like the server was not going to go away.

She was completely caught off guard when she opened the door, and Ellington stepped forward and announced, "I understand,

Cecilia. Now I completely understand your dilemma and it is appalling."

Immediately fear gripped CeeCee, and she wanted to ask what Winnifrey had told him, yet she could not speak.

Though her lack of words did not matter, for Ellington was set on speaking his mind. "This morning I was utterly rude for assuming I knew what you were speaking about. You were trying to tell me you could not live with the Roberts; particularly Winnifrey. Why...why, that woman is insufferable, and she treats you as if you were her private servant."

He reached out and took her hand as he apologized, "Cecilia, I am sorry to be so forward, but I cannot stand by and allow her to treat you this way. How can I, when her behavior is intolerable, it...it is downright repugnant. And as I said, I will not stand for it. How can I when it is plain to see she will make your life miserable?"

"Ellington please, you are plainly being too harsh. Winnifrey has her bad points, I agree, but she is not as atrocious as you seem to think. And what do you mean you will not stand for it? You do not even know me and have nothing to say about what you will or will not allow."

"This, I admit may be true, but Cecilia if you will spend some time with me, this will unquestionably change...,that is, knowing you,... not telling you what or what you can not do."

CeeCee smiled, she could tell Ellington realized he had been entirely too tyrannical, and now he was attempting to lighten his manner. Both fell silent for an uncomfortable time before Ellington finally asked, "Can we have dinner... together..., please?"

CeeCee weighed her options. Winnifrey would surely be furious with her, yet she really yearned to spend some time with Ellington. He seemed so very kind and he certainly was attractive, and the short time they have spent together has been entirely pleasurable. Besides, she liked the feelings his presence gave her, along with the way he treated her like a lady. With all this in his favor it was hard to resist his overture. Apprehensively she looked into Ellington's dark eyes and finally agreed, "Yes...Ellington, I will love to join you for dinner."

After she had spoken the words, she realized she had addressed him as Ellington, and how comfortably his name had rolled off her tongue. Quickly she repeated it several times to herself and liked the way it felt. Then once again she said it out loud, "Ellington...can you please give me half an hour to ready myself?"

"By all means," Ellington gayly chuckled. "I will be back in thirty minutes, Miss Cecilia Roberts." As he happily strolled away, he hummed a cheery tune.

CeeCee stood immobile for a full minute before she slowly closed the door then took off in a dead run for the closet. "What will I wear? Oh; my Lord, Winnifrey is going to kill me." *However, she thought, she is going to send me away as soon as we get home anyway, so what difference does it make what I do from now on.* CeeCee turned and studied the image in the mirror then added; "Besides I know as well as I know anything, Winnifrey will make my life unhappy one way or the other, so it is time I stop being afraid and take my life in my own hands."

CeeCee choose a lavender gown that Winnifrey had said she intended to pass her way one day. When Winnifrey had said this, she thought she would never have an occasion to wear such a frock. Yet now here she is standing before a mirror smiling at her glorious reflection.

She added one last hair ornament then smoothed the silky fabric. The gown was lovely, and her eyes sparkled with pleasure at the end result, "this is a dream come true," she whispered. "Please Lord let me have tonight..., wi...without any repercussions. Please, keep my secret, do not let Ellington find out I am a Negro."

She heard the light knock and fear gripped her chest. What was she doing? This is preposterous. Why did she let Winnifrey put her in this situation? Yet she knew why; Winnifrey was her boss and she was obliged to do whatever she said. *But soon all of that will end,* she thought, *since she is going to send me away.*

By the time she heard the second knock; her fear had been replaced by anger for Winnifrey and her threats. In a huff, she rationalized, "Winnifrey's deceptive games have ruined any chance of me having a normal life, so I deserve a little happiness if it comes my way."

CeeCee squared her shoulders and lifted her chin then headed for the door. This is her night and she is going to enjoy it at any risk.

Ellington sucked in a loud breath and whispered, "Cecilia..., you are breath taking. I believe from this day forward I will never let you out of my sight."

Her smile was full of delight and graciously she thanked him. Grinning like a fool, he tenderly secured her arm and wrapped it around his, though he never took his eyes off her lovely face.

Finally, CeeCee said, "Ellington."

"Yes, Cecilia."

"I believe it would be much safer if you watched where you were stepping." At this instant, she was amazed to see his cheeks flush slightly. Though it was not more than a second later when he broke into lighthearted laughter and agreed, "You are undoubtedly correct Miss Roberts, but I fear my mind has gone blank as I am flabbergasted by your beauty."

With this comment, she too blushed and shyly joined his laughter, as they quickened their steps down the corridor towards the main dining room. When CeeCee and Ellington entered the first-class dining hall she quickly glanced around to see if Winnifrey or Abigail were anywhere about. She exhaled a sigh of relief when she saw neither.

The whole time she waited for Ellington to secure a table she stood in awe and appreciated the rooms' splendor. She decided that the first time she had been there she was so nervous she had failed to look around; now however, she almost gasped at its grandeur. *Even the ceiling is magnificent,* she thought. She had never seen anything so extraordinary. Indeed, even the hotel in New York, as wonderful as it was, had not been so ornate.

This room with its artful images and lighting fixtures that shone so brilliant that their glimmered was fit for a King. She sighed as she decided she could never have dreamed of a room like this, since she never knew such extravagance existed. Each table was set with the finest China that was adorned with a royal inlay and the crystal and silver glistened to perfection. For an instant CeeCee could not help but be thankful she did not have to shine the pieces, for at home that was one of her responsibilities. Her thought made her shudder and since she did not want thoughts of home or her duties, she moved her sight to take in the room's inhabitants. There she noticed a gentleman with a tall shiny black hat on his arm. The hat matched his tuxedo and he looked so regal it took a deep breath in awe. She watched as he approached her and when he bowed his head in a respectful salute, she wanted to cry. Forever she had desired this life with all her heart, and now she feared she would never want to give it up.

Ellington stepped forward and offered his arm once again to CeeCee, and the ship's steward led them to a large table where the Captain of the ship sat. He stood to greet them and at once CeeCee turned to stone, instantly she felt inferior and lost her nerve and voice.

The Captain introduced several of the guests who sat around the table and Ellington nodded to each, while he noted that CeeCee had become rigid. He patted her arm for reassurance, though he himself began to feel uncertain and wondered if this was all too much too fast. Maybe they should have taken dinner alone, although he had hoped a crowd would lessen her anxiety. He wondered if instead, it had upset her. However, soon this thought was abandoned for CeeCee found her voice and whispered a gracious hello and sat herself confidently in the seat that was offered her.

CHAPTER TEN

C eeCee opened her eyes and stared at the ceiling for a long time. Had she only dreamed that she had spent the evening with Ellington Kempe? She smiled when she realized it had truly happened, and it was the most magnificent night she had ever experienced. It was perfect in every way even when she returned and cautiously entered the cabin, she was rewarded, Abigail and Winnifrey were not back from their evening of frolic. Yet it was only minutes after she had undressed and climbed onto the cot she used for a bed that they returned.

When they turned on the light, she pretended to be asleep and she heard Abigail tell Winnifrey, "No..., Winnifrey let CeeCee sleep. You can undress yourself this once." Begrudgingly Winnifrey agreed.

This night was heavenly, thought CeeCee as she once again started to recall it from start to end. Dinner was pleasant and filled with lively conversation where she listened but added little. After dinner she and Ellington had strolled the deck. They wandered from bow to ster; then to one side of the ship to the other with no apparent need to be anywhere except together. He asked if she would like to go dancing. And in truth she really wanted to say yes, however she was afraid they would run into Winnifrey and Abigail, so she said she was still not ready for large groups of merriment, and Ellington seemed to understand her inference.

Winnifrey's lie that her parents had perished in Africa favored CeeCee's new deception, and she in good order used it to her advantage. *This,* she thought, *will only be for tonight.* Then as the evening wore on, and her lies began to grow, she decided that maybe her fantasy could go on until they arrived in England. *It will only be for a few days and my lies can not harm anyone in anyway,* she told herself. *Then I will go back to being who I am, CeeCee Brown a colored maid for Winnifrey Roberts..., that is until she sends me away.*

That morning while laying on her cot feeling all the tender emotions Ellington had awakened in her, she wondered if in the end, she would be the one who was going to end up hurt. She had never been with a man, other than that time with Henry Dauber and the inexperience was befuddling. She did not know how she was supposed to feel, and she had no one to ask. But when Ellington kissed her hand and bid her goodnight, her heart leaped with joy, yet fear had engulfed her. His kiss bought a warm sensation she never knew existed. *Maybe,* she thought, *this feeling is what made Winnifrey so crazy.* She hoped not since she never wanted to be like Winnifrey. She pondered that thought before she moved on. She, herself, had witnessed Winnifrey chase after men, and more than once she wondered just how far Winnifrey let her indulgences go. No, she will not let herself turn into Winnifrey.

The next few days were spent dodging Winnifrey, since CeeCee was afraid her eyes might give away her true happiness. But soon her heart ached, because Winnifrey had now set her sights completely on Ellington. She recalled how her heart sank when she heard Winnifrey tell Abigail, "I had no idea Mr. Kempe was so wealthy. Why any girl would find herself fortunate to become Mrs. Ellington Kempe." She giggled and added, "And I imagine we both can guess who might be the best choice for such a prominent and rich gentleman."

Abigail only smiled at her sister's flippancy for she had far more important things to deal with. Since she and Henry had reacquainted themselves, they had become inseparable. And now her biggest fear was, as Winnifrey had once suggested, that her parents would send her away if they learned of the relationship. She had not planned to fall in love; however, there was not any doubt that that is what she had gone and done. If Winnifrey got wind of this, she would surely use it against her. This is why she had begged Henry to keep the romance a secret, for the time being anyway. He was not even allowed to tell his brother, Howard, or his friend, Ellington. If only Ellington would fall in love with Winnifrey, that would make her and Henry's life much easier. With this sentiment in mind she decided that she and Henry should help the relationship evolve and the sooner the better.

Surprisingly, Abigail realized Winnifrey was still prattling away so she tried to concentrate on her sister's words. "Yes, I think I shall insist that Ellington and I spend the day together. I will refuse to take no for an answer and if you, Sara, Howard and Henry can stay your distance, maybe we can properly begin our courtship. I say you all have been quite smothering. Why we have not had a minute alone! How is one expected to build a relationship if we can not be alone?"

Abigail noted Winnifrey had listed their names with her and Henry on either side of Sara and Howard, so this meant she was still unaware of their feelings. Though that did not surprise Abigail; Winnifrey rarely noticed other people. She was always too interested in herself to be bothered with such trivial concerns of other people.

"Lets' see," said Winnifrey, "we can picnic on deck. That would be lovely, and maybe play a board game or two. Of course, there are several other activities we can decide on later." She giggled again as her mind focused on one particular activity. After several seconds of hesitancy, she continued where she left off. "Yes, by the end of dinner, sweet Abigail, I shall have him fully infatuated. Without a doubt, I will have him eating out of my lovely little hand by evening's end." She tittered and added, "From there on I am sure, he will spend the rest of our trip trying to figure out how he can win my heart forever."

Abigail was sure her sister was overly confident. She herself had witnessed how unresponsive Ellington had been towards Winnifrey. Yet she and Henry will do their best to encourage the circumstances, so maybe that will help. Abigail weighed Winnifrey's confidence then settled, "Winnifrey," maybe you should take it less ardent," Abigail cautioned. "You certainly do not want to scare the poor fellow away."

Winnifrey briefly eyed Abigail as she considered the suggestion before she decided, "You know nothing about men, dear Abigail, and at times, I wonder if you will ever attain a husband with such ignorance. Though I am sure Father will be able to secure a suitable, if not a choice mate when all else fails."

Hurt by the remark Abigail fell silent and moved her attention back to the book she was attempting to read, though her mind promptly strayed and settled on Henry. She had told Henry, as soon as Winnifrey laid down for her afternoon nap, she would sneak away. She could hardly wait to distance herself from Winnifrey and her ill-mannered mockery. *Winnifrey,* she told herself, *has grown into the sort of woman, that if she were not my sister, I would avoid or not associate with at all. Though I do love her dearly, I, at times, dislike her greatly.* This fact saddened her, yet there was nothing she could do to change it and Lord knows, she had tried. She especially disliked the way her sister treated CeeCee; she was just awful towards the girl. She had asked her time and time again that she not treat CeeCee as her own private slave. *"Slavery has been abolished for years,'* she told her sister, *and treating a person as such certainly shows ill-manners....* Nonetheless Winnifrey continued this dreadful practice.

Abigail laid her book aside. Soon again she was daydreaming about Henry and their next meeting two hours from now. She could hardly wait for Winnifrey to lay down for afternoon nap so she could slip out. Meanwhile with the thought of Henry, Winnifrey, along with everything else, became less important.

E llington took a sip of the cold coffee, then sat the cup back in the saucer with a clang as he pushed them both aside. "Henry, please tell me. I know you knew Cecilia years ago. Has she always been so composed? Or is it because she is still mourning her parents, or do you think she is simply not interested in me as a suitor? I hope not, I truly find her irresistible."

"As did I, Ellington. And to tell you the truth, I too, was rebuffed. I am afraid, dear friend, that Miss Cecilia Roberts is elusive if not a complete mystery. Yet I would guess, that in fact, that is part of her charm. Would you not agree, my friend?"

"Yes, you are probably right, Henry." Ellington pulled the coffee cup back in front of him after the Steward filled it to the brim. Cautiously he stirred the dark black substance, and after a bit he looked up and asked thoughtfully. "Henry, is it my imagination or are you and Abigail becoming tight?"

Henry said nothing; he was asked by Abigail to be elusive about their relationship and he did give his word that he would not say anything, even to Ellington. Though in reality he wanted to scream it from the bowsprit of the ship, that he, Henry Dauber, had found the most wonderful woman in the world, and he loved her desperately and she, him. However, he did not let these words pass his lips. Instead he pondered what Abigail had said about drawing Ellington's attention towards her sister so they could be free to spend more time together.

After he swallowed the bite of fruit he had disengaged from the grapefruit on his plate, Henry looked up and saw that Ellington was waiting expectantly for an answer. He laid the fork on the plate and said without acknowledging Ellington's question, "Now Winnifrey..., I would

Say, is quite a different story from Cecilia. She is a passionate young lady, who I noticed has a deep interest in you, my friend."

Ellington smiled, he was aware that Henry was avoiding his question, but out of respect for his friend's privacy, he did not mention the obvious circumvention. Though he did hesitate while he searched Henry's eyes for a clue, then decided it was none of his business. So, he moved on and examined Winnifrey's similarities to Cecilia, there were few if any. She was an alley cat compared to Cecilia and he smiled almost instantly as his mind pictured Cecilia's sweet face. After a second or two his mind again moved back to Winnifrey, and his face soured. He was still angry with her for the way she treated Cecilia, though Cecilia disagreed with his opinion that she was treated poorly by the Roberts, especially Winnifrey, yet he still believed it true.

Henry waited, then finally asked, "Well?"

"Well, what, Henry. What do you want to hear? That I am interested in Winnifrey Roberts? That my friend is a waste of time; she is interested solely in my money."

"Come on, Ellington most women are interested in your money. At, least give the girl a chance."

Ellington studied Henry before he asked, "How does my interest in Winnifrey concern you, Henry? Are you suggesting, I change my interest in Cecilia over to Winnifrey? Hummm, is there any special reason why?"

Self-consciously Henry moved to pick up his fork before he answered, "It does not concern me at all, Ellington. I only wanted you to weigh your interest."

Each, and every night Ellington asked CeeCee to join him for dinner, yet she made an excuse along with an unhappy apology. She knew if she kept Ellington away from the dining room and Winnifrey, their secret would soon be learned so she encouraged his attendance.

As for Ellington, he begrudgingly excepted her excuses and ended up having dinner in the dining room with his friends and

Winnifrey, due solely to Henry and Abigail's conniving. Though as soon as everyone moved to the ballroom, he excused himself and hurried away to meet Cecilia by the stern.

Each night after her dinner tray arrived, CeeCee snuck away from the cabin to meet Ellington. They would talk for hours about everything in the world. Even seagulls entered their conversations, no subject was avoided…, except CeeCee's personal life.

A few days before they were to arrive in England, Ellington admitted he was in love with Cecilia. When he said the words out loud, he ended them with, "I can not live without you Cecilia."

His announcement was unexpected, but his words were beautiful and they broke CeeCee's heart into a million pieces.

She had never considered this predicament and she wondered if she should tell him the truth, but then he would hate her. This she could not endure. In truth she had fallen in love with him as well, and she could not bear the thought of him seeing her in her true light. For she was sure he would hate her for the deception, as well as her hidden identity.

Ellington waited and his heart skipped a beat when he saw the fear in her eyes. Desperate he begged, "Cecilia, please, do not shut me out… please, I love you. Together we can face anything. Please say you will be my wife."

CeeCee felt the panic as it engulfed her and she wanted to run away before she burst forth with the truth, but he held her hands tightly and all she could do was pray silently. *Oh, dear God, is this my punishment for lying? Please do not hurt him. It was me… all me… not Ellington. He did nothing wrong.*

She heard Ellington's words again, "Cecilia, please marry me. You need me and I would be honored to take care of you forever. You will never want for anything. I am a wealthy man, Cecilia. You will have a mansion filled with servants and if you want, you will never have to put up with the likes of Winnifrey again."

Ellington words echoed in her mind, *a mansion, servants, why she herself is a servant, how can she have a servant?*

Suddenly she thought of Winnifrey and how she was going to send her away and because of Winnifrey and her lies, she did not belong in either world. White or Negro...she was neither and belonged nowhere, and because of this she was going to hurt the only man she ever loved.

All at once and without forethought CeeCee made her decision. Winnifrey was not going to hurt her any longer. She was going to take what she had always wanted. Quickly she said one last prayer for forgiveness, then asked, "Ellington, are you sure, are you absolutely sure? I am penniless. My parents' death has left me dependent on the Roberts for support who are related only distantly. I have no other family, Ellington. Are you positively sure, Ellington? You must be certain!"

"I have never been surer of anything in my entire life, Cecilia.

I swear you will know my love for the rest of your life and lack for nothing. You will need no other family Cecilia. You will have me and all my comforts from now on."

CeeCee closed her eyes and bit her lower lip before she hastily said, "Oh God, Ellington. I think I would love to be your wife more than anything I have ever wanted in my entire life. But are you sure?"

He started to laugh, not only from relief, but also at her question.

She was as unsure as he had ever seen her, and he threw his arms around her as he tried desperately to reassure her. "Cecilia, I am not a man who gives into whims. I am not only sure that I love you; I am absolutely positive, I love you, and my family will love you as well. Why any person in their right mind would fall in love with you. And I..., I assure you, I am in my right mind, and I truly want you as my wife."

At the mention of Ellington's family, a new fear erupted and CeeCee again wanted to weep. She had fooled Ellington because he was blinded by love, but what about his family? Surely, they will guess the truth. What was she going to do? And what about Winnifrey? She will tell my secret. There is no way she will let her Negro maid marry the one man she wants for herself.

Ellington felt her go limp in his arms and he pulled away to look at her face. "What is it, Cecilia? You look as if you have seen a ghost?"

A tear touched the corner of her eyes and she cried, "I can not marry you, Ellington."

"Why are you saying this? Of course, you can, and you will. You already accepted and I will not release you," stated Ellington." He eyed her for several seconds, before he said, "something is frightening you. Is it the Roberts..., Winnifrey..., who? Cecilia, please tell me."

CeeCee smiled between her tears. She had never felt so loved before. Suddenly she realized Ellington would protect her at any cost. No one will doubt her, because he will not let them, and as for Winnifrey..., Well she herself will have to handle her and all her threats... even if at this very moment she could not begin to think how. She sighed and vowed silently, *Over and above that, I will do whatever it takes to marry this man. God, I am sorry; but I truly do love him, and I want to be his wife."*

Winnifrey paced the floor several times before her irritation erupted. "Oh, where is that man?" she muttered. Ellington had excused himself as soon as they were seated at their table. She scanned the ballroom to see if she could spot him. "Where is he," she seethed inwardly while she stamped her foot under the table.

When he left, she had asked if he were coming back and he had mumble something under his breath. She was sure it was an assurance that he would only be gone a short time. She quietly complained to herself since no one else was seated at the table. "Oh, Ellington Kempe, you are exasperating. Everyone is out on the dance floor except me, what must people think?"

So far, she weighed, I have tried everything I can think of to get his attention and up to this point nothing has worked. She had thought until her head ached on what her next move should be. He must possess some weakness, something she can use to her advantage, but what?

At that moment Winnifrey caught sight of Henry across the dance floor. He was dancing very near Abigail, closer than... "Nonsense," she told herself, "they are simply two old friends enjoying each other's company." She re-examined the two a second time; then fully dismissed the notion that they had become closer than she briefly feared. Then relief spread across her squinted forehead as her glance fell back on Henry. He is a gorgeous man; she silently told herself. Then immediately she smiled at the image that popped into her mind. Unequivocally she connived. "If all does not go well with Ellington, I can surely reset my sights on, Henry. Yes indeed," she mused, "it will be a cinch to obtain a proposal from Henry Dauber. He is such a pussycat..., he will not be at all as difficult as, Ellington." She contemplated then decided; he has always been infatuated by my beauty. He will not be as good a catch as Ellington, but far better than most. Though I shall not worry, for I am sure Ellington will eventually come around.

Winnifrey walk back and forth while Abigail disrobed and hung up her gown. "Abigail, lay that out for CeeCee to hang. Wherever is that girl, I need to ready myself for bed? I *swear*, Abigail, she has become increasingly more difficult to handle."

"Winnifrey, please do not use such language; it is wicked. And as for CeeCee, you can not expect her to stay locked in this room twenty-four hours a day. Besides as long as she agrees to only go out at night you should leave her be. Besides, I am sure she will not get into any trouble on her own, she does not want to be caught any more than you want her to be. You, yourself, would see this if you were not so overwrought about Ellington."

Winnifrey plopped herself down upon the settee. "Abigail..., I cannot believe he did not come back. What is the matter with him? He is perplexing to say the least. I cannot tell if he is interested in me or not..., *yet* I cannot imagine why he would not be."

The look she gave her sister was a plea for an answer. Despite, Abigail had none. As far as she could tell Ellington was simply not beguiled by her sister's splendor. As a matter of fact, at times he

seemed to dislike her greatly. She had asked Henry about her obser-
vation and he had agreed and said that he had also witnessed this
behavior. Yet he had no clue on why Ellington was so distant or
held this frame of mind.

Henry said that this conduct was truly unlike Ellington's usual
self and that he had been extremely private this entire trip. Henry
had also rendered that as hard as he has tried, he had not been able
to guess what was on his friend's mind, except he was sure it was
not Winnifrey.

With this so apparent to her and Henry, yet implausible to Winnifrey, she began to feel slightly sad for her sister and she moved
across the room to sit down next to her. Abigail drew her close and
softly patted her back as she promised, "Winnifrey, it is not the end
of the world if Ellington is not the man you marry. You are young
and there are many more eligible men just as handsome..., if not as
rich as Ellington. So please, Winnifrey do not fret..., you will find
your true love." As she said the last few words Abigail felt a warm
pleasure for, she in fact, had found just that in Henry.

Once Abigail's words were considered, Winnifrey became immediately indignant. She did not like her sister feeling sorry for her
and she glared at Abigail before she hatefully shot back, "What do
you know of love? You are a mere child with no experience in life
whatsoever."

Abigail still feeling bad for her sister tried once again to sooth
her distress. "Winnifrey, I do not have to experience love to know it
will come your way. For you are beautiful and an undeniable catch
for any man, and if Ellington can not see this, it is his loss, not
yours."

"Yes, yes, of course Abigail, you are right. You are absolutely,
correct, and Henry for one finds me altogether enchanting and he is
a decent catch. Maybe it is time I turn my attentions back on him.
This would surely be Ellington's blunder and Henry's triumph."

Abigail sat silently stunned. Had she heard her sister correctly?
Was she intending to go after Henry...? Her Henry?

Before Abigail could get her question straight in her mind the door unexpectedly flew open and in entered an obviously gleeful CeeCee. She looked as if she were floating as she danced around in circles humming. It was several seconds before CeeCee realized she was not alone and when she did, panic covered her face. She stopped and stood frozen in her tracks.

Winnifrey immediately became miffed at CeeCee's happiness and rose to face her and asked, "What in God's name is the matter with you girl?"

Abigail excitedly inquired, "What is it. CeeCee? What has made you so absurdly rhapsodic?" When CeeCee did not answer, Abigail immediately stood and hurriedly began to offer an excuse, "Oh, CeeCee, I see we probably startled you, it is obvious that yo...you..."

But before Abigail completed her amends, Winnifrey still upset that her evening had gone so unsatisfactorily, and now here is her colored maid more joyful than she, burst out angrily, "Where in heaven have you been?"

CeeCee opened her mouth to speak, but Winnifrey was not about to hear her or any of her regretful explanations. She directly moved to the onslaught so she could destroy CeeCee happiness. "CeeCee, you are a poor excuse for a maid servant, and I will not stand for it any longer. You will not step out of this cabin until we dock in England. Do you hear me? For no reason, whatsoever; will you step foot beyond that doorway." Winnifrey pointed angrily at the door that still stood wide open. "You have completely taken advantage of the situation, and I will no longer stand for it."

CeeCee, conscious of Winnifrey's loud voice, feared she would be heard in the outer chambers and hurried to close the door. By the time she completed this task her mind had accepted the full reality of her situation and she shuddered in fear. She was not ready to confront Winnifrey. How is she to do battle with her? Winnifrey is far cleverer than she and she will most certainly win. There is no way she can possibly convince them to let her become Ellington's bride.

CeeCee willed her body to turn and face her adversaries, yet it stood frozen. Nothing moved as she stood there facing the door with her back rigid against the sharp gaze of Abigail and Winnifrey. Her mind raced in search of the right words that could make them understand that she had not planned this. She never intended to fall in love especially with a white man. It was only minutes before she had been confronted, that she thought that the strength of their love would help her prevail. Now in the face of her enemy, the first idea that filtered through the mass of thoughts that now overloaded her mind was that she had been silly to accept Ellington's offer and tomorrow she will tell him so. Her mind was wild with rash thoughts, *I can never confess the real truth, that I am a Negro maid for Winnifrey. I will simply tell him I decided I am not in love with him.* With this conclusion, her heart leaped, and she wanted to fall to the floor and perish.

Winnifrey's impatience with the girl snapped and she screamed, "CeeCee, answer me, NOW!" However, she did not pause to let the girl, who now turned to face them, reply. Instead she took her evening's disappointment out on CeeCee. "You scamp, you disgust me. You have been out with a man. Am I not correct, CeeCee? I refuse to have my maid the scandalous gossip of this ship. You are not going to be a tramp and under my employ another minute. Pack your cloths CeeCee for you are going where all the coloreds belong, below and away from decent folk."

Aghast, Abigail stepped forward in an attempt to thwart her sister's rampage, "Winnifrey, please, you do not know what you are saying. Surely you can give CeeCee a minute to explain."

"I will not give CeeCee anything. I have given her far more than most colored folks ever get or deserve, and she has done nothing except taken advantage of me. I will not be the fool any longer. She is going below where she belongs. There she can dally with any man she pleases."

"Winnifrey," Abigail begged, "think of what you say. We can not admit that CeeCee is a Negra. What will that do to our credibility?"

With this statement CeeCee for the first time could see a way out, and she at once rediscovered her voice. "Winnifrey you are wrong. I have not taken advantage of you. It is you who have used me for unsuitable causes, and you who had taken advantage of my vulnerability. Over, and over again you have put me in situations to benefit yourself. Winnifrey Roberts, it is you who have ruined my life and now I belong nowhere. I do not belong with the negros or the whites, and that is all because of you..., you Winnifrey, you. Yes, Winnifrey you and only you are the one who put me here today. Which, I doubt would be surprising to most since you have been self-serving your entire life."

"CeeCee, you watch your mouth, or I will call the Steward and have you hauled away immediately."

"You can not, Winnifrey," cried Abigail. "Everyone will find out about CeeCee and I cannot bear this."

For the first time in CeeCee's life she lost all fear of Winnifrey and with this, an ample rush of strength flowed through her body. "That is correct, Winnifrey," said CeeCee, as she pushed her chin out to show her new defiance and stepped even closer. "You can not have your world find out that you have made a fool of them."

"Yes, Winnifrey, see, even CeeCee understands."

"Oh hush, Abigail, I will not be threatened by our Niggar maid."

"But Winnifrey, Henry can not find out. He will despise me."

Winnifrey eyed her sister for several seconds before she asked, "Whatever do you mean by that, Abigail? Surely you are not trying to say that Henry cares for you. Do not be ridiculous."

Still upset by Winnifrey's earlier disclosure that she wanted to take Henry as a suitor and now her current show of disrespect, Abigail in a huff shouted, "Yes! Yes, Winnifrey, that is exactly what I am saying, and I will not let you ruin my life because of your excessive self-indulgence.

You are only angry because Ellington has not asked for your hand in marriage and now you are taking it out on us."

Suddenly CeeCee burst into laughter. She had forgotten momentarily that Winnifrey wanted her Ellington. Now with all the confrontation this struck her as funny and she could not stop herself from laughing.

Her laughter of course angered Winnifrey even more, and she turned once again on CeeCee, and threatened. "You...you are a disgusting little Niggar girl and you had better close that mouth, or I will slap it close."

This threat was more than CeeCee could stand. Suddenly all the bent up anger that she had concealed all these years exploded and she shouted, "You, Winnifrey, will never ever touch me or threaten me again, and as for Ellington Kempe, he will never ask for your hand in marriage...."

Scornfully Winnifrey interrupted CeeCee's confrontation and declared, "CeeCee, you know nothing about Ellington and what he will or will not do. You are simply jealous because you will never have anything in that dreadful existence that you call a life."

Again, CeeCee threw her head back and laughed. She almost choked on her laughter while she cast her own discernment, "Well, Miss Winnifrey Roberts, that is where you are wrong. Though I am not surprised since you are wrong so often. You see, I do know what Ellington will and will not do. For he is the gentleman I was with this evening and let me tell you he will never marry you..., because he wants me, he wants to marry me!"

Abigail and Winnifrey immediately fell silent. Both girls stared at CeeCee as if she had gone insane. Finally, Winnifrey choked on a giggle that sounded closer to a sob, "CeeCee, that is disgusting. A Niggar can not marry a white man, especially a man like Ellington. Why that is ridiculous...and impossible! You are despicable and a spiteful Niggar, CeeCee Brown, to even imply such a thing!"

Abigail finally found her voice and whispered, "So you are the reason..., you are why Ellington, has been so bewildering lately."

With this declaration Winnifrey stood stunned as her eyes quickly glance from face to face. After a long pause she finally found her tongue and threatened, "I will not allow such a thing; it is revolting. And I will make sure you go to prison if you even attempt it, CeeCee."

With that threat CeeCee immediately became sorry for her outburst and she reached in the depths of her mind for a defense. Momentarily her strength wavered, and she decided there was no way she could beat Winnifrey. She was wrong to have even tried.

Suddenly her eyes met Abigail's and she was surprised to see compassion. She did not think her love for Ellington was repugnant.

Promptly CeeCee's strength returned in full measure and she chose her words wisely instead of in anger. "No, no Winnifrey. No, you cannot and will not do anything. A scandal like that would ruin your family. Afterall if you recall, you are the one who introduced me to Henry as your *cousin.* I expect after learning the truth he would attest to this and if needed, I even have more witnesses. Ellington for one and let us not forget: Sara, Howard and Doreen to mention a few."

Winnifrey's face was red with wrath and she kicked at Abigail's shoes that lay on the floor in front of her. CeeCee smiled slightly as she continued, "Your father's name will be a joke amongst his business associates and of course, we must not forget you and Abigail. If your conspiracy is learned, you will never find a husband. And..., and I dare say, this may even bring doubt to your own heritage Winnifrey."

"Oh, Winnifrey," cried Abigail, "this will kill Mother, and, and Fa...father..., he, he will surely kill us. Please do not say anything. I absolutely love Henry and have no wish to live my life without him."

"Abigail, I have no choice..., we cannot stand by and let a Nigger marry a wealthy white man. Why she would be perceived as our equal; surely you can not accept this?"

Winnifrey, I am as unhappy about this as you, but what choice do we have. Surely you can see that Ellington will not marry you either way, and if you look at it in a certain light, this will be his chastisement for rejecting you."

"Abigail," cried Winnifrey, "do not say such a thing. Ellington has not rejected me. CeeCee is nothing more than a simple whore to him, and once he has his fill of her, he will be back begging for my forgiveness and my hand..., I... I am sure of this."

"Then that is all the more reason to keep silent," retorted Abigail, "inasmuch as Ellington will never come back to you if he learns the truth."

Winnifrey fell silent and began to move from one side of the room to the other and back again. At one point she hesitated momentarily to study CeeCee before she seated herself again on the settee. Her lovely face puckered with displeasure and after a short spell of sorrowful self-deliberation, she stood and vengefully asked. "So how do we accomplish this absurdity? Surely you can not ask us to support your deceit. CeeCee, you will be completely on your own."

"I ask nothing of you except to leave well enough alone. Ellington, as well as the others, do not suspect anything and will not if you keep your mouth shut."

"CeeCee," asked Abigail, "how can you do this to Ellington? If you go through with this nonsense and he finds out that you are a colored girl, which he no doubt will one day, he will be devastated. He will hate you for making him the laughingstock of England. Surely you can see this?"

Her voice lightened and she moved closer to CeeCee and surmised. "It is understandable that you would hunger for a life such as we live, CeeCee. Though rest assured, you will fail..., you are completely uneducated and ignorant of society. In view of all this, it is unlikely you will succeed in fooling anyone longer than a tea party."

With a giggle Winnifrey smugly added, "Why I doubt you would even know how to drink properly from a teacup. You see CeeCee, I fear you have begun to believe you are what you portray. Despite you are still and always will be a colored maid servant...," She; laughed cruelly and added, "and nothing more."

CeeCee bit her tongue so not to speak. She knew it was best to let Winnifrey believe she would fail, and that Ellington will soon be back under her wily powers.

At this time Abigail stepped in and wisely praised her sister's sensible choice. "You are absolutely correct Winnifrey and CeeCee will no sooner be settled in before she is asked to leave, and as for us, we will be none the worse for the feign."

"Yes," agreed Winnifrey, "and CeeCee will be on the streets living the life she so deserves, a whore nothing more but a whore." Self-satisfied she again turned to CeeCee and asked, "You do realize CeeCee, that once you make this move there will be no coming back?"

CeeCee nodded and Abigail hurriedly asked, "How are we going to explain to Mother and Father. I am sure they will ask for CeeCee's whereabouts?"

All three stared at each other. No one had thought beyond the quarrel. When CeeCee spoke, her voice sounded thick and it broke halfway through her suggestion, "Maybe we can say tha...that...that I... I was offered a position on board ship.

"Do not be silly, CeeCee," shot Winnifrey.

"I know," screeched Abigail, "we will simply say we offered CeeCee's services to our escort." She laughed when she continued, "After all, Winnifrey, you yourself said she is deathly ill."

Winnifrey gave her sister a dirty look, but agreed, "Yes, that would probably work temporarily, then what?"

"Well... after a spell of silence, CeeCee can pretend to have someone write and say she found a position in England."

Winnifrey glared at CeeCee, then finally conceded, "All right then that is our story and CeeCee, once you write that letter, I never want to hear from you again. Then you must never breathe a word to anyone that you are a negro.... that is, until you are back with your own kind."

Once again CeeCee said nothing and only nodded her head in agreement. She had two days to figure out what she was going to tell Ellington.

CeeCee was beside herself with worry for there was no doubt Ellington would wonder why Abigail and Winnifrey, not to mention Mr. and Mrs. Roberts, would not be attending their wedding.

But more importantly once arriving in England, Ellington expected her to stay with the Roberts. She had no idea how she was going to explain their abandonment of her. Nor could she guess where she would stay, since she knew no one in England. There was no way she could ask Winnifrey because she refused to even speak to her since their confrontation. Abigail was also unfriendly; however, she did occasionally speak to her when it was out of necessity.

After watching Winnifrey mope around the cabin Abigail took control by wisely suggesting that Winnifrey avoid Ellington the rest of the voyage. "In case," she said, "your bitterness gets the better of you and you vindictively reveal the truth."

This was a great relief for CeeCee. Nonetheless in the end Winnifrey's spitefulness turned out to be more helpful to CeeCee than Winnifrey ever would have wanted it to be. As a matter of fact, it turned out to be the answer CeeCee was looking for.

Ellington noticed Winnifrey and Abigail's avoidance and concluded that the Roberts were snubbing his true love. Yet worse, he overheard a remark Winnifrey made to Sara, '*that some people marry out of their station,*' which further fueled his animosity toward the girls.

Soon it all came to a head. It was the night before they were to enter port. Everyone's luggage was being shuffled about and CeeCee's small bag was mistakenly placed with Winnifrey's. Ellington happened to be approaching their cabin to ask if anyone needed assistance with their baggage when Winnifrey booted at CeeCee's bag and ordered, "Remove this rubbish, or I will have it thrown overboard. I will not have your hand-me-downs near my fine possessions. And since you will not be lodging with us any longer, they need not be in our pile anyway, so remove them immediately."

From over Winnifrey's shoulder CeeCee saw the expression on Ellington's face and she realized he had heard the entire conversation. At once her cheeks turned flush with embarrassment.

Winnifrey at the same time took note of CeeCee's coloring and knew her anxiety must indicate Ellington's nearness. Sharply she turned to face him, and, on her lips she wore a brilliant smile, though only for an instant. For Ellington swiftly came to CeeCee's rescue when he grabbed her bag and announced, "This is true, for Cecilia will be a guest at Kempe Manor. There, I dare say we will not have the misfortune of running across you..., or your family, Miss Roberts." He turned to face CeeCee and cordially asked, "Cecilia, may I take your arm? It will be my pleasure to escort you to the stateroom for a cup of tea. With CeeCee securely on his arm, he then turned back to face Winnifrey and politely said with a mock smile on his lips, "I bid you a good day, Miss Roberts."

CHAPTER ELEVEN

C ecilia felt her stomach flitter and she prayed that she would not heave. This was the same feeling she felt most of the day as she questioned continuously if Ellington would doubt his decision. *What if he changes his mind about marrying me and leaves me standing on the dock, what will I do then? What had I been thinking? Why did I accept his proposal? Surely Winnifrey was right and I will end up on the streets. How does one live a life of lies with the man she loves and expect that he will never learn the truth?* "No, no" she silently told herself, "I cannot let this happen. I must not let Winnifrey's evil prediction hinder my judgment. I must stay alert or..., or I will end up just as she threatened, on the streets as a whore. If Ellington ever finds out I will surely..."

"Cecilia, it is time to disembark. If you can point out your trunks; I will have my driver, Raydell load them. We have several hours in the carriage before we arrive at Kempe Manor, I hope you will not mind the discomfort of the ride. My mother had no idea that I was bringing a guest and she most always sends a carriage for me instead of an automobile." He snickered while he added, "She feels the long ride will clear my lungs of America's tainted oxygen.

She is a dogmatic Englishwoman who rarely gives merit to the United States. At times I wonder if it is mostly a front since she has so many stateside friends."

Cecilia laughed lightly as the panic inside her grew; she had not heard a word Ellington had spoken since he asked after her trunks. She had not thought of trunks; her only luggage was the bag that Ellington now held in his hands. As she stumbled for an excuse she thought, *this is the beginning of my life of lies. This time I cannot put the blame on Winnifrey. This lie is mine alone and it is I who must bear the burden."*

Her smile widened to cover her guilt and she explained, "I have no other luggage, Ellington. That is one reason I stayed in my cabin so often. My trunk was lost or stolen in New York and I had no time to replace it."

"Well, fret not my dear. My Mother's seamstress will whip you up a completely new wardrobe in no time at all. This will be an opportune time to experience England's finest courtier as well as pleasuring my mother at the same time. She looks forward to any excuse to have Mrs. Illicent in for cuttings."

Ellington chatted cheerfully as they strolled towards the departure ramp. He seemed unaware that they stood at a complete stop several times. And more than once she noticed a number of excited passengers trying to push ahead of the cluster of which Ellington seemed simply unaware of. This she noted was charming and something Winnifrey would have never stand for.

Disembarking was slow since the crowded ramp was so full that at times she could barely see before her. But when they finally sat foot on Liverpool's soil, she was immediately surprised by the smells as well as the view. *Even the air smells different than Virginia's,* she thought.

There was no scent of sweetness from damp grasses or musk from the moist green pecan trees. The pungency was thick here and the air was filled with a disagreeable foulness. The odors were many and some very much undistinguishable, which she guessed came from the full capacity of the docks, in addition to the bustling streets beyond.

On one side of the docks the commotion was fearfully stirring, as crewmen from the ship hustled around yelling orders to other workers on board. At the same time, the noise on the streets was earsplitting. Automobile horns honked at the horses that pulled carriages and blocked their way, while merchant's voices shouted over the noise to offer their services and attract business their way.

CeeCee had never seen such lively activity or as many people in one place before. Many were offering foods right off their carts. Suddenly she was distracted by a strange hoot of a horn from behind and she turned to catch sight of a man on a bike that was larger than most she had seen. The bike pulled a small carriage behind it and the skinny little man bellowed an ear-shattering, "Service! Service, anyone need service!"

An obnoxious screech from a woman suddenly surprised CeeCee. And at once she recognized the voice to be Winnifrey's and this drew her attention away from the funny little man and onto her former employer. Winnifrey, followed by Abigail, then Henry, was coming down the plank and was barking orders at the crewman who was unloading her trunk. The sight of her brought back the realization of her loss along with a measurable amount of insecurity. She had always thought of Winnifrey as her friend, and no matter how bad Winnifrey treated her she never dreamed that one day she would be her enemy. Sadly, CeeCee lowered her head then quickened her step. She had no wish to encounter Winnifrey...or the Roberts who would surely be there to receive their darling daughters.

On the ride through the city Ellington pointed out several landmarks. Then asked if there was anything at all that he could get her before they left the city. "For once we entered the countryside there will be only an occasional farmhouse," he cautioned.

CeeCee shyly thanked him for his thoughtfulness and said she would simply like to enjoy the views. She was mindful of all that was going on around her and she was overwhelmed by most of it.

Yet what was particularly on her mind, was how her life had changed so drastically in such a short time. This fact daunted her.

Silently they road through the streets until the populace grew thin, then became barren. Shortly they entered a greener world with fields of flowers and tall grasses that moved to and fro with the wind. Here the skies were bluer and the air much fresher than the streets of Liverpool.

The carriage picked up speed and a light wind blew across her face; it held a slight fragrance of flowers and for the first time she felt a hint of homesickness. She was going to miss Virginia and she wondered if she would ever get to see her family again. She yearned to hug her sister and taste her mother's peach pie. Her father was a quiet man. Yet he always had a story, which forever covered him as a young boy and his life with her aunts, uncles, and of course her grandmother before she died. CeeCee felt the warmth of Ellington's hand as it covered hers and she smiled but said nothing.

CeeCee had been silent most of the day and for a time Ellington wondered if maybe she was having second thoughts, and this worried him greatly. Even though her smile was still filled with affection, he also saw a trace of fear. He pondered this until he decided it was her nerves that burdened her so. He had a suspicion that she was much shier than she let on. He patted her hand to comfort her; nonetheless he said nothing for he wanted to respect her privacy.

After a time, the air began to hold a slight coolness and CeeCee settled that it came from the large mass of trees that looked like an orchard. They were in the middle of nowhere and she sat forward and strained to get a better look, and Ellington chuckled at the question that slowly crossed her face.

"My dear Father," he explained, "has forever wanted an apple orchard and this is his attempt. It is so far from the manor because Mother was adamant that he planted the trees as far away from the house as possible. As she put it, 'she did not want the smell of the rotted fruit, nor be reminded of his daft dalliance with nature, and his peasant's interest.' As you can see, she was correct about the rotted fruit; Father's endeavor has not at all been successful. Although there is a time of year the trees do look lovely and the blossoms of course give, a pleasant scent. However, they have never been a bearer of any edible fruit. Though to be fair, I might add this failure is an uncommon incident; my father rarely fails. He is truly a remarkable man as you yourself will soon find out."

CeeCee heard the fondness in his voice; it also held a well seeded respect for his father. This, she suspected was a trait he sustained for whomever he loved, because she had also heard the same intensity when he spoke of his stepmother. She hoped that one day she too would truly earn his respect as well as his love. She smiled into his dark passionate eyes and recognized that they now held a visible desire, and she immediately blushed. While shifting uncomfortably she lowered her gaze to her gloved hands and quivered with apprehension.

Ellington's momentary waver in self-control brought about a befuddled moment. He saw that his desire must have frightened CeeCee, and in no way, did he ever want to make her feel threatened. He completely adored her and he cursed himself for his coarseness. "Certainly," he uttered to himself, "I am mature enough to know how to behave with a lady."

After Ellington's display of proclivity, he looked to be disquieted and CeeCee's heart went out to him. He was truly a gentleman and she did not fear his natural tendency for she was sure he would restrain himself. With this reassurance she let herself relax for the first time in days. After a while she asked, "Ellington, are we near your manor?"

Relieved that she seemed undisturbed, he relaxed. "Yes, my dear, we shall be there within the next quarter of an hour."

CeeCee shivered with uncertainty, then asked, "Will your parents mind an unexpected guest?"

Ellington had noticed her tremble and reached for a blanket behind the seat and laid it across her shoulder while he answered, "No, by no means, Cecilia, my Mother loves house guest. In fact, I am sure you will not be the only guest she will receive this weekend. So, I warn you my dear, you better brace yourself for a lively bout."

Anxiety registered in CeeCee's eye's and immediately he continued, "Cecilia..., you will love my Mother and Father as they will love you. So please, do not be concerned. This is now your home too, remember that."

Within minutes of their arrival CeeCee knew all that Ellington had said was true. His parents were wonderful as they warmly welcomed her into their home. And as soon as they learned that their son's house guest was to be his bride, they enthusiastically welcomed her into their family.

His mother, Sara immediately began to cry and his Father Delemare laughed and threw his arms around his son's shoulder and hugged him tightly. Suddenly both turned and swallowed up the apprehensive CeeCee. CeeCee was completely unaccustomed to open affection and she reddened with embarrassment, and everyone delighted in her sweet innocence.

Afterward Sara Kempe, who asked CeeCee to call her Sara, commanded, "You my child must be exhausted from the long ride. I am terribly sorry that you had to endure a carriage ride. If I had known you were coming, I would not have hesitated to send an automobile."

"Mother, Cecilia and I enjoyed the time alone."

Laughing Sara dismissed the comment with a wave of a hand as she retorted, "As I am sure any man would. Despite that fact, I as a woman can assure you Cecilia is tired; to say the least." She turned to face CeeCee and asked, "Am I not right, child?"

Delemare did not wait for CeeCee's answer. He immediately moved to take charge while he admonished his wife's forward behavior. "Sara, please do not smother the child. You are going to scare her away. It is obvious she is overwhelmed. So why not just show her to her room. If she wants to rest; she will. If she does not, she will not. Once she feels refreshed, she can decide for herself whether she wants Ellington to show her around the manor or not."

Delemare turned to CeeCee and added, "Familiarity will help you become more at ease with your new surroundings."

Unsure CeeCee smiled and Sara retorted, "Delemare, as always you are certainly correct though autocratic, my dear. Yet I will do as you suggest and show Cecilia to her suite."

"Good," said Delemare, "Meanwhile, we have other guest that Ellington and I will attend to."

Ellington laughed and kissed his mother. "I see nothing has changed since I have been away. You are both still impossible."

Sara patted his cheek and replied, "Admittedly, it is something we pride ourselves on, Sweetheart. Though more important, when you show our future daughter in-law about, see that you do not over exhaust her.

We must not have Cecilia sluggish for her debut at our dinner party tonight, so I suggest you refrain from showing her the complete grounds until tomorrow"

"Cecilia, did I not I tell you Mother would have a house full of guests? And knowing her, as I no doubt do, you will most certainly be on display this evening, so I assure you, you, my dear will need your rest."

The thought of rest and solitude sounded wonderful to CeeCee. She was already overwhelmed by all the fuss. The stress of guarding her every word was much more than she had anticipated, and right now all she wanted was somewhere to hide. At this moment, the seclusion of her own room will be much more welcomed than she hoped any of them would ever guess.

When Sara led CeeCee to her suite that she labeled, a bedroom, she asked, "Will this suit you, my dear? This has the best view of the estate and a private bath."

At once CeeCee felt a weakness in her knees. She had never in all her days ever been in a bedroom so lavish. As she fought to govern her delight, Sara's question registered, and for an instant CeeCee thought of Winnifrey. How would she have addressed such opulence? Ultimately, she seized control and breathed an impassioned reply, "It is lovely, Mrs... Sara..., and it shall suit me fine."

Sara smiled warmly and replied, "Well, you make yourself fully comfortable and I will have your bags brought up immediately."

Before CeeCee could explain that she had little to bring up, Sara had exited the room.

Gawking at the closed door in a dreamlike fog, CeeCee finally pleaded, "Nooo, not again, feet... move feet, move." Yet she was afraid to move in fear she would wake and find this was all a dream.

From the other side of the room she heard the loud tick of a clock and without moving a muscle she shifted her eyes in the direction of the sound. The time piece was lovely. Its creamy colored cast was painted with tiny delicate rosebuds and trimmed in gold. The fireplace mantle it sat on was also creamy white with golden garnish.

CeeCee inhaled, then released the breath as she told herself, "See..., see CeeCee if you can hear the clock and see it. This must be real. Ellington is real and this room is real. Oh God, I do not know how to live like this. "Surely Winnifrey was right," she said. "I will fail because of my ignorance."

Slightly discouraged she slowly stepped around the room, which in fact included three rooms and a wardrobe closet. In the sitting room sat a crimson velvet lounge and matching carved wood tables on either side. On top sat beautiful crystal lamps. An overly stuffed canopy bed filled the bedroom area near to capacity and the private bath had an elevated tub. The rooms were all decorated in the same theme as the clock and CeeCee felt intimidated by its luxury, so she remained standing in silent awe. Her feet ached and she wished she could sit down, but with the room's loveliness so majestic she remained upright. Several minutes' past before she heard a light knock at the door, and in marched Sara with a beautiful gown draped over her arm.

"Cecilia, please I hope you will not think me forward, but Ellington has informed me that you have lost your luggage in New York. Or was it on board ship. Either way I am sure it does not matter; you are still without a dress. However, I must say, I have heard of similar tales on both accounts and at times I question if there is a dupery amongst the ship's crew. Regardless, since we appear to be the same size, I have brought you a few of my new garments. I hope you will accept them. My seamstress will be by next week and she will fit you for a new wardrobe. Meanwhile you will need a gown for this evening's dinner party. And of course, you will need clothing for the next few days." By the end of her statement several maids entered the room all caring clothes respectfully over their arms. Each girl with great effort laid the garments they held on the bed for CeeCee's inspection. Then quickly they left the room, all except the last one who stood stiffly at the end of the bed.

"I will also have riding breeches and boots sent up, since I have no doubt Ellington will want to show you the estate on horseback," added Sara. "Alas, this is Emmy she will tend to your needs, Cecilia."

With these words CeeCee found her tongue and gasped, "Oh no, really that is not necessary...." When she saw the confusion on Sara's face she quickly added, "I do not wish to be a bother, Sara."

"Nonsense Cecilia. This is your home as well as ours, so anything you need will be at your bid."

CeeCee's heart sank; she had already failed. There is no way she was going to pass for a lady, especially if she could not comfortably except the aid of a servant. Dispirited she walked over to the bed and touched the garments that lay across it. With an extra effort, she smiled and forced her voice to sound confident as she said, "Thank you, Sara, you have been overly generous."

She lifted her head to face the white girl that stood where she herself should have been standing and requested, "Emmy, will you hel...hang up the garments before they winkle." She had caught the word *help* before it escaped and so not to say please; she bit her tongue.

Sara said, "Wonderful," and hurriedly excused herself.

At this time, Emmy moved swiftly to hang the gown that Sara had lain across the overstuffed chair. "As soon as the clothes, is hooked, Mum" she asked in a tongue that was strange to CeeCee ears, "would cha be liken a cup of tea. Or would my lady like ta freshen up abit first? Mum, I can hava bath drawed fortwith."

CeeCee hesitated only momentarily while she tried to decipher the girls' words, thereupon settled on the word tea, and agreed, "Tea, yes tea would be nice."

As soon as Emmy left the room CeeCee ran over to the wardrobe room and pulled out the moss green dress. It was beautiful; it was the palest of greens and the fabric shimmered in the light. This is when she noticed a necklace. It matched the gown perfectly. Sara must have forgotten that she hung it on the clothes rod along with the gown. CeeCee turned the jewel upward and immediately gasped at its exquisiteness. The stones that decorated the links in the chain were large, but in a strange way they looked dainty around the larger one in the middle.

Painstakingly CeeCee removed the piece from the hanger. Timidly she slipped the jewels around her neck, then studied the reflection in the mirror. "Yes," she decided, "Sara must have forgotten the necklace was attached to the rod. For this is a piece that is far too expensive to loan a stranger." Again, she touched the pendant that hung from the gold links, surely Sara did not intend for her to wear it. She caressed the stone that rested against her neck and whispered, "This is much too exquisite for someone like me...." A light knock at the door brought her back to the here and now, and she felt a warm crawl inch up her back and neck. She felt like she had been caught doing something wrong and when Emmy entered the room her cheeks were flushed with self-consciousness.

Hastily Emmy sat the silver tray that held tea and cookies on the table in front of the lounge, while she quickly explained, "Oh Mum, I'um sorry..., I shoult hav sat yaur jewelry out afore I fetched yaur tea, sorry Mum, I ain't of clear mind. This be ma first time ta be a lady's handmaiden. And me, I wish ta do it well, Mum."

The girl fidgeted for an instant then hurried over to the closet and removed a velvet bag from one of the rods. As soon as she turned to face the now composed CeeCee she explained, "Mrs. gave ya several more pieces far ya, Mum." She stood back but stretched her arm outward toward CeeCee. The bag hung from her hand and she mumbled, "fer your inspection, Mum."

CeeCee stood there not quite knowing what to say. Emmy looked expectantly while she waited for her to open the bag. After an awkward moment the girl finally lowered her head and said, " Xcuse ma manners, Mum...,I'll give ya somp priviacy." Without another word she quickly moved to pour CeeCee's tea.

CeeCee felt unworthy of such respect. Immediately she began to search for the right words to apologize for making the girl feel bad; then she realized that that would be improper. So instead she asked, "Emmy, if you will excuse me, I would like some time alone."

Emmy bowed and scampered from the room. Once she was alone CeeCee rushed over to the bed and sat atop the lovely spread that covered it. She waited only a second before she dumped the jewels upon it. She snatched up the first piece and examined it. In her entire life, she had never held a treasure so ornate. Just the thought that these were real jewels and that she would actually wear them was unbelievable. The prospect made her trembled and her heart thumped an extra beat in excitement while she studied her new treasures.

It was an hour later when Emmy knocked softly then waited for CeeCee's invitation to enter the room. After CeeCee's behest, she immediately entered and said, "Mum, Mr. Ellington, is requestin a jaunt, if ya ere up to it. If ya be, he surely is hapbe ta show ya about the manor."

"Yes, Emmy, please let him know I will be down in ten minutes."

"Yes, Mu...Miss Cecilia," and again Emmy scurried from the room.

CeeCee sat at her dressing table staring at her image. Even the reflection that stared back was unfamiliar to her. She had been studying this guise for the past hour and hoped that she could live up to what *it* appeared to be. She couldn't help but question if she had the courage it would take to continue this facade. Her insecurity had mushroomed after Emmy left her alone with the velvet bag of jewelry. At that time, the truth of what she had chosen to do hit her like a bolt of lightning. She tried to fight off all her misgivings, but Winnifrey's threat, *you will fail because of your ignorance,* kept creeping to the surface of her mind. CeeCee searched her eyes and then her face, "At one point will Ellington guess?" She asked the image in the mirror. "Will he see that I am nothing more than a liar and do not deserve his respect or his love?"

When no response came, she answered for the counterpart, "No, no CeeCee, he must never learn the truth. From now on, you are not only lying to protect yourself, you are saving Ellington from heartbreak..., for surely it will hurt him deeply if ever learns the truth."

She stood and smoothed her clothing, then lifted her chin to represent a lady's stance. "I am a lady and that is what the world will see. Winnifrey or the likes of her, will never bring me down. I am strong, smart and in love and that is how I will succeed," she determined.

CHAPTER TWELVE

C eeCee met Ellington at the bottom of the stairs. *He looks so handsome,* she thought. And when he touched her hand to lead her in the direction of the stables, her heart fell to her feet. I am truly in love with this man and I will do everything to make him proud of his choice. He will not be sorry he married me.

The steed Ellington had mentioned on the ship was truly everything he said. She was stunning white with a golden sphere between her hazel eyes; that went to the tip of her pink nose. She was well kept, and her coat held a polished luster that shone; it was plain to see she was a pride filled mare. And when the steed saw Ellington, she gave a snort and scraped her hoof to the ground. She energetically dashed from one side of her stall and back again, then neighed loudly. There was no mistake that she was excited to see her master. CeeCee laughed at the horse's antics, whilst she related, "Ellington, I believe you have an admirer."

"Yes, you are correct, she always has had a warm spot for me. I raised her since a colt. My stallion, Eros sired her."

"She is beautiful, Ellington and it seems she has a wonderful disposition."

"As does her owner," he answered.

CeeCee smiled but remained silent. Finally, Ellington added, "She is yours, Cecilia. A token of my affection, I know you will love her as much as I do you."

CeeCee gasped, "Ellington no, no you can not...,"

"I can and I will, Cecilia. Freya is yours, and I hope you will not deny me this pleasure by not accepting my gift."

CeeCee struggled with her conscience while she asked herself, *does a lady accept a gift like this, if so, how... and what do I say?*

She had always wanted a horse of her own, the only riding she had ever done was on Briarpatch. The old horse was named after his coarse hair, which she could painfully attest to since she always had to ride him bareback. Briarpatch was the horse that the workers use, he was old and blind in one eye, but she loved him just the same.

At this time CeeCee noticed that Ellington was still watching her as he waited for her answer. She released the breath she held and giggled nervously then immediately scolded herself for behaving so foolishly. She chastised *this is exactly how Winnifrey acts when around men.*

After more time than she feared it should have been, she smiled her pleasure and thanked Ellington for his kindness. "Thank you, Ellington. You are more generous then you should be, but are you sure you want to give such a prize away? She is so beautiful."

"I am sure I want you to have her. I believe that she was meant for you since you both are so exquisite. Even her name reminds me of you."

"Her name, questioned CeeCee?"

"Yes, Freya. Freya, is the Greek Goddess of love."

She blushed at his compliment and continued her acceptance, "Thank you, Ellington, for the complement and the gift. I will cherish both forever."

"As I will you, my dear Cecilia," answered Ellington.

CeeCee could see that Ellington wished to kiss her and she wanted his kiss as much as he did hers, yet she was not ready. Their relationship was too new and in view of her fear of being found out, she had decidedly reasoned that any intimacy they shared might give her away, since she was sure a white person's touch was different than hers.

Consequently, they stood there for an awkward moment before Ellington broke the silence, "Well, as Mother earlier accused, I would love to show you about the estate on horseback, though I fear it will have to wait." He moved back toward the manor as he added, "Instead let me show you around the manor."

CeeCee quickened her step to keep in stride with Ellington's as he became her guide. "The estate has been in our family for over a hundred years. My great-grandfather had it built as a wedding gift for his bride, my great-grandmother, Becca. She was a tiny little woman with a big soul and great-grandfather doted on her. It was said that he loved her so deeply that he rewarded her cherished love by granting her every whim."

When they entered the house, Ellington hesitated as he questioned, "Let me see, where should we start...? Do you have a preference?"

CeeCee shook her head slowly for she had no idea what a lady would want to see first.

Ellington smiled at her bashfulness and added, "How about the parlor? That is always a good place to start."

The parlor was lovely and larger than the parlor at the Roberts plantation. The drapes where dark red, *almost as dark as a beet*, thought CeeCee. There were several small couches all situated in what resembled a circle and a game table sat in the corner of the room. She walked over and touched one of the ornate game pieces; each piece was a work of art.

Ellington asked, "Do you play chess, Cecilia?"

Chess thought Cecilia. *This game does not sound familiar. Is it a woman's game?* She then decided she could safely answer, "No, I do not, though it does appear to be interesting. Maybe one day you will teach me."

"I would be delighted and with your quick wit, I believe you will master the game in no time at all."

CeeCee smiled at his appreciation as she turned to admire the rest of the room. The furniture looked old and the wood was dark and appeared to be quite heavy. At once she remembered what she had learned about antiques while at Brenau and asked, "Are all these antiques?"

Ellington's face instantly registered approval and he praised her awareness, "Yes..., how keen of you Cecilia. They too have been in my family for generations. Most of the portraits on the walls where painted by an uncle, Frederick Chancier. He was married to my grandmother's sister. He was a well-respected artist in his time though never famous. This room, I assure you, will be where you will be spending a great deal of time over these next few weeks."

CeeCee's expression registered confusion and Ellington added, "My mother, she is very fond of tea parties and as I explained earlier, she is very British, so I promise you will have your fair share of introduction party's over the next few weeks....,so, say to acquaint you with our friends and society. Again, I assure you, you are in for a treat, my dear, but you may want to hide yourself in the parlor for a brief reprieve."

CeeCee's face radiated a smile, but inside she was frozen in fear. *Tea party, she had never been to a tea-party. Only watched as she fanned the ladies or observed the girls at Brenua from across the room. Surely, she will flounder and all these creature comforts will be lost to her forever.*

Ellington's voice pulled her from her somber thoughts as he further explained, "Tonight you shall meet a handful of these fine ladies, and I dare say, if you are to be ready for this evening, I better hurry this tour along."

Ellington showed her the waiting room, drawing room, game room, breakfast room, and then the dining room which was large and elegant. He moved to the library where the walls were filled with more books then she had ever seen in one place. She had no idea that so many people wrote books.

When CeeCee sucked in a loud breath Ellington turned to question her, "Are you alright, Cecilia?"

"Oh yes, I am fine Ellington. I can hardly wait to begin reading these. Ellington, there are so many."

"Cecilia," Ellington said in a voice that registered surprise. "I knew you were well read, but I had no idea your love for books. I proclaim that this will be your favorite room. I will at once have a comfortable chair designated as yours as well as a writing desk sat up in front of the window."

CeeCee questioned, "A writing desk?"

"Yes, in case you are ever so inspired."

"Oh Ellington, you tease me."

"I assure you I am not teasing you, my dear."

CeeCee touched the leather bonding on a copy of Charles Dickens, A Tale of Two Cities. Breathlessly she whispered, "Oh, Ellington, that indeed would be a priceless gift."

He smiled at her rapture, then reached for her hand. Again, he said, "Come, there is more; I want to show you the garden. That too, you will treasure. Mother has a love of flowers; there is not a garden around that hers cannot put to shame."

At last they stood in the foyer, "Well that is most of the downstairs, Cecilia. He sighed and clapped his hands together, "So I guess my tour is completed, and I certainly I do not wish to overexert you, so I will let Mother show you the upstairs tomorrow. I imagine this has been a full day for you and you still have a dinner party to attend this evening."

CeeCee's energy and interest was fully awakened and hurriedly she assured him, "No, please Ellington; I am fine."

"The only room left downstairs is the office. The laundry and sewing rooms, are in a separate building near the stable and the stream. Of course, there are the storerooms off the kitchen, but these rooms will certainly not concern you, unless you have a desire to see the likes of the kitchen."

CeeCee thought of her mother and then asked, "I would like to see the kitchen, if that is alright?"

"Of course, and please feel free to explore any room at any time. This is your home, Cecilia. As for now, I will be happy to guide you around the kitchen."

The kitchen was big, as big as the dining room, kitchen and sitting rooms back home at the Roberts. There were at least a dozen women scurrying about busily preparing foods. CeeCee was surprised to see so many different foods being prepared. There were huge hams and birds of all sizes, most she did not recognize. They certainly did not resemble a chicken or turkey.

Ellington saw her look of astonishment and said, "Yes, it is a sight to behold. Mother likes to treat each guest to his or her favorite dish. That is why there are so many dissimilar foods being prepared at one time. By the way, Mother asked me to find out and report your choices to the staff so they can have them on hand. And if you have a selection for tonight, I am sure there is still time to prepare it."

CeeCee swallowed the lump in her throat. She did not want to say what she favored most. She thought it too simple for the likes of this kitchen and staff. Chicken and dumplings! Would they even know what it was, let alone how to prepare it? *What was that dish Elizabeth Bartlett spoke of*, she asked herself?

"Mother guessed a Virginian would prefer ham. I favored a stew," added Ellington. "So, which one of us is close," he asked?

She relaxed her guard and reveled in his eagerness to please her. "You, you are Ellington," she answered. "I do enjoy a good chicken and dumpling *stew*. Though I am sure this would be completely unfamiliar to your staff."

Joining in her laughter he agreed, "This may be true, but if at all possible, you shall have it for this evening's meal, my sweet." He bowed and said, "If you will give me a minute, I will let Cook know of your choice."

Ellington disappeared across the room and entered a short hallway that lead to a small chamber. CeeCee watched as he began to discuss her choice. Then her eyes moved away to explore the rest of the kitchen while she waited. It was filled with every convenience she had ever read about. She was sure her mamma would have loved a kitchen like this.

The baking shelves in the two hearths were large and the space that encompassed the room was vast and brightly filled with light from its many windows. She noticed daylight was beginning to dim and she wondered what time it was back home. *Yes, indeed Mamma would have died for a kitchen like this*, she thought.

Later back in her room she pictured every room and tried to recall what Ellington had said about each. She wanted to appear at ease with her surrounding this evening. "If I accomplished this," she told herself, "then people will be less apt to question my heritage. Tonight's dinner party will be my first real test...., what if I fail...? I pray I am up to it"

The dinners on the ship where difficult enough, but here as Ellington's new love, she feared all eyes would be on her. Most assuredly, she will be drawn into the conversation more, this she can be certain of because Ellington would see to it. "Oh, dear sweet Ellington, you are so kind." mare

With this thought she remembered his earlier gift. She loved the mare. "Freya," she whispered the name, "Goddess of love. What a splendid name for such a beautiful mare."

She never in her entire life ever thought she would own such a steed; she is extraordinary. CeeCee stood and walked over to gaze out the window towards the stable where the horse was corralled. Soon she would be the mistress of her own house. *Will it be anything like this she wondered?* She and Ellington had not spoken of such details. Yet she was sure he was accustomed to luxury and had no intention of living in a less opulent environment. Winnifrey said he was very wealthy. *Will I be up to the task of running a large house?* She had always been on the side of taking orders, never giving them. *I will have to watch Sara closely and learn as much as I can. I cannot fail Ellington.*

She saw a carriage nearing the manor and decided, *it is time for me to ready myself for this evening's performance.* With this conception, she realized that this was going to be her life from now on.

She will never again be CeeCee Brown, Negro maidservant for the Roberts family. She will be playing the part of Cecilia Roberts, a lady..., and then of course Cecilia Kempe, Ellington's wife, and Society Woman. By that time, it should no longer be a game or a dream, it will be her reality...*if I do not fail.*

She heard Emmy enter the room and she announced, "Mum, I'em ere ta ready ya fer the evnin.

E mmy smoothed the back of the dress and said, "Miss Cecilia, I em seein yer ar a lovely lass in Mrs. Sara's attire. Aye ye ar, and I say, Mr. Ellington fer shere will plum die filled wit pride this evnin, sherly he will. Yes Mum, the most envied ladies ar to be ere tonight and I'em guessin yer ar gonna be turnin a head ar two, yes ye are."

"Thank you, Emmy." CeeCee really liked Emmy. In this short time, she had adapted to her broken English. She reminded her of Viola, though she is white not dark brown like her sister. But she is happy in herself like Viola and she has no desire to be anything more than what she is. Since Emmy was so comfortable with herself, it made CeeCee less guarded. She felt she could be at ease with her and she would not judge her if she made mistakes.

"Miss, ar yer ready fer er necklace?"

"Give me a minute, Emmy."

"Yes, Mum."

Miss Cecilia was stalling, and Emmy recognized this. She attributed it to the lady's engagement jitters. She had never been engaged herself, although many of her friends had been, and they, too, were awful nervous when it came time to meet friends or family. As for Miss Cecilia, she could not guess how it must feel to in her shoes. Mr. Ellington is quite the catch, far better than the likes of her will ever hitch.

C eeCee stood at the top of the stairs trying to will her body to move forward. She knew everyone, including Ellington was waiting for her in the drawing room. She was already later than she felt was respectable, yet it was still impossible to make her feet move. After a time, she breathed inward deeply then pushed her foot forward. Slowly she proceeded one foot after the other down the staircase until her foot touched the last step. At this point a new panic gripped her. *Winnifrey said she will fail, that she will never be a lady. No matter how hard she tries, she will still be a colored servant.*

"How do I do this? Can I do this? Stop CeeCee," she silently scolded herself. "You are better than Winnifrey. She was born into an easy life and makes no effort to better herself. You are here because of Winnifrey's stupidity. She used you for her own cause and you simply benefited from it. Fate has given you the opportunity to be everything you dreamed of all your life. That is..., if you keep your wits about you."

"There you are, Cecilia," said Delemare, "my you look lovely this evening. I can see why my son is as fidgety as a penned foxhound.

I assure you your presence, as well as your beauty, will be a welcome relief for him and our guest. Embarrassingly, Ellington's eyes, as well as his mind has been focused on nothing aside from the doorway in anticipation of your entrance." He laughed before he added, "Regretfully I must confess his conversation thus far has been entirely half-witted."

CeeCee wrapped her arm around Delemare's extended arm and smiled demurely, just the way she had been taught so many years before. Her voice was barely a whisper when she said. "I am sorry for my tardiness. I promise I will try my best to expel your son's abandoned state of mind."

Delemare laughed again and patted his future daughter in-law's hand. She was indeed everything Ellington had described.

When they entered the drawing room, CeeCee immediately felt faint. This is where she had forever wanted to be, in the presence of ladies... as their equal.

Ellington moved toward them as soon as they entered the room and playfully teased, "Father, I should have guessed that you alone would be the one to find my beautiful fiancée since you are always drawn to beauty."

"That I can not deny son," quipped Delemare.

"Cecilia, my love, I warn you Father can be a rascal. He will easily steal your heart if you do not stay on guard," he laughed.

"Ellington, my boy, you are as perceptive as your wonderful mother, and I dare say, I most surely will never get away with a damn thing with the two of you around."

Everyone in the room laughed at the two men's bantering as they casually gathered around Delemare, Ellington and CeeCee.

Ellington kissed CeeCee's hand and whispered, "Cecilia, you are not only beautiful, you are as always a breath of fresh air."

Sara hurried to stand next to Delemare and declared, "So here is our honored guest for this evening. We were beginning to worry my dear.

Though I admit this is most naturally overwhelming and I too might have attempted to avoid an entrance as long as possible."

"Now, Mother," mocked Ellington, "anyone who knows you well, recognizes that you have never been what one might call *timid*. I trust I am safe in revealing that you would definitely use any opportunity to be the center of attention and that most certainly does include being late to make your grand entrance."

Sara laughed goodheartedly and admitted, "I absolutely adore having you home again, Ellington. You do tend to keep your Father and I in line. Now let say we introduce this lovely creature to our friends."

CeeCee grasped at once that everyone accepted that she was shy, and this she decided could be the answer to her prayers. The less she was expected to say, the less chance she would make a mistake. Winnifrey herself had said this very thing and this may well be the key to her success.

Sara wrapped her arm around CeeCee's shoulder and whispered, "You look lovely, dear," before she announced, "Miss Cecilia Roberts, these are our lovely friends, Mr. and Mrs. Keppel. He is a charmer and she is truly delightful. Both are always a joy to visit with."

The gentleman Sara indicated was by all standards quite handsome. He stood tall and slender and wore an impressive uniform. Immediately upon the introduction he stepped forward and gave a slight bow. Then asked, "Please, will you address me as George, Miss Roberts, and my wife, Alice. She will insist on her first name as well. As I can assure you will the rest of this merry group."

At this time, his wife moved to the forefront and offered a hand and smiled her welcome before she said, "My word, Ellington, you have positively chosen a lovely woman. It is so nice to make your acquaintance, Miss Roberts."

Sara extended a slim white hand to draw her guest to the forefront and continued her introductions. "And this is Ellington's dear friend, Mr. Radcliffe Wilhouse and Miss Molly Zooker. She is also an American..., from New York. And of course, my dear cousin, Ethel Collier, and her eldest son, Edmond, and next to them is Eunice Sneed.

"CeeCee smiled and concentrated on the words she had practiced in front of the mirror. "Thank you all for such a warm welcome, and I too, would like you to address me by my first name, C... Cecilia."

Suddenly, the group engulfed CeeCee and Ellington as they congratulated the two. They asked questions so fast that neither Ellington nor CeeCee could answer a one. Several inquired when the nuptials would take place and where. CeeCee was speechless and Ellington came to her rescue with a quip, "Please I just got her to say yes. Let us not frighten her away by moving too fast."

CeeCee wanted to throw herself in Ellington's arms and kiss his handsome face for his protective instinct. It was heartwarming and timely since she was not prepared to answer so many questions so quickly. Her mind had not been trained to think that fast. This she told herself will be your first assignment, *learn to think clearly under scrutiny. These women are clever, and in their mind's eye they will certainly see you as the fake you are.... if not careful.*

The next morning when CeeCee stirred she heard the odd whistles of birds from afar and she opened her eyes with a start. Her strange surroundings at first did not make sense. Where was she? Then her memory came clear and she smiled. Last night had been wonderful.

Everyone was so kind, and she enjoyed the conversation enormously, even if she herself did not utter more than ten words all evening.

Unexpectedly she was aware that someone was in her room and she pulled the quilt up and under her chin as she peeked around the room. She heard the sound again and realized it was splashes of water. Suddenly the door to the bathroom opened and out sauntered Emmy.

The girl immediately saw that CeeCee was awake. She smiled brightly as she merrily said "Goot mornin, Mum. I brought yer mornin tea as well as a few tea biscuits, Mum, I wadent shere if ya be taken breakfast or not. I hope these'll do ya."

All at once Emmy's eye's widened as well as did her grin and she chuckled with excitement. Her voice was full of delight when she said, "I heerd ya made quite a showin last night, Mum. Mr. Ellington, he's been walkin about da manor in a state tat louks like a hapay rooster....I dar say."

CeeCee sat up and giggled too. She felt like a schoolgirl about to share secrets with a friend and she asked in a doubt filled voice, "I did? Oh, it was a lovely evening, Emmy. I loved every moment of it."

"Ya, I'd say fom wat I heerd, Mum, tat it was a gay time. Wat is mer, Mr. Ellington, first thing he asked, is fer me to let em know wen ya be up and about. He; I say, is lookin forard to a ride in da countryside. My guess Mum, he's eager ta show yau wat hem has ta offer ay. Ar yau up ta it, Mum?"

CeeCee scrambled out of the bed and excitedly acclaimed, "I most certainly am, and tea and breads will do me fine, Emmy." CeeCee stopped speaking when she realized she was standing barefoot and, in the nightdress, Sara had given her. Immediately she decided she did not care and hurried toward the bath as she held the coverup over her shoulders that Emmy handed her, "Please, let Ellington know... I will be ready before the hour is up. Oh," she said more to herself then to the girl watching her, "what do I wear?"

"Yar not ta worry Mum. I laid yar clothes out, Mum."

CeeCee splashed in the warm water as she marveled at how wonderful life has become in such a short time. Ellington awaits her. She did not fail him last night like she feared she would. I am a lady, I am truly a lady no matter what Winnifrey says..., I am.

She gazed out the window then back at the mirror to study the outfit she wore. The riding attire was expensive that she was sure of, and the fit *was* perfect. The boots, though a little large, were comfortable as well as attractive. Even so, the whole ensemble made her feel rather showy. She took a deep breath and released it as she slipped the hat on then smiled, "If only Mamma could see me." Though, in truth she knew her Mamma would never understand. *Negras should know their place,* she heard these words from her Mamma more times than she ever heard anything else. Viola believed these words as much as their Mamma did so she, too, would not understand. "Papa." She smiled when his image came to mind. He was different; there was a time when he wanted more too. Then, he was also gifted with a strong mind. But circumstances did not allow him his dreams, so he grew comfortable with the life he had. *So, why did I get this need? Why do I strive to be what I am not?*

She gave herself one last check over and saw that her smile had faded and quickly she replaced it. "Now Miss Cecilia," she told herself, "you have a wonderful man waiting for you, not to mention a beautiful white steed, so let me see that lovely smile." She smiled at herself in the mirror then rushed from the room as she sang, "Oh Freya, oh Freya, here I come, I can hardly wait to ride you through the hills of Kempe with my one true love, Ellington Kempe, La-La-La-La-La...."

Ellington had been correct in his discernment of his mother's prospective agenda. And unfortunately for the stressed laden

CeeCee the next several weeks were spent attending afternoon teas between two and four at the manor. Or on occasion she accompanied Sara on a visit to an estate of one of her many acquaintances.

Surprisingly, fitting in was much easier than CeeCee ever imagined it could be. No one questioned her lineage. Mostly because Ellington had informed Sara of her parent's demise and her lack of family thereafter. And Sara in turn enlightened her mélange of friends, who kindly avoided the subject of family; out of respect for CeeCee's recent loss. This fortunately saved CeeCee from the unpleasant family inquiries that usually popped up in most rudimentary conversations.

Set free from this burden CeeCee began to concentrate on her etiquette. She was truly thankful for the opportunity to sharpen her social grace. She had come to realize that all her education was a waste if she could not choose the right fork or comfortably wipe her chin with a napkin. From what she remembered of the young ladies at Brenau, a person could be shunned for a lack of sophistication. Since Sara considered her social status highly regarded, CeeCee suspected that any ill conduct from her future daughter inlaw would not be well tolerated.

The weeks passed and life was lived in a flurry. Sara and she had not only attended social engagement after social engagement; there were fittings, then re-fittings for her new wardrobe. Finally, CeeCee breathe a sigh of relief, when the garments passed Sara's final inspection. Soon after, as a gift, Sara arranged for her to have her hair coiffeur. The thought of this frightened CeeCee, for it was completely new. She had never seen a person get their hair barbered. She had heard it mentioned before, but what it entailed she did not know. From the minute the man offered her a seat, then tousled her hair, she held her breath and did not breathe evenly until the procedure was completed. She feared, surely this man will guess the texture of my hair is coarser than a white person's, and then she would be found out. Yet he seemed oblivious to anything except his art. For which she was absolutely grateful.

Frequently the days were also filled with pleasurable rides and picnics with Ellington, but at night it seemed there was an endless series of parties. Her favorite was the small dinners with Ellington, Delemare and Sara together with special close friends of the Kempe family.

It was several months after her arrival that CeeCee realized that she had become comfortable with her new routine and Kempe Manor. By this time, she had also come to realize that her feelings towards Ellington had grown into a deep love. Not only for Ellington, but his family as well. Though she still missed her family terribly, the busy routine distracted her longing for them and home.

It was soon after this recognition that Ellington brought up the question of setting a wedding date. He suggested, "August! August is a month that seems to fit a wedding, do you not agree, Cecilia?"

CeeCee remained silent. "This," he said, "will give you and Mother time to ready yourselves." In jest, he offered, "I hear there are a slew of things a woman must do before the joyous occasion." He laughed before he continued, "If it were a man's charge, the affair would be no more than an exchange of rings and a honeymoon. Thank God for women and pageantry," he teased.

CeeCee's face turned bright red and Ellington laughed and said, "Please excuse my crudeness. I did not mean to embarrass you, my dear sweet, Cecilia."

CeeCee smiled but made no effort to respond. Ellington's tease was not what upset her. It was the question of the wedding date that caught her off guard. Of course, she knew the question would come to pass one day, but for some reason she was not prepared for it at this time. Her alarm, she realized, must have shown on her face for Ellington soon reacted to her silence.

"Do you feel a year is enough time for you to prepare Cecilia? If not, we can make it longer? I certainly do not wish to take advantage of the situation or to dictate to you in any way. I can tell you are a free-spirited woman and that, I genuinely enjoy and hope never to change..."

"No, no Ellington..., started CeeCee, "that is not it at all."

Disturbed he asked, "You have not changed your mind, have you?"

Self-consciously she whispered, "No, no Ellington, I without question love you. I do want to be your wife. I yearn for the day I will be yours.... I... I am sorry if I made you feel uneasy..., I..., guess I simply did not expect...." Her voice failed her and faded away.

He recognized that she was frightened, and his heart went out to her. After a minute or so of awkward silence Ellington moved to touch her cheek lightly as he whispered, "Cecilia, I do understand. This is a time when a young lady needs her mother. I am sure Sara intends to be there for you..., but...still..., that is not the same, is it?"

He hesitated and waited for her to at least nod her agreement before he took her hand in his and continued, "You barely ever mention your parents, so I know little about them. Though I can see you loved them greatly..., and I am sure your pain is never ending...."

He stumbled on his next words before he comfortably finished his declaration, "Cecilia, Cecilia...I...I love you and I truly am aware that my love can not replace your parents..., but I do hope it will help fill that void one day."

His dark eyes searched hers and when he found what he was looking for he concluded, "I love you, Cecilia and I promise I will wait until you are ready to become my wife."

Tears rolled down CeeCee's golden cheeks. She did not attempt to hide or wipe them away. She, in her entire young life, had never known that people loved like this. *Mamma and Papa worked hard, and they loved Viola and me, but never once had she seen any kind of affection between the two. And rarely did they bestow any on her..., or Viola. Even the Roberts, who openly showed Winnifrey and Abigail love, rarely offered it to one another. She had thought such love only existed in the books she read. Up till now she thought it was all fantasy. But now, now she was not sure. How can she be the recipient of such love, certainly she did not deserve it?* All these misgivings ran through her mind like a stream rushing to its nadir.

Ellington tenderly wiped at her tears with his fingertips and she saw how much they upset him. *He must have misread their meaning,* she thought. Suddenly a small voice called out from the depth of her soul, "Ellington, sweet Ellington, you are too kind. You are gentle and sweet, and you treat me far better than I deserve." In her mind, she added silently, "I am an impostor, a liar, and you have not a glimmer of a suspicion. How can I not grant you all that you wish?"

A few days later CeeCee, on her eighteenth birthday she mailed the illusory letter that Abigail had suggested she do before she left the ship. She falsely stated that her employer had written the letter for her. In the letter, she told her parents that she decided to except a permanent position in England. She figured this was the last time she would ever get a letter to her parents and Viola, since neither knew how to read or write. So, she took the opportunity to tell them how much they meant to her and that she missed them fiercely and she ended it with. *You will be in my thoughts and heart forever, your loving daughter and sister, CeeCee Brown.*

She cried herself to sleep that night and when she slept, she dreamed of Winnifrey. She was chasing her with the letter in hand and as she waved the pages in the air she screamed, "Niggar, Niggar... CeeCee you are nothing, but a Colored girl and you will never be anything else. And everyone is going to find out.... I promise you will fail because you are ignorant, and you will lose Ellington, as surely as I am me."

The next morning CeeCee awoke earlier than normal. Without hesitation, she jumped out of bed. She had no intention of waiting for Emmy to ready a bath. In haste, she splashed the sweet-smelling water from the night before to her face and dressed hurriedly. She wanted to escape the barriers of her room as quickly as possible. For some reason, this morning these confines made her feel imprisoned.

She hurried downstairs and entered the garden through the large double doors in the parlor. At last she stopped and scanned the immediate area. Once she decided she was alone, she inhaled a deep breath of morning air and let her shoulders lay lax. The garden was beautiful in the morning's sun lighted mist. She inhaled again and blew the breath between her full lush lips. Slowly she stepped out of the shadows and began to wander the cultivated area. Her heart felt heavy with remorse and she held her hand to her bosom while she questioned if she had made a mistake. Was she an evil person to have taken advantage of Ellington's irrational state? Afterall love does put a person at a disadvantage. She had heard Winnifrey spout this declaration many times in the past as she claimed victory over her latest conquest? Though she too was in love, so maybe this did not hold true for her situation. Even though her hunger to be a part of Ellington's world also played a great part in her decision..., as did love. Was she amoral like Winnifrey accused? Tears glistened in the corner of her eyes and she paused in hopes to control the ache in her heart. *I must think of something other than myself,* she thought, *or I will surely cry.*

She moved her attention to her surroundings and admired a flower that almost held a violet hue, yet it was white. She wondered what it was and made a mental note to ask Ellington. At the thought of Ellington her heart winced and filled with pain once again. "Oh," she whispered, "oh, Ellington."

After her brief lapse, she regained her composure again. Yet still she felt desperate for someone to confide in. Finally, she asked, "Little flower, can you please help me..., please? I never meant to hurt anyone, especially Ellington. I only wanted to live free..., and as a Negro I am bound...., not with chains, but certainly by human culture. And without question my mind and ambitions would be stifled, of this I am sure. I... I, as a Negro would never be allowed to be anything more than a servant. I know you can not understand this because you live in a world where beauty is a way of life. But in all life, this is not the same, certainly not in a colored's world." CeeCee turned slowly in a circle and swiftly viewed the garden's elegance then grumbled, "See lovely flower, this is all new to me and...and, I do not wish to lose it. I made my choice and even if it was made in haste or not for the right reasons, I am sure I was right. Besides, there is no turning back... I have gone too far."

Alas, she hung her head as she pondered her thoughts; then whispered once more to the tiny flower she now caressed lightly, "I so want to be like Sara...., and one day you will see, I will be." Her voice rose a pitch and in frustrated anger she cried, "And I shall have no regrets, do you hear me...?" Quickly she turned to see if anyone had heard her words and felt a sudden relief when she saw that she was still alone.

Disheartened, she seated herself on a stump that Ellington said was once a flowered tree. He said Sara had ordered it cut down because it drew menacing insects. Again, she moaned, "Oh...,"and whispered, "Ellington." As she finally came to terms with the fact that she was simply trying to justify her decision. "I guess I needed to say the words aloud, so I will know that they and all that surrounds me is real, and amoral or not, I have no intention of giving it up."

That evening while on a stroll after dinner she told Ellington that an August wedding would suit her fine.

Ellington was pleased and for the first time he kissed CeeCee tenderly on the lips. Afterwards he whispered, "Thank you, Cecilia. I love you and I promise; you will never regret your decision. After one more kiss he said, "Let's go tell Mother and Father. Mother has been frantic lately as she waited for us to set a date. I asked her to let you make the decision on your own and in your own time. I can only imagine how hard that has been for her. Being respectfully silent is not one of Mother's common characteristics."

Sara was beside herself with happiness and immediately began to list a multitude of parties that must begin at once. Then quickly she moved to the question of a wedding dress. "Cecilia, do you have a family dress?"

When CeeCee did not answer right away Sara quickly added, "If not my child, I most assuredly would be honored to have you wear my family's. My Mother and her mother before her wore it as I my-self did. And since I do not have a daughter, I would love for you to wear it."

"Thank you, Sara, I would love to" uttered CeeCee.

Delemare, kissed CeeCee on the cheek and tears where in his eyes when he said, "My dear, I could not have chosen a better match for my son. You and he shall be quite happy; of this I am sure." With a wink he added, "And I trust, you and my son will afford us a house full of grandchildren."

Panic immediately grabbed CeeCee; she had never even thought of a family. How can she have children? Her mamma's Papa was white, and she turned out to be as dark as their black cat, Gravy.

Delemare noted that CeeCee was stunned by his comment and laughed at her innocence. "Do not worry yourself my dear, Cecilia. We can wait. No reason to hurry a family along."

Everyone laughed when CeeCee gave an uncomfortable silly giggle, yet for her the fear was deep and very real. Children was an issue she had forgotten to weigh. She knew nothing about conceiving a child only that they were born."

Sara wrapped her arms around the disturbed CeeCee as she scolded her men. "Can you not see that this is a subject that should be discussed in private or by women alone? Now you two stop this at once or I shall have to cudgel you both."

Delemare laughed casually, but Ellington apologized sheepishly for their boorishness. Thenceforth Delemare asked, "Sara and I have a request. We are in hopes that you will consider staying on at Kempe Manor. We have talked this over the past months and came up with a remarkable plan. We have decided the entire east-wing can be remodeled for your primary residence. We do understand a woman needs her own home, but if you agree we will make sure Cecilia has such of sorts."

Sara clasped her hands together and begged, "Oh please, my darlings, say you will? You have filled this manor and our lives with such joy. I hate to think of how forsaken this place would become without you. Cecilia, I promise you can have anything you want my dear, just name it. Is that not correct, Delemare?"

"Indeed, it is my dear," Delemare hurriedly agreed.

As Sara continued without a hint of doubt. "I am most assured that our draftsman can build anything you may desire. Not only that, Delemare will see that you and Ellington have your own entrance. So, see, in all fashion it will be your very own home."

Ellington uncertain turned to face CeeCee who had not uttered a word since Sara's solicitation began. He searched his future bride's eyes in hopes of interpreting her thoughts and feelings. Finally, he saw what he was looking for and his own eyes filled with relief. He gave her a wink to show his approved consensus and she in turn, did the same. At which time they both swiftly turned to face Delemare and the anxious Sara.

Ellington's voice wavered between a pretended distaste and skepticism when he said, "Well..., I would have to say..., that..., is an interesting proposal... Mother and Father.... And in all honesty.... uhm...well... I assure you..., it will be our pleasure to agree. Do you not agree, Cecilia?"

Tittering gaily CeeCee tried to force a solemn face when she hem-hawed before she answered, "Oooh..., I dooo.... most certainly agree, Ellington." With the giggle she could no longer suppress she continued, "I believe it is perfect. Ooh, Sara and Delemare, it is more than perfect, it is an amazing offer."

Sara and Delemare studied the pair while they weighed their antics. The two had, for a period, convinced them that their request would be denied. With that possibility they were already looking for better augments to convince them otherwise. But after a briefness Delemare realized that their answer had been yes, and he shouted a loud flabbergasted, "Fine, that is just fine." Relief spanned his entire face as he placed a boisterous slap on his son's back. He had thought he would have to work much harder to get them to stay and with his apparent pleasure, he continued. "We will begin renovation at once. As soon as the plans can be drawn up and if you, my dear, Cecilia, have any special request please bring them to our attention as soon as possible."

"Yes, yes indeed," cried the teary-eyed Sara as she grasped her hands together in thankfulness and repeated her husband's last statement, "Yes, yes, my dears. Anything you want, anything at all."

CHAPTER THIRTEEN

The year past with such speed that it left CeeCee breathless and when Delemare announced at dinner one evening, "I am told the east-wing is to be completed by the week's end, and here it is only July, a month before the wedding." CeeCee remained speechless, her life was nothing like her life in Virginia and at times, it intoxicated her. Ellington recognized that his wife to be was slightly overwhelmed and he entwined his fingers into hers and squeezed lightly for reassurance. At once he saw that this had lessened her fear, and he returned his attention to his father while he continued his announcement. "I must say the rejuvenation has done wonders to the old dwelling. I can only believe Great-grandfather would not see it as the same place. It has every modern aspect the new day has to offer which should please you greatly, Cecilia. Though I fear with this most apparent, your staff will be the envy of ours. Why dear Sara, we may even have a rebellion on our hands."

"Well," smiled Sara, "since this is something we need to thwart before it begins. I suggest we have Mr. Hardcore continue his work throughout the rest of the manor. Do you agree Delemare?"

"Your response, my dear, is exactly what I anticipated and that has already been arranged," he grinned his self-satisfaction then continued. "Mr. Hardcore will begin the day after Cecilia and Ellington's nuptials, since you, Sara, will be busy with these prior obligations until then."

"This is wonderful news," answered Ellington, "with them completing the project early, it will give Cecilia and I ample time to choose furniture. As of yet we have not ordered a single piece. We must begin this task at once Cecilia. Since it will take some time for the pieces to be constructed and delivered."

"It is quite trying to match a couple's taste and if the carpenter is to have your choices finished by the time you return from your honeymoon, we must start immediately, right after dessert," added Sara.

CeeCee unclear of what ordering furniture might entail insecurely nodded her head in agreement. Will she know how to furnish a house? A manor has so many more rooms and many pieces were needed to fill the empty spaces. Will she know what is appropriate, or what Ellington would appreciate she asked herself?

Though she soon learned that none of this mattered because in truth the choices were to be more to Sara's liking than hers *or* Ellington's. Yet since she was overwhelmed with the particulars of woods and their durability along with the different designs, many she never heard of, Sara's help was a welcomed relief. Particularly with the antique pieces that CeeCee admired greatly, but knew little about, Sara's knowledge was very much appreciated and without a minute's hesitation CeeCee agreed with whatever Sara favored.

A week before the wedding Ellington declared that he had booked passage for him and Cecilia. They would travel through the Far East for their honeymoon. He said, "Cecilia, I remembered you said you had an urge to travel. So together we will begin in Asia. I hope this will please you?"

CeeCee wanted to cry with happiness though dread numbed her. She did not know the full intent of a honeymoon, but she did know what married people did on them and her deepest fear was that she would be with child before she came back to Kempe Manor. Though instead of airing her fears, she graciously thanked Ellington for his wonderful gift.

That evening Sara took CeeCee by the hand and said, "If you gentlemen will excuse us, Cecilia and I will be in the garden. There are several last-minute details we need to discuss."

Once in the garden, Sara, a very exceptional woman for her time. In a gentle, but factual way, explained the reality of womanhood to Cecilia. She started by acknowledging that she had noticed that CeeCee had fears and as they walked between the prolific buds in the gardens, she attempted to ease her future daughter in-law's concerns. In the end, she whispered, "You will learn love can be what you make it, my dear. You and Ellington will also find that the act of making love can be as recreational as it can be fruitful." Sara noted CeeCee's doubt and continued, "My dear Cecilia; you have nothing to fear, for if Ellington is anything like his father and I am sure he is, he will be a very thoughtful and tender lover. You will have many years of pleasure and happiness."

Ellington and CeeCee were married the morning of August Eleventh, 1904, in the little chapel that sat in the middle of the forest of Kempe estate. Immediately following, was a lunch and reception, then the couple left for London. There they would spend several days before they sat off on their Far East tour. CeeCee was far more nervous than Ellington could see, but she kept in mind what Sara had told her. Soon she learned that she had nothing to fear, for what Sara had predicted came to be so, and they had a wonderful honeymoon night.

Six weeks later when the couple returned to Kempe Manor, CeeCee found that Sara had hired a full staff for the east wing. Emmy was among the selection, which truly pleased the newlywed since she had grown fond of the girl and considered her, if only in mind, a friend.

CeeCee was also filled with relief because earlier that day she came to realize that she was not with child and she thanked God for his gift.

It was soon after their return that Delemare decided that it was time for Ellington to take over as head of Kempe shipping, which meant weeks at a time away from home. CeeCee had mixed emotions. She was happy for Ellington, yet she would miss him terribly when he was away. Although this also meant there was less chance of her becoming in a family way.

She knew Ellington wanted a child and it hurt not to be able to give him one. She knew she had no choice; she could never become impregnated. *What will I do if I ever become...?* This thought haunted her dreams and continually entered her mind throughout her days. With Ellington away Sara offered her many distractions, yet her heart was heavy with loneliness for her family as well as Ellington. So, many a day was spent in the serenity of the library writing the words she could not say.

It was the September after their first year that CeeCee received a letter from Abigail. The letter was cool and not a bit friendly. It was sent to merely inform CeeCee that she and Henry were to be married the same month she received the letter. And even though Henry and Ellington were friends, she would prefer if he and she did not attend the ceremony. To insure this, she sent no prior announcement, she said, '*I will leave you to your own explanation, Cecilia. Also,* she wrote, *once Henry and I marry we will live in London, so I fear we will frequent the same places, not to mention, like friends. Therefore, I am sure we will run into you and Ellington in the future. I hope you will remember yourself and make the encounter as agreeable as possible. Earnestly yours, Miss Abigail Roberts.*'

CeeCee felt an ache for Henry and Ellington's lost friendship. It was all because of her. *Why do I have to be burdened with this guilt,* she asked herself? *All I want is the freedom to love the man I choose.* But she knew very well why because Ellington was not granted the same freedom of choice. For the woman, he loved was not real and if he had known this, he would not have married her. And for certain he would leave her in a second if he ever learned the truth. So of course, she will do just as Abigail had instructed. Henry's friendship will forever be an unavoidably lost for Ellington.

With a whimper, she started to crunch the paper together to toss into the fireplace to burn; however, she looked down at it once again before she did so. Surprised grabbed her as she noticed a scribbled line at the bottom of the page. In haste, she unfolded the letter and began to read *P.S. Viola married Lemule Man some months past and is now with child. Your mother is well, and your father is at times in ill health.'*

"That is, it, no more than enough to make me yearn for more. But, yet enough that I am thankful to know," she spoke these words under her breath, but loud enough to be heard.

"Tis everthing upright, Mum."

CeeCec jumped; she did not hear Emmy come into the room. "Yes, of course, why would it not be?" She realized she had snapped at the girl and changed the tone of her voice as she added, "I am afraid I miss my husband. Please excuse my harshness. I am not myself today."

"Yas Mum, it tis understandable. I maself surely woult not be anymuch better. Fact tis, I maself surely woult let the man out of ma sight. I woult be followin em round the world and back agan."

CeeCee stared through Emmy as she evaluated her words. Emmy eyed her for a minute then doubt filled, she asked, "Can I gets ya somptin Mum?

"Yes, yes you can. I want to book passage to New York. Do you know where Sara is? I am sure she will know exactly what I need to do."

"Ah, ya goin to yur man, a wise choice I mus say, Mum."

For an instant CeeCee re-evaluated her decision. Then quickly walked across the room and out the door as she said, "Never mind, Emmy, I will find her myself. You can bring some luggage to my room, two bags should do nicely."

CeeCee eyed the letter then shoved it in her pocket and hurried up the stairs as a delighted Emmy murmured from behind, "Surely I be gettin em, right naw, Mum."

Two days later CeeCee was on a ship headed for New York and Ellington. She sent a telegram to inform him of her plans like Sara suggested, but did not wait for his return response as she had also proposed. CeeCee did not want to hear that Ellington preferred her not to travel alone. That she should stay home and wait for his return.

The trip was smooth and uneventful, which gave her the much-needed time to think and plan. She intended to visit her Mamma and Papa and hopefully Viola if she lived nearby. But she did not know how to go about it without running into the Roberts.... or worse, Winnifrey. And what could she tell Ellington. He knew she would not want to see the Roberts. She could say that she decided to mend the rift.

However, when she arrived two and a half weeks after her telegram was sent, her husband was nowhere to be found. Although there was a message from Sara, '*Cecilia..., received a message from Ellington the day after you left. He asked that you delay your travels to New York. He will let you know when a good time is. As for this trip, he is going to be in the field most of the time. Port to Port business, I believe he called it. Please beware, New York is an ungodly place for a beautiful young woman alone.*

Love, Sara.

CeeCee stood in front of the desk clerk who had handed her the message. Distressed weighed upon her heart and was easily seen on her face. The very thought that she was alone with no idea where to find Ellington frightened her. *Why he has no idea I am even here,* she thought, *since the clerk said he left right after he sent the telegram. I hope Ellington will not be angry with me, since this is a foolhardy situation, I put myself in.*

The clerk stood in wait while CeeCee decided what to do. There was a gentleman behind her who coughed lightly in hopes that she would excuse herself for he could be serviced. Suddenly the tenacity of the old CeeCee resurfaced and she lifted her chin and ordered, "Well, I am sure my husband has a suite. Have my bags brought up immediately?"

The clerk did not move, and she raised her voice slightly to show she would not accept his disrespect, "WELL."

"Yes, Mrs. Kempe, I will get your key and have someone escort you to your room promptly. Harvey! Mrs. Kempe's luggage," he yelled.

CeeCee looked over her shoulder at the man who had coughed earlier, and he was holding back a smile as he tipped his hat courtly and said, "Good afternoon."

CeeCee nodded her head and turned back to the clerk, "I will need a car and driver. Have them here tomorrow by seven a.m., no make that six."

"That will not be a problem, Mrs. Kempe, is there anything else?"

She glanced once more over her shoulder at the man who stood behind her and in a lower voice mumbled, "No, that is all for now." Then hurried after the young man who carried her bags.

With Ellington, out of town this may work out to her advantage, she thought. With him away on business she will be free to do as she pleases. If she moves quickly, hopefully she will be back before his return and he shall never be the wiser. "Yes, this is much better," she told herself as she followed Harvey into the elevator.

"Excuse me," asked Harvey and she realized she had spoken aloud.

"Never mind," she whispered then silently reprimanded herself for the unguarded moment.

The next day she was in the lobby at five-forty-five anxiously awaiting her driver. She paced the carpet before the fireplace until she noticed a man and woman observing her with weary interest. At once she stopped and sat down in a velvet armchair that face the door. There she stared at each person that entered until she saw who she trusted was her driver. She stood and watched as he approached the desk to make his inquiry and when the clerk pointed in her direction, she moved forward to meet the man halfway.

The man at first appeared to be youthful yet when he removed his hat and asked, "Mrs. Kempe," she saw specks of white throughout his brown hair.

"Yes, my bag is over by the door."

His look held a question and she added, "We shall be away several days. I need to go to Richmond, Virginia. Will that be a problem, Sir?"

"No, no Mrs. Kempe, not at all." Then he hurried to the doorway to retrieve the bag.

The journey was exhausting. It took over twelve hours of continuous driving before they hit Richmond's city limits and another hour to find a place to stay. By the time CeeCee released her driver for the night she felt her body ache with stiffness, yet it was filled with a flood of emotional excitement. She had a yearning to press on and see her parents tonight, though she knew this would be a ridiculous attempt.

After some thought, she decided that even if she did not know where to look for her sister, it might be wiser to try and find her first. She grappled with that and her desire to see her parents, but she assured herself, seeing Viola first would be the wiser thing to do.

The driver followed her to the cottage she had rented for her stay. He unlocked the door and set her bag just inside the doorway before he asked, "Is there anything else, Mrs. Kempe?"

Too tired for words she simply shook her head, "no."

The driver started to walk away and she asked, "Sir, there is... one thing more." He waited while she thought about her plan, then quickly she asked, "Before you pick me up tomorrow, I would appreciate if you could run an errand."

"Sure, Mrs. Kempe and what might that be."

"I need for you to locate the whereabouts of a Mr. and Mrs. Lemule Man. Miss Viola Brown before she came to be Mrs. Viola Man, and she used to live at the Hershal Roberts Plantation; other than that, I know nothing more. But if you can find where the Man's live, I will pay you well for the information. I will want to visit with them tomorrow afternoon if you can procure this information. So please plan on picking me up at noon."

"Yes, Mam. I'll do my best to find them for ya. Goodnight, Mam."

CeeCee was up before daybreak and took a walk as she watched the sun rise. Soon after she sat on a bench and watched as the warm heat began to dry the morning's damp mist while she began to contemplate her doubts. They had begun to surface after she settled in last night and continued late into the night. Now here she sat with the same questions tormenting her as she surveyed the orange light that filled the sky. Finally, she asked herself, "Will I be welcome?"

As far as Viola, Mamma and Papa knew she had accepted a position in a house in England. How can she explain her visit? A servant did not make enough to travel abroad. Of course, she will tell Viola the truth, just like she always did, but Mamma and Papa.... I hope Viola will not be too disappointed in me; although I am sure she will be angry. "Oh Viola, I have truly, truly missed you, it will be so nice to see you."

When she heard, the driver's knock she already had her handbag on her arm and was ready to go. The first thing she asked when she opened the door and faced him, "Did you find her? Did you find, Viola?"

"Yes, I did. Well, I think I did Mrs. Kempe. Matter of fact, they live not far from town. It looks like Lemule Man works at the mill, loading. We should be there in less than thirty minutes."

The man seemed uncomfortable and instead of moving toward the car he stood fast. That's when CeeCee noticed he looked embarrassed. She waited and when he did not say anything more, she asked. "Sir, is there a problem? Is Mrs. Man alright?"

"Oh yes, Mrs. Kempe. No problem with the Mrs. other than being bigger than a barn with child."

"Well, then what is the problem, Sir?"

"Well, Mam, you being a lady I'm not sure if I should be takin you out to the Nigger quarters. I don't believe it's safe. That's if I have the right people. These ones is Colored. Did ya know that, Mam?"

CeeCee suppressed her anger and looked down at her dress. She had worn her least extravagant garment, yet she was sure it was still far better than anything her sister owned. Finally, she faced the driver and ordered, "Sir, my safety is none of your business and I assure you if it were, I still would not ask you permission."

"Sorry Mam, I was just concerned. Niggers aren't always the most decent folks."

CeeCee gave him a dirty look and wanted to ask, *I am a Negra, do you think I am not decent,* instead she said, "I am ready. Now if you do not mind, I would prefer you keep your comments to yourself." She did not add *Sir,* since his prior comments destroyed all respect, she had earlier held for him.

"Yes, Mam."

The trip was awkward and silent, yet it was still far better than listening to the drivers' unfavorable remarks. When he slowed the vehicle, then pulled to a stop, it was in front of a group of small wooden shacks just off the roadway. CeeCee remembered this area; she had visited relatives there some years before. This was a part of town she hoped she or her sister would never have to live in. These structures held none of life's comforts and if she remembered correctly, they often held no essentials such as a fireplace or stove to cook or warm the often-empty rooms. Many of the folks slept on cots they put together in the corners of the rooms. The walls were made such that they rarely held out the wind that howled through the cracked and broken old wood. But still the landlords charged dearly for their property, and most families were forced to share living quarters.

CeeCee sat inside the car for several minutes while she gathered her thoughts and courage. Meanwhile a group of squealing colored children crowded around the automobile. She searched their faces, then moved her gaze to the adults that stood outside the shanties until she recognized her sister's. Slowly she moved from the security of the car and made her way towards the woman that bulged with child.

When Viola saw her moving in her direction; she did not move to greet her. She looked confused. Then suddenly, recognition stung her face and she ran and threw her arms around her sister as she cried, "Na it aints you, I knows it aints you, CeeCee Brown, is it re-allys you?"

Eventually CeeCee pulled away and laughed while she cried, "Viola you are as big as a house."

Viola still crying kidded, "Well yous jes hold tat tongue, for you aint notin mor an bone wit skin. Comon in CeeCee, so I can fatin ya up some. I tells ya, I nev'er woulda dreams a seein ya agin. Com comon girl."

Viola immediately moved to put on a pot of chicory. Then pulled out a loaf of bread and some cheese along with a half-eaten pie as she said, "Straight fom Mamma's kitchan. I ramemba's how's ya lovs them pies, CeeCee."

"Thank you, I have missed them almost as much as I missed you, Viola."

CeeCee's eyes moved around the small, but clean space. Viola had made the hovel a home. Several of the pieces where hand me downs from Mamma, which were hand-me-downs from the Roberts; the rest she assumed was the same. They made small talk until Viola sat a cup of chicory and a plate in front of CeeCee and ordered, "Eat-up."

The chicory was something CeeCee had not tasted in a long time and had forgotten how bitter it was. The first swallow had to be forced down and for an instant, she missed her tea. She wished she had thought to bring some for Viola to sample.

Viola sat her plump stature down and grinned at CeeCee for the longest time before she asked, "Wheres cha get such a purty dress, CeeCee? Did the lady ya works fur givs it ta ya? How didcha git here, CeeCee? Is ya back ta stay? How ya git a car to brings ya out ta us? Most a em white boys don't lik comin out to the quarters."

CeeCee wanted to cry with happiness; she had missed her sister terribly. "Viola, I promise I will tell you everything. Although right now I want to know how Mamma and Papa are. Are they well?"

"They be doin good, CeeCee." Lordy, CeeCee ya sounds jes like a real lady. My ya shur looks purty."

CeeCee smiled to acknowledge the compliment and took her sister's hand and asked, "Are you happy, Viola? Is Lemule a good man?"

"Oh ya, I's happy and Lemule he's a real good man, hard workin an all. We aint got lots, but we's got mor em som."

CeeCee offered, "I can change that Viola. Will you let me?"

Viola gave CeeCee a strange look then questioned cautiously, "CeeCee..., wha kina job has ya got tat ya can hep us?"

CeeCee poured the dark fluid of the chicory into Viola's chipped cup, then began her story. Viola viewed her sister with slight distrust, but never said another word until the very end of CeeCee's disclosure. Which ended with, "Please understand, Viola. I had no choice. I had nowhere to go. Winnifrey was going to send me away to be a servant for another family."

"So ya weds ya a rich white man for ya aint hasta work. How da ya live white, CeeCee? Yas colored. CeeCee, ya cants change tat."

"Viola, I could not live like this," CeeCee waved her hand about the cabin, "and be happy..., please understand?"

"No, I caint, CeeCee. Ya turns aganst ya own folks. And I's caint say fer sur, but I think tat ya best not be seein Mamma an Papa. Cause ya machief will surley hurt em hard. Papa he be gitin on, an Mamma, well she don't need no heartache ta add ta her life's burden."

CeeCee spent the better half of her visit trying to get Viola to forgive her. Finally, about the time Lemule was due home, Viola caved in and promised she would consider it, but she said she would never accept that she married a rich white man. And no, she and Lemule will not take any gifts from her in any form.

"Ma Lemule's a proud Colored man, CeeCee, an he don't needs no hep and the same wit Papa," spouted Viola in a controlled but angry tone. "Now ya betar gits goin CeeCee, before Lemule gits home. No needs upsetin em, no needs at all."

Heavy with disappointment CeeCee hugged her sister and kissed her good-by. When she opened the door and stepped on the wooden box that was used for a step, she turned and asked, "Can I come and see you again?"

Viola loved her sister, yet she was not ready to fully forgive her antics and as far as she saw it, CeeCee's acts were a form of betrayal. She chose white folks over her own kind. Still and all she gave in once again and agreed, "Yas, buts not fer awile. Wates til afta the baby coms. I needs som time."

The visit was less than what CeeCee had hoped for. However, she was happy that she was able to spend some time with Viola, if not Mamma and Papa. When her driver pulled into the driveway to drop her off at the Inn it was supper time and as distressed as she was her stomached gnaw with hunger. She realized that the little she had at Viola's was all she had eaten all day. The driver opened the door and she hesitated before she moved to get out. The drive back had as well been in silence and she weighed whether she wished to speak now. Finally, she said, "Pick me up at six am. I want to return to New York. Is there a diner nearby?"

"Yes Mam. There's a nice dinner house a block down and to your right on Main."

She said nothing more, just turned to walk toward Main Street.

The driver hurried an offer, "Mam, maybe I should drive yo...."

CeeCee ignored him and his offer and continued to walk.

The next evening when CeeCee arrived back at the Plaza Hotel in New York she shoved a handful of bills in the driver's hand and informed him that she would no longer need his services, then hurried away. The driver looked hurt and bewildered, but this was not her concern. She was worried about Ellington.

While she waited for the passenger elevator, she prayed that he was not back from his business travels since she needed some time alone. She hesitated when she unlocked the door to their suite, however she was rewarded with empty darkness. Without turning on the light she threw her bag and purse on the bed and plopped herself down as well. Her heart still ached with sadness for what she felt she had lost. She was glad Ellington was not here to see her so upset. "How would I explain my pain," she asked? And after a minute she answered herself, "With lies, with more of my lies."

That night she cried herself to sleep and in the morning, she felt the same as she did the day before. She forced her sluggish body out of bed and filled the tub with warm water. She read the label on a bottle, it claimed to sooth aching limbs, so she poured it generously into the tub. After a quarter of an hour of soaking she still felt the same. "Your claim is unworthy," she muttered annoyed. Ungratified with the oil's result she jerked a towel from the rack and irritably wrapped herself in its comfort.

After she settled in the comfort of a robe she curled up on the couch and decided to order breakfast but as soon as she laid the mouthpiece back in its cradle, she immediately retrieved it. She was not hungry, so why eat? She started to cancel the order then remembered Viola's words and thought better of it. Her sister had been right; she has lost far too much weight. Even Sara recently commented on this very fact. CeeCee heard a squawk and realized it was from the speaker; "Hello...Is anyone there? Can I help you?" Suddenly she realized that she was still holding the phone. Embarrassed she whispered, "No, no thank you," and laid it down with a clunk. Immediately she stood and moved to stand in front of the bow window. *It looks like rain,* she thought. "CeeCee you have to get a hold of yourself. What if Ellington comes back and you are in this state?" Yet this did little to change her mood. Dispirited she stared at the streets below, "Oh Ellington, how I wish I could experience your understanding..., what a foolish thought," she snapped. "This is the road you chose, Cecilia Brown, and when you did so, you understood what it was in itself. You knew you were walking away from everyone. Yet, sadly, I had no idea how alone I would be," she cried.

Finally, the bustle on the street below distracted her and for a bit she forgot her pain-ridden heart and started to feel better. By the time breakfast was completed she admitted in a grim voice, "This life I am living was my choice, and feeling sadness for the relationships I have lost..., or the isolation I must endure to keep it, will simply be my burden. *This,* I confess is truly a lot less than many others have suffered in the past. But..., still I fear my loss will be greatly felt."

She studied the ring on her finger. Ellington had been generous with his gift and for an instant her heart cried out, *CeeCee, you are unfair and selfish. He gives you everything and you in turn give him nothing, not even honesty.* "I love my family, but more; I love Ellington. He and his family have been so kind, and I pray I will never have to give them up.

Ellington was surprised to see her when he returned that evening. Though he was not angry like she feared. He simply laughed with pleasure and asked, "My little adventuress, what have you gone and done?"

CHAPTER FOURTEEN

T he next couple of years were chaotic. Ellington, once he recognized CeeCee had a flair for the social aspects of business,
he decided his wife was better utilized at his side than at home
alone. So, she began to accompany him on most of his business
trips. This period was a wonderful time, yet it also increased
CeeCee's fears of becoming pregnant, since being together magni-
fied her chances of an accidental pregnancy. Although she did read
everything, she could on modern techniques to prevent such consequences, yet she knew nothing was foolproof. Consequently, she
agonized each and every month until she knew she was safe while
her poor Ellington waited in hopes of a child.

Each year she had visited her sister and on the second trip she
was finally allowed to meet Lemule. He was a big man with a heart
to match and it was obvious to see he loved her sister dearly.

Their daughter Jasmine was barely over a year when Viola
found she was again with child. This was about the same time
things began to get harder for Lemule. Work hours at the mill grew
less and less for colored folk while a white man's hours and wages
increased. Still Viola refused to let her spirit be dampened and con-

tinued to reject CeeCee's offers of help or gifts. No matter how much CeeCee begged her sister to be practical. "If not for you, then for the children," pleaded CeeCee. Viola's comeback was always the same, "We'll makit on aur own, CeeCee, witout yar hap, ar yar handouts."

It was two years to the day of CeeCee's receiving Abigail's announcement letter that she and Henry were to marry that she and Ellington attended the Opera in London. It was a glorious night and they were socializing in the colonnade with several couples, two of which happened to be new acquaintances. Ellington had met several remarkable people since he had become interested in the stock market, and their social calendar had soon grown to where they spent more time in London for social engagements. This evening was splendid and CeeCee, for the first time let her guard down and enjoyed the freedom of new friendships. She did not fear her words or that her secret would be revealed, and she laughed freely when Mr. Bickford spoke of a misfortunate investment that his wife Clementine still tormented him about. Then suddenly in the middle of his decree the gentlemen glanced over CeeCee's shoulder and whooped, "Henry, ole boy. How the hell have you been? The Mrs. and I have not seen you in ages. Clementine, it is our dear friend Henry and his new bride."

Ellington turned first and by the smile on his face CeeCee knew it was Henry Dauber who most naturally was with his bride, Abigail. CeeCee caught herself when she realized she was frozen in fear and immediately scolded herself, "CeeCee, there is no reason why you should feel less than you are. You are as much of a lady as Abigail ever was." She pasted a smile on her lips and turned to face Henry and Abigail. Instead she came face to face with Winnifrey and a gentleman she had never seen before. It was quite evident that he was well acquainted with the now smirking Winnifrey, for he held her arm casually but possessively, over his.

Abigail looked downright paralyzed standing next to Henry, who stood between her and the cynical Winnifrey and her gentle-

man. Henry's face registered surprise before it beamed with pleasure when he recognized not only his old friend Mr. Bickford, but
CeeCee and Ellington as well. It was clear he was thrilled to see
Ellington and the two immediately threw their arms around each
other as Ellington chuckled, "Damn, Henry damn." When they
pulled away from their jubilant embrace he continued, "Married life
certainly agrees with you..., and it does as well for you, Abigail. I
say you are downright glowing."

"That my dear friend is because my sweet wife Abigail, will be
blessing us with our first child in a few months."

At this time Winnifrey stepped forward and spoke her first
words of vengefulness, "I can only assume that you have not been
blessed by such, for surely Cecilia would not be here today."

Everyone fell silent and eyed Winnifrey with question since her
voice dripped of contempt and her statement made little sense to
most. At this instant Abigail stepped forward and saved the moment. She finished her sister's supposed thought with a stiff but
gay, "Yes, yes indeed, I imagine it would be most difficult to leave
one's child in the care of a nanny. Even for a simple outing to the
Opera. I too, without a doubt will feel the stress, though I hear it is
only with the first child that one has such doubts."

Winnifrey gave her sister a nudge but added nothing more on
the subject. Henry eyeing the peculiar antics of his wife and sister
in-law chalked it up to the particulars of motherhood and mumbled
causally, "Ellington...What do you say we meet for cocktails after
the performance?"

Ellington put out by Winnifrey's impertinence was about to
refuse, when CeeCee forced a happy smile and accepted, "That will
be delightful, though we can only stay for one. Ellington has business first thing in the morning."

"So, one it is," said Henry, "we will meet you across the street.
As for now I suggest we find our seats, or the show will start without us."

Through the entire Opera CeeCee dreaded the upcoming encounter, she knew Winnifrey was not finished with her. She should

not have accepted Henry's invitation. "Though," she told herself, "I cannot hide from her forever. It is inevitable that we will run across each other from time to time. Henry and Ellington are friends and their friendship deserves respect and Winnifrey or no Winnifrey, I intend to support it."

Winnifrey was ready for CeeCee as soon as Ellington and she arrived. She turned to the gentleman she was with, who was at least a head shorter than she and twenty years older and announced, "Albin, Ellington was my first love. Why if it had not been for Cecilia's *conniving*, I am quite sure he and I would be happily married this very day."

The group grew quiet while they waited for CeeCee's reaction, but instead Albin mercifully spoke up, "Now, now my sweet Winnifrey, and where would that leave me? You know my life would not be complete without you," he teased as he winked at CeeCee and Ellington.

"And besides Winnifrey," spoke Henry, "I am sure it was I who was your first infatuation, not Ellington at all."

The attempted light-hearted diversion went over Winnifrey's head and she bluntly continued, "Yes, yes that may be so, but that was nothing more than a flirtation, Henry. In truth, it was Ellington who was my intended. We would have made a fine couple and surely someone of

Ellington's position needs a wife such as I, someone with affluence and agreeable pursuits. I am quite sure Cecilia knows little about how to keep a gentleman of such distinction happy. So, I say in truth; I would have been a much more suitable choice...but Cecilia used...."

This time Albin ignored his wife's rudeness and interrupted her in mid-sentence as he stood to offer a hand towards Ellington. "Albin William Cortney here, please excuse my wife. At times she does tend to carry on a bit."

Ellington nodded his agreement while he properly introduced Cecilia and himself. Then asked, "How long have you and Winnifrey been married Albin?"

Albin's smile was weary when he answered, "Less than a year; though I fear it does seem longer."

Winnifrey again did not get the just of his meaning and laughed gaily. She was the center of attention, and negative or not, this made her giddy. "My you two do tease," she remarked and again giggled with pleasure.

The waiter poured champagne into the last glass and Henry lifted his and said, "To old friends."

Afterwards Ellington returned, "And to new beginnings."

Everyone clanged their glasses and muttered their agreements, and immediately thereafter Winnifrey began once again, "I hear your father has stepped down and you are now administering Kempe Shipping. How nice for you, though I imagine this is when a proper match does come in handy. A good wife can be so beneficial to a man and his business. Do you not agree, Albin?" She did not wait for Albin's input and continued. "Dear Albin, is heavy in the stock market so he dearly appreciates the advantages of a good background. He also owns several large insurance companies in the United States as well as abroad. We travel to England on business quite often. Ellington, I hear you travel to New York frequently? Why, we would love to have you out to our estate for a visit. It is quite vast, and I dare say we have more than enough rooms to make your visit comfortable."

It was obvious the invitation was solely for Ellington; CeeCee was not included in the mention. Ellington took offense at once, though CeeCee squeezed his hand as not to worsen the situation. She saw his jaw tighten, but he respected her intended request.

Abigail throughout her sister's exchange remained closed lipped and after Winnifrey stopped to take a sip of her Champagne, Henry and Ellington began a pleasant chat.

Abigail stayed silent and only nodded here and there throughout the conversation. CeeCee attempted a smile when she saw Abigail's eyes momentarily rest on her, but she quickly looked away without returning the gesture. Meanwhile Winnifrey's gaze fell boldly on CeeCee. Her squinted eyes burned with hatred while they darted from her to Ellington and to her again. After a bit CeeCee moved her gaze to Albin, who now sat quietly at Winnifrey's side. She wondered why someone as kind as he would have chosen a woman so full of animosity. Maybe Winnifrey was right; by marrying the right person he benefited from her family's name and connections.

CeeCee returned her attention to Winnifrey and instantly a new fear gripped at her chest. Winnifrey had noticed that she had been observing Albin and her fury was apparent. At once a collage of Winnifrey's hurtful words from years ago, assaulted her, *you will lift your skirt for any man..., whore..., no man is safe with you around.* And as untrue as these words were then and today, her cheeks still burned with unwarranted embarrassment. Whereas it was directly followed by a flow of relief when she heard Ellington announce, "We, I am afraid, must be on our way."

Her attention moved back to him and the entire group, as she in a practiced voice and without forethought asked, "So soon....," immediately she swallowed her words.

"No," shot Winnifrey, "Ellington..., we barely had time for a visit. You must not take leave; I have greatly missed your wit awfully. Is that not so, Henry? I have often wondered on Ellington?"

Ellington stood with his answer, "That may be so, but it is late and as much as I enjoyed my visit with *Henry* and *Abigail*, Cecilia and I must be on our way."

This time his direct implication had not gone unnoticed and Winnifrey immediately took offence and retorted, "Dear Ellington, I believed Cecilia's lack of formal sophistication has rubbed off on you. How sorrowful for us who have to endure it."

Albin, who had finally decided he had enough of his wife's rudeness, turned on her and admonished angrily, "Winnifrey, please! Can you not remember your place? Now hand me your wrap, we, as well, are leaving."

He turned to face Cecilia and Ellington and bowed slightly as he apologized, "Cecilia, Ellington, please excuse my wife's ill manners, I am sorry to say I have no excuse for her disagreeable behavior."

Winnifrey snatched up her coat as Albin had ordered, but in defiance she threw CeeCee a disgusted look. Immediately thereafter, she graciously smiled an attractive smile towards Ellington who did not return the gesture. Nor did he acknowledge Albin's apology when he withdrew from the table. Instead without another utterance he nodded to Henry, then Abigail. He wrapped CeeCee's coat around her shoulders and mercifully directed her from the table and Winnifrey's unyielding attacks. In the background, they heard Winnifrey's, "Well I never. And Albin's, "That surely can't be so, Winnifrey."

CeeCee was completely relieved the evening was over. She had wasted no time in retrieving her cloak and handbag when Ellington suggested leaving. Now she trembled as they stepped out into the cool night air and she breathed her first deep breath of relief since their first encounter. Ellington kissed her hand and said, "I am sorry that you had to put up with that, my dear. That woman is evil; I fear I should never leave you alone with her. It is hard to believe that she and Abigail are sisters, or that you are related in anyway..., thank God it is only distantly."

CeeCee smiled and kissed Ellington's cheek, but said nothing. She knew Winnifrey had every right to despise her and if he knew the truth he would as well hate her.

The latter part of the evening had been insufferable, but it turned out to be a valuable lesson for CeeCee. Now she knew that Winnifrey was someone to truly fear. Her spiteful nature had taken over all her dignity. If she could tell the world that Cecilia Kempe had been CeeCee Brown her colored maid without hurting herself or Abigail, she would do so in a heartbeat. *How foolish I was to forget my place when it comes to Winnifrey or even Abigail. I am and always will be nothing more than a Negro in their eyes, I will never be an equal. I promise, I will not make that mistake twice. It is wise to stay clear of Winnifrey. Her feelings are too close to the surface and that will put Ellington and our relationship in danger, whenever she is near.*

It was a few weeks after the unfortunate night at the opera that CeeCee received a letter from Abigail. She, from the start, politely rebuked CeeCee for her acceptance of Henry's offer of cocktails and said, *'In the future, if we ever do run across one another, please do not further the visitation. It is not at all that I care how it will affect you, though I trust that once dear Ellington learns the truth he will pay flagrantly for your immoral behavior. And most certainly your life will be changed forever. Regardless, I worry mostly about what these circumstances, if ever brought to light, might do to Henry and me, not to mention our child. What I ask is for you to keep in mind that there is more than one life at stake here. So be mindful Cecelia. When you are placed in a predicament such as last month's, you must expedite your departure.*

Mrs. Abigail Dauber

PS: Your father passed in his sleep last week. Your mother is doing well.

CeeCee stared at the words. They were sharp and to the point. Abigail made no attempt to be kind or tranquilize with the announcement of her papa's death. The words stung at her heart and she wanted to cry. Not only for her lost, but also for the words she remembered from the past. Abigail's lack of compassion disclosed that she still felt the same as Winnifrey and she had years ago when she expressed the sentiments, *Why don't be silly, CeeCee, colored folk do not have such feelings.*

It was not too long after this curt tiding, that CeeCee became ill. She chose to miss the trip to New York with Ellington even if it meant she would not see Viola and share their time of sorrow. At first, she attributed her illness to the stressful news she received of her papa's death and not being able to mourn him openly. Though soon she began to fear the worse.

"No, please Lord not now, I cannot handle more," she prayed and prayed until Ellington's return. By then she knew the Lord was not hearing her cries and she and Ellington were going to be parents.

Delemare and Sara where off on an extended holiday and would not be back until after the New Year. Ellington was extremely busy with the ship line business and though he was concerned about CeeCee's discomfort, it never occurred to him that she was pregnant. He had all but given up hope of them ever having a child.

Emmy was the only one who asked, "Mum, do yau suppose yau be wit child? My Auntie was overly ill wit her Thornwald."

"Emmy, please do not suggest such. I am sure it is nothing more than a touch of influenza. And I do not want Ellington to get his hopes up, so do not suggest such in his presence."

"Yes, Mum, I was jest hopin yau might be, tat's all."

"Well, I would appreciate if you do not go about the Manor spreading gossip."

"Yes, Mum."

Once Emmy left the room, CeeCee scooted out of bed and looked in the mirror. Her face was pale and as of late she had lost several pounds. She was on the thin side anyway, but this loss made her look raw-boned and slightly unattractive. She smoothed the cotton gown over her stomach. She did not look full-bellied; maybe she was wrong. Maybe she does have a virus and it is simply refusing to relinquish its hold. *Could all this alarm be for not,* she wondered?

She flattened the material against her skin once again and thought, "How many months could I be if I am indeed pregnant? Oh Ellington, this should be a happy occasion. What have I done to you? Soon you will hate me... and our colored child."

Ellington stayed home for three weeks and CeeCee did everything she could to appear in good health though she was sick with worry. She avoided riding Freya until the day before Ellington was to leave on a return trip to New York. This time he planned to be away for at least two months, and she yearned to go with him. But instead she made several excuses why she should not. Although she did promise to join him as soon as she completed her prior obligations. That night she felt a stir in her belly, and it frightened her more than she ever believed it could.

She lay unmoving next to her husband and listened to his every breath. He would disown her soon and all this would be gone. She had grown to appreciate her freedom. The luxuries he had given her were many and very much appreciated. Though she recognized she would miss him far more than any of these loses, yet she still desired to keep them all.

Ellington stirred and CeeCee smiled when he laid his arm over her stomach. *If I can only tell you Ellington...*, "What will I do?" she asked herself. "Where will I go..., home? I no longer have a home. Will I end up on the streets as Winnifrey predicted? Oh, Viola I need to talk with you. I need to think, and I cannot."

The next day when Ellington kissed her goodbye, he asked once again, "You promise you will come to me the minute you are free?"

"I have previously promised Ellington. Remember I came to you when you ordered me not to, so I doubt I would not when you so willingly beckon me."

"True, this is true," he whispered against her cheek, "but I already miss you madly."

"I love you my dear husband! Be safe. Now off with you."

She watched until the dust from his car faded and the quiet was thick and lonely. Again, she felt a slight stir and she prayed, "Please do not let him be hurt Lord? Ellington is a good man; I should be the only one to pay for my sin."

She walked into the parlor, pulled out her journal and wrote several pages before she called Emmy in and announced, "Emmy, pack me several bags, I decided I will join my husband after all."

"It be a fine decision yau come ta, Mum. Will ya be leavin this day?"

"Yes, Emmy, have everything ready by noon time."

Emmy hesitated and momentarily studied CeeCee's expression. Something sounded strange in her voice and this troubled the girl, but after only a brief delay she agreed, "Ya, rite way I will, Mum." Then she scampered off toward the stairway as she threw one last questioning glance at her charge. Something was not right, yet it was not for her to question Mrs. Kempe or her actions.

CeeCee went to London and spent several days walking through London's Park and Regent Park Zoo. She stared at the mothers with their newborn babes and watched as toddlers screamed with delight at the animals about. Her heart yearned to hold her and Ellington's baby, but her decision was made this was never to be.

The next day she left for Virginia in search of Zoa Darcus. CeeCee recalled the whispers she overheard as a child, '*Zoa, the mid-wife could safely rid a woman of her undesired pregnancy with little or no complications.*' "Zoa, she decided, "Zoa is the only answer to my problem."

Viola was thrilled to see her sister. But immediately after her welcome Viola wailed, "Ma lord, CeeCee, watcha ailin wit? Ya looks liks a scarecrow."

CeeCee wasted no time. The months of holding everything in burst like a dam that was weak from the constant pressure of its heavy load. "Viola, my life is near over. I am being punished for my sins and now Ellington's going to learn the truth, and he will hate me forever."

Viola backed away and searched her sister's eyes for the answer she knew was not there. Finally, she asked, "Why dontscha sit, CeeCee, an tells me bouts it?"

Jasmine, who was three and a half, walked in carrying Erla Hattie, Viola and Lemule's second child, named after Lemule's Mamma Erla and his Aunt Hattie. Viola at once scolded, "Jasmine, ifs ya dont put tat childs down, she aint nevea gonna learns ta walk. Now you goes outdoors and play."

CeeCee smiled and touched Jasmine's face as she ran by with a happy squeal. Her baby sister immediately started to scream and Jasmine halted at the door and her smile was replaced by a serious pout.

Viola without delay urged, "Git now, go on, she be alright, Jasmine." And the child flew out the door with not so much as good-bye or see ya later.

Viola laughed at her daughters' eagerness, "Ya wouda think tat child's Erla Hattie's Mamma way she carry on. I is guessin she gonna be a good mamma one day wit a whole lota kids."

With this remark hanging in the air CeeCee dropped down on the old wooden chair that sat in the corner of the room. The space that surrounded her reminded her of the room she and Viola had shared as a child. No colors: everything was drab. The walls held not a painting, family portrait or otherwise. The furniture, what little they had, was dark wood and old; much of it was either chipped or scratched. These things never seemed to bother Viola; she appeared to be happy, her children were happy and so was Lemule.

Intensely burdened with stress CeeCee felt her head swoon, frightened she stood up, then fell immediately to the floor. She heard Viola gasp and cry out "Oh ma lord, CeeCee, wha...."

That was the last word she heard and when she opened her eyes sometime later, she was on her back atop a bed. The quilt Mamma made for Lemule and Viola's wedding present was spread over her and an old woman was next to the bed peering at her anxiously. When she saw CeeCee's eyes flicker she moved closer. Her black eyes were as black as she was, and they darted back in forth while she studied CeeCee's coloration. "Hummm, she looken awfa pale, Viola." She peered into CeeCee's half opened eyes as she mumbled under her breath, "Hummm..., I's see, uh hu." Her presence or her manner did little to ease CeeCee's anxiety. As soon as the woman realized that her patient was coherent she grumbled, "Cecea Brown, whacha doin ta yaa salf. Yas tryin ta kills ya an ya kid."

CeeCee did not recognize the woman and she smelled of strange odors which instantly made her stomach lurch with a desire to vomit.

The woman sat back and wrapped her arms around her full bosom and cracked a half grin which showed a mouthful of empty spots where teeth use to be. "Yas aint knowin me, huh? Well, I's certainly knows ya. I wa witcha when yas was bought inta tis world, missy. I's yau papa's sista, Bell."

She moved forward again and examined CeeCee's eyes once more, then went on with her chiding. "CeeCee it aint good ta be travlin whens cha so fas alongs wit child. Ya can hurts ya bot."

CeeCee sat up and asked, "Where is Viola?"

"She makin som soop. Froms da looks of it, yas not been eatin. Rite?"

"Please, I want to talk with Viola."

"She be hare, jes ya sit here an wat, child."

When Viola entered the makeshift room, she carried a large bowl of soup and half a loaf of bread. She sat the bowl down on the table near the bed and ran out and came back a minute later with a knife and a bowl of jam along with a pitcher of water. "I aint gots no milk or butta, wont til Lemule gits home, so I hopes ya dont minds wata, an som boiled fruits."

"Do not make a bother. Viola..., I am fine, honest, I am not hungry."

Bell, coughed in disagreement and Viola said, "Nat til Bell say so. Naw eat."

"I said I am not hungry and how do you know I am with child...," she asked Bell as she started to remove the blanket that half covered her and stopped. Her dress was scooted up to her hips and lay in disarray about her. Startled she glanced up at Viola, then at Bell. "What...wh...."

"Yas, CeeCee, I checked ya. An I says yau is difnitly wit childs. And I's will alsa says ya not much longa ta go."

CeeCee fell silent; she had no idea how long she had been pregnant. These past months have been crazy, and she had to admit she had not watched as closely as before.

Bell could tell that CeeCee was scared and moved closer to the bed and asked, "CeeCee Brown, is ya not wit da fatha?"

Bell did not ask if she was married. Not many of the colored folks that lived in these parts married. They simple chose a mate and lived together. In their eyes, they were married, but in the eyes of the law this was not recognized.

CeeCee choked, "Viola, please?"

Viola understood the question immediately and answered, "No, CeeCee aint wit no man, Bell. If she be wit child, she surely be in trouble."

At the finish of her sister's statement CeeCee sat up. "I want this baby gone. I want it out of me. BELL!"

Bell shook her head, "No, CeeCee, yas pass tat."

"No...! Zoa Darcus, she can help..., I heard people say, she can help."

No, child..., not naw CeeCee. Yas will be killin the child and yarsef."

"I do not care," she shouted.

Viola cried, "CeeCee, whacha sayin?"

"Viola, you have to understand. I cannot have this baby."

"Na, CeeCee, wha I's undastands, is yaus gone an turns yaself inta Winnifrey. Ya aint seein notin exsapt wa ya wants. Neva mind if its hurtin anabody else."

"No Viola, you are wrong. Bell..., tell her, you are older and wiser. You know a woman alone with a child can not survive on her own. I will be treated like a Whore."

"Tats maybe hows its should be," spoke Viola.

Dumbfounded CeeCee stopped all argument, "Viola!"

Viola looked at her Aunt and said, "I thanks ya fer yas tim, Bell."

Bell looked at CeeCee for a space of several minutes before she nodded her head at Viola and walked from the room. After they heard the door slam hard, Viola turned to face her sister. "CeeCee Ias neva been sa ashamed afor. I's glad Papa aint heres ta knows ya. He neva hered the truth, so I's glad hees in da ground, iggonant of his CeeCee an all her doins. An asfer Mamma she aint neva gona know, cause I's'ill do everthin ta keeps it from her."

Viola looked saddened as she shook her head in disbelief and after a deafening silence she continued. "Ans since ya gon an burdoned me and my..., wit ya sin, I'is gonna speak out, CeeCee. I's not gonna stand by an letcha kill a baby."

"Viola...Viola, I do not have a choice. I do not want to live without Ellington. I love him and he will not except a baby that comes out black."

"Ya cants be sur tat it be black color, CeeCee!" cried Viola.

"No," whispered CeeCee, "though there is a very good chance it will be. And if so..., I will lose Ellington...., for surely he will throw me and the child into the streets."

"Well, ya caint go killin a baby cause ya scared, CeeCee."

"Ellington wants a child with all his heart, Viola..., and I want his baby. Yet if I have it, I may lose everything. I cannot chance being put out on the streets especially with a child. If this child has a trace of Negro heritage Winnifrey or Abigail will certainly point it out to Ellington. Why are you having trouble understanding this, Viola?"

CeeCee, yas da one tat not undastandin. Tis aint no mor bout ya. Its da child."

"No, Viola, no, I can not, and I will not..."

"Then ya givs da baby ta me. Me an Lemule can taks it as ar own."

"You can not be serious," asked CeeCee. "You can barely make it as it is. And how would you explain it?"

"Dont needs ta explain notin, hapens all a time. Folks jes help others out.

"Why would Lemule want to be burdened with another man's child?"

"Cause hes a good man, is all," Viola stated proudly.

CeeCee closed her eyes. She could not speak; her head ached and so did every part of her body. After a minute Viola moved to sit on the edge of the bed and sympathetically. She wiped at the tears that were streaming down CeeCee's cheeks. CeeCee forced her eyes open when Viola said, "Jus lisin, CeeCee. I knows ya thinks it be easier if yas loose da baby, but tat aint liklay gonna happen. So's ya stays wit us til ya has it an sees what color it is. Bell says that aint fer off, an I aint seen wen she be wrong. An if its colored, ya leaves it here and goes home ta ya man."

CeeCee cried, "What if it is white, how do I explain to my husband I have baby, his baby?"

"Well, known ya as I does, ya will comup wit somten, CeeCee."

"Viola, think..., how do I explain my absence?"

Viola stood and picked the bowl of untouched soup off the table, "I's goin warm da soop. Ya do som thinkin, CeeCee. Do som real hard thinkin, ya har me. Then we can talk agan...later."

Chapter Fifteen

Before the night was over CeeCee wrote a letter to Emmy and explained that she fell deathly ill on her trip to New York and was admitted to a hospital as soon as she arrived on land. The doctors had advised that she stay in bed and rest for at least a month. She pleaded, *Please Emmy, do not worry Sara, Delemare or Ellington with this matter. Ellington is very busy with his work and does not need to be burdened further with my illness. All I ask is for you to mail the two letters I have enclosed at different dates and I shall be home fit and happy before he is. Please understand I will feel much better if I am not a bother to anyone. I trust you will respect my wishes. In confidence, Cecilia Kempe.*

CeeCee accepted that this was a bit chancy, yet she was aware that Emmy was a romantic and she would put this into a positive light. She would make CeeCee a heroine, a woman in love that decided to sacrifice her own self to loneliness to save her husband from the weight of her burden.

Bell was correct in her prognosis that CeeCee would deliver early. She was hardly showing a bulge when she had her baby girl. The infant was skinny, and her legs and arms were long and scrawny like her father's. The instant she was born she filled her lungs with air and bellowed so loud that it could be heard outside the house where Lemule waited with the girls. "Her squealin," laughed Viola "is warin tha world shes som on ta reckon wit."

Afterwards CeeCee slept for two days. She slipped in and out of her haze, but she favored the warmth and safety of slumber. At times she even pretended she was asleep when Viola entered the make-shift room to check to see if she was awake. Finally, towards the end of the second day Viola moved a wooden box next to the bed. Inside laid the whimpering child and CeeCee was soon awakened by the now insistent wailing. At first when she heard the wails, she did her best to ignore them and covered her ears with her hands. Unfortunately, as uninterested has CeeCee was in the newborn, Jasmine was not about to let the baby go unnoticed. She scrunched up her face and put it only inches away from CeeCee's and firmly asked, "Aint cha gonna be a Mamma?"

Tears immediately flowed down CeeCee's face and the little girl wiped them off with her dress hem and said, "Mamma says she gonna be ar lil sista. Is dat right, Aunt CeeCee?"

With these words so innocently spoken, CeeCee knew all that she needed to know. Her baby was colored. Ellington would never get to know his child and she would never live her life as her mother.

The next morning Viola opened the windows to air the room. She moved to the baby's bed and lifted her out of the wooden fruit box and laid her against her shoulder as she patted her tiny back. She moved and stood in front of the bed where CeeCee still tried to pretend she was asleep and demanded, "I says its time ya welcoom tis child."

CeeCee forced her eyes opened and stared at an angry Viola who held a wrapped bundle in her arms. She scooted upward and weakly answered, "Why, she belongs to you. She is yours Viola. Jasmine told me..., she is colored."

"So, so is I. Is ya tellin me ya dont love me CeeCee cas I's colored."

CeeCee blinked and wiped away the tears before whimpering, "No Viola, I love you dearly," and slowly she reached out for the baby. She held it for several minutes while her heart pounded rapidly against the small creature. Finally, she opened the wrap around the baby's tiny face and saw a miniature brown Ellington staring into space. Her heart lurched and she quickly glanced up into her sister's smiling face and said, "I do love her. Viola, she looks like Ellington."

"Well, I neva sees ya Ellenton, but she sur is one prutty child CeeCee. And she gots lots a gumtion, jes like yas do."

CeeCee wrapped the wee little fingers around her forefinger and asked, "What..., what did you name her, Viola?"

"Well, I was guessin ya mit wanta be da one ta do that."

"Me?"

"Uh huh."

Excitedly CeeCee asked, "What, what do I name her? I never even thought...."

Viola's laugh was filled with relief and happiness as she teased, "Ya'll think a somten known ya."

Together CeeCee and her sister decided on Molly Amber Man. Although she did favor Sara, she decided, "It is best to keep all connection by name or otherwise away from the Kempe family. It will be safer for all concerned," settled CeeCee.

She kissed the baby's forehead and whispered, "Molly, please understand..., I do love you, but this is best."

Before CeeCee left she insisted that Viola and Lemule let her help support Molly Amber. She said each month she would send a letter with money inside. After days of argument Viola agreed, but only if it was a minimal sum. She argued, "CeeCee, ya has ta rememer, we is poor. An we aint gonna be explainin why we has more en we should. Aint good fer Molly. Aint good fer Lemule. An folks'll wonder."

CeeCee had to agree Viola was right. But she begged, "Viola, if there is ever any reason you need me, please send this letter. Everything is ready; you simply have to mail it."

"I's promise. CeeCee, ya aint gotta worry, me an Lemule'll tak good care a Molly Amber lik she be ar own."

CeeCee arrived home, only days before Ellington and the day after Delemare and Sara left on another long holiday. She was glad that she had some time to herself before she had to face her husband.

CeeCee was relieved that she had been right in her judgment and Emmy did as she assumed, she would and protected her secret with grace and pertinacity. As far as anyone knew CeeCee was with her husband, and Sara and Delemare never even thought to think otherwise. They had simply taken it for granted that if their daughter in-law was not there at Kempe Manor, she was with Ellington. Emmy had dutifully mailed the letters CeeCee had sent her. And when Ellington wrote to CeeCee, she hid the letters until she could hand it to her charge. CeeCee was thankful for her loyalty and increased her wages accordingly.

The first month away from Molly Amber was a strain and Ellington noticed his wife's apprehension and decided they needed a holiday.

"Cecilia, I do wish you would put your charities on hold. They are taxing you and the strain is quite obvious and if I may, I would like to suggest we join Father and Mother in London."

She smiled at Ellington as she remembered the excuse; she used for not joining Ellington in New York was her charity work, and now that she was not quite recovered from Molly Amber's birth, he took it for granted that these same labors were fatiguing her now.

"I will try Ellington, though it is extremely hard to say no at times," lied CeeCee. "Though I appreciate your concern and I agree, a trip would be a wonderful respite."

It was on this trip that CeeCee became aware of the turmoil in England. She and Ellington had dinner with his dear friend, Radcliffe Wilhouse. During dinner, he proudly announced, "I have recently become a First Lieutenant in the Army, and I intend to serve our country until all chaos in Europe is settled. However, in all honesty, I fear it will become far worse before it is better."

When Radcliffe spoke CeeCee could see the look in Ellington's eyes and it frightened her. He was immensely interested in his friend's commission and asked far more questions than CeeCee felt comfortable with. It was very unsettling and before dinner was over, she decided to let her objections be known as soon as they returned to their suite.

The evening air was beautiful, but it held a slight chill. Yet she opened the doors off the balcony anyway and moved to stand between the doors while she gazed out at the Royal Botanical Gardens. She struggled to repress her fears though it was obvious she was troubled.

Ellington watched his wife from inside the suite. He sensed her uneasiness and after a time he walked up behind her and wrapped his arms around her waist for comfort. Finally, he asked, "Cecilia, what is it? You have not been yourself tonight. Are you feeling ill?"

CeeCee remained silent and laid her head back against his chest. She could hear his heartbeat and for some reason that comforted her so.

After a time, she said, "Ellington, I am sure I am being silly, but for some reason I feel frightened. I love you and never want to lose you and..."

"Sweetheart, why in the world would you ever think that you could lose me? I am here and always will be."

"Ellington, I saw the longing in your eyes?"

He turned her around and asked, "Longing?

"At dinner, tonight. When Radcliffe announced his appointment, you...you, I saw that you too, wanted to go and fight for your country." She shook her head in hopes of escaping the image that now re-appeared. "The thought of you in danger..., oh...Ellington, do you have a desire to fight at your friend's side? Please tell me I am wrong. I could not bear to lose you."

"Cecilia, my dear sweet, Cecilia. You will never lose me, because God could never be that cruel to someone as kind and exceptional as you."

With these words CeeCee's heart grew heavy. She truly loved her husband and continually lived in fear of losing him, and she was very aware that he had avoided answering her question.

It was only after Ellington slept that she let herself feel the raw fear that surrounded her. She lay unmoving by his side. The darkness engulfed their room and she saw the devil as he danced about in the shadows and sang, '*Liar, liar, liar. Liars' never win.*' She knew this to be true, liars never win, and neither would she. To avoid the taunting vision and his hurtful words, she moved to lay on her side.

She smiled as she watched Ellington's chest as it moved up and down with each breath he drew. This bought her a warm comfort and soon her mind wandered and settled on Virginia and Molly Amber. She wished Ellington could know his daughter. *He would be a wonderful father,* she thought. *But that is not to be, and it is best to stay away from impossible dreams.* Her daughter's face floated across her mind and she smiled. Soon after she drifted off to an uneasy sleep to dream of war and the many pains it brought.

It was a year before CeeCee was able to return to Virginia to see Molly Amber and she cried when she realized how much she had missed. In her mind, Molly Amber was still an infant not this toothless urchin crawling across Viola's floor. The older girls, Jasmine and Erla Hattie, giggled and tickled their sister until she was screeching in delight. In the end, Viola yelled for the older two to go outside and to give her and their Aunt CeeCee some peace of mind.

When the girls ran out the door, Viola laughed and said, "Tem girls aint eva gonna leave tat child be. Shes a light in der life." Molly Amber gurgled and giggled as she climbed on top of CeeCee's lap. Immediately she hugged her neck and placed a wet kiss upon her cheek as she pulled at CeeCee's curls.

"She sur is a lovin child, CeeCee. Aint no one who dont love her, mostly Lemule and she em."

Molly Amber heard Lemule's name and screeched, "Poppa! Poppa!"

CeeCee enjoyed her visit but it was over way before she was ready to leave. She wanted so much to stay longer, but Ellington would be back in New York in two days and he expected her to be there. So reluctantly she left Molly Amber and a piece of her heart in Virginia.

The following year's visit was hard and far worse than CeeCee could have imagined. Molly Amber did not know who she was, and she avoided CeeCee as much as she could. When CeeCee was ready to leave she felt a deep ache for all she had missed and wondered what her next visit would bring. She reached out to kiss Molly Amber goodbye and the child buried her face in Viola's shoulder.

It was shortly after the return of this visit that CeeCee received a letter from Winnifrey. As soon as CeeCee recognized the return address she became frightened and sat the letter aside. Why would Winnifrey write her? Whatever it was it had to be bad; this she could be sure of.

That evening after dinner she went out to the terrace and stared at the moon. Finally, she told herself that she would not let Winnifrey frighten her in her own home and she hurried to her room to read the letter.

At first Winnifrey pretended friendliness and most of what she said was pure gossip.

Dear Cecilia,

I do hope all is well with you and dear Ellington. It has been ages since we last spoke. I am sure life is treating you far better than you deserve.

Your Mamma is getting on in her age and my mother is talking about replacing her since she has become so forgetful, which I suggested to Mother, is far more burdensome than need be. But I am sure this is none of your concern. However, Viola does show an interest and visits her regularly. Matter of fact, just the other day she dropped by with her brood. My I have not seen her for ages. But I must admit I was not the least bit surprise when I noticed another child was on the way. Anyhow, that got me to thinking and I could not recall her carrying her third child. And those of us who know Viola pregnant, knows she usually grows to an unattractive proportion. Moreover, that youngest child, for some unseemly reason appears familiar to me, but who can say why? Maybe one day the reason why, will come to me. If it does, I certainly will let you know.

    Mrs. A. W. Courtney

Winnifrey's letter was a threat and CeeCee saw this right away. She had seen Molly Amber and figured it out. What was she planning? Would she simply torture her by hanging the threat over her? Or would she be cruel and tell Ellington? CeeCee knew she had to do something, yet what could she do from afar? She could not think of anything, for Winnifrey held all the cards. She could ruin life for all concerned if she so desired.

It was six months after that dreadful letter that CeeCee was able to get back to New York with Ellington. Ellington was going to be tied up with business in Vermont for several days and asked CeeCee to accompany him. She could see his disappointment when she said she had errands to attend to. Yet there was no way she could tell him the truth. As soon as they said their good-byes, she headed for Virginia and Molly Amber.

The door stood wide open and there were flies buzzing about when

CeeCee knocked on the open door and yelled, "Viola, are you in there?"

She heard a frail reply, "I's here."

Concerned filled CeeCee and she rushed through the doorway. The instant she saw her sister she cried, "Viola what is the matter with you, are you ill? Where are the babies?

"CeeCee aint ya go worrin, Molly Amber's fine. She be wit Primo."

"Who?"

"A goot friend, CeeCee. She lov ma kids lik her own."

"What is wrong, Viola? You look awful."

"Its ta baby..., its gone, CeeCee..., and I aint doin well as I should be, tats all. But I's gitten bettar."

"What does the Doctor say?"

"Ain't see no doctar, ya know no doctar gonna see a colored girl, CeeCee."

CeeCee hesitated, she knew Viola was right, but she could not think of what to do. Viola attempted a show of strength by pushing herself to a sitting position. Once up she caught her breath and added, "CeeCee, sit, I's gonna be fine, aint no reason ta worry. Molly Amber an da kids..., they..., gonna be home wit Lemule. Then ya can spend tim wit yaur baby. She sur is grown."

CeeCee spent the rest of the day caring for Viola and as the day went on, she seemed to get better. By the time, Jasmine ran through the doorway with Lemule only steps behind with Erla Hattie in one arm and Molly Amber in the other, Viola was sitting up and smiling.

Molly Amber was three and a half years old and a ball of high-strung energy. It was easy to see that she was as smart as a whip and a disposition that instantly won you over. Her face, heart shape with high cheek bones was the image of CeeCee's, yet darker in color, though her eyes were unmistakably the same yellowish-brown. No wonder Winnifrey recognized the child as hers.

CeeCee enjoyed every waking moment with Molly Amber, and while she slept, she marveled at her tiny features until the wee hours in the morning. It was good to see her so happy. Viola was correct when she said that she was growing like a weed. She was going to be tall like her papa and again CeeCee wished Ellington could know his child.

When she was ready to leave to go back to New York and Ellington, Viola was up and about. Though CeeCee had her doubts that she was as hearty as she pretended to be, and when Primo unselfishly suggested that she care for her and the kids for the next few days, CeeCee insisted that her sister accept the offer. The driver stared straight ahead as he waited by the roadside. Everyone stood at the door and kisses and hugs where plentiful while CeeCee secretly stuffed a handful of bills into Primo's hand and said, "In case

Viola needs anything, if not... you spend it on something nice for you and the kids."

Her sister's objections interrupted their conspiring with a loud "CeeCee! Ya knows wat I sa."

Chuckling Primo added as she accepted the bills. "Yas don't has ta pay for my hep. I loves Viola lika sistar." Turning to face Viola she argued, "But da money'll surs comin handy."

Viola thought for a minute but could not argue with the truth, so she said nothing more on the subject. Instead she hugged her sister one last time and bid her a tearful goodbye.

Primo laughed at her victory and scooped Molly Amber into her arms for another kiss and CeeCee smiled with relief all the way to the car. She liked Primo. She was a good-hearted caring woman, who laughed often and kissed or hugged each child whenever they were in arms reach. Molly Amber had squealed with joy with each show of affection. This and the fact that Viola would have more time to rest, gave CeeCee a great deal of comfort. Especially since Molly Amber had been a chore for her these last two days! She had no doubt that all three young ones together would certainly be a wearisome task for her ailing sister.

CHAPTER SIXTEEN

*1*913, England was still in unrest, but the turmoil that surrounded the country was even greater. CeeCee worried every day that Ellington, who was overly concerned about the humanitarian aspect, would want to involve himself wholly. He stayed in constant touch with his friend, First Lieutenant Radcliffe Wilhouse. She recognized that he had become more involved in public organizations that fought to eradicate the growth of several unpopular militant groups. His involvement she heard was dangerous and she feared for his safety, but he reminded her often that it was his duty to protect the home front, even if only by conscientious acts.

She herself read everything she could on the matter and hoped that she would be able to sway him in the event he decided to take further action. Still with all this awareness she was not prepared for the day in late 1913 when Ellington came home with a uniform. She urged him to reconsider up to the day he left to join his unit three weeks later.

The day Ellington left, CeeCee felt like he took her very being with him and she wandered around the empty house in despair. It would be months before his return and her heart ached with endless hopelessness.

Sara tried her best to cheer her and Delemare said it was Ellington's duty as a young man to protect his homeland and she should respect that. Yet she could tell that he too was worried for his only son's safety.

After the holidays Sara and Delemare left to spend a few months abroad and CeeCee decided to go see Molly Amber. There was nothing to complicate her visits now so she could stay as long as she liked.

Once she arrived in New York her despair was replaced by excitement. This was going to be the first time she could spend unlimited time with her daughter. She spent the first day shopping for Molly Amber and bought her several dresses and two pair of shoes and a coat for the remaining winter days. She hoped everything would fit; it had been months since she had seen her and at the time Molly Amber was growing like a string-bean. Of course, she also picked out several items for Jasmine and Erla Hattie. She even bought a dress for Viola. Which she had no doubt, that Viola would argue was too extravagant for the likes of her. She was sure she would also scold her for spoiling the girls, though this thought did not detour any of CeeCee's purchases.

The next day her heart felt lighter than it had in several weeks and she hummed a happy tune as the driver she had hired drove her to Richmond. She pictured Molly Amber chasing June bugs and giggling at the cricket's tune like that last night they spent together, and her heart swelled with pleasure. When the scenery grew familiar her heart began to pound with eager anticipation. She could hardly wait to hold her baby and feel the weight of her precious body. As soon as the car stopped, she jumped out and ran up to the door. It was closed so she knocked hard. She waited several minutes before a lady she did not recognize answered.

CeeCee waited and when the lady did not introduce herself, she said, "Hello."

Confusion crossed the lady's face, but her friendliness was apparent when she said, "Howdee, what can I do fer ya, Mam."

"I am, CeeCee, I am here to see Viola, is she here?"

The woman studied CeeCee's face and then looked her up and down. Afterward CeeCee could see the woman's confusion. She could not figure out why a white lady was asking for a colored woman, especially a poor one. Finally, the woman remembered it was none of her business and she stepped aside to let CeeCee enter.

Once inside CeeCee felt a strange unfamiliar feeling and turned to ask, "Is my sister here? Where is Viola?"

By this time sadness had replaced the curious expression and the old woman said as she pointed at the chair nearest CeeCee, "Sit Mam, please."

At first CeeCee did not move. It was plain to see something was wrong and she was afraid if she sat, she would be forced to hear what it was. For a time, she searched the woman's eyes, after the brief hesitation she bravely moved forward to face the woman's words. She was only inches away from her face when she stopped and demanded, "Where is Viola? Where is my sister?"

"Ohh, my. Its you CeeCee Brown.... My chil I's sorray, but yaur sista, she ben dead since March."

CeeCee's head grew light and she reached out and grabbed to hold unto the table that sat in the middle of the room. Her mind wanted to ask if she heard the woman correctly, yet she knew that she had. Suddenly another fear gripped her, and she screeched, "Molly Amber! Where is Molly Amber? Where are the girls? Where's Lemule?"

The old black woman said nothing for what seemed like forever. All she did was shake her head back and forth and CeeCee wanted to grab her and shake the words out of her. Instead CeeCee screamed, "WHERE, WHERE ARE THEY?"

Finally, the old woman answered the questions, "I dont knaw, Mam. I jes moved in hare a couple a month's back. Me and my man dont know wheres Lemule. He took the youngons and left. Jes packdem up and headed out. He took Primo wit em. She be real excited ta be goin, but didin say where ta."

CeeCee's head was swimming and she could not think. What should she do? Someone had to know something. Then she thought, *Mamma, Mamma will know something and so will Primo's Mamma.*

She looked at the old woman again and bellowed, "Do you know if Primo had any family?"

"Na, aint hear'd a none. From wha I know a Primo she ben a warm lovon woman, ifs ya gits wha I mean. Not many folks social wit har, since she been round here. So, we aint know much abot har. Har last mans left som months back, times ben hard fer har. Viola an Lemule aint cared none wha folk say bout har, em both ben good ta har, an Primo, she was here for ya sistar til da end. An CeeCee, Primo, she sur lov em kids and Lemule. She gonna make em a good woman, an a mamma fer em kids. Ya aint needin worry none. She gonna tak care a em all, real good."

CeeCee dropped her limp structure onto a chair while she thought *this chair is nicer than what Viola and Lemule had. Why,* she wondered, *would this thought stand out among the hundreds that are scurrying through my head?* Suddenly she became conscious of a lump in her throat, it felt thick and hard and made it difficult to swallow. Her chest ached from the fear that gripped it, yet she could not cry. She lifted her head and calmly said, "I have to go see my Mamma..., Flower..., Flower Brown. Do you know her? I...I am sure she will know where Lemule took my dau...dau, took Molly Amber... and the girls.' CeeCee stopped when she realized she was rambling. That's when she noticed the woman's face had grown grim again. Immediately she wanted to scream, *WHAT! STOP THAT, STOP LOOKING SO TRAGIC, STOP!*

"Chil I knows ya Mamma, an she caint halps ya. She aint be thinkin no more. Har minds gon way. Jes happen one day, right afor Viola passed. She be livin wit Bell fer a while; now she wit her uncle's boy Jasper, near da woods. But it aint matta who she wit, cause she aint knowin nobody no mor."

With this news came the tears. *Nothing I ever felt before or could ever feel again will hurt as much as this,* she thought. *Oh God. Where is my baby? Where is Molly Amber?* Suddenly she heard wailing and realized it was her own voice that was echoing throughout the small cabin. Her eyes darted from the old woman's face to the door. She wanted to run, to escape this wrenching pain that was tearing at her heart. Nevertheless, she stood motionless, sobbing while her mouth moved up and down as if she were speaking, yet no words came.

The old woman moved closer; then wrapped her arms around the distraught CeeCee. She held and rocked her back and forth while she murmured softly. "Jes is life chil. Yous caint do notin bout it. Lord, he jes taks som tim. We alls gotsta go someday, som jes earlier den others."

Willa was the old woman's name and CeeCee welcomed the comfort she gave well into the next morning, when the old woman led her by the hand down the road to Bell's old neglected shack.

Bell was the only person who knew the truth about Molly Amber and being with her helped. CeeCee cried tears for the loss of her sister, mamma, and daughter. While Bell consoled her the best way she knew how. With plenty of sweetened sassafras tea laden with warm milk, and buttermilk biscuits. As well as plenty of religious song and bible verses, she had learned from the old colored preacher at the church by the river.

It was evening before CeeCee finally asked, "Bell, how did Viola die? Last time I saw her she was doing much better."

"Ya, she be doin good. Wen she gone an git herself wit child all-ova agin; it wadin long afta dat da lord took da child. As hard as I tried CeeCee, I wadint able ta stop har bleedin and soon she be gon too."

"Lemule he wa a brokin man. I wa mighty scared fer em. But Primo she be real good fer em, an em kids." Bell's aged face was laden with deep pain and she let the tears roll openly down her cheeks as she shook her head sadly. "I aint knowin much bout

Lemule an Primo's doins, only wat Primo say afore she an Lemule gone."

Bell stood and walked over to the wood burning stove and retrieved the stained pot that held the sassafras tea. Once she filled CeeCee's cup again she continued. "Primo wa pleased tat Lemule wanted har fer his woman. Real happy ta be goin wit em and the kids. She sa they was goin West ta be farmers. She sa Lemule, he com in ta som monay. Enough ta buy em a farm. Ya sir, Viola wa right. Primo shes a good woman and she gonna stand by Lemule an dem kids. No doubt bout it."

CeeCee wanted to ask her why she let them take her baby, but she knew why so she did not ask the question. She stayed for three weeks and asked everyone around if they knew anything about where Lemule was headed. She was close to the point of giving up when she remembered a service she once read about. So, she left Bell and her tender sympathy and went to Richmond to find a private detective agency.

Once she located what she thought was her only hope, she found that the agency was not interested in her case. Finding colored folk was not a high priority, especially if a family moved on their own accord.

Desperate, CeeCee offered a large amount of money if they could at least locate, Molly Amber, and this too was refused. The only explanation given was, "Them damned colored folks, they just don't have recorded records like white people. So, its damned near impossible to track them down, Mam."

Overwhelmed with loss and filled with discouragement, she stayed in Richmond for several more days before she returned to New York. That night in the dim light of her suite she unpacked her lone suitcase. When she reached the bottom her throat tightened, there sat three little dresses; one for Jasmine, another for Erla Hattie and a pink lace for Molly Amber, all, which, laid atop the lavender frock for Viola. At once she grabbed up the garments and held them close while she cried for hours. By the next morning she decided to go back to England. There was nothing left for her in the States only memories and hopelessness.

CeeCee had not been gone eight weeks, but upon her return she found England changed and her fears for Ellington grew to new heights.

Hostilities were throughout the country and war was becoming a daily reality. *I can not lose Ellington, too.* CeeCee lived with this constant thought and often her fears woke her in the middle of the night. Each time her body was soaked with perspiration and her mind was filled with fears from the dreams she could not remember. She lay awake gasping for air while she desperately tried to recall the mental images that had frightened her so. Soon these same obscure impressions began to haunt her in day as well as night and all too soon the signs of her stress became clearly visible.

The darkness around CeeCee's eyes startled Sara and Delemare when they returned from their three-month excursion. Her appearance was so shocking that without a moments' hesitation Sara ordered her to bed and asked Delemare to get the doctor posthaste. The doctor prescribed a medication and rest, but CeeCee knew these would do no good. What she needed was nowhere to be found.

It was a month later that she was awakened in the middle of the night by a touch of a hand and she knew without opening her eyes that Ellington was home. She kissed and held him so close that he begged for air. As soon as she realized her strength, she released him at once and his recovery was instant. Likewise he, without a minute's hesitation, returned his own barrage of fervent kisses upon which she teasingly struggled, yet soon relinquished any resistance. Soon both were aroused beyond control and without further foreplay they both surrendered fully.

Afterward Ellington lessened his hold but did not release her and she realized that he was still hungry with desire. Playfully she teased him while he laughingly fell against the soft layers of bedding and pulled her atop of him. Such passions where not forsaken until well into the evening when a dire need of sustenance finally fatigued them. At this time, they tiptoed down the darken stairs into the kitchen and loaded their arms with food and drink. Then hurried back to their bed of passion to quench the need for nourishment before once again satisfying their desire for each other.

In the days that followed Sara and Delemare could not believe the change in CeeCee. She was her old self again. To celebrate this, along with the return of their son, Sara invited a group of close friends for a long weekend party.

CeeCee once again felt life was worth living though soon her world was shattered again. It happened on the last night of the weekend affair. Delemare raised his glass in honor of his son. Ellington thanked him and the guest for making this a memorable occasion. Then immediately he announced that in two weeks he would be reassigned. He would join his fellow fighters in the trenches near places unknown to all present.

This time even Delemare begged his son to reconsider; yet all pleas fell on deaf ears, for Ellington was determined to do what was best for his country. "Men are dying for freedom and I shall do my best not to be one of them, but I'll be damned if I won't be beside them while they fight, Father."

Delemare recognized that in Ellington's tone of voice was a deep admiration for those who had given their all. He was loyal to his country as well as to his armed comrades. It was obvious no words he could speak would lessen that virtue, so he did not try.

The day before Ellington was to return to his unit, he and CeeCee mounted Eros and Freya and road the Estate. When Ellington announced, "As a boy this was my favorite spot, Cecilia, I would love to share it with you. Do you mind if we picnic here?"

CeeCee nodded her agreement. To her it did not matter where she was as long as he was near her.

Ellington dismounted and hefted the picnic basket and blanket off Eros' back. After he spread the coverlet, he tenderly lifted his wife to the ground while at the same time he kissed the lips he still hungered for. He was pleased and instantly relieved when she eagerly met his passion.

Yet as soon as he loosened his hold an anxious look had replaced her smile and she scurried away too busy herself with the basket. He watched as she pulled the treats that Sara had lovingly cooked for him and CeeCee. Sara rarely entered the kitchen, but Ellington favored her creations to Cook's, so she surprised them with a basket filled with his favorites.

CeeCee wanted this day to never end though she was very aware of each minute that seem to come at such great speed that it filled her with gloom. She did not want their last minutes to be cheerless, but today she had little control over her feelings.

Ellington lowered his tall frame to her level and touched her hand tenderly before he pulled her to him and whispered, "Cecilia, please, do not be sad," and he kissed her until she was happy again. Eventually they made love on the lush green hilltop that centered the grounds of Kempe.

Later that evening, CeeCee held Ellington close and softly cried into his shoulder as she begged him once more not to leave her. Ellington attempted to comfort her by caressing her tenderly and whispering sweet words of solace, though for CeeCee the words fell greatly short.

During this time dampness crept into the air and soon nighttime swallowed the trees that surrounded them. Shadows danced about as they lazily listened to the many sounds that girdled them. Cecilia leaned back against Ellington's naked chest and felt the warmth of his breath when he kissed her neck. His hands moved swiftly to cup her breast as he caressed them lightly and his lips fell to her bare back as he tasted the warmth of her body. When she shivered, he stopped and draped a blanket around her naked shoulders while once again brushing his sweet lips against the back of her neck. At this time, all words were forfeited and for a time only love spoke.

Eventually the silence was broken, and Ellington once again made an effort to explain, "Cecilia, I want you to know I love you more than life itself, and this is why I must go. I want you..., and our children, we hope to have one day, to be free. Freedom is..., a gift we all take for granted. But we are wrong in our assumption that it is simply owed us, for this path has been seeded by the blood of many men and women...and sadly, even more shall fall in the future. But..., in all truth, my blood is something I will gladly give if it means you are safe and out of harm's way. I love you, Cecilia."

Oh, dear Ellington. No, your dropped blood will not free our daughter, thought CeeCee, *for she is a Negro, and Negros barely know freedom.*

CHAPTER SEVENTEEN

———— ❦ ————

With Ellington gone to war, CeeCee again began to mope around the Estate. Sara tried to involve her in her volunteer work, but she was listless and had no interest. She said her body ached and she slept more hours than she was awake. One night about three months after Ellington had left, she was awakened by a great pain, which was replaced by many smaller stabs. This lasted for several hours. When it was so bad, she could barely stay silent any longer, she called out for Emmy who ran to get Sara's help. By morning, the pain stopped, and she had lost her and Ellington's second child. She mourned the lost child, yet sadly she was thankful, though with all her recent loss she wondered if this was her punishment for living a lie.

While CeeCee waited for the war to end and Ellington's return, she worked with Delemare at Kempe Shipping. She managed the books and scheduled what crossings she could. Most all their ships were engaged in the war and since business was hard to come by anyway, this really did not matter. She enjoyed the shipyard and it helped to pass the time, but her mind was never far from her losses.

Yet, for some reason being near Delemare made her feel closer to Ellington who she missed desperately.

Ellington wrote often, though time seemed to move at a snail's pace between letters. And to Sara, she often complained that the post lacked in its service especially for its military personnel.

Her life had become a tedious merry-go-round and her only rewards were the furloughs Ellington occasionally arranged. Yet despite the joy his visits brought her, she feared them greatly. Her biggest concern was the same as it always was, that she would become pregnant. This fear troubled her constantly and once again she secretly began to read everything she found on new birth control methods, which she soon found was near nothing and almost impossible to find. Most of the materials fell just short of suggesting abstinence. However, it was obvious her past practices had failed her greatly and the cost had been harshly painful. She briefly considered the pamphlets suggestion, before she wadded it up and threw it into the rubbish bin.

Though in 1915 she read of a woman in New York who wrote a magazine called, The Woman Rebel. Along with an encouraging pamphlet on birth control called, Family Limitations. These leaflets, once acquired, enlightened her in a way she had never been before. The woman's name was Margaret Sanger and CeeCee thought she was the first true voice for women. Whereas Sara thought her words aggressive and troublesome, and pleaded that CeeCee change her reading preferences.

With Ellington away, her interest grew to include and support several newly formed groups. One such was the NAACP, the National Association for the Advancement of Colored people. This organization was founded by W.E.B. Du Bois, and a group of negros as well as white folks. This gave CeeCee the much-needed hope that Molly Amber's future was not as dire as hers would have been in the negro world.

Women were also starting to voice a fight for rights, and she decided to join in since this too was the only way she could procure her daughter's future. However, she soon became aware that the negro man's rights were far less than even a white woman's rights were, so she was sure a negro woman's rights were even lower. This thought was discouraging, although in the end it made her more determined. She decided to use the Kempe name along with her position to strengthen her fight for education of colored and under-privileged women.

Sara thought her daughter in-law's efforts were brave and praised her for taking on such an unpopular cause. But soon her praise lessened, and she began to discourage her involvement since she feared public rebuke.

CeeCee refused her advice and continued her work, even though she became less vocal about it around the manor. Still in due time Delemare communicated his similar feelings along with his opinion, "A cause such as this is a waste of time, Cecilia. A poor woman, colored or not, has little interest in education and I dare say your persistence will be a wasted effort."

CeeCee felt disappointed in Delemare and in her arguments. She knew his words were not meant to be hurtful, but in truth, he was simply ignorant on the true facts about Negros. In the end he admitted, "I know I have little knowledge of the wants and needs of a Negro. And since my opinion is based solely on the judgment of others it may very well be feeble. Despite, I must say, I trust their conclusions and believe that they are much closer to the truth than your innocent beliefs are, my child. Consequently, if I may point out, you are not only a woman..., but, a pampered one at that. So, I dare say, you have even less understanding than I of a negro's need."

CeeCee wanted to laugh and cry at the same time. She bit her lip and struggled not to reveal the truth; that she knew far more than *he* or

Sara could ever imagine. That she indeed *is* a woman and a Negro woman at that, and only through her own conniving and self-education was she a pampered one.

Which, if she may remind him, had fully earned, and won his respect with all her extensive abilities. Why he himself had admitted this more times than once, and at one point he even declared that she was intelligent and capable enough to run the whole damned company without him. *Yet,* she pondered, *would he think the same if he knew I was a Negro?*

It was the morning of July 16, 1916 and CeeCee was in the library working on some papers for Delemare. He requested she complete the figures by noon since he had a meeting at two, and he wished to go over them beforehand. She had just pushed the last page to the side when she heard a peculiar noise from the foyer. Minutes later Delemare walked in with Sara close behind him. At first neither said a word, yet their faces disclosed shock and CeeCee's first thought was, *Winnifrey told them, they know my secret.*

The silence in the room was thick and when she could no longer stand it, she stood to face what she assumed would be their rebuke. That's when she noticed the letter in Delemare's hand. From what she could see of the page, it carried an inlay that resembled black lace and suddenly her knees wobbled in weakness. The fear that clutched her chest was suffocating and desperately she tried to force out the question that choked her, yet she so wanted to suppress it. Then she realized her lips were parted and moving, but nothing had come out. She gasped, then simply whispered his name, "Ellington...?"

Silence stretched before her. Finally, Delemare sadly nodded and her legs crumbled beneath her. Delemare opened his arms and moved swiftly across the floor, but not in time to catch the anguished CeeCee, and as she drifted downward, she considered, *I thought I felt my worse pain, though nothing has ever hurt as much as this. God, there is nothing more you can take..., except me, and that I pray for and would gladly welcome.* Suddenly she heard her voice as it wailed a prayer out loud, "Please lord, please take me too. I cannot live without him." After this statement, her mind ceased to think, and she stared up towards the ceiling. Sara and Delemare's grievous faces registered for an instant as they stood over her calling her name. Then her eyes went blank and she saw nothing; it was as if they were strangers and she was a barren piece of flesh.

The pain that had engulfed her was paralyzing like nothing she had ever encountered before. From afar she heard Sara's screams, but did not react and when Delemare asked if she needed a doctor, she never acknowledged his question. She just stared into space as if the emptiness held the answers to whatever she required.

The next few days CeeCee moved in a daze. She remembered the funeral, but it was as if she floated above and watched in the safety of obscurity. She heard Radcliffe Wilhouse say that Ellington was shot down at the battle of Somme and that he was truly a hero. Though none of that really mattered to her; he was gone that's all she heard.

The priest whispered words of intended comfort and she stared through him as if he were not there. He waited and when he saw that she was not ready to come out of her protective nullity, he patted her hand. Then turned to leave but first he whispered something in Sara's ear, who then moved immediately to her side.

Soon after everyone started to leave and finally, she sat alone with Sara, Delemare and Radcliffe. When she could no longer stand their hovering, she stood and walked from the room. As the door closed behind her, she heard Delemare say, "No Sara, let her be."

When she was in the courtyard, she stood very still until she was sure she was alone, then took off in a dead run for the stables. There she ordered that Eros and Freya be saddled. At which point she rode off in such a fury that the stable hand wondered if he should ride after her or call someone to watch over her.

CeeCee rode like the fires of hell was about to engulf her until she found the hill that Ellington loved. There she swayed then fell from her saddle onto the damp grass. Weakened with grief she closed her eyes. Soon she began to envision Ellington was there and was holding her once again. Step by step she relived their last time on the grassy slope. When Eros snorted and trampled the ground, she knew he understood her pain.

Everyday CeeCee rode Freya while Eros jostled the mare from behind. They gallop the grounds for hours at a time while CeeCee pretended Ellington road the horse behind her. This was her only comfort and soon Sara informed Delemare that she was concerned about her health, that their daughter in-law was near a breakdown. She suggested a trip but CeeCee refused; she would not leave her refuge or her phantasm behind. She had stopped all interest except her riding for this is where Ellington lived.

Her sanctuary lasted for six weeks. It was a day like every day before and she rode to the top of the hill. When she reached its peak, she halted Freya and spread her arms to embrace the wind. At this time Eros nudged the mare from behind and he neighed. Without forethought CeeCee turned to speak to Ellington and saw that his saddle was empty. Suddenly his death was real and there was no more escape in the saddle of Freya. Slowly she turned the horses and moved them towards the stable as tears fiercely rolled down her face. When the stable hand clasp Freya's harness she looked down into his eyes and saw his pity and she cried outward, "Please, please get Sara."

This day was the first time she felt the tears and truly mourned Ellington's death and the last time she ever rode Freya.

CeeCee was not quite thirty years old and a widow and once again she did not know where she belonged. Although it was not long after she accepted Ellington's death that dear Delemare put her fears to rest. It was the two-month anniversary of Ellington's death. Earlier that day she had visited his grave in the family cemetery and told him about their daughter. She ended her confession with, "Ellington, Molly Amber was so like you and now I wish I had been brave enough to share her with you."

When she returned to the house that afternoon Sara suggested they all have dinner together in the main dining room. It would be the first since Ellington's death. CeeCee had grown accustomed to taking her meals alone in her sitting room and she hesitated before she accepted.

At six o'clock sharp CeeCee forced herself down the stairwell. When she entered the dining room, she saw that Cook had prepared all her favorites dishes. There was a mélange of strange foods on the table. They ranged from quail, meat pastries, and gateau stuffed with fish, to corn pone, stewed tomatoes, and fried okra which CeeCee remembered Sara and Delemare greatly disliked.

CeeCee's immediate reaction was surprise, though this was quickly replaced by pleasure when her eyes fell on the large bowl of lima beans and ham hocks. She smiled and sighed happily, "Oh my, cornbread and lima beans. I cannot remember the last...." Her voice fell off and her eyes glistened with tears when she recalled her last time was at Viola's table, yet she beamed, "Sara you...Delemare, I cannot believe this...how...where..., oh my...thank you. This is so thoughtful."

Both Sara and Delemare brightened with great gratification. CeeCee could see that they were pleased by her reaction. They were glad they went through the much needed effort it took to get the vegetables, since this was the first smile that had lit their daughter in-law's face since that dreadful morning of July 16.

All through dinner Sara carried on idle chitchat until Delemare tautly coughed lightly; then suddenly she fell silent. After a moment and no one spoke CeeCee looked up to face four vigilant eyes. Instantly her pleasure was replaced by anxiety and she waited while she took short little breaths to ease her fear. Again, Delemare coughed; it was obvious that he felt uncomfortable with what he had to say.

Finally, Sara said, "Well."

And without further delay Delemare began to speak. At first it was slowly, then rapidly, "Cecilia..., I... we...we do not know...well if you have...ah... Well, have you given any thought to future plans?"

Again, Sara spoke, and her voice held a hint of exasperation, "Delemare, please."

At first Delemare looked confused, then he understood his wife's implication and moved on. "Oh, yes. What I mean to say Cecilia, is well...dammit. What I am so fretfully trying to say Cecilia, is we love you.

We love you as if you were our own child, and we wish... very much, that you will stay here with us..., at Kempe Manor. This is your home as well as ours and we hope that you realize this."

The fear that had gripped CeeCee when she heard Delemare's first words disappeared. She had been afraid that they were going to ask her to leave and her relief was evident.

Sara immediately echoed Delemare's words, "Yes dear, we love you. We want you to stay here with us and not go back to the States."

Her last comment startled CeeCee, for she had not given any mind to future plans, and certainly not returning to the States.

Delemare smiled when he saw the relief on CeeCee's face and immediately he felt encouraged and hurried on with his proposal. "I... we...Sara and I, would also like to suggest that you continue your work at Kempe shipping. You make life remarkably easier when you are there..., and in truth I would hugely appreciate the help. I am quite sure you have noticed that this old man is getting slower. Unfortunately, I fatigue much sooner then I use to, so your assistance is truly needed, Cecilia."

CeeCee smiled while she strained to control her tears. Finally, she felt composed enough to answer, "I love you both, too, and yes I would very much like to stay. Here, is where I feel Ellington and it would pain me greatly to leave him... behind...." Her memory pictured Ellington's face, and for a moment her mind refused to move on. At last, the clouded image dissipated and was replaced by Sara and Delemare's tender smiles. She knew they understood her hesitation and she was thankful that they did not intrude. After the brief silence CeeCee straightened her back and sat taller in her seat to show a strength that she was not sure of, though this fact was not evident in her voice when she answered Delemare's proposal. "As for Kempe shipping, I think ...I am sure.... I would be happy to work for you, Delemare. I will do everything I can to pay you back for all that you have done for me."

"You owe us nothing, Cecilia. You have given us much more than we can ever give you. Plus, you gave our son twelve wonderful years. Ellington loved you more than...," Sara's voice died out and a tear rolled down her cheek. The room fell silent and Delemare reached out and touched Sara's hand and then reached for

CeeCee's. No more words were spoken for nothing more needed to be said.

CeeCee welcomed the long hours at Kempe Shipping. At first, during the week, she stayed in a lodge near the shipping yard. But soon she missed Kempe Manor and the illusory presence of Ellington, so she moved all the yards' paperwork to the library at home. From that day on she rarely left the manor only to visit Ellington's grave site or an occasional call on Eunice Sneed, Ellington's favorite cousin by marriage, and a woman that she, too, had grown fond of.

Eunice was nine years older than CeeCee and was an only child. Her parents died when she was barely seventeen and she had briefly moved in with Sara and Delemare who were distantly related, yet closely entwined through friendship and family. Eunice, likewise, had only one child, a boy named Edward after his father. His father had passed on some years back and Eunice doted on the boy. Edward was at present, away, attending Oxford. He had just recently announced his engagement to a wonderful girl named Anne Sweetbriar. CeeCee loved Anne from the minute she met her and very soon, the girl became a substitute for the much-missed, Molly Amber. This was one reason CeeCee, every so often, ventured out to visit Eunice. Who received regular visits from her future daughter in-law Anne.

It was during one of these visits that CeeCee learned that Anne and Edward wanted to have a large family. Though Anne admitted that this might not be an option, since Edward wanted to teach, and teachers did not earn a large salary. CeeCee immediately thought of Viola who was poor, but never gave a second thought about having a large family. She wished she had, for then she would still be alive today, and Molly Amber would be within her reach.

That day, after CeeCee left Eunice and Anne, she felt a sadness that she could not dismiss. She longed to find her daughter, yet she had no idea how to carry out such a task. She feared she would never see Molly Amber again. This notion was new, something she had never even considered until now, and she prayed towards the heavens, "Lord, please let her be safe and loved. Ellington, please forgive me and watch over our daughter."

This is when she thought of her work with the NAACP. She had involved herself for Molly Amber's future, and since Ellington's death, she had ignored her pledge to pave a better life for their daughter. "This," she promised, "will change. Molly Amber, I promise I will not let you down again."

It was this day upon her return home that she learned the war was over. After Sara had enlightened her, she without a word, ran upstairs and locked the door to her room. In the loneliness of her and Ellington's chamber she cried incensed tears, while she accusingly read every letter Ellington had ever written her. Each time she laid a finished letter aside she asked, "Why did you have to die? Why Ellington? Why did you have to be brave? I needed you far more than your country did?" But by the time she read his final words, she understood him and his sense of duty much clearer than she ever had before. She also came to terms that her pain and anger was not at him, but only at the fact that he died. Like so many others, he would not be coming home. That night she packed away his letters and vowed to make herself worthy of his love. In his life she had failed him greatly, but in his death she will not. "Once you told me you would happily spill your blood to keep me and our children free. I thought at the time that this would not help the daughter you did not even know. Our daughter, Ellington, Molly Amber..., but I was wrong, Ellington. I promise your death will not be in vain. I will do everything I can do to help our daughter's freedom, and your death will not be an empty one, my love."

CHAPTER EIGHTEEN

Delemare never fully recovered his strength after Ellington's death, and when the flu epidemic hit England in 1918, he succumbed to its feverish assault in late April. Twenty-one months and twelve days after Ellington's funeral, they laid Delemare to rest in a grave next to his only child.

Sara was comforted by CeeCee who never left her side. Though soon she too was ill with the fever, which gave Sara little time for grief while she tended the needs of her daughter in-law. After three and a half weeks CeeCee finally sat up in bed and weakly asked, "Sara, are you okay?"

Sara did not answer instead she plumped CeeCee's pillow and poured her a fresh glass of water.

"Sara, please do not fuss. I am feeling stronger. I can manage on my own. It is you who needs care, not I. I should be up soon. Now go and lie down, Emmy can tend to me. This is a time for grief..., for your grief."

"No Cecilia, I am fine."

"Sara, you have not had a minute to yourself since Delemare's funeral service. You need time to grieve; it is unhealthy if you do not. Sara, you must shed tears to ease your pain." CeeCee lifted Sara's hand to her cheek and squeezed it close. "Sara, please listen. When Ellington died, you were so good to me; now let me repay that kindness. I want to take care of you so let me."

"Cecilia..., you are a lovely young woman and truly I thank you for your concern, but I am fine. In my own way I have come to terms with Delemare's death." Sara fell silent. After a bit she smiled then went further, "Cecilia, I loved Delemare from the moment I met him, and I believe beyond a doubt, that he is...was a man to be thankful for. Of course, I will forever be grateful and cherish our time together, but for now I must go on. You yourself Cecilia, unknowingly taught me this, and that is what Delemare requested of me."

"Going on is a fact you cannot escape Sara, but still you...."

"Cecilia, please hear me out. There are things I must tell you. Delemare and I talked of this many times after Ellington's death. Delemare was keen and somehow, he always knew the future. He knew he would not live much longer, and since he was fifteen years my senior, he worried I would spend too many years alone after he passed. So... we...well we made plans together."

She stood and started to move around the room. *Nervous energy* thought CeeCee as Sara moved from one side of the room to the other. *She is not as strong as she likes me to believe.*

Finally, after Sara weighed her thoughts she continued, however she did not stop her restless steps, "See..., Cecilia, my entire life has been lived as a fortunate woman. And this is not wholly due to my husband's extensive fortune. I, on my own am a very wealthy woman. My holdings are as vast if not superincumbent to Delemare's. Because of this, I possess several large estates, one in which I favor. It is located in the midst of Berkshire, not far outside of London. There, my family goes back as far as anyone has recorded annals."

Sara fell silent and studied CeeCee before she moved onward. "Cecilia, I shall never want for anything. And as for Delemare and his many possessions...," she swept her hand around the room to indicate their surroundings, "these were all meant for Ellington." She hesitated and moved closer towards CeeCee before she added, "and since Ellington is no longer with us, it shall all go to you."

CeeCee gulp, "NO! Sara you can not. This is yours."

"Cecilia, it is already done. Delemare and I saw to it before his death. I will go back to Berkshire and live. This is what I want, that is what Delemare wanted and that is where I belong."

Sara moved swiftly to close the gap between her and CeeCee. Then sat carefully on the bed next to her. She moved to take her hand in hers, while she stroked away the dampened hair that had stuck to CeeCee's face. There were tears on CeeCee's cheeks and more threatening to spill over from her eyes. Sara kissed the center of her forehead lightly then added, "Sweetheart, please do not be sad. This is what I and Delemare wanted. You are a part of Kempe Manor as I am a part of my home in Berkshire. I know as well as Delemare did that you will love and care for this estate. So please, please put a smile on that lovely face, for you are now the proud owner of Kempe Manor...along with Kempe shipping."

CeeCee choked, "What? Kempe Shipping?"

"Yes, my dear, you heard me correctly. You have worked awfully hard to keep Kempe Shipping in the black as Delemare often said. So, you shall continue to reap its rewards. You, Cecilia, with the aid of several legal aides Delemare appointed, will run the yard. You, my dear, will always have final word on everything, and all of its profits will go to you and you alone."

CeeCee was shaking her head, "No Sara, no... please.... Sara...Sara, Kempe Shipping belongs to you. You are Delemare's widow; you should own his property, not I."

"Now whatever would I do with a shipping yard, Cecilia. Why even its day to day routine is beyond my comprehension, and you, I dare say, are quite comfortable handling the most difficult matters. Now let's not hear another word." She stood and patted her daughter in-law's hand. Then she swiftly headed for the door as she added, "I will be right back with a pot of tea and a bun. I am sure you have had your fill of consommé."

By the time CeeCee was up, Sara had already packed and was ready to leave for Berkshire. She said the manor was too confining without Delemare's lively presence, and she wanted the comfort of her own estate and family. Within days of her recovery CeeCee stood at the door of the manor while she watched Sara's car fade into the early morning fog. Once Sara's driver drove the vehicle out of sight CeeCee turned to face her own loneliness. The place she was sure, would not be the same without Sara and Delemare. Since Ellington's death they had been her saviors now she wondered, *what will I do?*

The first week after Sara's departure, CeeCee contacted the lawyers that Sara had mentioned Delemare had appropriated to assist her in the running of Kempe Shipyard. She requested that all records pertaining to the company be brought to the library at Kempe Manor. There she organized the new office of Kempe Shipping and there is where she spent her days and most of her nights. When she was not working, she was reading or entering notes in one of her many journals. This became her daily routine.

With the war and the flu epidemic over, the British eagerly began to restore their surroundings and for most, life became as it once was. Soon CeeCee found party invitations a frequent part of the printed matter that arrived with punctuality every Wednesday at mid-day. Without consideration each and every one was sent back with a thank you, along with her regrets.

Now and then a friend would make an effort to orchestrate an encounter with a Count or Lord, who just happen to be in town and available. CeeCee without deliberation, rejected all overtures.

She was not interested in a relationship. She was still in love with Ellington.

Eunice Sneed urged her to get out and join the world around her, but CeeCee's excuse was that she was extremely busy with Kempe Shipping. The only invitation she accepted was to Edward and Anne's wedding, and this was only out of love and her loyalty for Anne.

It had been eighteen months since Sara's return to Berkshire and CeeCee still missed her profoundly. Each and every time she did anything, she would ask herself *would Sara do it this way?* Occasionally she received a note or card from Sara, but no visits. Sara begged her forgiveness and explained that she could not face Kempe Manor without Delemare. For CeeCee it was different, yet she still understood, since she herself could not bear to leave the manor because Ellington's presence was everywhere.

It was two years after Delemare's death that CeeCee received a card with a note imploring, *'My dearest Cecilia, please come to Berkshire. I have become engaged and am having a party to celebrate. I have met a wonderful man and I want to share my happiness with those I love most. The gentleman, Lord Weston has also lost his consort, a woman he truly loved deeply, and he respects my feelings for Delemare. This is a rare opportunity for a woman my age and I plan to grasp it enthusiastically and enjoy it wholly. Please Cecilia, please be a part of my joy, please come to Berkshire. Love Sara.'*

CeeCee carefully contemplated the invitation in her hand. Three weeks earlier she had unenthusiastically sent her acceptance card to Sara's personal secretary, but only after days of weighing her options. Ultimately, she decided she loved Sara and to show her devotion she would attend the gala. In truth she was indeed happy for her dear friend, even if she dreaded taking part in the celebration. But that was the only way to demonstrate her love and support.

She moved closer to stand over the bed. It held several dresses that were spread across the bed cover waiting for her inspection.

Upon accepting the invitation, she had realized that she had nothing to wear and summoned her seamstress. She had not needed anything so elaborate as a party gown in ages. CeeCee touched the softness of the chiffon. The gown was lovely; the fabric was textured in a way she never seen before. The color was a soft rose and the waist was garnished with laced roses. The bodice was looser than what she usually wore, although the seamstress informed her that this was what fashion now considered fitted.

CeeCee turned to face the oval mirror that stood in the corner of the room. She smoothed the material of the dress she wore over her hips. Her waist was a size larger then when she first met Ellington, though at that time she was far too thin. Her eyes moved and lingered on her hair. She had paid little attention to her appearance over the past few years, and she still styled her hair the same as the day she received the news of Ellington's death. He had loved the thickness and shine of her hair. *I wondered if he had known it was the hair of a Negro, would he have still yearned to caress it. Molly Amber's hair was as thick, yet hers was tight with curl. Molly Amber. She is eleven today. How she missed her, oh God, how I miss Ellington.*

Her eyes again moved to the bed and she scrutinized the gowns that the seamstress had created. She stopped and studied the one of satin. The emerald green would have been lovely against Molly Amber's skin tone. Soon, she will want dresses like this, will she receive them? Chances are..., no. Most Negros do not attend parties that require such lavishness, and she doubted that Molly Amber's life had changed enough that she would now....

Suddenly she heard the shuffle of Emmy's feet and she turned to greet her. The expression on the girl's face showed that she was still in pain from a recent fall where she sprained her back.

"Good-mornin Mum. Cornelius is bringin a dress case up da stairs for yaur gowns. Shouldt I let hem in?"

"Certainly, Emmy and please sit, you should not be on your feet."

"No, Mum, I be fine. I need ta be packin ya things up, Mum."

"Nonsense...," Suddenly CeeCee remember Abigail and how she used to insist that she help with the chores. This had always upset CeeCee. She worried that someone might see or that Abigail would decide that she no longer needed the service of a girl, and she would lose her job. For that reason, without further argument CeeCee backed away and stood out of Emmy's way. And without delay the girl began her task.

As soon as Cornelius entered the room CeeCee saw a light in Emmy's eyes flicker and she smiled. She had thought that Cornelius was sweet on Emmy, and now she could see that it was the same for her maid. This pleased her, Emmy had not yet found a man of her own and from what she knew of Cornelius, he would be a good husband for Emmy.

CeeCee turned and started to leave the room then asked, "Emmy, will this trip be too much for you?"

"No Mum, I be truly eager ta go, Mum. I ne'er been ta Berkshire."

"Very well, just have everything ready by seven in the morning. I do want to get an early start. Cornelius, you will be my driver this trip."

Cornelius' face lit up and he grinned ear to ear as he said, "Yes Mam, sure thing."

Emmy also grinned and happily acknowledged, "Very goodt Mum, everathin will be as ya say, first thin in the mornin."

CHAPTER NINETEEN

I t was wonderful to see Sara. Her eyes shone with happiness and her warm reception made CeeCee instantly glad that she had accepted the invitation.

The first night Sara held a small dinner party which consisted of a few close friends. One of which was Radcliffe Wilhouse. This was the first time CeeCee had seen him since Ellington's funeral, and even longer since she had seen him out of uniform. Therefore, at first his identity escaped her since the transformation was so incredible. It simply did not register that he was who he was, Ellington's dear friend. He looked so mature and dapper in his finery, and she almost introduced herself when he first approached her. But when he said, "Hello Cecilia, you look extraordinary this evening. It's nice to see you out again."

She at once recognized his voice and the image of him standing over Ellington's grave as he said, *he died a hero* echoed in her ears. It took her several minutes to compose herself. Radcliffe recognized her alarm but remained silent until she was ready to speak. When she did, CeeCee immediately apologized. "I am sorry, Radcliffe, I..., I guess you simply surprised me."

"Please, no need to apologize, I could see that you didn't recognize me and with our last meeting being so climactic..., well it's quite understandable. You were merely caught off guard."

The rest of the evening was pleasurable and several times CeeCee found herself laughing out loud. She could not remember the last time she enjoyed herself and before she closed her eyes that night, she admitted that it was nice to feel alive again.

Lord Weston turned out to be everything Sara had described and the next day he, along with Sara, Radcliffe and CeeCee spent the morning galloping the foothills of Sara's estate. Then after a light meal on the lawn, they all returned to their rooms to retire for a short nap, for the evening was promised to be lengthy, to say the least.

The night's gala was set to begin at seven and it was now six-forty-five. CeeCee knew she needed to finish readying herself, but she could not move. The last twenty minutes she had sat motionless, spellbound by the reflection in the mirror. Finally, she tried to convince herself, *you will survive this. The gathering last night had gone smoothly, so..., so will tonight's. But then,* she argued, *the gathering last night was small. A large party is far more difficult; this is a challenge I do not want to contend with.* She told herself her nervousness was due to her lack of recent social experiences. She had not been in a large crowd since before Ellington's death and that had been more than four years ago. She shuddered when she realized that all her old insecurities had resurfaced. She felt helpless to fight them and she thought, *I am not the woman everyone believes I am.* Instead she felt she was once again, the little colored girl born and raised on the Roberts Plantation. "When I was young, I only pretended to be a lady.... A white lady," she whispered.

But that was only pretend, she answered in her mind...*then again, is not everything I do or ever done, pretend? Am I inferior; simply because I are not white?* All at once a new fear gripped her, *will I embarrass Sara, what if I do not remember how to act..., everyone will find out that I am an impostor.* Her eyes brimmed though they remained wide as they studied the image that stared back at her. *I am what everyone sees..., I am,* she wanted to scream. *Why can't they see that I am a lady...? Ellington did.* "Or did he," she asked softly, "maybe he merely loved me enough that he failed to see the truth? Then... she asked, "Certainly, he would not have loved me if he knew the truth?"

Ellington, you had always been my courage..., and now I am forced to stand alone. "Is that why I hide?" she asked the image. "Because I am weak without him?"

She hoped not for Ellington's memory deserved better than that. He had always been proud of her and thought of her as an independent woman, and that he encouraged. Even his last letter broached the subject as he praised her deeds at the shipyard. She can not let him down..., not now. If anyone finds out the truth about her, his memory will be tarnished forever.

Gradually CeeCee began to feel the strength of Ellington's love. Soon she squared her shoulders and sat taller. Now that she was armed with new resolve, she gazed at the reflection in the mirror and once again assessed the image. Her hair was lustrous from the two hundred strokes it received earlier, and her cheeks held the much-prided pink tinge they always did. The rose-colored dress was unique and fit well, complimenting her figure to its peak. Unexpectedly her expectations for the future were re-ignited and she declared, "I am strong," and she deemed, "I am, what I always wanted to be, a lady..., a well-educated lady with standing. Now, thanks to Ellington and Delemare I can afford to be a fighter as well. I am Mrs. Cecilia Kempe. I am no longer that poor colored girl; that dares to remain and cowers within me. Nothing can hold me back except fear, and this I will not allow." She stood, then stretched taller and firmly related to the reflection that stared back. "I will not let you down Ellington." Suddenly she was drawn back to reality, by a light knock at the door and a soft "Mum ar yau readied," pulled her back from her meditative state. She gave one more smile to the reflection then answered, "Yes..., Yes, Emmy I am indeed ready."

R adcliffe met CeeCee at the doorway of the ballroom and immediately offered his arm as he warmly chided, "You, Cecilia, are going to make my evening very challenging."

Her face instantly registered surprise, then was replaced by a simple smile full of question. At this time, he immediately pushed on, "For you are, as always, a beautiful woman. But tonight, I must admit you have gone a bit further, for you are frankly radiant, Cecilia, and being that this is quite evident, I am sure I will be forced to fight off all your admirers. Simply so I, myself, may have a few moments of your time."

"And you, my friend, are a gracious gentleman, although at times I feel you do bestow excessive compliments. Yet, it does present a lady with the most pleasant of welcomes. However, appreciated, I doubt I will need your gallant valor. But if required I will happily accept your intended chivalry..., and I thank you in kind, for your generous flattery."

Radcliffe laughed at CeeCee's lighthearted response, then he swiftly maneuvered her through the crowded doorway. His moves were confident, and he eased between several groups before he stopped and discreetly whispered. "Before we get to far from the beverages, can I get you a glass of champagne or sherry?"

Even though CeeCee presented a carefree mien, Radcliffe recognized that she was slightly nervous. Still and all this was no surprise, Sara had informed him earlier that this was the first time the young widow had ventured out on her own since Ellington's death. She also indicated that she may be less than perfect company. Yet, in his opinion, aside from her nervousness, yesterday, she was quite entertaining and thus far tonight she has handled the situation remarkably well. He guessed that Sara might have underestimated Cecilia's strength, because as far as he had observed in his past encounters, Cecilia had always come off as a fighter.

Within minutes of her arrival she proved him right for her tension diminished and her old confidence returned. She was full of clever puns and was quite engaging in her informal conversation.

After dinner Radcliffe and CeeCee enjoyed several dances before she rejected his offer of a fourth dance. Then excused herself with a lighthearted laugh and a promised, "I will be back after I freshen up a bit. Please, do not look so forlorn, Radcliffe, I promise I will be back shortly."

It was when CeeCee was on her way back to Radcliffe that she was suddenly stopped by a clutch of her shoulder. Startled she turned and started to ask, "What is the meaning..." then fell silently stunned,

Winnifrey's face was full of hostility while she still gripped CeeCee's shoulder tightly.

The immediate sight of her and her apparent anger frightened CeeCee and she released a little whimper, "Oh..., oh.... Winnifrey." Then promptly she caught herself and asked, "What, what is the meaning of this, Winnifrey?" Though she did not hesitate for an answer before she continued, "I was not aware you were here. I did not know you were family or a friend. Why are you here?"

"Dear me, of course I am related, Cecilia. Is not every one of aristocracy who lives in England related in one way or another?"

CeeCee simply stared; she did not interrupt Winnifrey's response that was clearly hostel. CeeCee did not wish to start anything.

Winnifrey's smile was unkind as she moved closer and went on with her critique, "Oh dear CeeCee, you are still so simple. What a shame that you people are so slow, and yes, *Cecilia*. I am a distant cousin by marriage..., Abigail's marriage that is. Therefore, I belong here far more than you, a dull unimportant colored girl."

CeeCee gasped and Winnifrey laughed with pleasure; she had succeeded in disturbing her rival. After she threw her head back in laughter, she immediately regained her restraint and threw CeeCee a disgusted look. At this same time, she scrutinized her up and down then added. "My, my, widowhood certainly does agree with you. I, on the contrary, was terribly distraught after hearing of dear Ellington's demise. Though..., from what I have witnessed tonight, it has done little to eradicate your old behaviors. Yes indeed, and once again no man is safe whenever he is within arm's reach of Virginia's own Niggar whore, CeeCee Brown.

Why I say, if your family had any idea they would simply die of embarrassment. Though I dare say, most are already dead. And since your Mamma is quite out of her mind..., well never no mind." A wicked laugh escaped her lips and Winnifrey suddenly moved even closer and asserted, "You know Cecilia, I think you may have gotten all your crazy notions from your insane mamma."

CeeCee held her breath and refused to let Winnifrey's hate to goad her. Winnifrey had turned into an evil bitter woman and with this performance, it seemed she was out of control. So CeeCee decided it was best to remain silent, for anything she said would surely only trigger further anger. On the other hand, she soon realized that her silence did the same.

Winnifrey realized that CeeCee was not going to give in to her needling, so she pushed further, "Yes, I heard that you lost a child not long after you lost your dear sister. I was deeply saddened to hear about *poor* Viola."

CeeCee sensed that Winnifrey was not speaking about the child she miscarried, but about Molly Amber. And Winnifrey's voice purposely held no remorse about the lost child. *This is a deliberate intent to inflict more pain, thought CeeCee.* Despite, CeeCee's face showed no emotion and she remained silent as she desperately tried to stay calm.

"Yes, I was truly sorry for Viola's Negra man," added Winnifrey. "And I told him just that when I paid a visit to his grieving family. At the time he was still mournful, red-eyed and stress filled. Yes, I would say he was just plain pitiful. However, his mournful face soon changed to panic when I mentioned your name. I tell you Cecilia, you colored folk are just so easy to read. I guess because you are so simple-minded. Any which way I immediately eased his burden. I quickly explained that you and I are such dear friends that we never keep secrets from each other. I knew everything there was to know about you. Yes, he stood there open mouthed and dumbfounded. What a simple man! That is until I told him that you recently sent me a letter telling me that you were going to take Molly Amber away from him. That you intended to take her back to England the very next time you came to the States. Why, you would not believe the horror that swept over that simple Negra man's face. I tell you it would have broken your heart, Cecilia. Well, as you can guess it certainly did mine. Anyhow, me being the tender-hearted soul that I always been, I immediately understood his alarm. I mean, he sincerely loved that child, and did not want to lose her like he did his mate, Viola."

CeeCee could see Winnifrey was clearly enjoying herself and meant to inflict as much pain as she could. So, she prepared herself for the next blow, but she was in no way ready for her following words.

"For that reason, I advised him to take his family and leave Virginia, posthaste. Why I swear Cecilia, he looked downright confused..., that is, until I handed him a handful of bills. I am sure far more than he had ever seen at any one time, let alone would earn in a lifetime. Why he at once fell to his knees and bawled like a baby. Cecilia, I tell you, it was downright heart-rending. I guess some Negra's know how to be thankful and others...well you know. Anyway, I would say, that makes two babies you lost? Is that not correct, Cecilia?"

Winnifrey shook her head at the stunned CeeCee. Then she immediately added with an evil snicker, "Yes, I would have to say God takes all from those who are not worthy, would you not agree, Cecilia? After all I am sure *He* frowns intensely on deception. And passing for a white woman...well, I would guess that has to be the largest form of dishonesty, would you not agree, Cecilia?"

CeeCee's head was swarming and she gasped for air and choked on it. "Why, why Winnifrey? What have you done?" Her mind pounded one question after another until she felt sick to her stomach, and all Winnifrey did was stand there hideously smiling at her. She was enormously happy with herself and pleased with her success.

CeeCee's mind repeated the words of Winnifrey's indictment, *God takes all from those who are not worthy, would you not agree, Cecilia?*

Winnifrey had always been mean, but now she had turned into a vicious woman who was filled with hate. *She blames me for what she perceives she lost when I married Ellington. There is no doubt that if Ellington were here tonight, Winnifrey, without concern for anyone, would have informed him of her lineage and Molly Amber's existence.*

Suddenly CeeCee remembered a letter Ellington sent her not long after Henry and Abigail had their third child. He said Henry had confided that Winnifrey lost several babies and was openly blaming Albin and his age for the miscarriages. Yet in truth it was CeeCee, Winnifrey blamed; she could see it in her eyes. *She blames me for all she's ever lost and the only way she could retaliate was to take my child.*

Rage filled CeeCee as she faced every fear and threat Winnifrey had ever bestowed upon her. It was far too late, but finally and without reservation she faced Winnifrey, the woman who had always stood in her path. In her voice there was no mistake that she now hated the woman that stood before her, and when she spoke her voice dripped with contempt. "And who would know about God's wrath more than you, Winnifrey? You lost every man you ever thought you loved along with every child you ever conceived. So yes, I agree Winnifrey, God does take from those who are not worthy."

CeeCee thought Winnifrey was going to slap her but instead she stepped even closer and seething with venom she whispered between her teeth. "CeeCee, I will not have the pleasure of watching you burn in hell, but at least I have been given the privilege of seeing you suffer in life. And I promise you, you will never again see that little Niggar child of yours again." In conclusion of these words Winnifrey gave her an angry shove, then stomped off in an exaggerated huff.

CeeCee did not move; she stood there shaking and feeling sick inside. Her eyes were fixed on the back of Winnifrey's stature while at the same time trying hard not to cry. She had once loved Winnifrey and she had hoped that one day her love would be returned. She had envied her position and vied for her friendship, but as Viola had long ago predicted, that was not to be. They were worlds apart and Winnifrey's anger was because she had dared to crossover that line.

A hand touched CeeCee's shoulder and she jumped, then sharply turned to meet Sara's tense smile. Her eyes revealed a deep concern and when she spoke, she did so in a cautious calculated manner, "Are..., are you all right, Cecilia?"

CeeCee wanted to ask how much she had heard, but from the love and respect in Sara's eyes she decided she did not have to. And when Sara moved closer to hold her for an instant, she knew her answer, she was safe. However soon Sara's words erased all visions of refuge. "My sweet child, I am afraid it is time you to move on. You need to separate yourself from Ellington and his memory. This will be best for all concerned." She backed away and lifted CeeCee's chin and continued, "Cecilia, I love you and always will. But I am old and cannot protect you as Ellington would have."

She assumes Ellington knew, thought CeeCee.

"Financially, Cecilia you are well taken care of, so make your life count. Do not end up bitter and mean like Winnifrey. She is a very unhappy young lady and she will make your life miserable if you let her." Sara touched CeeCee's cheek gently as she considered her next words. Upon her decision she explained, "I will have your bags prepared and you shall leave first thing tomorrow morning. The rest must be your choice. Now come and say your goodnights you need your rest."

CeeCee followed Sara and in a hazed like state she bade her goodnights. Radcliffe looked immensely disappointed, but he accepted her plea of a headache and said he would see her in the morning at the breakfast table.

Emmy could sense that something was terribly wrong as she helped CeeCee out of her dress, and with CeeCee's next words proved her instinct was right. "Emmy, I want our bags ready to leave by five in the morning, so be here by four to pack. Now you may go."

"Mum...?"

"Go Emmy, please go."

She was not herself this was plain to see and concerned Emmy offered to fetch a pot a tea and a powder for her headache. CeeCee absent mindedly refused the overture. Emmy hesitated then upon deciding that there was nothing she could do she left her charge sitting at her vanity staring into the mirror.

The tears would not come, yet CeeCee suspected that they were about to burst forth any minute. *Was Sara's dismissal an act of support or displeasure,* she asked herself? *She said I should move on. I can not. How can I leave Kempe Manor, where Ellington's memory is everywhere?*

The next several months CeeCee immersed herself in Kempe Shipping. She tried hard not to think about Sara, or Radcliffe and that last evening they spent together. Thus far, he had requested several visits and each and time she immediately rejected his request. She had not seen him the day she left Berkshire, and he worried that he had offended her in some way. This she did not contradict since she thought it was best believed.

It was seven and a half months since Sara's party and a month after her wedding. CeeCee did not attend the wedding, she was not invited. Sara had advised that since Winnifrey was certain to be present, it would be best if she did not come.

The day had been a long difficult one since it was also the anniversary of Ellington's death. A lonely night stretched before her and she sat at her desk in the library sipping a glass of sherry while she attempted to busy her mind with a book. The silence throughout the house was deafening; then suddenly she heard a sound. It was the exact sound she heard the day Delemare and Sara burst into the room to tell her of Ellington's death, and she froze. A feeling of deja-vu overwhelmed her and she looked up to see a vision from the past which was paralleled by a shadow of Ellington. There upon it immediately faded. She stared at the empty space for over an hour hoping for its return. Finally, a new realization engulfed her. She had been living in the past and for a person who no longer existed. '*It is time you move on. It is best for all concerned,*' Sara's words from months ago repeated themselves. And for the first time CeeCee realized that she had been right, *it is time.*

Chapter Twenty

After CeeCee's vision, a fresh new energy had emerged, and it coursed through the halls of Kempe Manor. Even Emmy's mood ranged from extreme happiness to low spiritedness. She was thrilled that she and Cornelius were going to be married in three weeks, however with Cecilia leaving her and Kempe Manor her heart wept. The thought of her never seeing her charge again was weighing on her mood. In two days, her lady would be leaving England, and this made her days heavy with sorrow. She had grown to love CeeCee dearly over the years, and she would miss her greatly.

Anne and Edward Sneed had moved into the main wing of the house a few days prior and would now be her new responsibilities. "I like both Sir Edward and Lady, Anne, extremely," she explained to her betrothed. "Yet I will miss Mum awfully much. Why must she take leave I wonder?"

Cornelius wrapped his arms around the teary-eyed Emmy but said nothing since he too was saddened by the departure.

Once CeeCee had decided that she must do as Sara had recommended, she immediately began to take action. First thing the very

254 · ELLEN M. FOSS

next morning she summoned Cornelius to take a message to the recently wedded Sneeds.

T he following Tuesday, she, Edward and Anne, sat in front of the fireplace sipping tea as she presented, "I have decided that Kempe Manor shall be your new home. Of course," she insisted, "I will pay a substantial allowance to maintain the Estate's vast holdings. This way no encumbrance shall befall you. To sum it up Edward, your dream is to continue teaching and Anne, you want children. From what Eunice has recently told me you are now with child; with this arrangement we can all have what we want.

At first Edward refused, "Kempe Manor," he said, "is your home Cecilia and that is what Delemare and Ellington intended it to be. We thank you, but we cannot except your generous offer."

"Yes, you are correct, Edward. Ellington wanted his home to be *ours.*" She stood and moved to stand in front of the fireplace and her voice was faint when spoke again. His *dream* was that it be filled with love, happiness, and the laughter of many children. Sadly, for us the latter was never achieved." Suddenly she smiled and her tone grew cheerful, "Though with your help in the end we can fulfill Ellington's dream. Edward, Anne..., if you accept and take care of Kempe Manor you will be doing me a great service, and I will forever be in your indebtedness. See..., your youth, devotion, and merriment, is what Kempe Manor needs. Please do not deny me this. It will be best for all if you accept this offer."

"But Cecilia..., Anne started.

Yet before she could speak CeeCee finished, "I promise you Ellington and Delemare would approve," rendered CeeCee."

Finally, after hours of long-winded deliberations the Sneeds conceded and agreed to maintain the property for CeeCee. She promised to have the lawyers draw up the necessary papers and have them delivered as soon as possible.

Once the question of Kempe Manor was settled CeeCee arranged a meeting with the lawyers at Kempe Shipping. Her objective there, she was sure, would be much easier to obtain. The lawyers, she decided, would simply run the business as they always have. Any major decisions would be presented to her in New York.

The meeting went as expected, until she was ready to excuse herself. "Oh," she said, "I have one last request, Mr. Archer."

"Yes, Mam?"

She thrust a handful of papers in his direction and continued, "I would appreciate it if you could draw up this trust for Edward and Anne Sneed using these particulars."

Mr. Archer and Mr. Williamsam, the lawyers Delemare had appointed to assist her in the operations of Kempe Shipping, quickly glanced though the papers she had handed them. Mr. Williamsam muttered under his breathe, "Well..., this certainly is a generous offer, Mrs. Kempe. Are you quite sure? I think this may be slightly impulsive since it is so overly generous. One must be quite clear of emotions when drawing up a contract of this sort."

CeeCee ignored his deduction and added, "The Sneeds are unaware of the full enclosure, Mr. Archer. And for the time being it shall remain as such. Do we understand each other, Mr. Williamsam, Mr. Archer?"

"Indeed, Mrs. Kempe," answered both.

"And Mr. Archer, I want every particular followed."

"I will see that they are Mrs....Mrs. Kempe. But you are relinquishing all claim to the property... are you sure?"

"Yes, Mr. Archer, I am assigning all rights of Kempe Manor to the Sneeds' and their heirs, along with the allowance specified."

"Are you sure that is what you want, Mrs. Kempe?" asked Mr. Archer once again.

"Quite sure, Mr. Archer," answered CeeCee in a purposeful tone.

NEW YORK 1922

T hings had changed in New York since she had last visited and CeeCee was surprised to see so many Negroes. She had heard that a number had left the farmlands to move to the city, but she had no idea of the enormity of the shift. It was said that the jobs were better and so was the pay. She hoped they were correct: she certainly wished them luck. Though in reality, at this point in her life she had given little thought of them or their needs for some time. Her past affiliation with the NAACP or any other action that helped her lineage, had been dropped long ago. Six years had passed, and Molly Amber and Ellington were hardly more than an aching memory. Her life no longer had a purpose or direction. To her, her existence had grown insignificant and she lived it as so in isolation.

The suite she purchased was in the nicest part of New York City, so she did not see the poverty that most Negros lived in. Her empty life went on for several more years before she was forced to open her eyes.

At the time she faced that all were not as fortunate as she; and that many lived as no human should have to. *Again,* she thought,

CeeCee Brown you had forgotten who you were or where you had come from.

That day had begun like every day since she came to New York. She read her morning newspaper over a cup of tea while she nibbled on the toast that room service had served her. It was when she turned to the last page that she noticed a small article at the bottom. It was a picture of a Negro child. Her slight body lay on the filth of a back alley near a large trash bin face upward. Her eyes were opened, but they held no laughter or feeling; there was nothing but dark emptiness. The paragraph below it read that the girl was fifteen years old and was dead from an apparent abortion attempt. This in itself was not the reason it made the newspapers. The article said that there were hundreds of such cases each year. But this warranted a mention because the girl had left a note. It named the son of a prominent white businessman as the father of the child she carried. It also said that he arranged the botched procedure. Of course, all responsibility was denied by the boy who was a second-year student at a well-known university. Even though several witnesses did concur that the girl's story was true. The boy's story was accepted as the truth. No further investigation was pending, reported the officer in charge.

CeeCee studied the face that looked void of all feeling. She was a pretty girl though she was much thinner than any pregnant person should ever be. She was close to Molly Amber's age and this saddened her deeply. *Innocence often disregards the poor,* she thought.

"Who is going to protect these young women?" She muttered under her breath, "Who"? Sure, she was aware that there were clinics, but if a Negro girl was pregnant and frightened, would she go to a white man's clinic? If she herself had not had Viola and Bell to thwart her abortion attempt, Molly Amber would not be alive today, and as much as she missed her, she still was very thankful for the years that they had shared.

Her eyes moved back to the picture for one last glimpse and when she started to lay the paper aside, she saw the girl's name,

Rose. Rose fit the girl; she was as pretty as any flower she had ever seen.

The picture of Rose haunted CeeCee for days and on the fourth day, in the wee hours of the morning she realized why. She had made a promise to help pave a better life for Negroes and she had not fulfilled her promise.

She had done nothing to make her and Ellington's child a better place to live. She had not only let Molly Amber down she had also let girls like Rose down. This was a mistake she never intended to make again, and she whispered into the dark night, "I will do all I can to make a woman's word as significant as a man's, and a Negro as worthy as any white being."

Days later the driver looked confused, but he did as CeeCee ordered and drove slowly through the streets of Harlem. At one point she yelled, "Stop! Then said, "Never mind, go on." Soon another yelp filled the car, "Here. Stop here!" And when he did, she immediately jumped out of the vehicle. Her driver hesitated, then hurriedly locked the car and rushed after the fast paced CeeCee.

"Mrs. Kempe, Mrs. Kempe, I don't know if this is a wise thing to do. These streets aren't safe for a man alone, let alone a woman and a rich white woman at that."

Her driver's name was Manny. He was tall and lean and always looked unshaven, though she had never been around him when he did not smell of shaving creme. What's more she knew from his past two years of service that he held no dislike of other races; he was simply stating a fact. But since she was not afraid that someone would do harm to her, she merely quickened her steps and did not acknowledged his remark. Instead she mumbled to herself, "If that happens, no one will be any better off, and that is not my goal."

Manny gave her a strange look but quickened his own steps and followed her up the street. Several doors down she finally stopped, "Here," she said, "this is where it shall be. "It is perfect..., yes this will be ideal." Then she turned as quickly and hurried back to her car. The confused Manny followed respectfully in silence.

It was one year and a day that on that very spot in Harlem that the Harlem Rose Clinic opened its doors for their first Negro patient, a sixteen-year-old who was seven months pregnant and living on the streets.

CeeCee watched discreetly from a side widow, as the girl stood across the way for several hours before she cautiously entered the building and mistrustfully asked, "Couldcha hap..., ma belly hurts."

The clinic boasted its own Negro doctor and several nurses of the same descent. Besides medical treatment it offered such services as birth control instruction and protection as well as placement assistance.

CeeCee was extremely proud of the clinic's success but kept a low profile. This was a safe haven for the Negro woman, and she wanted to keep all eyes focused on that alone. The further away she kept any white influence the safer the women would feel. From the shadows she spent her time furthering her cause and again she became actively involved in the NAACP.

Soon after Harlan Rose Clinic's success CeeCee found herself being invited to many different women's organizations as a key speaker. These affairs involved a lot of travel around the country. At first, she was startled by the difference between the states. The western and northern parts of the country were far more accepting of the black population, than the Southern States were, yet all showed some prejudices. Some were less tolerant of race and openly disregarded the rights of Negros. The southern vocabulary often included and addressed such individuals as Nigger, Blackie, Colored, Jig a boo, Spade or Darkie. They had no respect for a black person or their ability to be a capable human being.

Their behavior sickened CeeCee and she realized that she had forgotten what it was like to live as Negro. She had experienced life far too long as a white person. Though, in truth, even before that she had lived in the protection of the Roberts Plantation and was not aware of the many repression's others lived under.

At these southern states, she was applauded when she spoke of a woman's right to be considered equal. But rarely was she given the same applause when she spoke of a Negro woman's right to be equal.

Many times, she was disheartened and wondered if her intentions were futile. She questioned if she should quit her campaign. Her objective was to enlighten all women, not just white women alone. At one point she had to admit to herself that at these functions she touched only the rich, who seem to care very little about the black race and its struggles.

The final straw came when she was at a rally in Mississippi and without thought bent down and kissed a black infant. The lady behind her was aghast and said, "My word Cecilia, you kissed a Nigger baby. I certainly had no idea you where one of those Nigger lovers."

CeeCee's heart sank and she realized all her words thus far have fallen on deaf ears. For this woman saw nothing, only the color of the infant's skin. The child was not more the six months old and already she was burdened by the color of her skin.

After that rally CeeCee returned to New York downhearted. All she wanted was the refuge of her apartment. There she stayed alone, where she was safe and away from ignorant people and their hurtful words. *No one can hurt me if I stay in isolation. The protection of home...,* she thought, *is the only place I can be me. For underneath, this skin is a black person as dark as any other. My heart bleeds for the pain they suffer. Yet here I am hiding in my protected refuge.*

CHAPTER TWENTY-ONE

S he had been in New York for ten years and had made no close friends only casual acquaintances. She befriended her much revered Margaret Sanger soon after she opened Harlem Rose Clinic. Yet Margaret traveled so much CeeCee rarely saw her. However, since she was conscious of the risks that close relationships could bring, their friendship stayed as a work associate more than a friend. CeeCee still lived in constant fear that someone would find out her true identity and reveal it to the world. *Closeness,* she thought, *usually gives birth to certain intimacies.* Her mind immediately shifted to Ellington and their ten-year marriage and she whispered, "And this is something I cannot bear...." *Nor can I afford,* echoed in her mind."

I t was rainy outside, and winter was in the air. She needed to return several calls though she still felt antisocial and decided for now she wanted nothing to do with the interaction of conversation. She had finished her newspaper and started to read an article in *Time* magazine. Then she pushed it aside and picked up her edition of *Claude McKay's, Harlem Shadow.*

CeeCee had just settled on a page when her doorbell chimed several quick trills. At first, she thought of not answering, but reluctantly pushed herself off the davenport to answer its call. She peeked through the peephole to see who was there. She was surprised to see Donna Maxford nervously moving from one foot to the other as she rubbed her hands together. CeeCee quickly covered the peephole with her hand and instantly felt silly. No one from the other side was able to see in, and she knew this. Yet she felt exposed and slightly vulnerable by the intrusion.

Donna lived down the hall and had been attempting a friendship for quite a while, even though CeeCee continuously hampered her endeavors.

At first CeeCee weighed whether she should pretend she was not home, then concluded that would be rude and opened the door, but only a crack, since she did not want to invite her in. She had had her fill of rich white woman, especially of the Southern origin, which Donna Maxford clearly was.

Donna perked up as soon as she saw CeeCee's face peek around the doors edge. "Hi, I was afraid you wasn't home. I know how much you travel. I sure hope I'm not disturben ya all. But my heaters on the brink and the repairman won't be here for another hour or so. I was hopin you wouldn't mind enterainen me for a bit. Just till he gets here, then I'll be out of your hair, I promise. Can I come in?"

CeeCee hesitated yet she had no idea how she could politely refuse a woman in distress, so she backed away from the door and opened it wide. Donna slid pass while CeeCee smiled tensely. When CeeCee closed the door, she braced herself before she turned to face Donna who had stopped at the end of the hall while she waited for her host to join her.

Her smile was as wide as the doorway she stood in. "Thanks," she said, "I didn't want to sit in the lobby for an hour or more. And since it's so dreary outside I wasn't about to go outside, beside what can ya do in about an hour?"

CeeCee nodded her understanding but did not express an opinion. Donna made a quick scan around the entryway then dutifully followed CeeCee to the living room. "Holy cow, this sure is a nice place. It looks like you brought half of Britain back with ya. Nice art."

"Thank you," replied CeeCee with no added comment.

Donna hesitated then seated herself on the divan next to the book CeeCee had been reading. "Well, anyhow I love your taste, I see you're also into antiques. My daddy used to sell that stuff, but nothing as fine as yours." At this time, she snatched the book off the sofa's cushion and read the cover aloud, "*Harlem Shadows, Claude McKay,* umh..., have ya read, *Home to Harlem*?"

Without waiting for CeeCee to respond Donna continued, "It's a great book to read. But..., I tend to believe, *Song from Jamaica* was his best work. That, of course is my opinion, which ya might take note, I got plenty of." She laughed at herself then went on, "Anyhow, I think he mighta overlooked some of the real problems in that society. It seems most mighta been held back a bit. Though what do I know? Do you read a lot, Cecilia? I love a good book."

Suddenly CeeCee burst into laughter. This woman was exhausting, yet exhilarating at the same time, and her book critiques. *Well,* thought CeeCee *it certainly does put her in a different light.*

At this point CeeCee realized that she had done the exact same thing that she had despised in others. She had judged Donna by the color of her skin. She had decided that since she was white and rich, she would be prejudiced and uncaring. CeeCee smiled at her own ignorance, then asked eagerly, "What can I do to make your stay comfortable? Can I get you some tea, or a sip of sherry?"

"Tea? Well, that sure sounds good. I would be mighty pleased to have a cup of tea, with ya."

Donna was about five feet three or four and slightly plump, although the extra weight was well distributed. Her blue eyes sparkled with energy and when she laughed, they crinkled at the edges. Her laugh-wrinkles, which usually revealed a woman's true age only added to her attractiveness, and complimented her pretty face. Her laughter was boisterous and louder than any refined woman should be.

Her spiritedness was catching and soon CeeCee found her guard slackening, and she, too, was eagerly expressing her views on McKay's writings. Moreover, for the first time in her life she felt the beginning of a true friendship. She genuinely liked Donna and her artlessness. There was no pretense in her, and her expressions were refreshing.

After room service delivered CeeCee's order, they settled in front of the fireplace with their cups of steaming tea and sweet breads to munch.

Donna sipped her tea as she watched the fire roar while CeeCee stoked the wood in the huge hearth. Donna's silence was somewhat un-nerving after her blast of enthusiasm, and CeeCee turned to see if she was okay. She could see the woman was in deep thought, as she too was contentedly thoughtful. The last twenty minutes had been quite enjoyable and filled with something she had not experienced since Sara's friendship.

Minutes later CeeCee was brought back to the present when Donna warmly voiced, "Cecilia, you are such a lady, well versed and all. I..., I seen ya speak once on television. I like that ya speak your mind. I think if more people did, we'd all be better off."

CeeCee smiled her agreement and thanked her for the compliment. Then she noticed that Donna's face had grown serious and she sat forward as she decided to express more of her feelings.

"Cecilia, I'm from Texas, and am not a cultivated lady like most of yaur Southern Bells. So, if I ever offend you in any way whatsoever, please just say so.... up front, okay? See, I like ya and I would be happy if I could be yaur friend. But I got some bad habits, not ta mention my Texas drawl and New York tongue mix..., so, well to say the least, at times I confuse people. Sometimes people even take what I'm sayin wrong. I figure that's one reason I'm so unpopular with the country club set." Apprehensively she laughed at herself, then added, "Yau'd think bein here four years I woulda catched on by now, but like my Stanley says, I'm just plain country. Lucky for me, that's all right with him."

Donna stopped long enough to take a bite of bread and a sip of tea, then continued. "Stanley and me, we been married twenty-two years. I still think he's the handsomest man I ever seen. Even though we got two kids he still treats me like a newlywed. I tell ya, a girl can't get any luckier than that."

She studied CeeCee for a few seconds before she asked, "Both our kids are away at school.... I know yau're a widow, Cecilia, but ya all got any kids?"

CeeCee was alarmed by the question and for a moment she did not know how to answer. She wanted to say yes, but a yes answer would require an explanation, so instead she asked. "Would you like some more tea? I am sure yours is cold by now Mrs. Maxford."

"Donna... call me Donna, and I'm sorry..., for bein so nosey. I don't mean nothin by it, I guess it's just my friendly nature, like Stanley always says."

"No, please do not apologize...," boldly CeeCee added, 'it is simply a sensitive topic."

"Then that's a subject we'll avoid," replied Donna.

"Thank you, Donna and will you please call me, CeeCee?"

"I'd be proud to, CeeCee."

There was an awkward minute then Donna jumped in and said, "Why don't I tell ya bout me and Stanley."

"Yes, why not, answered CeeCee?"

"We met in Texas, not far out of Houston. I was not much older than sixteen at the time and was waitressin in a little cafe near the oil fields. That's where Stanley worked. He was a driller and the best lookin boy I ever saw. But he wadant just handsome, he was smart too. Course I never guessed he'd go so far, but he sure enough did. By the time our first was born he already had a productive oil well of his own.

Wadant much, but it was producin. I never imagined and my daddy was downright staggered by the fact, cause he thought Stanley was justa no good, and no way good enough for his lil ole

Donna. I'm sure, Stanley bein five years older than me plus already a divorced man, didn't make my daddy any happier."

Suddenly Donna gave a hoot and said, "Boy, he sure did have ta eat them words some years later. I tell ya, CeeCee, that didn't help him any which way in the happy department. My daddy, he don't' like bein wrong"

Donna shook her head as she smiled sweetly, "Me and Stanley, we both come from poor families. But my family was a might poorer than Stanley's. Some even called us, poor white trash, but we never paid no mind. Our hearts are good and that's what counts in the end. Though..., once me and Stanley moved to New York, cause of Stanley's oil refinery business..., ya know, the exportin of it. Well we found out money is all that counts. Old money that is. It's downright hard to get accepted here if you ain't known by the right people. Which I'm sure you ain't gotta worry bout none. But some little ole Texan gal like me, surely does. No matter though, I certainly ain't gonna give up. One day I'm gonna be just like one of ya all."

CeeCee laughed and declared, "Let us hope not. You are perfect the way you are Donna, and please; do us all a favor and never change."

From that day on, Donna became CeeCee's constant companion. It was not too long after when Donna joined her friend in her efforts for woman's rights and education. The two traveled around the United States and hoped that one day their words would change the world. Donna worked in the background. She scheduled the meetings and ran the office while CeeCee spoke at rallies for the rights of woman and men of all races.

With the threat of war in 1939 the efforts for equal opportunity of all races became an unpopular topic and when World War two began, all interest for their cause dropped. All efforts went towards the support of the American troops.

This time CeeCee refused to stand by and let the men fight alone. She volunteered for the Red Cross and went back to her beloved England as an interpreter. Since she spoke English, French, and some German, she was a valued aide to the Red Cross Medical teams and assisted in communications with injured troops.

After the war ended and CeeCee returned to New York, she felt her cause was less important than she had before she went to England. She had watched young men and women die. "There is no difference in color or gender in death," she told her dear friend, Donna.

Although Donna continued to argue that they needed to start their cause again, CeeCee refused to pick up the gauntlet to begin the movement. She said, "I am too old and tired. I am no longer up for the fight."

It was not until McCarthyism was well on its way out, did CeeCee face the importance of causes like hers. Again, she put forth an all-out effort to advance the rights of colored people and supported the NAACP. And in May of 1954 when the United States Supreme Court ruled segregation illegal, she stood proud amongst the courtroom spectators. Though when a black man slapped the back of another black man and said, '*We did it, never again will we walk in the shadows.*' CeeCee wanted to cry for she realized she would never be out of the shadows. As far as the world was concerned, she was *white*. The only pride she could feel was as a white, Cecilia Kempe, fighting for the rights of Black Americans. This saddened her, but the choice had been made many years before, and as unfair as it may have seemed, she was far more effective as she stood, than if it were known that she, Cecilia Kempe, was indeed a Negro woman named, CeeCee Brown. Yes, this fight was far from over and her value, as it stood, was still greatly needed.

Chapter Twenty-two

"**D**onna, I am not a young woman. I need my rest; I have no business going to parties on New Year's Eve or anytime."

"CeeCee, you're an ole poop head and you have no idea what you miss by staying locked away in your apartment. The only time you go out is to attend a rally or a speakin engagement. You need to widen your horizons."

"I am quite happy at home and being alone...."

"Nonsense. Now get dress, we are goin shoppin to buy you a new dress." "Donna, I do not buy dresses at stores and you know that."

"CeeCee Kempe, I never realized you were such a snob."

Stanley interrupted their argument by adding his two cents to strengthen his wife's demands, "Might as well give it up, CeeCee. Ya know as well as I do, that once Donna settles on an idea, there ain't no changin it."

Donna's and Stanley's daughter Rachel agreed as did her husband Peter. Their two children Miles and Carolyn laughed and teased, "Give up, Aunt CeeCee. Give it up." As the baby in Rachel's arms gurgled his support.

Lambert, Rachel's younger brother and a clergyman tried to be a mediator as always, light-heartedly kidded, "Come on now, leave Aunt CeeCee alone. She has the right to make her own decisions. If she prefers to stay home, let her. I'm sure together we can make our own good time."

"Oh, sure *Lammie pie! A*lways choosing Aunt CeeCee's side," teased Rachel. Then to her husband she muttered, "I can only imagine his idea of a good time. My guess is, it would equal one of Aunt CeeCee's teatimes." Then to CeeCee she pleaded, "I promise you, Aunt CeeCee, he knows even less about New Year's Eve parties than... than..., than say Charley here, who, if I may remind you, is only two months old."

CeeCee laughed at their antics. She loved Donna and her family and even more so when they all got together for the holidays. Soon all would be leaving and returning to their own daily lives and she will miss them greatly. She watched Rachel tickle Charley's tummy and a pang of desire tugged at her heart. She always wondered if Molly Amber had children. She had never told Donna about Molly Amber, but she was sure her friend sensed some hidden secret. CeeCee was sure she would never have guessed the complete truth.

The party was huge. It seemed everyone in New York had attended, and CeeCee wished she had not. She sipped the Champagne that Stanley had brought her, but it tasted bitter, so she disposed of it on the first tray that passed by. She was on her way to the buffet table when she heard a soft sociable, "Hello, Cecilia," and turned to face a much older Abigail.

Her first instinct was to be frightened. Yet Abigail was smiling. Her eyes were friendly and held no hint of threat, so she smiled back.

"How are you? You certainly look as lovely as ever. I see age has not weathered you as it has some of us," declared Abigail.

CeeCee relaxed her guard and answered, "I am very well, Abigail. You have no room to complain about the consequences of age. You look wonderful and if I may add, incredibly happy."

"I am, thank you. Henry is a wonderful man..., and our children.... Well, we are fortunate to say the least."

"And so, you should be. I always thought you and Henry were perfect for each other."

Again, Abigail smiled softly, then after a slight hesitancy she said, "CeeCee you have turned into quite a woman. From what I hear, you are doing great things for women all over the world. I wish you continued success."

Tears touched CeeCee's eyes; Abigail said *woman*. She did not label her as Negro, Black or a Colored woman, only a woman. This was the greatest tribute she could have given her. This is what she wanted for all her race, to be accepted for their achievement, instead of judged by their skin. CeeCee dithered before she regained her composure and whispered, "Thank you, Abigail."

Abigail nodded and turned to leave then stopped and uttered, "CeeCee. . .."

CeeCee waited and when Abigail said nothing more she asked, "What...what is it Abigail?"

"I... I just want you to know, I had no idea about your child.... CeeCee. Winnifrey told me what she did to you. I just want you to know, I think her act was despicable. She had no right and I know you will never forgive her, and you have every right. . ., but if you can please try to understand. She is a tortured woman CeeCee. In her mind she has concluded that she has lost so much, and her way to deal with her contrived pain, is to blame others for the anguish she suffers. Unfortunately, you have always been one of those others."

Abigail tittered momentarily before she spoke again, "CeeCee, Winnifrey is of a weak soul...and to be truthful..., weak mind. I fear this will worsen in the months to come. You see..., Albin..., he, he is not well. The doctors say he will not last more than a few more months.

Winnifrey has no idea, since Albin has decided it is best that she not be told. That, I can and cannot agree with since I understand both sides. However, either way she will need a lot of support. CeeCee..., I fear for her awfully. Winnifrey has always had so very few friends and even less as of late. She has become increasingly difficult and most avoid her. With Albin's death, I am sure she will become even more wretched since she does not do well without a man."

CeeCee said nothing her heart was pounding so loud; she wondered if Abigail could hear it as well.

"CeeCee, I only tell you this..., for you can know God is punishing Winnifrey for her terrible deeds. She has not gone untouched." Abigail stroked CeeCee's cheek lightly and said, "Good night, Cecilia," turned and walked away.

CeeCee watched Abigail leave through tear filled eyes. She wished she could have said something, but what was there to say. At this time Donna stepped in front of CeeCee blocking her view of the departing Abigail. Concern immediately filled Donna' face, "CeeCee are you okay? You look like you just saw a ghost."

CeeCee refocused her vision on Donna, then smiled as she answered, "No, no ghost, Donna, only an angel."

From behind, CeeCee she heard the call of, "HAPPY NEW YEAR," and she whispered, "I hope so."

The months passed and CeeCee busied herself with the clinics she had funded. Two in Mississippi, one in Georgia and one in Pennsylvania and of course her beloved, Harlem Rose in New York. The desire for education on birth control was growing, but not as rapidly as the needs were in the poorer communities.

CeeCee continued to speak at teas, luncheons and women's groups, but once again she felt she was not touching the right circle. "How can I make a difference," she asked Donna, "if those who need it the most, can not hear our message?"

"CeeCee you are makin a difference and in a roundabout way, the people that need to hear what your sayin, do. The clinics are busier than they've ever been, and more are askin questions about birth control," reassured Donna.

Rachel who recently joined their fight agreed, "Yes, Moms right, Aunt CeeCee, each day more and more are becoming aware. Women, no matter what color, need to take charge of their lives and this begins in the bedroom. If we don't demand the right to govern our own bodies, how can we expect to handle our lives? How can we grow as a person?"

CeeCee smiled; she remembered when she had that much energy and grit. Rachel's passion was right out there for the world to see. She, herself, could never have been free enough to express it as strongly to the world. Yet years ago, Ellington had mentioned that he was proud that she was an independent woman. *But he only knew half the story,* she thought, *as does most all who know me.*

"Yes, Rachel, you are right, and we shall teach them how. Not only how to control their lives, but how they can control the growth of their families," responded CeeCee. "We will have to change our strategy and go where the people who need us are. Parks, laundromats, food lines and churches. We will hand out leaflets in grocery stores until the management hauls us away. My friends, we are going to the streets."

Consciousness was growing and in 1955 when Rosa Parks refused to give her seat up on the bus. CeeCee was full of pride for the young girl.

CeeCee knew the voices of those that spoke out for equality, and they were being heard loud and clear for the first time in their lives. They were determined that the world would hear them and move towards the change they begged and fought for. Cecilia Kempe's notoriety along with others who choose to stand in the front lines grew.

The newspapers loved her, a white society woman fighting for the under privileged and they dubbed her, White Soldier of Minorities. They said she was brave, but in truth that was a lie. It was those of color that stood in defiance who were the brave ones. These fine souls chose to fight in open view of the world. She, many years prior, had chosen to hide behind a mask. The mask she fought behind was the well protected armor of her pale skin. No, she was not brave; she had chosen the coward's way out.

CeeCee read the printed matter that Donna had brought her on birth control pills. Afterward she looked into the eyes of her old friend and said, "This will make all the difference; now we must move on.

Donna nodded her agreement and CeeCee fell silent. Donna waited and said nothing while CeeCee remained quiet and thoughtful. After some time, she looked up and commenced to speak her mind, "Donna... I... am old and who knows how much time I have left. There are things I must do...before that time."

"Yes, we have to fight for..."

"Yes," she interrupted Donna's words, "we need to make this world a better place... for all. None of us will be free until we are all free. Our children and their children must learn this lesson."

Donna studied CeeCee. She had such a strange look on her face, and this worried her friend. She assessed it while she evaluated what CeeCee had just said and what she might have meant. Finally, she sat forward and replied, "Well, then I guess we better get started, where do we begin, CeeCee?"

CeeCee smiled at Donna. She was a loyal friend and had always remained true to her word. She never asked more than what CeeCee was willing to provide. "First, I must start with myself. I have some unfinished business to attend to.

Again, Donna studied CeeCee's expression, then asked, "Can I help?"

"Not unless you know a very good detective."

"A detective?"

CeeCee avoided the question and answered with. "Then...once I have completed that task, we will join the fight towards civil rights. Martin Luther King, Jr. and the likes, need our help. We all must see that ignorance does not prevail."

CHAPTER TWENTY-THREE

Juliet stood by the sidelines and watched as the paramedics worked skillfully, yet it was plain to see their anxiety, so she turned to leave. At a time like this a reporter was certainly not something CeeCee needed, and she headed for her car.

"Juliet! Juliet!"

Juliet had moved several steps in the direction of the parking lot when she realized it was her name that was being called. She turned to see Mary Lou running towards her, so she stopped to wait for her to catch up.

Mary Lou sounded like she was winded when she reached her and took several quick breaths before she said, "Juliet..., did ...you get your story? Did you get anything?"

"Nope," Juliet shook her head. "She started to tell me about herself, but after a few comments I realized she wasn't making any sense. Soon after she fell silent...then I noticed her breathing had become shallow. That's when I called for help. Did she ever regain consciousness," asked Juliet?

"Only for a few seconds," replied Mary Lou, "she mumbled something about, "ignorance can not prevail." Then she fell back into unconsciousness. I'm sorry you didn't get your story, Juliet. It seemed so important to CeeCee. She talked of nothing else for days."

Juliet smiled her thanks and turned to leave. She unlocked the Saab's door and threw her equipment in the back seat. At this time, she heard herself being hailed a second time and turned expecting to see Mary Lou again. Instead it was a woman she'd never seen before. She was carrying a box and from the way she was carrying it, it looked heavy. Upon her approach she immediately asked, "Juliet...Juliet Powers?"

"Yes," she answered, "I'm Juliet. What can I do for you?"

The woman appeared to be in her late fifties. She had a large protruding nose that seemed larger than it was because her face was so thin. Juliet guessed that her dark hair, which was full of grey and pulled tightly back into a bun, did nothing to defray the sharpness of her unattractive features. However, her eyes were warm and friendly, so Juliet immediately forgot all, but her friendly smile.

The woman exhaled relief and sputtered, "Wonderful, wonderful! I'm glad I caught you. I was afraid I missed you, Mary Lou said you left some minutes ago."

Juliet's face revealed her distraction as she threw her purse in the car while she waited for the lady to explain why it was so important to speak to her. The woman noticed her look of quandary and promptly stopped her rambling. "I'm sorry," she said, "Please excuse my rudeness." She reached her hand out from under the box that she held and said, "I'm Darnell Weaver... CeeCee's personal secretary."

"Oh, nice to meet you Ms. Weaver."

"Darnell will do," she returned in her nasally voice.

Juliet waited and after a pause Darnell continued, "Oh, it's the box."

"Box?"

"Yes, CeeCee's box. She said if anything ever happened to her that you were to get the box. She said it was all important that you read everything in the box." She then stressed, "Juliet, please, you must read every page. This was especially important to CeeCee."

After a brief hesitation Juliet lifted the lid on the half-opened carton and peeked inside. "Books," she asked?

"Journals," answered Darnell, "every journal CeeCee ever kept."

"But why? I mean why me...does she still want me to tell her story?"

"No, heaven's no."

Juliet waited, then finally burst, "Then what?"

"Oh, its' simple," replied Darnell, "She wants Molly Amber to know the truth."

"What, Mol... Molly...Molly Amber...my Grandmother?"

"Yes, Molly Amber. She needs to know the whole story."

"Why...my grandmother...., she's dead."

Darnell smiled, "Yes, I know. CeeCee knew that too. Juliet, please. Please, read the journals, then you will see. It took a long time, Juliet, but in the end, CeeCee came full circle."

It had been over 2 weeks since the death of Cecilia Kempe. Juliet stood over her grave and read the words that Rachel Maxford Hart, had requested to be placed on the headstone. It was in the name of her mother, Donna Maxford. She said her mother Donna had read them to her years ago and thought that they fit the relationship between her mother and CeeCee. She and CeeCee were the best of friends until the day of Donna's passing 10 years earlier.

To have known her was a great honor, to have her as a friend was even a greater privilege. Her goodness will live in our hearts forever. For she was truly one of God's chosen women.

Juliet read the sonnet several times then stood silent gazing unto CeeCee's resting place. Her heart was heavy, and she felt a tinge of regret. She wished she had known the old woman. But it seemed life had other plans, and in truth, the life she had lived; she would not have wanted to trade. Even for the privilege to call Cecilia Kempe.... Great-grandmother.

"CeeCee," she quietly whispered her name, then added, "Primo was a wonderful Great-grandmother and she loved her family wholly. And even if Ellington's love sounded like something out of a fairy tale, Lemule as ordinary as he was, was all a Great-grandfather should have been. My Grandmother, your Molly Amber, CeeCee. Loved them both dearly and talked of them almost daily her entire life. After the car accident that took Molly Amber's only child, my mother, Hanna, and my father, Jake. Grandma Molly Amber opened her arms and raised me with that same warmth and love she herself had received all those year ago with Primo and Lemule. Together we thanked the Lord for the time we all had together, and I will always cherish their memory's.

Yes, CeeCee, I heard you knew Molly Amber left us some years back, and I understand you missed so much by not knowing her. But I am thankful you never came forward and took away what was precious to her, her family."

She sighed deeply, then voiced, "CeeCee, from what I've learned you were an extraordinary woman and against all odds you accomplished astounding feats. Yet, I would not have traded any part of the life we, as a family, shared. Nevertheless, I wish we could have known each other.... yet thanks to your journals, today I understand you and your words better than I did when I first learned the truth." Juliet reached out and touched the letters beneath the eulogy. These were the words CeeCee had written and asked to be on her headstone.

Sometimes life's choices are not ours alone. Then... sometimes they are, and we have no one to blame but ourselves.

Juliet read the words out loud and felt the pain of their meaning. She and Darnell were the only ones left who knew the truth.

Her eyes filled and her voice choked when she said, "Great-grandmother, I was angry at first, I thought you took the easy way out and you were a coward. Then after reading more of your words...well.... Well, I guess it's true at first you had little choice, but later once past those first steps, your journey became selfish. Those steps were not taken for the betterment of anyone except for yourself. You hid behind the tone of your skin. However, most all your adult life was spent on redemption and for the very people you ran from. And for that, Cecilia Brown Kempe, I can only say, I genuinely thank you.

THE END

ELLEN'S BIO

For Ellen the urge to write had started long before her first book, with poems and miscellaneous writings. Her first effort was a short story named Kathleen/Catherine. To prove her dedication to the written word the story was typed out on a small portable Smith Corona typewriter, no computer screen, no spell check, no correction key or save or print key. She had gotten a response from Red Book indicating they liked her story but would preferer something more towards women's rights.

As the years rolled by Ellen authored **Kathleen/Catherine, One for the Money, and Murder by Proxy,** and in a different genre **CeeCee Shades of Black**. A prominent New York Agent was excited about her work and was eager to guide her through the publishing process when 9/11 happened and the publishing industry and her writing went on hold.

Today once again she is looking forward to marketing her manuscripts to the public.

www.ingramcontent.com/pod-product-compliance
Lightning Source LLC
Chambersburg PA
CBHW030322200626
46816CB00006BA/1894